A NEW DAY RISING

Books by Lauraine Snelling

Hawaiian Sunrise

A SECRET REFUGE

Daughter of Twin Oaks   Sisters of the Confederacy
The Long Way Home

RED RIVER OF THE NORTH

An Untamed Land   The Reapers' Song
A New Day Rising   Tender Mercies
A Land to Call Home   Blessing in Disguise

RETURN TO RED RIVER

A Dream to Follow
Believing the Dream

HIGH HURDLES

Olympic Dreams   Close Quarters
DJ's Challenge   Moving Up
Setting the Pace   Letting Go
Out of the Blue   Raising the Bar
Storm Clouds   Class Act

GOLDEN FILLY SERIES

The Race   Shadow Over San Mateo
Eagle's Wings   Out of the Mist
Go for the Glory   Second Wind
Kentucky Dreamer   Close Call
Call for Courage   The Winner's Circle

A NEW DAY RISING

LAURAINE SNELLING

BETHANY HOUSE PUBLISHERS
MINNEAPOLIS, MINNESOTA 55438

Published by Bethany House Publishers
A Ministry of Bethany Fellowship International
11400 Hampshire Avenue South
Minneapolis, Minnesota 55438
www.bethanyhouse.com

Printed in the United States of America by
Bethany Press International, Minneapolis, Minnesota 55438

Library of Congress Cataloging-in-Publication Data

Snelling, Lauraine.
    A new day rising / Lauraine Snelling.
        p.   cm. — (Red river of the north ; 2)
    ISBN 1–55661–577–9 (pbk.)
    I. Title. II. Series: Snelling, Lauraine. Red River of the north ; bk. 2.
PS3569.N39N49   1996
813'.54—dc20
                                 96–25355
                                     CIP

To the Round Robins and the Birds of Pray
for all their support and encouragement.

LAURAINE SNELLING is a full-time writer who has authored numerous books, both fiction and non-fiction, as well as written for a wide range of magazines and weekly features in local newspapers. She has written the GOLDEN FILLY SERIES and HIGH HURDLES for Bethany House Publishers. She and her husband have two grown children and make their home in California.

Minnesota north woods
February 1884

T imber-r-r-r!"

Haakan Bjorklund shaded his eyes against the sun glinting off the snow-capped branches and watched as the ancient pine crashed to its death. Branches exploded from the trees around and beneath as the monolith fell, sending a shower of long green needles and resinous pitch that followed the plunging tree to a snowy grave. Silence followed, a tribute to the death. One last branch, snagged on a companion giant, tumbled to the snow beneath.

"All right, let's get those branches stripped," the boss yelled.

Two men with a crosscut saw nodded and sent Haakan and his partner, Swede, the go-ahead signal.

"We got da ting ready for you. See you do so good." The speaker smiled, his cracked lips showing a missing front tooth. He'd lost it in a discussion over a card played wrong the night before. His right eye, only half open, sported a purple swelling left by the contender's fist.

"Ja, like that would be hard. You fellows couldn't get started sawing if we didn't wedge 'em for you." Haakan hefted the heavy ax he wore across his shoulder as if it grew there naturally. He stepped to the first branch, and with three perfectly placed cuts, he severed a limb equal to the trunk of a small tree. As he worked his way up the trunk, he could hear the process repeated on felled trees all around him. The virgin north woods were being leveled, tree by tree. Swede worked the other side of the huge trunk, and when they reached the end of usable wood, they severed the tip and rolled the log to finish cutting the branches half buried in the snow.

Haakan felt his muscles loosen, and despite the near zero air, sweat trickled down under his arms and the middle of his back. As the rhythm of heft and slam continued, his mind wandered back to the cookshack and the widow woman who ran it. She served pancakes so light the men nearly had to hold them down with a fork lest they float away. But it wasn't only her pancakes that drew Haakan's attention. Trading pleasantries with her at mealtimes had become the high point of his day. And when he could bring crinkles to the edges of her warm brown eyes and a smile followed by a laugh that even sourpuss Johnson couldn't resist, Haakan felt like he could defeat the entire crew single-handedly.

"Hey, Bjorklund, you gonna daydream all morning?"

Haakan snapped the last limb off by stepping on it and raised his ax to his shoulder. As they made their way to the next marked tree, he removed his whetstone from his pocket and honed the edges of his double-bitted friend. His father had always said dull axes caused more accidents than sharp ones, and this son had no intention of losing wages due to an injury.

As soon as he had enough money saved, he planned to propose to Mrs. Mary Landsverk and suggest they take their earnings and head west to homestead some land of their own. After fifteen years routing about the country, he was ready to tap into that dream of free land and a strong, happy family. The fact she had two small sons only added to her value, far as he could see.

When the steam whistle blew for dinner, he followed the rest of the crew over to the sledge and climbed aboard. While the others jawed and teased one another, he worked at the bits of his ax with his whetstone. It was about due for a real sharpening on the grindstone.

"Hey, Bjorklund, there's a letter for you." Cappy, a logger until he lost an arm on the ripping saw and now a bookkeeper in the office, passed down the rows of benches handing out letters to those fortunate enough to have relatives who wrote. "You got a girl hid somewhere we don't know about?"

Haakan thanked him with a smile that reached the edges of eyes blue as the fjords of his homeland. The Bjorklunds were known for the blue of their eyes and jaws squared with determination. He recognized his mother's handwriting. "Ja sure, this one, she's known me all my life." He stuck the letter in his pocket to be read in private. He hadn't heard from home for a long while. When he looked at the postmark, he knew why. This one had been mailed three months earlier.

He looked up to catch the smile of the young boy who refilled the platters of beef and bowls of potatoes for the hungry crew.

"More coffee, Mr. Bjorklund?"

"Ja, Charlie." Haakan held up his cup. "Mange takk." Over the top of the cup he caught Mrs. Landsverk looking his way. He raised the now full cup in a toast of gratitude and returned to his plate. He knew if he didn't hurry, he wouldn't get enough to fill his belly before they returned to the woods. As the men finished eating, the noise level rose accordingly.

Curses split the air over at the next table, causing everyone else to stop talking and listen.

"Not again." Haakan dropped his knife and fork and turned to see who'd started the commotion. But he knew without looking. Swede and Jacob were at it again.

Haakan got to his feet, cut his way between the stomping and cheering men the fight had drawn, and exited the building through the door nearest the kitchen. The shoveled path led to the outhouse. At least out here he wouldn't be forced to break up another fight. Just because he stood half-a-head above most of the men and could reach farther than any of them, he'd been deemed the peacemaker. He wore a cut lip to prove it.

Once he'd finished his business, he returned to the cookshack porch and drew his letter from his pocket.

"My dear Haakan," his mother wrote. "I hope and pray this letter finds its way to your hands and that you are well. Your far and I watch the mail for a message from you, but so long, now, we have been disappointed." Haakan sighed. He hated writing letters. What could he say to them? How many trees were cut, who beat whom in cards, and that two men were caught by a tree that fell wrong? One died and the other wished he had. Life in the north woods took all a man had to give and then bled him again.

"I pray that you have found a church where you can hear God's Holy Word and draw near to the foot of the cross." His mor had no idea how far and wide this land of America stretched and how many were the miles between towns. No minister came to this logging camp or to the mill downriver, and the farm where he worked one summer lay ten miles from the nearest town. No, a church he hadn't seen for more than a year or two.

After giving him the news of the family at home, she continued. "You remember your cousins twice removed, Roald and Carl? Both of them died in the terrible blizzard and flu epidemic last winter in Dakota Territory. I would have told you sooner, but I just learned of the dreadful tragedy myself. I believe you could be of help to their families and perhaps could spend Christmas at their farm. You are the closest family to those two poor grieving widows who are so young to suffer like this, and I know they would be beholden."

Haakan swung his arms to warm himself. He shook his head. Mor talked like he could ski right over to the cousins' houses and help them do the chores of an evening. He checked the date at the top of the precious paper. Sure enough, early November. Besides being so far away, he had steady work here. And if Mrs. Landsverk agreed with him, he'd soon have a family of his own. Perhaps they'd stop by the Bjorklunds on their way west.

The blast of the steam whistle forced him to stuff the letter in his shirt pocket and return to the front of the cookshack, where he loaded on to the sledge along with the others. Ignoring their banter, he thought about what it would be like to have a family of his own—a fine wife, sturdy sons to help in the fields, and golden-haired daughters who laughed like their mother. Fifteen years he'd been in America, and while he'd seen a lot of the country and worked any-where at whatever he found, he was no closer to the dream of own-ing land than when he left home.

"Hey, Bjorklund, you going to Hansen's tonight?" The sledge driver threw the words over his shoulder. Everyone stopped talking to hear the answer.

"Nei, I got better things to do with my money than fill Hansen's pockets."

"Ah, that ain't it. He's hoping to spend a bit of time with Miz Landsverk. Widow woman like her needs a man. Why else you tink she come to da logging camp?"

"Ja, but you better get a push on. I heerd she done got a beau."

Haakan felt like someone slugged him in the back with a tree trunk. He forced himself to turn slowly and look at the last man who spoke. Raising one eyebrow, Haakan waited for an answer to the question he kept himself from asking. Ears, so named for the ap-pendages that nearly waved in the breeze but for their frostbitten tips, nodded. "Dat's vat I hear."

Haakan shrugged as if it meant nothing to him. He knew they'd never let up if he showed any reaction at all. Keeping secrets was well nigh impossible when twelve men bunked in a ten-by-twelve room.

"Ah, he yoost repair tings for her 'cause he got nothing else to do." Swede, his partner and best friend, managed to stick up for him as usual.

Haakan had found the best way to get along was to keep his mouth shut and his fists ready. He used them rarely, only in emergencies, but everyone knew that when he started swinging, he meant business. He shut down many a brewing brawl on his reputation alone.

At each stop, more men bailed off and headed for the marked trees to be downed and stripped that day. As those felling the trees moved on, teams of horses skidded the logs to the clearing where they would be loaded onto sledges and hauled to the bank of the river. After the ice left the river in the spring, they'd be floated down to the main sawmill. Keeping the logs from jamming up took another kind of skill and daring as the logrollers jumped from one floating log to another, using their peavey, a pronged spike, to break things up. While he had good balance, Haakan had chosen instead to work in the mill itself, feeding logs into the buzz saws. The noise alone fair to deafened a man, but at least he didn't have to worry about a dunking in the frigid water.

Haakan, Swede, and Huey swung off the sledge at the end of the track. The three were known as the best team in camp. They wedged the trees for the sawmen, then stripped the huge pines with greater speed and fewer accidents than anyone in this logging camp or the three surrounding it.

Haakan paused and sniffed the air. "Snow coming."

Huey shook his grizzled head. "You be better'n anyone I ever met for knowing the weather like you do. Yoost smells cold to me."

"And piney."

The three slogged through the drifts to the next tree, marked with a notch about chest high. Within a few strokes they were back to their natural rhythm, and the blows of the axes fell precisely on beat. Haakan resolutely kept his mind on the task at hand. With the letter burning a hole in his chest and the nagging voice that said he'd lost the woman he loved, he maintained a speed with the rise and fall of his ax that would have felled a lesser man.

"Enough, man. What you tryin' to do? Kill us off?" Swede stepped back to watch the tree drop to the ground and mopped sweat off his forehead with a frost-encrusted sleeve.

Haakan looked at the third member of the crew to see him nodding and puffing hard. Plumes of steam rose and frosted his bushy eyebrows.

"Sorry." Haakan leaned on his ax handle, only then realizing his lungs were pumping like bellows. He looked up to see the first snowflakes drifting in the stillness. A last branch broke through the ice-crusted snow with a pop, while in the distance another tree crashed to its death. The forest wore that peculiar silver-blue look of winter's early dusk, when the sun has fallen beyond the trees but not yet fully set. Directly above, a gray cloud sent more snowflakes drifting downward.

"We should be able to down another before the team arrives."

"If they can find us. We got so far ahead."

"Even that lazy driver we got should be able to follow the felled trees." Haakan slapped Swede on the back. "Come on, I promise to let up on you."

That night in the warmth of the cookshack, Haakan tried to catch Mrs. Landsverk's gaze. Was she deliberately not looking at him? The thought made the possibility of the gossip being right even more worrisome.

As half the men shouted and shoved their way out to the straw-filled wagon for the hour-long ride to Hansen's saloon, Haakan bided his time, counting on her to come by again with coffee refills for those few who still lined the benches. Instead, Charlie, her young helper, carried the pot around.

"More coffee, Mr. Bjorklund?"

Haakan held out his cup. "There isn't, by chance, more of that dried apple pie in the back, is there?"

The boy's cheeky grin split his face. "For you, there just might be." He took the pot with him and hurried to the kitchen, leaving the man sitting farther down the table unattended.

With one finger, Haakan traced the red lines in the checkered oilcloth covering the table. Should he try to talk to her tonight or wait till morning? With it being Sunday tomorrow and half the camp hung over from their carousing the night before, breakfast was always served later and then dinner in the middle of the afternoon so the kitchen help had part of the day off.

"Here you go, sir." The boy leaned closer. "I din't tell her who it was fer. Herself's not in too good a mood."

Haakan thought of asking Charlie what was happening with Mrs. Landsverk, but a shout from the other logger stopped him. Besides, he'd never been one to ask a boy to do a man's job.

"Hey, boy, bring some of that coffee down here. You want I should have to fetch it myself?"

"No, sir." Charlie scooted off, but only after a wink at Haakan.

Haakan took his time over his pie, removing the letter from his pocket and reading it again under the light from the overhead kerosene lamp. The words hadn't changed. His mother surely did expect him to head for Dakota Territory immediately. And on skis no less, as if he'd had any time to make skis. He thought of the long hours he'd spent playing cards with the other loggers. Skis hadn't seemed important. Where would he go anyway? Deeper into the woods?

He scraped the last of the rich pie juice off the plate. He knew he should write his mother a letter. Since her letter had taken so long to arrive, she believed he was already there. Wherever *there* was. Surely she understood he had a life of his own to lead. As the eldest son, he'd always taken care of the younger ones, especially after his father died in a fishing boat accident when he was ten. Only after his mother remarried did he feel he could leave Norway for the new land. And now she expected him to run save the wives of two of his cousins, cousins so far removed he'd only met them once and their wives never.

A guilty conscience weighing him for not writing in so long, Haakan headed for the bunkhouse to get paper and pencil. Since the light was better in the cookshack, he returned and took his place again on the long plank bench. Besides, if he remained in the cookshack, he might get a chance to talk with the woman he'd been dreaming of.

"Dear Far and Mor and all my family, I am as well as can be expected and still logging in the north woods of Minnesota. I am sorry to tell you that I cannot leave here right now—your letter took three months to find me—as my boss depends on me in many ways. Perhaps I can travel west in the spring if they don't hire me on at the mill." He stopped and chewed the end of the pencil. What was there to tell them? He knew they didn't want to hear of the fights and drinking, the accidents, and the frostbite. What they wanted to hear was that he was married and raising a family. A shame it was, because deep down he really did like the logging life. He signed the letter "With love from your son, Haakan," and addressed the envelope, sticking the last stamp he owned up in the corner. The room had grown too quiet.

He stared at the now darkened kitchen. Mrs. Landsverk hadn't come to join him for a last cup of coffee like she usually did. He shook his head. There was trouble in the hen house for sure.

In spite of his concern, when Haakan fell on the rough bunk, sleep hit him on the way down. He heard the carousers return sometime in the wee hours, but since no fight erupted, he slept on. When he awoke, it was with the determination to confront Mrs. Landsverk, tell her he loved her, and ask her to marry him. The sooner the better. He crossed his hands over his broad chest and stared at the rafters above. Is this really what he wanted?

"Ja, it is!" He leaped to the floor with a thud, slapped Swede on the shoulder to wake him, and, still in his long red underwear, rattled the grate and added fresh wood to the nearly dead fire.

"Hey, keep the noise down over there!" The man in the corner added a few pungent words to the first, and the grunts from the others said they agreed.

"If you'd been sleepin' rather than drinkin', you'd be ready to greet this glorious new day." Haakan slammed the lids down on the stove with more than necessary vigor. He broke the ice in the top of the drinking bucket and ladled water into the kettle to set on the stove. Today he would wash and shave to greet his beloved looking his best. He dug out his last clean shirt, whistling a tune and dreaming of what was to come.

When Haakan entered the cookshack with his corn-silk golden hair still darkened by the water he'd used to make it lie flat against his head, a strange man in a black wool suit sat at the end of the bench closest to the kitchen. With one hand on his shoulder, Mrs. Landsverk was refilling the man's coffee cup. His hand covered hers and he was looking up at her with eyes brimming with love. The man certainly didn't look old enough to be her father. Where on earth had he come from?

Haakan tried to take a deep breath, but the ax that split his breastbone wouldn't allow it. He started to turn, but she caught his movement and, with a smile to dim a summer sun, said, "Come, Mr. Bjorklund, I want you to meet a very good friend of mine from home. We lived on neighboring farms growing up."

Feeling as if his life's blood were running down his shirt, Haakan did as she asked. After the introduction and a stiff handshake, which took every ounce of civility he possessed, he shook his head at her offer of coffee.

"Then I will tell you my wonderful news. Since his wife died,

Reverend Jorge has been looking high and low for me, and now that he found me, we will be married next week in Duluth. Isn't that wonderful?"

The axhead drove deeper into his heart. Haakan dipped his head in the briefest of nods. "I am very happy for the two of you. Now, if you will excuse me . . ." He turned and forced his legs to walk, not run, to the outside door, and he straight-armed it open. The resounding bang sent ice and snow crashing from the roof to the stoop. He headed out one of the skid roads, his long legs covering twice the ground as usual. When he was out of sight of the camp, he broke into a run, his corked boots spurting snow behind him.

By the time he returned to camp, he was no longer calling himself every kind of fool. His legs had cramped and forced him to stop more than once to stretch them out, but his breathing had returned to normal. No one could see the sweat still soaking his long johns. He looked like a man who'd been out for a Sunday stroll, but for the set of his jaw and the ice in his eyes.

It was his own fault, he knew, which didn't make it any easier. If only he'd spoken earlier . . .

The coming nuptials were the talk of the camp. One logger began collecting donations from each of the men so they could buy a present or give the newlyweds the money. Heaven only knew that preachers didn't make much. Haakan tossed in a dollar.

The night they left he won every hand at the poker table. No one dared argue with him.

By the end of the week, he had all but put Mrs. Mary Landsverk and the wedding out of his mind. Or so he thought. When the new cook—a man who closely resembled a potbellied stove—drove up with the supply sledge, Haakan said not a word. But then the few he'd uttered all week didn't equal the fingers of one hand.

Life in the logging camp continued at the same steady pace. A blizzard kept everyone confined to camp for three days, and by the end of the third, Haakan had ignored three bloody fights.

"What's with you, man?" the foreman asked.

"Nothing, why?" Haakan cocked one eyebrow.

"I counted on you to keep order around here. Now I got one man with a broken arm and ta other with cracked ribs. They was kickin' the life out of him, and you sat back and did nothin'."

Haakan crossed his arms across his chest. "I wasn't hired to be peacemaker." He didn't add, *And if you'd been sober instead of drunk on your bunk, you could have broken up the fights yourself.* But he must have thought it plenty loud because the foreman glowered back at him.

"The men respect you."

"Ja."

The foreman slammed his hands on the desk. "Don't expect no favors from me when it comes time to hire at the mill. You know they go on my say-so."

Haakan felt his muscles tense. Grabbing the man by the checkered shirt front and slamming him against the wall would only relieve the anger burning in his belly for now. It wouldn't solve anything. He'd come so close to joining in the brawl last night, he'd had to leave the bunkhouse.

In spite of his best efforts, thoughts of Mrs. Landsverk, now Mrs. Jorge, tormented him night and day. He hadn't realized he loved her this much or had so counted on her going west with him in the spring. If he'd had the sense of a mosquito, he'd have spoken sooner.

One day toward the end of March, he heard his name called above the din of men eating. Another letter. He rose to get the paper square and returned to his place on the bench. Two letters so close together. What could have happened at home?

He slit the envelope carefully and drew out the paper. Perusing it quickly, his heart sank. His mother sent another request for him to help save the widows. Surely there were plenty of men in Dakota Territory who wouldn't mind meeting up with a widow woman and working her land for her. He shook his head. It wasn't for him. He liked the logging life, and lumbering liked him.

Two days later, he woke up prone and found himself being hauled back to camp in the middle of the afternoon on the sledge.

"What happened?" He could hardly speak around the vise that held his head in a grip that continued to tighten.

"You was struck by a widow-maker." The driver spit a blob of tobacco into the snowbank. "You was lucky. Two inches closer and you wouldn't know nothing ever again."

Haakan gritted his teeth against the movements of the sledge, each one cranking on the vise handle, intensifying the pain. "Swede?"

"Just scratched up some. He had a sense of it and drove you forward with his shoulder. I seen it. That one was close."

Haakan lifted his hand to his head and drew it away covered in blood.

"Not to worry. That cookie, he'll stitch you up good as new. You

Norwegians got good hard heads."

Four men hauled Haakan off the sledge and carried him into the cookshack to lay him on one of the ten-foot tables. He closed his eyes against the agony, stemming the nausea rising in his throat.

"Easy, son, you'll be good as new when I'm done with you." Cookie pressed around the gash with gentle fingers. "Don't seem to be nothing broken, fer as I can tell. 'Course a crack in that solid skull of your'n could cause plenty problems too. Seen men go blind and deef after something like this."

Haakan clamped his hands around the edge of the table. "Just get on with it."

"Better go get the whiskey. This sure do call for it." The grizzled man's fingers continued their probing. When the driver arrived back from the kitchen with the amber-filled bottle, the cook took a slug himself and then poured some into the wound. The fire burning Haakan's head jackknifed him near upright.

He finally opened his eyes again to see Cookie waving the bottle in front of him.

"Drink up."

He'd never tried drinking lying flat on his back.

"Here, let me help." The driver worked his arm under Haakan's shoulders and lifted him carefully. With his other hand he propped the bottle at the injured man's lips. "Drink quick."

Haakan started to refuse, but when the cook ordered him to drink, he did. The liquid burned like wildfire clear to his gullet. He took a few more swallows, doing his best not to cough at the heat. It wasn't that he had never drunk, but nursing a drink through an evening of cards and chugging it down were two different things. He'd never seen any sense in being pie-eyed and sicker'n a dog the next day.

Right now he didn't care. He'd do anything to dull the vicious pain squeezing his head.

He passed out about the third stitch. From then on he would have a permanent part on the right side of his head. It wasn't perfectly straight, but then cracked heads rarely are. He woke up two days later to see Cookie peering into his eyes.

"Hey, son, dat's good." Cookie leaned back in the chair he'd pulled up to the lower bunk where they'd made the injured man comfortable. "You gonna feel right better soon. I ain't never lost a man I stitched up. Know your name?"

Haakan closed his eyes against the dancing firelight. Someone must have left the door open on the stove. His name? Of course he knew his name. Nothing came to mind, however.

"I see. Know where you're at?"

Haakan looked at the rough-sawn boards overhead, the patchwork quilt covering his body. Moving his head set the anvil to pounding again. He closed his eyes and let the questions lie.

When he woke again, he remembered everything. His name, the logging camp, and the swoosh of a falling widow-maker. That branch had done it's best to kill him, but here he was.

Sleeping, waking, and finally clear headed, he found thoughts of Mrs. Landsverk always drifting through. He should have made his intentions known sooner, before that Reverend Jorge had found her.

It took two weeks before he could rejoin his crew, and by then, much of the snow had melted in the first of the spring thaws.

"So, what you gonna do next?" Swede asked one day. "They already chose up the men to go work the mills. Didn't see your name on the list."

"I know." Haakan thought back to the scene with the foreman that night weeks ago. The man had a long memory. He rubbed at the scar on his head that glowed pink in the sunlight. "I think I'm heading west. I got some relatives who be needing a hand in Dakota Territory, and after I get them straight, I'll keep on going. I heard there's some mighty big trees in Oregon Territory and an ocean with fjords beside. What about you?"

Their axes continued the rhythm of branch-stripping as they talked.

"Ah, you know that neighbor to the west of the dairy farm where I worked the last two summers?"

"Ja."

"Well, she be needing some help, too. I'm tinkin' I might stay on there, if she needs me, a' course."

"Just don't waste too much time before you ask her." Haakan swung and cut clear through a six-inch branch. He pushed it to the side with his axhead. "If you care for her, just ask her right out."

"M-marryin', ya mean?" Swede stuttered over the words.

"If that's what you want."

"Ja, ja. That it is." Swede leaned his ax against a branch and wiped his forehead with a faded red bandanna. "I tink I may like felling trees better, you know?"

The two men looked at each other and shook their heads. Their laughter rang high, accompanied by the sharp ring of ax on wood.

Early one morning a few days later, Swede joined the men on the final wagon going to town. "You find your land, you write to me, ya hear?" he called as the driver slapped the reins on the backs of the two teams. "You know what town I be near."

"Ja, I will." Haakan waved a last time at the hooting and hollering men. *Should I be with them?* He shook his head and bent down to pick up his pack. It contained all his worldly goods, a knife, cooking pot, cup and small utensils, a change of clothes, extra socks, the Bible his mor insisted he take, fishing line and hooks, flint and tinder, and some food he'd begged from the kitchen. He'd topped it all with a quilt and a blanket all wrapped in a tarp he bought off the owner of the lumbering outfit. He shoved his arms into the ropes he'd fashioned, and with his ax firmly anchored to his belt, he started walking west.

A hundred paces or so up the drag road he turned and looked back. Shutters covered the windows. The buildings were all set on logs carved with up-turned ends to make pulling them easier. Soon teams would hitch up and drag the camp farther north to where prime trees still blotted out the sun. Would he make it in the west, or would he be back here again next fall just before snow-fly and asking for his job back? Or, just as they had hammered shut the doors of the buildings, was he slamming shut a time of his life?

"Widows Bjorklund, here I come. If I can find you."

The morning sun shone over his shoulder, casting his shadow ahead of him and leading the way to the western territories.

Skiing would certainly have been an easier mode of travel if he'd started west earlier in the season.

Haakan paused after crossing a swollen stream by way of a fallen log. Bridges like that were few and far between. He dug in his pocket for his last biscuit, hard as one of the pine trees he'd felled, and dunked it in the tin cup he'd filled with ice-cold water from a clean trickle. Starting a fire took too much time, and where would he find dry wood, anyway? While a couple of times he'd found a farm where he could sleep in the barn, most nights he'd spent wrapped in his quilt in the tarp.

Sometimes cold, often wet, he'd fought to keep the thoughts of Mrs. Landsverk at bay. What was the matter with him that he let her leaving bother him so? He called himself all kinds of fool and a few other names as well, but the memory of her smile kept coming back, especially in his dreams.

One night, howling wolves forced him to make his bed in the crook of a towering maple tree. He was so tired he tied himself in and slept anyway. Whatever had possessed him to start on this fool journey before summer, or at least spring, was well established?

He stopped to ask about the road he ran across, with grooves deeper than his knees, in the Minnesota rolling hills just before the Red River Valley.

"That there's the Red River carts' track," the storekeeper said. "Used to haul supplies north from St. Paul and furs south from the fur traders. Them big-wheeled carts could be heard for miles, they squawked so. 'Tween them wheels squallin', the oxen bellerin', and them French Canadians swearing, those long lines were something to behold." He ran his thumbs under his apron strings. "Now, I ain't got nothing 'gainst the railroad, but it ain't nearly as colorful as the Red River carts. You be needing some supplies?"

Haakan nodded and gave the man his brief list. After asking directions, he set off at a northwestern angle to catch the ferry crossing the Red River at St. Andrew. Unbeknownst to him, he'd swung too far south in his western trek. It wasn't long before he crossed the railroad tracks running north and south. How much easier his trip would have been could he have caught a train.

Ice floes still joined the flotsam of the Red River in full spate.

Haakan stood on the east bank and stared across the muddy river. Too high for swimming, that was for certain, besides being far too cold. None of the folks he'd talked with had mentioned a bridge except for the one down south in Grand Forks. The town on the other side of the river hunkered down like the falling rain might wash it away, just as the river had obviously done with trees that once stood along the banks. Water-logged trees bumped branches with each other and with those still standing as they bobbed their way to the river mouth north on Lake Winnipeg. Perhaps he should go upstream and catch himself a ride on one of those floating logs. Surely he could steer it to the opposite bank at some point.

Water dripped from the brim of his hat, some missing the tarp he wore like a poncho, and ran freezing its way down his back. He needed to find shelter of some kind, that was for certain. He watched from under the partial protection of a tree as the biting rain turned to snow.

A cable hooked around the trunk of the solid tree farther back on the bank disappeared into the swirling river. Looked like in the summer, at least, they had a ferry to take travelers across. As the snowfall thickened, the wind caught the flakes, driving them directly into his face. There'd be no crossing the river this night. The afternoon light was quickly fading under the onslaught of the snow and wind.

He had a choice to make: camp here and hope for a better tomorrow or return to the farm he'd passed a mile or so back on the road. Haakan shivered under the meager protection of his tarp. As wet as it was, he knew he'd never get a fire going. And the snow still lying in the shaded places was wet as a puddle anyway.

The big question was, would this miserable weather turn into a full-blown blizzard or just remain an irritating snowstorm? He rose from his hunkered-down position by the trunk of the tree and headed back in the direction he'd just come.

Only thanks to the early lit lamps did he see the house off to the left through the swirling snow. Even so, if the dog hadn't barked, he might have trudged right on by, so easy it was to lose track of the distance in the now heavily falling snow. As he walked up to the back porch, Haakan heaved a sigh of relief. He would be safe now from the unsettled weather. When a man answered the knock, Haakan greeted him in his accented English, then stated his request.

"Do you think you could let me sleep in your barn tonight? I've been traveling some time, and—"

"The barn! Heavens no, you'd nearly freeze out there. You come on in. Had supper yet?" While the man only came up to Haakan's chest bone, his welcome filled the porch and followed them into the warm and cheery kitchen.

"Let me take my boots off out here." Haakan pointed to the porch.

"No, no, it won't be the first snow that's made it fer as the rug. Though Mattie don't like it when I track up her kitchen floor. You make yourself to home, and I'll go get her." With a gesture to indicate the chair and the stove, the man charged out of the room and headed for the stairs.

Haakan could hear him calling "Mattie, darlin' " as he climbed to the second floor. After removing his boots and hanging his dripping tarp on the enclosed porch, he hung his coat and hat on the tree by the door. Perhaps after supper they would let him put his things by the stove so they would be dry by morning. He looked around the spotless kitchen and extended his hands to the welcome heat emanating from the cast-iron cookstove. Now this was what a home should look like. White wainscoting halfway up the walls with sky blue paint covering the rest. Glass-fronted cupboards for the dishes, and counters enough for several people to work at once. He eyed the coffeepot shoved to the back so it would still be hot but not bubbling. How long had it been since he'd had hot coffee. Days? A week?

"My land, what could you be doing out on such a night as this?" A woman, as cheery as she was round, bobbed into the kitchen and immediately pulled the blue enameled coffeepot to the front burner.

"I was hoping to cross to St. Andrew, but—"

"I know, I know, that lazy son of Sam's didn't bother to answer your halloo. But not to worry, you make yourself right to home here while I get something warmed for your supper. You look like you could use a good feed."

Haakan shifted his gaze to the man—he'd said his name was Ernie Danielson—who stood grinning in the doorway. Ernie shrugged and dug in his pocket, removing a carved pipe and placing the stem between grinning lips. He shrugged again as if to say, "She's always this way, just be comfortable." Haakan raised an eyebrow, but his attention immediately returned to the bustling woman when she shoved a mug of hot coffee in his hand and pointed to the table.

"Unless you'd rather stand here to get warm?" Her dark eyes smiled up at him, then she quickly bent and opened the oven door. "I know just the thing."

Before he had time to offer to help her, she'd dragged a chair over to the oven door and almost pushed him down onto it.

Haakan felt as though he were caught in the middle of one of those twisters he'd seen one summer. But with all her goodwill, he could only do as he was told and murmur "mange takk," chasing it with a thank-you as he recovered his new language.

"Not to worry, we understand some Norwegian too," Ernie said with a wave of the pipe he'd not bothered to light. He took a chair at the table, and a cup of coffee appeared almost miraculously in front of him.

Haakan felt the warmth of the oven seep through the blocks of ice he called feet. No more had the thought of wishing he could take off his socks floated through his head than Mattie—he still didn't know their last name—left her skillet and turned to her husband.

"You go get him some dry socks out of that drawer in the spare room. Yours would be far too small for feet of his size." She shooed her husband out of the room. "Now we can put your boots on the oven door for the night, and I can see your coat and hat need some drying too. Anything else?" She stopped her stirring and put a hand to her mouth. "Ach, I done it again, ain't I? Just take over and order everyone around."

Haakan looked up into her merry eyes and couldn't suppress a chuckle. "No, ma'am, you remind me so much of my mor that I feel like I just walked into the door of my own home. And I've not been there for over fifteen years."

"And where was that?" She turned the bread she'd set to toasting over the fire under the open front lid.

Rich, meaty fragrances rose from the now steaming skillet and tantalized his nose. His mouth watered while he sipped on the hot coffee. He could feel the heat clear to the heart of him. "North of Valdrez, Norway, in a little hamlet where no one who lives more'n twenty kilometers away has ever heard of."

"Ach, you miss those you love, I'm sure." She took down a plate she'd had on the warming shelf on the rear of the stove and ladled beef stew with carrots, turnips, and potatoes onto the plate. "You can eat here or at the table, depending on how your feet are warming."

Ernie charged back into the room and waved three pairs of hand-knit woolen socks at his wife. At her nod, he handed them to Haakan. "Put these on before you eat, and I can guarantee the food'll taste better. Hard to appreciate anything when your feet feel nigh unto freezing."

With another murmured thank-you, Haakan did as he was told. Then he got to his feet and took the plate and cup to the table. Ernie followed with the chair, and after settling their guest, the two older people took the two chairs on the other side of the dining table. Mattie set the kerosene lamp to the side, and with coffee refilled for all of them, they both took a cookie from a filled plate set in the center of the table.

"Now, we can just visit." Mattie dunked her cookie in the coffee and rolled her eyes as if this were her own bit of heaven.

Haakan felt sure it was. By the time he'd cleaned his plate after the heaping refill Mattie insisted he accept, he leaned back in his chair and sighed. "I'm thinking you saved my life this night."

"I doubt it. You look to be pretty self-sufficient to me. But you surely made our evening brighter. Until the spring work starts, we live pretty much by ourselves. Once we can get out on the fields, the men make their way back, and then we have a full bunkhouse and a cook to help Mattie, besides."

"Ach, how those men love to eat." Mattie's smile of reminiscence said as much for her love of cooking as it did for the men who enjoyed eating it.

Haakan could tell she liked having others to care for. The socks warming his feet said as much for her knitting skills. There were no bumps to cause blisters on unwary feet in the smoothly turned heel.

"How many men work here?"

"During the winter, just us and our foreman. As far as Bonanza farms go, we're pretty small, but the owners let us run it like it was our own. We repair machinery all winter long and get it ready so breakdowns won't slow us down come spring."

"What really is a Bonanza farm? I've heard all kinds of tall tales about the tons of wheat grown." Haakan leaned forward, propping his elbows on the table.

"There are hundreds and even thousands of acres in one farm. We can handle it since the machinery got so much better. The farms are usually owned by someone back East and managed by folks like us. We made them rich, we did. You be looking for work?"

Haakan shook his head. "I left logging in the north woods to come help some relatives of mine over on the Dakota side. Their husbands died a winter ago."

Ernie and Mattie swapped glances. "What did you say was your last name?"

"Bjorklund. Why? Do you know them? Kaaren and Ingeborg Bjorklund?"

"Well, I never . . . Small world we live in, for sure." Mattie leaned her elbows on the table. "Such a tragedy, them two young women left all alone like that. And that Ingeborg. She's some worker, that one."

"How do you know them?"

"Why, Ingeborg and her sister-in-law bring us cheese and butter, chickens, and produce in the summer. They sell to the Bonanza farm to the south of us, too. I don't know how they do it. And that little Thorliff, he's taken on a man's job, and he's only seven, or is it eight now?" Mattie turned to her husband for confirmation.

He'd finally gotten his pipe drawing and nodded around the fragrant smoke that wreathed his head. "Eight, I think. I surely hope they stood the winter all right. Of course, it helps now that Lars Knutson—he used to run a threshing crew—and the other Miz Bjorklund married last fall. They surely did need a man's help if'n they was to keep the land. Those two Bjorklund brothers was working fools, too. I told 'em they could come work for me anytime, but they was too busy breakin' sod."

Haakan nodded, grateful for the information. "I'm not surprised. Their father, Gustaf, has a fine reputation at home, and I'm sure he trained his sons to be like him." *I could have stayed in the north woods*, he thought, *or gone back to the farm I worked at last summer and saved myself a trip.*

"Yah, you Norwegians be good workers, that's for certain sure. As I said, if'n you want work, you come to me."

"I will think on it, but my mor would be mighty put off if I don't help out our relatives. I have a job back in the Minnesota north woods come winter, so perhaps I will stop on the way back." Haakan took one of the cookies when Mattie pushed the plate closer to him. "Thank you."

"Or you could come with the women when they bring their wares. I sure am hoping they keep coming. That Ingeborg makes the best cheese this side of heaven." Mattie smacked her lips and dunked another cookie in her coffee.

The three visited a bit longer, and then Mattie led the way to the spare room that looked more like home than any spare room Haakan had ever seen. A colorful nine-patch quilt covered the double bed, and a braided rag rug lay beside it on the dark painted wood floor. She set the lamp on the dresser and looked around.

"There are towels there in the commode, and there'll be hot water in the reservoir, should you be wanting to shave and wash in the morning. Heat will come up through the register in the hall, so you might want to leave your door open to let it in. Now, you have anything that is damp in your pack, you hang it on the rack to the side of the register. Ernie stoked the fire good so it won't be out by morning." She headed out the room and stopped at the door. "You sleep well now, you hear? You got nothing to worry about."

"Thank you, Miz Danielson."

"Mattie."

"All right." Haakan dropped his arms to his side. "But thank you, and I hope I can do something in return for all this bounty you've been so kind to share with me."

She shook her head and tossed a smile over her shoulder. "You already did." She went out, a chuckle under her breath.

Haakan stood there, questions ripping through his mind like a freshly sharpened saw through green wood. Never one to let things lie, he headed out the door after her. She was halfway down the stairs but turned when he called her name.

"What did I do but impose on your good graces?"

She looked up at him and shook her head. "Why, you're going to help out my friend, Ingeborg. And who knows what manner of good will come of that." She quirked her head, her round face beaming. "Would you rather have pancakes or johnnycake for breakfast, Mr. Bjorklund?"

"Ah, pancakes, I guess. Though whatever you make is fine with me."

"Good night, now."

Haakan stood at the top of the stairs shaking his head.

By the time he'd looked at the rows of plows, disks, seed drills, mowers, and binders the next morning, Haakan felt as though he'd been run over by three of the draft teams housed in the long hip-roofed barn next to the machine sheds. Never had he seen so much machinery in one place, and most of it he'd never heard of. No wonder the Bonanza farms were able to produce such enormous crops of wheat. The tales he'd heard weren't exaggerations, after all. Still, the truth was hard to believe.

Much to Mattie's dismay, he didn't wait for dinner but struck out midmorning.

"You just holler good and loud when you get to the ferry there at the river. Long as you're coming in the midday, old Sam will make that lazy son of his come across for you. It'll cost you two bits though." Ernie extended his hand. "Been fine meeting up with you, son."

Haakan grasped it and shook it, feeling as if he were leaving his family, and he'd only known these people less than a day. "I will see you in the fall, then. And thank you again."

The two men stood on the edge of the snow-covered road. While only a couple of inches had been dumped on the area, small drifts still ridged the white expanse and covered the fields as far as the eye could see. Off to the west, the trees lining the river shortened the endless horizon. In spite of the sun sneaking in and out of the high mare's-tail clouds, the ever present wind tried to blow their breath back down their throats.

"And I thought spring might be here with all the melting going on." Haakan shifted his pack.

"No, winter hasn't let go its hold yet. But you watch, tomorrow might be like a summer day. The icicles still be dripping." Ernie slapped Haakan on the arm. "Go with God, young man. I hope you learn to love this flat land as I do."

"Not much chance. I like hills and trees too much." Haakan raised a hand in farewell and started down the road. *You're a logger,* he reminded himself as he trudged along. *And that's what you plan to be until you have enough of a grubstake to get your own land. And it surely won't be in this flat stuff.*

As Ernie had said, when he hollered good and loud, a sturdy boy set out with a canoe to get him. While the current carried him some downstream, he paddled back to the road along the bank, ducking branches as he made his way toward Haakan.

Haakan dumped his pack in the middle of the craft and climbed in the bow. With the extra weight, the current didn't carry them as far, but again the boy returned close to the riverbank. Other than a grunt in response to Haakan's hello, he said not a word until they snugged up to the floating dock.

"That'll be two bits."

Haakan climbed out, retrieved his pack, and after fishing them out of his pocket, he dropped the coins in the boy's palm. "Thank you."

A grunt answered him as the boy tied the craft, prow and aft, to the cleats on the dock.

Haakan shook his head as he shouldered his pack and strode up the muddy, rutted street. He stepped out at his usual pace only to find himself flailing the air with his arms to keep from landing in one of the ruts. Never had he seen such slippery mud. And what he didn't slide in clung to his boots till his feet felt as though they weighed fifteen pounds each.

When he made it to the porch of the general store, he sat down to scrape the gooey black stuff off his boots. When banging them against the step failed to accomplish the feat, he picked up a stick and scraped it all away.

"Ah, yup. That's why we call that stuff gumbo. Sticks right to anything moving. Why, I seen horses drop from carrying such weights round their hooves."

Haakan looked up, then up some more to see the face of the man leaning against the post above him. He stood tall and thin like a tamarack with a face to match, his beard scruffy as tree limbs in the fall.

"Mud is gumbo."

"Ah, yup. And turns to rock when it dries out. You got to work it into submission sometime in between." A juicy glob flew past Haakan's ear and plopped in the puddle near his feet.

Haakan shifted off to the side. Where he came from one didn't spit near a friend.

"You here to take up farmin'?"

"My name is Haakan Bjorklund." Haakan rose to his feet and turned to face the leaning tree of a man. "I'm come to help out some relatives of mine, the Bjorklunds."

"They's dead. Lost in the flu an' the blizzard more'n a year ago."

"Ja, I know that. But I heard their widows can use some help. I come from the north woods in Minnesota."

"Ya look kinda like a logger." The man nodded.

Haakan waited, hoping the man would give him directions to the Bjorklund place. When none were forthcoming, he took in a deep breath. One could never fault the residents of St. Andrew for talking too much if Sam's son and the tree here were any indication. "You know where they live?"

"Ah, yup."

Haakan waited again. He quelled the rising impatience and rocked back on his heels. "Might you be willing to share that information with me?" He glanced to where the sun had hastened to its decline. Didn't look like he would make it to the homestead today, either.

" 'Bout half a day or more good walkin' to the southwest." Tamarack pointed in that direction, and a second glob of tobacco juice followed the first.

"How far before I can ford the river that flows in from the west?" Haakan was already wishing he'd had Sam drop him up river, beyond the mouth of the tributary.

"Ah, that'd be the Little Salt. It's runnin' high right now."

Haakan stuck his hands in the front pockets of his wool pants. He paced his words to match this laconic purveyor of local information. No sense trying to hurry this. "So's the Red."

"Ah, yup. Pretty nigh onto flood stage. Nothin' much git through till they abate some."

"Are there any marked roads?"

The tree looked at him as if all the sap must have run from his head. He shook his head and spit once more. "Ya foller the river till you git there." With that he shambled off the porch and disappeared around the corner.

"Mange takk." Haakan raised his voice, then snorted when no polite response answered him. He scraped some more mud off his boots on the step and mounted to enter the store. A bell tinkled over the door, and a plethora of smells—the same of general stores worldwide—made him sniff in appreciation. Leather and spices, kerosene and pickles, tobacco and new metal buckets, to mention only a few. He stopped for a moment, caught by the variety of goods stacked on shelves, hanging from the walls and ceiling, filling crates and barrels. Clear out here in what seemed to be the ends of the earth, if he had the money, it looked like he could buy about whatever he could dream of.

"Can I help you?" The man's spectacles shone as brightly as the dome rising from his hair. His apron, perhaps white in the beginning, now hung in gray folds from the string around his neck. As he came to greet his customer, the storekeeper reached behind and tied the dangling strings so the apron fit like it ought to.

"I . . . ah, I need two peppermint sticks and a pound of coffee." Haakan looked around, wondering if there was something besides coffee he could buy for Roald's widow. Perhaps that Lars fellow wouldn't appreciate a stranger bringing his wife a present. What would they be out of now after a long winter? Sugar? Of course. "Give me a couple pounds of sugar too and add half a dozen of those candy sticks."

As the man wrapped the items in paper, he looked up at Haakan from under caterpillar eyebrows. "You new to the Territory?"

"Ja, how can you tell?"

"I ain't never seen you here before, and I heard you asking Abe out there for directions to the Bjorklunds." He handed the packet, now wrapped in brown paper and string, across the counter. "He ain't one to volunteer much."

"I saw that." Haakan dug in his pocket for his money. "Know where I could stay for the night and maybe get a meal?"

"Well, Widow MacDougal runs a small hotel, but she took a trip down to Fargo for the winter. Won't be back till the riverboat runs. St. Andrew kind of closes up in the winter 'cept for me and the blacksmith. Guess you could try over to the Lutheran church. If the pastor is around, he maybe could help you. That'll be a dollar."

Haakan laid the money on the counter and picked up his parcel. "Mange takk."

"We don't get much travelers this time of year, what with the mud and rising rivers. Soon though, we'll have settlers moving west like fleas on a dog." He came around the counter and walked with Haakan to the door. Now that cash money had changed hands, it seemed to loosen the man's tongue. "You had a horse, he could swim you across the Little Salt, but without one, you're facing five miles or more before you can ford it. And then it'd be dangerous. You shoulda come before the ice went out."

"I'll keep that in mind." Haakan let himself out the door, the bell tinkling again.

"You'll find the Lutheran church couple blocks west on the outskirts of town. Can't miss it, white steeple and all."

"Thank you again." Haakan tipped his hat and followed the

boardwalk along the front of the next two buildings before he had to step back in the gumbo. His boots weighted up fast as he could step. Getting to the Bjorklunds looked to be a mite farther than he had thought.

When no one answered at the church or the small frame house beside it, he decided to keep on going west. There was no sense wasting the remaining hours of daylight. Surely there would be another farm along the way. The snow from the day before had mostly melted, so the road that followed the Little Salt River was clearly visible. Perhaps, he decided, if he stayed on the shoulder where grass from the year before lay brown and could be seen through the remaining snow, he wouldn't mud up so bad.

He spent the night in an abandoned sod house that had since been used for storing hay and feed. Wrapped in his quilt on the tarp in front of a fire, his mind traveled both backward and forward. Back to the logging camp and the pleasant times with Mrs. Landsverk, forward to a place he could now begin to envision. Living in a soddy would take some getting used to. Who was this Ingeborg Bjorklund, and would she even want his help, such were the things he'd heard about her?

Even though he hung his pack from a rafter, a mouse found its way in while he slept and scurried down his arm when he lifted the pack down in the morning. When Haakan checked the contents, he found a corner nibbled away on the packet from the store. Grains of sugar trickled out until he untied the string and rewrapped the package. He smiled, pleased that the creature hadn't found the coffee beans.

When he finally came to a place where the Little Salt River broadened out, and the road leading down to it showed there once had been a ford there, Haakan sat down on a tree trunk thrown up by the river and pulled a now dry chunk of bread and the remaining cheese from his pack. He studied both sides of the muddy river as he ate and surveyed the country around him, his thoughts flowing like the river before him. Off in the distance, he could see smoke from a chimney, but he was surprised to find so few homesteads, especially along the riverbanks. If water was such a premium in this area, why weren't the riverbanks more densely settled? Somehow he'd thought this area to be more populated, since there weren't Bonanza farms here, or so Ernie had said. Looking back, Haakan figured he'd covered near to ten miles and only seen three or four houses in all that time. Or did the sod homes fit into the prairie so as to disappear? He could tell where the sod had been broken in areas where snow had melted and showed dark soil rather than brown grass.

While his food disappeared rapidly, his stomach didn't agree that it should be full. He wrapped his tarp more tightly around the pack, leaned it against the log, and taking his ax he stepped up to one of the willow bushes. With a few quick swings, he cut himself a sturdy pole that stood several feet above his head.

He squinted up at the sun, rejoicing in the warmth on his face. If he owned a homestead near here, he told himself, he'd be down in the riverbed cutting logs. *Those sod houses look mighty sturdy, but I'd rather have a log one any day*. He sat back down on the log and removed his boots and socks, tucking them into the pack in the hopes to keep them dry. While he hoisted his pack, he continued to speculate about setting up a mill on the banks of the Red River. Surely there was call for lumber in this area. The Red had enough trees to supply boards for homes of wood, and glass windows could be brought in on the riverboat. Why, even the sod houses could use shakes for their roofs. He could set up splitting shakes.

Using the pole to prod the river bottom in front of him, he stepped into the icy water. "Uff da!" he gasped as the icy water swirled up to his knees, his hips, and then to his waist. He leaned against the current, testing each footfall to keep his balance. Certain he was going to have to swim for it, he breathed a sigh of relief when the pole showed an upward thrust to the river bottom. Slipping in the mud, he pulled himself up the shallow incline, and once on dry land, he leaned on his pole, his breath heaving in and out of his lungs.

Standing in the shelter of a tall cottonwood, he stripped down to his bare skin and pulled on the dry clothes he'd stored in his pack. Long johns, shirt, pants, and finally dry socks and shoes. He could hardly force the buttons through the holes or lace his boots, his fingers shook like he had the palsy. Leaping to his feet, he swung his arms, thumping himself on the chest and forcing his legs to move. He considered starting a fire to warm himself, but the thought of lost time made him pick up his pack and command his legs and feet into a trot. Between the sun and action, he knew he'd be warm soon.

He headed out in a southeast direction, knowing the Red River would keep him from going too far east. If he figured right with what little information he had, he'd hit the river north of the Bjorklund homestead or come right into the homeplace.

But dark caught him before he reached either the river or the homestead he sought. The wind at his back picked up a knife edge when the sun disappeared under the horizon. With nothing but prairie in sight, he huddled tighter into his wool coat and kept on walking. A dog barking brought him to a stop. Slowly, he turned to locate the direction. When he whistled, the barking turned to a frenzy. He turned due south and whistled every once in a while to keep the animal barking.

"That's enough, Shep!" a man's strong voice commanded. "Whatever's got you going on like this, anyhow?"

"Helloo!" Haakan called out and stopped to listen for an answer.

"Hello, yourself. Keep on coming, you're getting near." A lighted lantern pierced the darkness like a beacon at sea. "Welcome, stranger, you nigh unto missed us, didn't you?"

Haakan reached out to shake the man's hand. "If it hadn't been for your dog barking, I'd have gone right on by." He glanced down at the dog that stood by his master's knee, hackles raised and a rumble deep in his throat.

"Enough, Shep. Ya done good. Come on in. My missus will skin me alive if I keep you standing out here. She's already got the coffeepot heating."

"I hoped maybe I could sleep in your barn—"

"In the barn! Heaven's man, you want us both thrown out on our ears?" He turned and headed for the door. "Agnes won't hear none of that, let me tell you."

Haakan followed the man, ducking as he did to enter the sod house.

"Lookee here, Shep brought us some company, he did."

Before he knew what had happened, Haakan had been divested of his pack, coat, and hat and sat in a rocker in front of a cookstove that seemed to half fill the room. A cup of coffee warmed his hands, and a little girl stared at him from behind her bigger sister as if she'd never seen a stranger before. One thing Haakan knew for sure: he was welcome, and these fine people were as Norwegian as they came. He felt like he'd stepped into a small piece of home but for the close dark walls and the overlying smell of earth from the walls and floor. And they still hadn't even asked his name.

"Uff da," The woman murmured, seating herself on one of the benches along the trestle table. "Now what news did you hear in St. Andrew? Has the ice gone out on the river? They started up the ferry yet?" She took a swallow from her cup. "Surely will be a treat to have real coffee again. That's first on the list soon as the wagon can make it to St. Andrew. Sorry for the substitute. We use roasted wheat when we run out of the real thing."

"Give the poor man a chance to answer," Joseph said, waving his cup in the air. "How far you come, young man?" He looked to his wife and laughed. "Can't keep calling him young man, can I? I'm Joseph Baard, and this is Mrs. Baard, Agnes. We come from Ohio to homestead this here valley." He named all the children, who either grinned or hid behind another depending on their age. "And who might you be?"

"Haakan Howard Bjorklund."

"Bjorklund?" Mrs. Baard pushed back so quickly she nearly turned the bench over. "We got neighbors and best friends named Bjorklund. You related?" At Haakan's nod, she clasped her hands together in her aproned lap. "Thanks be to God! They sure do need some kin to help out."

"Roald and Carl were my cousins twice removed."

"You heard they died, then?"

"Ja, that is why I am here." Haakan described his trip from the north woods of Minnesota in a few short sentences, and then said, "My mor wrote and told me they needed help, and soon as the logging season ended, I started west."

"Thank the good Lord." Her smile lit the room. "Ah, me. Where's my manners gone? You had any supper?" When he shook his head, she ordered Penny, the older girl, to fetch foodstuffs from the well house while she set a skillet on the stove. Before many minutes passed with the two men visiting, she had a plate of chicken and dumplings in front of him, along with bread and butter and a pitcher of milk.

"And if'n you go hungry after Agnes is done serving, you got no one but yourself to blame," Joseph said. Turning to the children who stood staring shyly at Haakan, he ordered in a kind voice, "You young'uns get to bed, now. Mr. Bjorklund will still be here in the morning."

The sun had made it halfway to the peak when he left in the morning, much to his host family's sorrow. Haakan made sure each of the children had a peppermint stick to remember him by. Agnes clutched a small packet of coffee beans to her breast as if he'd given her gold and diamonds.

"You go on straight east now. Just follow the track. Runs right into Ingeborg's. Kaaren's house is a bit to the north. I could give you a ride, you know."

"I know. Thank you for everything." Haakan waved a last time and strode out the track. Two wheel ruts had cut through the prairie grass and down to the dirt. He walked on the ridge in the middle to keep from slipping in the mud.

The sun warmed his shoulders, trying to make up for the snow and rain. Overhead, a V of ducks beat their way northward, their quacking a wild music on the breeze. Brave shoots of green showed on the places where the snow had melted away. The trees along the banks of the Red River edged the horizon so flat Haakan wasn't able to tell how far away they really were.

Never had he seen such flat land. Like a tabletop, it spread far as the eye could see in all directions. To the south a spiral of smoke told of an intrepid homesteader and ahead another. Thanks to the Baards, he now had an idea what life had been like for the two missus Bjorklunds in the last year. Blizzards in the winter, and breaking sod, planting, and harvesting in the summer. How had they endured without bolting back to town?

As the sod house and barn came into view, only the smoke feathering from the chimney said someone was home. Not far to the north lay the second sod house and barn like Baard had said. A caramel-colored dog with one ear straight up and the other flopped forward charged out from behind the barn and barked three times. He stood with one white front paw raised, his tail fanning the breeze. He barked again, more insistent this time.

"Paws!" a boy's voice called. The dog looked over his shoulder and wagged his tail again.

The boy came round the corner of the sod barn, followed by a woman carrying a small, gowned child with near-white ringlets on her hip. Her hair caught the sun and gleamed like a crown of gold. Tall and straight, she strode toward him, her welcoming smile warm as the spring sun.

Haakan caught his breath. So this was Ingeborg Bjorklund. Nothing anyone said had prepared him for this vision of a Viking queen.

Early April

God dag. Mrs. Bjorklund?"

"Ja."

"I am Haakan Howard Bjorklund, recently of Minnesota." He set his ax on the toe of his boot and removed his hat. "My mor wrote from Norway and said one of our relatives needed a hand. Since logging was done for the season, I came to see if I could help."

"You have the same name as us." Eight-year-old Thorliff stepped forward and looked up—way up. Tall for his age and already showing signs of future broad shoulders, the boy held his ground. Hair that couldn't decide between white gold and deep blond, whether to curl or lie straight, fell in one swatch over his right eye in spite of the porkpie hat that should have kept it in place. Pants and shirt showed thin wrists and ankles of winter white.

"Ja, your father is my cousin twice removed." Haakan felt as if he looked into a mirror when he saw the boy's eyes.

"Was," Ingeborg said softly.

"I know." He looked into her eyes, seeing the sheen of unshed tears. "I'm sorry."

Ingeborg nodded. "I have the coffee hot, and dinner is nearly ready. Would you like to join us?" She laid a hand on the head of the boy who stood slightly in front of her, guarding both her and the baby with his wide-legged stance. "This is Thorliff." With her other arm, she raised the chubby toddler on her hip. "And this is Andrew."

Thorliff ducked his head only enough to be polite. While his mother welcomed strangers, he clearly held his regard in reserve.

The dog walked forward on stiff legs to sniff the pant leg of the intruder. While his tail waved, it was obvious he, like the boy, expected the stranger to prove himself before being accepted.

Haakan glanced from the woman to the son to the dog and back. Her smile caught him in the chest like an arrow driving home straight and true. "Mange takk." When he turned slightly to remove his pack, a low rumble came from the throat of the dog, still watching him with careful eyes. Haakan stood straight again and spoke to the boy. "I have something for you in my pack, if you'll call off your dog."

Ingeborg laid a hand on Thorliff's shoulder. "Tell Paws it is all right. This man is a friend."

Thorliff studied the stranger for a long moment before he did as asked. "Paws, good dog. Come here." The dog looked back at his master, up at the stranger towering above him, and back to Thorliff.

"He takes good care of his family," Haakan said, extending his hand, palm down for the dog to sniff his knuckles. "I had a dog like this when I was a boy. He never left my side."

Thorliff nodded. "Paws guards the sheep, too."

"May I?" Haakan signaled to his pack.

"Ja, he will not hurt you." Thorliff slapped his thigh. "Paws, come here."

Paws finished sniffing the proffered hand, wagged his tail again, and turned back to the boy, checking over his shoulder to make sure the stranger didn't overstep his bounds.

"Good dog." Thorliff bent enough to ruffle the dog's ears and received a nose lick in return.

Haakan slipped his arms from the straps on the pack and reached inside the top flap. He pulled out the remaining peppermint sticks. "I thought a boy might need a treat after such a long winter." He held out the candy, one for Thorliff and another for Andrew.

Thorliff tried to act as if he didn't hold with candy sticks, but the gleam in his eyes gave him away. He took both sticks with a mange takk and handed one up to Andrew. When the baby only waved the red-and-white stick in the air, Thorliff put the end of his in his mouth and sucked on it. "See, Andrew, like this."

Andrew studied his brother's actions. When Thorliff pulled the end of the stick out, held it up, and put it back in his mouth, Andrew licked his candy first. His blue eyes grew round, and a grin split his face. He closed his mouth over the treat, making an O to match his eyes.

"Good, huh?" Thorliff giggled at the baby's chortle.

Both of them held the candy sticks in their mouths, grinning around them.

"It looks to me like you have won their hearts already." Ingeborg grabbed the baby's waving hand before the candy could land in her hair. "Mange takk. Not many would think of bringing the children a treat like that."

He stared down into gray eyes with a gaze so direct he felt she could see right through him. A straw hat hung on ribbons down her back, leaving the coronet of golden braids as a burnished crown. A few freckles already dotted her nose, mute testimony to her love of the sun, and the strong chin spoke of determination unfettered. When she smiled, her whole face glowed, lighting her eyes and crinkling the edges. He saw no shy miss here, but a woman of strength and courage. And when she smiled, he could do no less in return.

"Come, we will have dinner soon." She started toward the house. "I was washing the lamps outside since the sun begged me to." She pointed at a bench that held a pan of soapy water and several glass lamps.

Haakan met her grin with one of his own. "Begged you to? I like that. I wouldn't want to stay inside today either. Do you think spring is really here, or will we get another blanket of snow?"

"I don't know. I have learned to just appreciate each day as it comes, and after a long winter like we—I've had, I don't want to waste a moment of the sun's warmth."

❧ ❧

She skirted the mud patches, kicking up snow with the toe of her boot as if she could barely keep from dancing. She felt like twirling, like taking Thorliff by the hands and whirling him around, then doing the same with Andrew. To think God had sent them a gift like this visitor on such a splendid day.

Those eyes he had, eyes she hadn't seen in such a handsome face since they buried Carl. While Thorliff, too, had the Bjorklund eyes, there was something to be said for such eyes in a tall, broad-shouldered man. She'd heard of measuring a man's breadth by ax handles, but never had the picture been so real. The ax looked to be a continuation of his arm, the way he handled it. The cleft in his chin made his strong jaw even more manly.

She had so many questions to ask, but since Kaaren would want to know the same answers, she would wait until after dinner. The waiting would not be easy, though.

She felt a giggle rising in her throat. What if she'd been wearing britches? He most likely would have taken one look and run clear back to the north woods. She jiggled Andrew on her hip, keeping one hand ready to protect her hair.

"Velkommen to our house," Ingeborg said as she stepped into the dimness of the soddy. She paused a moment to let her eyes adjust. *Thank the good Lord I did the dishes and straightened up before I went outside.* On the way to the table, she pulled the coffeepot closer to the heat, then settled Andrew in a chair with a box on it. Taking the dish towel draped over the back of the chair, she smoothed it around his tummy and tied a knot behind the chair so he wouldn't fall off. "Have a seat," she said, motioning to Haakan with a sweep of her hand.

⚜ ⚜

Haakan followed a pace behind so he could watch her. While she looked every inch a woman, from the crown on her head to the black wool skirt damp at the hemline from melting snow, he had the feeling it would take little encouragement for her to join the boys in a game of tag or a footrace. She didn't act like any widows he knew.

Once seated at the square table, with benches on two sides and chairs with hand-turned spindles at the others, he could tell by the delicious smells rising from the oven and the kettle she stirred on the stove that she was no ordinary cook.

His stomach rumbled in anticipation.

Ingeborg poured the now hot brew and set a cup of it on the table in front of him.

"Mange takk." He watched her smooth grace as she turned the loaf pans out on a towel spread on the counter of a cabinet of sorts that was set against the sod wall by the stove. Shelves beneath and above gave her a workplace and storage for kitchen goods.

"That bread smells like a piece of home." He took a sip of the scalding brew and looked around the sod house. A trunk decorated in the Valdrez style of rosemaling sat in a place of honor under the one window. Beautifully carved shelves lined both sides of the deep enclosure. Two rope beds were attached to the rear wall, sharing a post in the center. Colorful quilts and several elk hides covered the mattresses. An oak rocker, turned spindles for the back and topped with a carved header, showed the pride of the maker's workmanship. Curved arms with a roll at the end told of the hours spent in making the chair a thing of beauty, not only a necessary furnishing. A picture flashed through his mind of the woman, so busy now with setting out the food, sitting in that rocker with a babe to her breast. He felt a flush start down at the base of his neck.

He forced his gaze to the sacks hanging from the rafters, the few remaining bundles of dried herbs, and the lengths of wood stored there to dry and season. Obviously Roald had held the same love of wood and creating beautiful and useful things from it as did Haakan himself. Shame there weren't more windows so the dark walls didn't crowd in on one. He shook his head. What must it have been like to be cooped up in here with a young boy, a baby, and the screeching wind day after day? How did she get out to care for the livestock in the winter months?

The question burst forth in spite of his personal admonitions not to be inquisitive. "How did you manage through the blizzards?"

Ingeborg turned from the stove where she'd been adding more wood to the firebox. "You mean with the cows and sheep?"

"Ja, and the boys. By yourself?"

Ingeborg wiped her hands on the underside of her apron. "We strung a rope from the house to the barn so we could follow it when the snow was so bad I couldn't see my hand in front of my face. You learn to do that early on, or you never make it through the winter. We melted snow for the animals to drink when they could not get out to the trough. It was much easier this year since we had the well. We used to take the animals down to drink in the river where we kept a hole chopped out for them." She handed Thorliff the plate of sliced bread to place on the table. "One good thing about the snow, we never ran out of water, though keeping enough melted was a full-time job. Thorliff has done the work of a man since his father died. I couldn't have managed without him." She patted the boy on the shoulder. "Thanks to the good Lord, we made it."

Haakan shook his head in amazement. Privately he doubted the good Lord had as much to do with it as did her sheer strength of will and Norwegian stubbornness. But then, he'd never been one to trouble the Lord with the events in his life. He'd decided early on that he'd rather take care of things himself than try to depend on one he couldn't see and who caused such pious and sober faces of a Sunday morn. Contrary to the pastor's and his mother's preaching those years ago, he'd always felt the bird choirs and the wind anthem in the trees a better way to worship if there really was a God like they'd insisted.

When she had all the food on the table, Ingeborg asked Thorliff to lead grace. Haakan joined in the old words he'd learned at his mother's knee. "E Jesu naven, gor vi til brod. . . ." It had been a long time since he'd heard the verse. He knew if he'd taken time to say grace at the trestle tables in the cookshack at the logging camp—packed shoulder to shoulder they'd been—he'd have missed out on the bowls and platters of food being passed down the line. Too, he'd have been in for a healthy dose of ribbing. Haakan had earned his reputation for strength and fairness the hard way—by his hands.

They were halfway through the meal when he remembered. "Oh, I have something for you." He pushed his chair back and retrieved his pack from by the door where he'd set it when he came in. Along with the packet of sugar and coffee, he held out the letter the man at The Mercantile had sent with him. "I'm sorry. I forgot to give you this sooner."

Ingeborg clasped the letter to her bosom. "From home! A letter from home!" She raised shining eyes to thank him. "What a treat you have brought us. We'll all have to take this over to Tante Kaaren's to read after dinner." She laid the precious envelope down beside her plate and fingered the tied brown packet. "And what is this?"

"Open it, Mor." Thorliff leaned forward, elbows on the table.

"I wanted to bring you a gift but didn't know you, so this was all I could think of." Haakan took his place again and raised the cup to drink.

Ingeborg unwrapped her package. "Not more peppermint sticks, I take it?"

"No." He looked at Thorliff. "Sorry."

Ingeborg sniffed. "Coffee." She opened the packet and brought the bag up to her nose. "It smells heavenly. I've been hoarding the few beans left, now we will have plenty."

"Mor, what is in the other pack?" Thorliff asked, his eyes on the brown wrapped parcel.

"I don't know. Do you want to open it?"

"Can I?" He looked from Mor to the visitor. Haakan nodded and Ingeborg beckoned for Thorliff to come stand beside her.

"Be careful," Haakan cautioned.

Thorliff caught his bottom lip between his teeth as he cautiously pulled each fold of the parcel open. When the white granules lay before him, he raised questioning eyes to the man across the table.

"Wet your finger and dip a taste."

The boy did as told. "Sugar! Real, white sugar." He grinned up at his mother. "You do it." She tasted the treat and rolled her eyes in delight.

"Ah, sugar and coffee. And we were all out of honey, too. You couldn't have thought of anything better, Mr. Bjorklund. Out here we never take coffee or sugar for granted."

Or anything else, Haakan felt like adding.

Andrew banged his spoon on the table. "Me, me." Ingeborg dipped her finger in the treat again and put the tip of it in the baby's mouth. Andrew grabbed her hand and sucked again on her finger when she tried to withdraw it.

"That is one smart little fellow. He knows a good thing when he gets it."

"And he don't let go." Thorliff sneaked another quick taste and grinned at his mother when she frowned the teeniest bit and shook her head.

"We will put this away for a very special treat." She rewrapped the packet. "What do you tell Mr. Bjorklund?"

"Mange takk," Thorliff said, flashing a grin at the same time.

"I believe since we are related by marriage, no matter how distant, you could call me Haakan." He looked across the table at her, willing her to agree. Why did it make any difference to him what she called him? After all, he would only be here until fall, and then he'd return to the north woods. He ignored the questioning of his mind and waited for her response.

Ingeborg nodded. "All right. And I am Ingeborg. Soon you will meet Kaaren—she was Carl's wife—and her new husband, Lars Knutson. He ran the steam threshing machine and the crew that came through here in the fall." She looked down at the packet in front of her. "Kaaren's two little girls died in the same flu that took Carl."

"And Roald?" He called himself all sorts of names for asking.

"Inadvertently. After Carl died and the blizzard let up, he went to check on some of our neighbors. The northern blizzard came back, and we think he was stranded in it and died. He might have fallen prey to the flu . . ." Her voice trailed off. She sighed, a sound that tore at his heart. "We'll never know for sure what happened, just that he never came back."

Haakan caught himself before asking the question that burned in his mind. *You mean to say he left you and your children alone? To fend for yourselves in the storm?* "I'm so sorry. You needn't talk about it if—"

"No, I'm finding it easier now. Talking about it seems to help, somewhat." She cut a piece of meat for Andrew and fed him a bite. "So, how was your journey from the logging camp? Did you walk all the way?"

"Ja. And while I saw rich and beautiful country, the next time I would like to take a train." Haakan entertained them for the rest of the meal with tales of his travels and life in the logging camp. But when they began talking of relatives, Thorliff lost interest.

"Mor, can I go outside?" Shifting restlessly on his seat, Thorliff leaped in when there was a pause.

"Ja, that you can." Ingeborg looked up from moving her fork around. She looked over to Andrew to find him with his cheek on the table, sound asleep. "Ah, what have I been thinking? You go draw water for the sheep, and after Andrew wakes from his nap, we will go to Tante Kaaren's."

On a "Ja, Mor," Thorliff flew out the door, whistling for Paws as he went.

"Would you care for more coffee?" Ingeborg stood to pick up Andrew. His head lolled on her shoulder and one finger made its way to his mouth.

"I could go help Thorliff."

"If you like. I'll clean up the kitchen and then show you around the farm. The sheep are Thorliff's special charge, so he will delight in introducing you to his friends."

Haakan pushed his chair back. "Mange takk fer matten."

"Velbekomme." Ingeborg was already bending over to lay the sleeping child in one of the beds.

Haakan followed Thorliff outside. The haunting song of geese passing on their way north made him look up. Just to the east, silhouetted against the deep blue of the sky, the flock in V formation seemed to stretch from one horizon to the other. Never had he seen so many waterfowl flying north as he had since he entered the Red River Valley. His fingers itched to take one of the pieces of wood from the rafters and begin looking with his carving knife for the flying goose imprisoned in the wood.

Ingeborg kissed the baby's soft cheek and laid him gently on the rustling corn-husk mattress. "Sleep well, den lille guten, sleep well." She stood and kneaded the small of her back with her fists. Andrew was getting awfully heavy to carry like that. Most of the time he climbed up in bed by himself, but then usually he didn't fall asleep at the dinner table with his face in his plate. She returned to the work counter and took a damp cloth back to wipe off his face.

"Uff da," she muttered as she straightened again. "What kind of a mother are you?" She shook her head and stopped at the table to stack the dishes. Knowing the water was cold in the dishpan on the bench outside, she went to bring it in. Haakan was cranking the handle at the well to bring up the full bucket, with Thorliff setting the empty pail on the well's rim.

The song of the wild geese attracted her attention, too, and she shaded her eyes with her hand to see better. She knew if they'd set down close enough, she could bring home fresh meat for supper. The thought of striding through the woods on a hunt set her heart to thrumming. Even though hunting wasn't considered part of women's work, she had become very good at bringing home game, thus leaving the men free to break the sod. While Roald had tolerated her hunting, Carl had been the one to teach her how to shoot the heavy gun and where to find the game trails. While it didn't take a great hunter to find sufficient game in this region so rich with wild life, Ingeborg knew she was better than the average marksman. Wasting shells had earned her a stern reprimand from Roald, so she took careful aim before shooting.

Perhaps today was not a good day to hunt. If this man was really going to be here for the summer, she'd best not shock him too soon. *It might keep him from staying*, she thought. *Now if I really want to drive him away, I'll just don my britches, and he'll head back for the north woods fast as his feet can carry him.*

Back in the soddy with her hands in the sudsy water, she allowed her thoughts to turn back to Roald. He would have been more than pleased to have a cousin come and offer to help for the summer. He would try to talk the man into staying, unable to understand why anyone would not want to homestead in Dakota Territory. Of course, if Roald were here, Haakan would never have arrived. Had Roald known of this relative in the new world? Of course, the Bjorklund family tree had so many branches around Nordland, it would take a genius to keep track of them all.

She finished drying the dishes and put them away. After a glance at Andrew to make sure he slept on, she went outside, grateful for the warm sun that nearly blinded her in its intensity. She raised her face to the heat of it. Why did the sun of spring feel so much more friendly than the sun of winter?

She brought the last of the kerosene lamps inside to fill and trim the wicks later. The chimneys now gleamed like they hadn't all winter. Polishing them in the sunlight revealed streaks to buff away not visible in winter's dimness.

On her way back and forth with the small chores, she smiled and waved, letting Thorliff show the guest around the farm and introduce him to the livestock. The sod barn was bursting at the corners with all the animals that now shared its protection and the corrals at either end. Ewes with their lambs—Thorliff had already docked all the tails—and now the grown sheep were due for a shearing. The lamb crop had been good this year, reminding Ingeborg of the time she finally turned back to the Lord to beg forgiveness and accept His gift of love and healing. Her winter had indeed been a long and dark time of the soul. She still missed Roald, of course, sometimes deeply; but the pain of it had lessened, and the bitterness she'd harbored those many months was gone. *Praise be to God!*

Finished inside, she joined Thorliff as he took Haakan outside to meet the oxen, the horses, and the lone mule—the other had died with Roald in the blizzard. The three milk cows—two heavy with calf while the third was still producing—and the six-month-old calf came to have their heads scratched and stretched their necks for the stroking they so loved. This year they would have two sows, since they'd kept one of the gilts to breed come spring. They shared a boar with the Baards, as they did a bull and machinery. One neighbor to the north had a heavy stallion, so Ingeborg's dream of providing stock for the families heading west was becoming close to a reality.

"We have seventy acres ready to plant," Thorliff said proudly. "Mor can bust sod good as any man."

Ingeborg gave a wry smile at the raised eyebrow from their guest. "You do what you have to in this country."

"And we ain't going to lose our homestead, are we, Mor?" Thorliff puffed his chest. "Since we now got a ride-on plow, soon as my legs are long enough to reach the pedals, I can plow, too. I already know how to drive the team."

They leaned on the slender tree trunks, stripped down for poles, that comprised the corral for the cows and horses. Out across the prairie they could see more rich brown dirt appearing through the snow.

"You have a good start here." Haakan rested his chin on his hands, his hat tipped back, and a curl of blond hair caught on his forehead. He nodded and put one foot up on the lower of the four rails.

Thorliff nodded in return, as if talking man to man like this was an everyday occurrence.

Ingeborg felt her heart bursting with pride in this son of hers who worked so hard and had assumed a man's responsibilities long before his time. She knew he seemed so much older than eight, with a seriousness that left little room for the boy to come out and play. He needed someone his own age, like the Baard boys when they all met for schooling.

She heard a lusty wail from the house. "Andrew is awake. Why don't we go over to Tante Kaaren's now and share our letter and our new relative."

"Tante Kaaren bakes the best cookies in Dakota Territory," Thorliff added. "You'll like her and Lars."

Andrew sat howling in the middle of the bed, but the minute he saw his mother, he clamped off the tears and waved his arms, ready to be picked up. While he could walk well enough, Ingeborg was grateful he hadn't taken to climbing out of the bed and coming to find her. She even thought about creating a gate to put in the doorway, so if she didn't hear him right away, he couldn't get out and get lost on the prairie.

"Den lille guten," she said with a smile, always telling him what a good boy he was. She had come too close in the winter of her rebellion to giving both boys away to Kaaren's care. "Come, let us go visit Tante Kaaren." She scooped him up in her arms, took the letter off the table to put in her apron pocket, and headed out the door. Each time she went out again, she marveled at the warmth that hadn't yet penetrated the soddy. The thick dirt walls kept the house cooler in the summer and warm in the winter but didn't change temperature easily. Perhaps by the fly and mosquito season, they could put a screen door in place and another screen over the window. Such a treat that would be.

"I could carry him for you." Haakan turned from his study of the western horizon when she came out the door.

"I . . . I don't know. He's not used to strangers." Ingeborg looked from the man to the child who clutched her around the neck. "He can walk, but it takes so long to go the distance with his toddling steps. Besides, he gets mud all over."

"I can ride him piggyback." Thorliff stopped throwing the stick to Paws long enough to volunteer.

"Here, den lille guten, come for a ride." Haakan extended his hands, palm up.

Ingeborg thrilled to hear him use her very words for this little one, the first child of her own womb. She held Andrew loosely and leaned slightly forward in encouragement.

Andrew studied the face of the man, as if trying to learn his character through the inspection. He wiggled in his mother's arms, clamping an arm around her neck for an anchor and waving a pudgy fist in the air.

"Go on, son, it's all right." Ingeborg spoke softly, laying her cheek against his.

Andrew sighed as though he'd made a major decision and leaned forward, grasping Haakan's thumb with one hand. The grin showed all five of his teeth and was accompanied by the incessant drool that went along with teething.

Haakan settled the baby on his hip, wrapped in a strong arm, and they headed across the field to the sod house about a hundred yards away.

"The boundary line between the two homesteads goes right down the middle here, and this way we are able to help each other more quickly. The first year on the homestead, we all lived in the one soddy we built later that summer. Roald and Carl first spent all the time they could breaking sod, since a house wasn't as necessary."

"What did you live in?"

"The wagon. Once we could sleep on the ground, it was much easier. Baby Gunhilde was born on the ship coming over, so that first winter in the soddy we had four grown-ups and two children."

"And you are still friends?" Haakan shook his head in amazement.

"More than friends. Kaaren and I are deeper than sisters. We saved each other and fought together for our sanity—and our salvation." Ingeborg didn't elaborate any further. Instead she pointed to a spiral of smoke still farther north. "It is easier now with more neighbors. Why, Kaaren taught school during the good days of fall after the harvest was done and during the winter. Agnes Baard taught us all to speak English."

"You do speak English?"

"Ja, somewhat. But Norwegian is much easier yet. There are so many words I do not know, and those I learn, I soon forget."

"Then we will speak English." Haakan bounced the baby to make him laugh.

"Velkommen. Velkommen." Kaaren met them before they'd even reached the door.

The greeting almost took away the concern Haakan's statement caused. Why was it men had a habit of always giving orders like that? Could a man help her and not take over? Was it possible?

Ingeborg returned the greeting and introduced their new relative, but the questions kept bubbling up like stew set on the stove to simmer.

4

Norway

I cannot bear to let him go."

Gustaf Bjorklund rolled over under the quilts that cocooned the aging couple and wrapped an arm around his shivering wife. "But we have no choice. They need him in Amerika, Ingeborg and Kaaren. They cannot save the land without men to help them. If they lose the land, we lost our fine sons for naught."

"It is too high a price." Bridget wiped her tears on the pillow slip.

"But we knew when they left we would never see them again. I thought we understood that."

"Ah, but, Gustaf, just knowing they walked the same earth kept Roald and Carl within my heart. Now they are gone, and so is a part of my heart."

"But . . . but we will see them again. They are not gone forever."

"I believe that too, but . . ." She sighed, a mother's sigh that sobbed of love and loss. "Mayhap in some small corner of my mind, I dreamed I would see them again on this earth. That one day, before we died, we, too, would journey to that new land and visit our sons and their sons."

"You want to leave Norway and move to Amerika?" Gustaf shot straight up in bed. "Surely you don't mean that."

Bridget laid a hand on his shoulder, pulling him back under the warmth of the goose down quilt. "Nei, I could not leave our home here, not for good. But to visit, ja, that I could do."

"You would make that long journey, visit, and then return?" Gustaf choked on the words, as if they were too tough to chew, let alone swallow. "You think we are made of gold, then?"

She shook her head and sighed again. "Surely, I of all people know that is not true. But I talked with Solvig today. She and Haldor are going to Amerika. And not to stay either. She says she was born Norwegian, and she will die Norwegian, in her own land, in her own bed. But they will see their children again before they die."

"We do not even have the money to pay for all of Hjelmer's ticket, let alone fares for both of us. Besides, if we had so much ready kroner, we have two daughters who talk of marrying men in Amerika, and they haven't emigrated there yet either." He rolled over so his back was to her. "Go to sleep, Bridget. You must have been sipping the dandelion wine or some such."

Bridget rolled over on her back and let the tears leak out the corners of her eyes and into her ears. Why was wanting to see her children again such a terrible thing? Just because they lived halfway around the earth, should she put her love for them out of her mind and heart as if they'd never been? Is that what Gustaf did?

Since Johann and his wife Soren had yet to have children, and Kaaren's babies had died in the influenza, little Thorliff and Andrew were her only grandchildren. Ingeborg wrote so seldom. How were they? Thorliff would be seven, nei almost eight, by now. And Andrew, she knew, had the Bjorklund eyes, and Ingeborg hadn't cut his curls yet. Thank the good Lord for Kaaren who kept them informed. They were growing up without their bestefars and bestemors. Ingeborg's parents could no more leave for Amerika than could she and Gustaf. They still had small children at home.

She let the dream of visiting continue. They weren't too old for the journey, were they? Other than a twinge or two in the knees when the fog set in, she had never been one to complain. And Gustaf, why, he could still work circles around the younger men. And if he didn't want to work on a farm, surely there were townspeople who wanted fine furniture or had things in need of repair. Since Johann had taken over much of the farming chores, Gustaf had spent more of his time with his wood tools. It was a shame that many of the trunks he so lovingly created had emigrated and left them behind.

She sighed again. Surely she wasn't thinking of emigrating. Surely she wasn't. She was thinking only of visiting, wasn't she?

Hiding her lack of sleep behind a ready smile and the knowledge that Hjelmer would soon be leaving, Bridget bustled about the kitchen preparing breakfast. By the time the porridge was set with thick cream and the coffee poured, the others had trouped to the table. So few remained at home. Johann and his wife, Soren, Hjelmer who couldn't wait to leave, Augusta who hired out so often they rarely saw her, and Katja the baby, who was only twelve. Bridget had finally removed one of the leaves of the table so it wouldn't stretch so far, an empty reminder of those no longer present.

Before she sat down, she had counted the kroner and the coins in the octagonal box set high in the cupboard. She brought the red, tightly lidded container to the table with her. Gustaf looked at her with one raised eyebrow before folding his hands for grace.

"I Jesu navn, går vi til bords . . ." The age-old words echoed around the table as they all joined in. At the "amen," Hjelmer reached for the plate of sliced bread in the middle of the table.

Taking two pieces and passing the plate on to his sister, he eyed the box in front of his mor. The money for his ticket, what there was of it, lay hidden in that box. All of them had been contributing whatever they could earn. As it had for the others before him, his passage to Amerika was taking all the family resources.

"I'll pay you back, you know." Hjelmer spoke around a mouthful of porridge.

"Like the others?" Gustaf frowned at his youngest son. "You think you will do so well you can just send money back to Norway immediately?"

Hjelmer had the grace to duck his head.

"You think the others have not done their best, even to giving their lives?"

As his father's voice rose in volume and deepened at the same time, Hjelmer shook his head.

Bridget put her hand on her husband's arm. These two, they did not always see eye to eye. Perhaps she should have been more strict with this youngest son, but with his merry laughter and teasing spirit, he'd been able to get around her more than the others. Each of their children was so different in temperament, how could it be thus when they all grew up in the same house, and she tried to treat each of them the same?

But in appearance, Hjelmer was a younger version of Carl, with dark blond hair that still curled when damp and shoulders not yet widened with manhood. And like the others, the Bjorklund eyes of deep blue caused the neighborhood girls to look at him with hope in their eyes. The fishing boat had left its mark on him in the Tshaped scar to the outside of his right eye. Katja said it would drive the girls wild.

And now, Bridget had watched him since he returned from Onkel Hamre's fishing boat. The experience hadn't taken the starch out of him as his father had hoped. Instead, he'd been very good at things of the sea, or so Hamre said. Gustaf said he thought they received such a good report because Hjelmer kept even the hardened fishermen laughing.

"I'm sorry, Far, that's not what I meant at all," Hjelmer apologized.

Gustaf glowered from beneath bushy eyebrows. His very beard seemed to quiver at the supposed insult. "I think this Dakota Territory will take you down a peg or two. The Bible says, 'Blessed are the meek.' You must keep that in mind. A little humility is good for the soul."

"Yes, Far." Hjelmer nodded.

Bridget shook her head. She was never sure with this son if his instant contrition went deeper than the skin on his face or not.

The rest of the meal passed in silence, since none of the others wanted to incur the wrath of their father.

When Johann started to rise, Bridget gave a small shake of her head, and he settled back in his chair. She cleared her throat, a signal that she had something to say. All eyes fastened on her.

Opening the box, she began to speak. "You know how often we have counted this store of ours. With the additions of last week"—she smiled at each of them in thanks for their contributions—"we now have almost enough. When you deliver those two trunks—the paint is now dry enough—and get paid, that income, along with the money from the linens Soren so beautifully embroidered, will leave us lacking only funds for food."

"I can work for that. I know I can." Hjelmer let his words trail off at the look Gustaf shot his way.

Bridget continued as if no one had interrupted. "The same family that ordered the trunks has asked if I will sell my spinning wheel, and I said yes. The offer was too good to refuse."

"Your spinning wheel! Mor, not that. You said you would never sell it." Hjelmer half rose to his feet. He looked from his mother to the spinning wheel that sat in the corner, always in a place of honor. Gustaf had made it for her as a wedding present, and the song of the wheel had been a lullaby to all the babies, first in the cradle and later at their mother's knee.

Bridget sent Gustaf a look pregnant with a plea for understanding.

Gustaf raised one bushy eyebrow, and his eye flickered in a wink. "I will make her another. A new one of cherry wood, no longer scarred by years of use and the bangings of children."

"Perhaps they would wait and take the new one." Hjelmer stumbled over his words.

"Ja, and miss the boat they are so anxious to board. Would you wait?" Gustaf placed his hand over that of his wife. "I will begin immediately when I return from delivering the trunks, one of which will include the spinning wheel."

Hjelmer sank back down in his chair. Was this voyage already costing more than he could afford to pay?

Gustaf looked around the table. "Can anyone think of anything else that might be sold?"

Soren shook her head. "Nei, but I will begin to bake the sea biscuits that Onkel Hamre requires for his fishing fleet. Hjelmer can chew on those all across the sea and even in the new land. He won't starve."

"If he doesn't lose them," Katja said, covering her chuckle with both hands.

Hjelmer glowered at her as he sat down again at the table. He took the last slice of bread off the plate and covered it with apple butter. "I haven't lost anything for a long time."

"You will have to watch out for those who take advantage of emigrants like yourself. Remember what Ingeborg wrote about the ways people trick innocent ones out of money and goods, even their tickets."

"Far, I will be careful. I'm not some dumbhead like the Hagen boys."

" 'Pride goeth before a fall.' " Gustaf's words carried the voice of doom. "Don't you forget that."

⁂

Within a week, Hjelmer found himself at the port of Kristiansand, waiting for the ship to begin boarding. He kept one bag thrown over his shoulder and clenched the other with fingers of iron. His little sister's teasing words "Don't lose your things" still irritated him. It was true he had lost a number of things through the years; but he had become a man since then, and a man didn't misplace or lose the very things that would keep him alive and well, things like food and clothing, tickets and money. He couldn't wait to write her a letter from Dakota Territory in Amerika to say he had arrived safe and well with all of his possessions.

As he followed the other heavily burdened emigrants down into the hold of the ship, he shuddered at the darkness and the dank smell. Would the ship from Liverpool to New York be this bad?

The pitching North Sea didn't bother him, only the feeling of being boxed in. But the train trip across England opened new vistas undreamed of. He felt like a child with his nose plastered to the window, trying to see all the perfectly ordered farms, the hedgerows, and the compact fields of green grass or dark soil prepared for spring planting. His brief glimpses of dirty factory towns and puffing mills made him grateful for the clean air of home.

The ship, while not the largest berthed along the docks of Liverpool, made all the others he'd boarded so far seem more like rowboats. Three smokestacks were added to the sailing masts and rigging, promising a swift voyage. Like cattle, the emigrants were herded aboard and down to the dark hold. Steerage, the least costly way to travel, had sounded like an adventure, but now, Hjelmer felt his first quiver of doubt. While the bite of disinfectant overlaid other smells, the stink of vomit, excrement, and despair permeated the wood and thus the air. Open hatches let in a semblance of fresh salt air, but the boy wasn't deceived.

Babies wailed, women and children cried, and fathers tried to keep their families together in the rush for the bunk room. Three and four tiers high, sized like roughhewn coffins rather than beds, the bunks filled the space. Aisles so narrow that a man's wide shoulders scraped on both sides divided the remainder of footage.

"They treat the cattle better'n us, and we paid good money for these tickets." The man who'd claimed the bunk below Hjelmer's muttered his complaint.

Hjelmer nodded. He heaved himself up into the space he'd staked out as his own to let a family of four squeeze by. How he wished he had been at the head of the line and grabbed a bunk where he could at least see the sky when one of the hatches was opened. The dark seeped from the walls like a malevolent beast seeking to destroy all hope. How could he handle the dark and cramped quarters for seven days, and that only if they weren't delayed by storms? Kerosene lamps guttered from posts on the main aisle, their stench adding one more layer to the stew of odors.

After the last emigrants made their way down the companion-way, the rumble of the steam engines that already made the floor-boards quiver changed timbre. The hatches slammed closed, and with a shudder the huge screws commenced to turn, and the ship eased away from the dock.

Someone began to pray in a loud voice. The language was German as far as Hjelmer could tell, and the tone held fear and foreboding.

Hjelmer piled his bags at one end of his bunk and leaned against them, stretching out his legs. While he had a book to read, the light was far too dim for such an activity, likewise for the carving of the bird he'd started while waiting in line. Never one to be idle, he felt himself begin to fidget by the time the vessel reached the open sea.

He knew when that happened because he felt the difference in wave pitch. His months on the North Sea with Onkel Hamre had taught him much about the weather and waves. The huge steamer plowed through the swell, but not without some rise and fall motion. It wasn't long before the smell of vomit dominated the air, already dank from the number of people breathing, coughing, and crying.

A little girl in the bunk across from him hadn't stopped her tears since they boarded.

Hjelmer thought to Katja at home. She would look on the voyage as a grand adventure and soon be entertaining all the children within earshot with the stories that flowed from her fertile mind.

A sigh of relief went up when the hatches were opened and one of the ship's crew bellered, "All you down there, line up and come topside while the weather holds."

Someone must have understood his words, because as soon as a few climbed the steep passageway, others followed. Hjelmer grabbed his carving and knife and joined the line. He should have practiced his English as Roald had written, but no one on the fishing boat spoke the new language, and he'd not bothered to locate a teacher once he returned home.

Two other young men joined the line behind him. He turned with a grin and an outstretched hand to introduce himself. When they answered in Swedish, Hjelmer switched to that language. Since Norway lay under the auspices of Sweden, Swedish had become the official language of Norwegians also and was taught in the schools.

"Do either of you speak Amerikan?" he asked.

They shook their heads. "They said we didn't have to learn it, that we will get along just fine with our own language. Learning Amerikan is a waste of time."

Hjelmer shrugged and stepped up onto the deck. Drawing in a deep breath, he made his way over to the rail. Never had he been so grateful for the wind and spume from the tips of the rollers as the ship's prow cleaved the waves. If he never went below again, he wouldn't mind at all. Except to get his belongings, of course. Were they safe below? The thought hadn't entered his mind until this moment. And his father had cautioned him repeatedly about protecting his bags. Surely no one would dare steal from other emigrants while on the ship. There was nowhere to hide.

He found a nook in the lee of one of the funnels, sat cross-legged on the deck, and took out his wood and knife. As soon as he finished the seagull, he planned to start carving spoons. Mor said a woman always needed more stirring spoons, so he thought to make a set of different sizes for Ingeborg and Kaaren. He knew he should be carving hammer and chisel handles for working the forge, but he'd learned early that people appreciated gifts. The bird, that was something else. His fingers itched to create images of the wild creatures he saw, so an eagle on a limb and a puffin on a rock were some of his creations that lined the shelves of his mother's house.

"Hey, mister, what you doin'?" The little girl who'd been in tears now squatted in front of him, her arms crossed on her knees.

Hjelmer held up the bird. "Carving."

"Ain't that pretty." She reached out a cautious finger to smooth it over the extended wing. "Where'd you learn to carve like that?"

"Practice. My father taught me in the beginning."

"My father don't do such nice things."

Another child joined her, and soon Hjelmer sat in the midst of an admiring audience.

"Tell me about the bird." The little girl crossed her legs, mimicking the way Hjelmer sat. Others followed suit.

Hjelmer wrinkled his brow. Here, he'd thought to have a moment to himself, and now he had an audience who wanted a story, no less. "Well, it is a seagull. You've seen them all around the docks and some are even now above us." He pointed to the white gulls shrieking and crying on the wind and in the rigging of the foremast.

"So." The children's gazes followed his pointing finger.

"So, soon we will leave the birds behind, and now I have one to remember them by. Where I am going in Dakota Territory, I'm sure

there are no seagulls." As he talked, he continued to roll bits of shavings off the emerging bird.

A bell clanged somewhere. Parents came by and took their children off with them. Finally, a crewman stopped. "Time to get below
now."

While Hjelmer didn't understand the words, he recognized the
signal. "Ja, I go." He put the bird in his pocket, gathered up his shavings, and followed the human herd below.

That night, after a supper of soup and hard bread, he lay on his
bunk and let his thoughts fly home on the back of the west wind.
He could see his family gathered around the oval oak table in the
warm kitchen, redolent with the flavor of lamb stew and fresh bread.
Perhaps Mor had made fatigman, dusted with cinnamon and sugar.
The coffee would be rich and hot.

Somewhere aft, a concertina struck up a polka, joined by the
strains of a fiddle. While there was no room for dancing, the music
lilted the length of the vessel and helped salve the remembrances of
home.

They could have used the music in the morning to cover the
unpleasant sound of vomiting. The seas had roughened, bringing
with it the agony of seasickness.

Grateful for his sea legs, Hjelmer spent every moment he could
topside. When the ever present wind bit so deep that his shaking
hands refused to hold the carving knife, he walked the decks and
visited with other young men who did the same. Whenever he heard
someone speaking English, he stopped to listen. A few words became obvious. "Good-bye, hello, hey you, yes, no." One couldn't go
far with such a limited vocabulary. But none of the other emigrants
seemed to care about learning the language. Like the young men
he'd met the first day and continued to see, all stayed within their
own kind.

The third day out, Hjelmer came upon a card game. Thanks to
the tutelage of the fishermen on Onkel Hamre's boat, Hjelmer had
gained real skill in the games of chance. In fact, some had said he
was gifted. He didn't need a second invitation to join in.

They sighted land on the eighth day, eight of the longest days
Hjelmer had ever endured, even with the distraction of playing
cards. He stored his winnings in the pouch with the carved seagull
and wrapped them in his extra shirt. Slinging one bag over his
shoulder and clutching the other now lighter because of his eating
some of the rock-hard biscuits, he reached the passageway before

most of the others. On deck, he joined the crowd at the rail facing south. As they steamed into the harbor, scaffolding and construction equipment nearly covered a small island near to the shore. Workers swarmed over the site, and the clang of hammers and shrill of saws carrying on the breeze could be heard over the now diminished engines in the hold of the ship. Barges loaded with lumber, gravel, and sand butted up against the piers like piglets nursing on a sow.

He made his way to the bow and caught his breath in amazement. Before him lay the city of New York, glimmering in the sunlight reflected off a thousand windows. Buildings as tall as the highest pine trees of Nordland, and taller yet, marched into the distance. As the ship he rode eased its way into the berth, he couldn't absorb the sights fast enough. Tall ships, squat boats, barges, flags of every stripe and nation, long piers, men of every shape and color. Such bustle, hurrying, shouting. Never had he seen such pandemonium.

The first-class and second-class passengers left the ship first. The steerage held back until all the baggage was removed. Finally, in orderly lines, the emigrants filed off the ship and up the crowded pier to solid land.

Hjelmer strode toward Castle Garden, where they'd been told the officials would pass them through. Once through the line, he planned to head for the railroad station and board the first train west.

Suddenly a piercing scream rent the air.

Hjelmer swung around. A cry for help sounded the same in any language.

The scream came again. Sobbing and screaming.

Back along the pier a woman leaned over the edge and pointed to the water.

Hjelmer dropped his bags and sprinted to the edge of the pier. Down in the water, filmed with oil sheen and cluttered with flotsam and jetsam, a small child thrashed and sputtered.

Without a thought, Hjelmer dived in. He surfaced, shaking his head to throw the water out of his eyes, and treading water, he looked around. Two strokes and he had the child in a strong grip.

"I have you, easy now." He murmured the words, not caring if the child understood or not.

Dark terror-filled eyes peeked out from dripping hair that curled on the child's forehead.

Someone threw him a rope. He grabbed it, pulled the child close to his chest and let them haul him back to the dock. With fingers shaking from the frigid water, he knotted the rope under the child's arms and patted the heaving chest. "You will be all right now."

Another rope flopped in the water beside him, and he pulled himself up.

Standing on the dock, dripping water and shivering in the wind off the river, he accepted the mother's thanks.

"Velbekomme."

He ducked his chin into his chest. Someone wrapped a blanket around his shoulders. "M-Mange takk." He could hardly speak, his teeth chattered so hard.

Hjelmer nodded at the comments of gratitude and appreciation flowing from the emigrants gathered around him. He started back to where he'd dropped his bags. He had to get into some dry clothes before he caught his death of cold.

The black seabag, the leather carpetbag that held his train tickets, his winnings from the card games, and all his worldly goods were nowhere to be seen.

5

Thorliff," Kaaren said, brushing a strand of sun-kissed hair from her forehead, "run out to the barn and get Onkel Lars." She turned to her guests. "He's working with the forge, and you know how noisy that can be. Here, sit down, sit down, and we'll have coffee." When she turned to the stove, Ingeborg stopped her.

"No, we have the coffee and visit later. First, we have good news. Mr. Bjorklund brought a letter from home. Mr. Mackenzie gave it to him at The Mercantile." Ingeborg drew the precious envelope out of her apron pocket. "See?"

"Oh, how wonderful." Kaaren flashed their visitor one of her warmest smiles. "It is so long since we have heard anything." She sank down on one of the four chairs at the oilcloth-covered table. In this home, too, were evidences of a man handy with his hands and a piece of wood. While many homes had only stools or chunks of wood to sit on, these chairs had spindles set into upper and lower curved backs. The carved rocker by the gleaming cookstove wore a colorful patchwork quilt, and beside it rested a bag of yarn and a half-knit piece.

Ingeborg studied her sister-in-law's face. Kaaren was looking pale, like she didn't feel good at all. While Kaaren was careful to always wear her sunbonnet, this was not just the creamy tinge of protected skin or the pallor of winter. Dark smudges lay under her tired blue eyes as if she'd smeared coal dust there. Her skirt gaped at the waist of her always slender frame.

"So, Mr. Bjorklund, how did you happen to come clear out here? You said you were from Minnesota?" Kaaren asked eagerly.

Haakan told her the same as he'd told Ingeborg and turned when another man entered the soddy.

"Well, hello, sister. I hear you brought us company." Lars stooped to step through the doorway as Haakan had. When he straightened, he removed his hat and hung it on a row of pegs by the door. With one hand on Thorliff's shoulder, Lars extended his other to greet the visitor. "I'm Lars Knutson, and I am glad to hear I have another relative, in a round about sort of way."

While the men greeted each other, Ingeborg stood with her hands on the back of a chair and, without meaning to, compared them. One dark and one fair but both tall and broad of shoulder. Haakan could measure his by the span of an ax handle. Wind and sun had carved both faces into rugged maps of experience, and they each wore the square jaw of determination, tempered by ready smiles of greeting. Even so, they reminded her of two dogs on first meeting, stiff legged, prancing around each other but with tails wagging. Would they be able to work as a team for the summer? Of course, each would be breaking sod on the separate homesteads, but plowing, seeding, haying, and harvesting were done in partnership, even with the extra team and machinery of the Baards.

Would they resent her working out in the fields, too? The thought of being cooped up in the soddy day after day, after she'd become accustomed to weeks of freedom in the sun working the fields like a man, dressed in britches like a man, hunting, and bringing home the meat, made her flinch. Could she bear going back to women's work only? Did she need to? After all, it was her land.

It surely wasn't as if she didn't have enough to do around the farmstead. There were chores enough for three women.

"Ingeborg?" Kaaren's soft voice broke in on her woolgathering.

"Ja." Ingeborg blinked and took in a breath, careful not to release it on a sigh. Surely she'd learned the lesson of not trying to add tomorrow's trouble unto today at her mother's knee. "Let us enjoy the letter. Kaaren, you read the best"—she extended the envelope—"you read it."

Kaaren nodded. "Why don't you all sit down. Thorliff, you take Andrew and sit in the rocker." Carefully she slit the thin paper and withdrew two sheets, covered both sides with script so close together not a space was wasted.

" 'Dear Ingeborg and all our dear ones. I cannot begin to imagine how hard this time has been for you, but we can all rest assured knowing that our Lord is there with you in the midst of all the heartache. If it were not for the knowledge and faith that He is caring for you and us, I would have died of a broken heart, as I know you would have, also. One day we will see our loved ones again, if we don't lose heart.' "

Kaaren paused and wiped her eyes with the corner of her apron.

Ingeborg tried to keep the tears that burned behind her eyes and at the back of her throat in check, but it was not possible.

A chunk of wood dropped in the firebox of the stove, breaking the silence that filled the soddy. Andrew reached up and stuck his finger into Thorliff's nose, a trick he'd learned recently that usually brought on a giggle.

"Andrew, don't." Thorliff looked over and caught his mother's nod. When she smiled through her tears, he sat back and wrapped both arms around the baby, setting the chair to rocking with one foot.

"Sorry." Kaaren sniffed and continued. " 'We are all well and working hard to earn a ticket for Hjelmer to come to you. He hopes to leave as soon as spring visits us here in frozen Nordland. If all goes as planned, he will arrive sometime in mid-April.' "

"Hjelmer is coming." Ingeborg looked over at Haakan and Lars. "He is the youngest brother of Roald and Carl. It is hard to think of him as more than a gangling clown, but four years would make him nineteen, a young man now." She stopped. "Mid-April. He could be here anytime."

"In the beginning, we had planned to send money for one of our brothers or sisters to emigrate each year, but so far that has not been possible." Kaaren continued the explanation. "My sister Solveig would love to come too, maybe soon." She returned to the letter. " 'I wait with patience to hear from you, that you are bearing up and continuing to rejoice in Christ our Savior. Your loving family, Gustaf and Bridget.' "

Ingeborg felt a stab of guilt. She should write more often, but the time flowed faster than a mountain stream in full spring spate.

After Kaaren finished reading the letter, they sat for a moment in silence. Then Kaaren pushed to her feet. "I will get the coffee."

"And cookies?" Thorliff raised a hopeful smile.

"Thorliff." Ingeborg's tone and frown made him duck behind Andrew. But when all the adults laughed, he grinned and shrugged.

"I think Mr. Bjorklund would like to taste the best cookies in the territory. Maybe in all America."

"You rascal." Kaaren tweaked his hair. "You could talk a bird out of a tree, let alone get cookies from an aunt who loves you." She handed the letter back to Ingeborg, her eyes begging to read it again later. Turning to Haakan, she said, "So, tell us all you have been doing since you came to this country. How long has it been?"

Haakan answered her questions and those of the others and nodded to Thorliff after taking his first bite of Tante Kaaren's celebrated cookies. Thorliff lifted his own in response and gave a crumbly grin.

"So, you say you have come to help for the summer." Over the rim of his coffee cup, Lars studied the man at the other end of the table. "When would you head back for the north woods?"

"I need to be there just after the first snow when the ground has begun to freeze. We cut trees all winter and float them down the river to the lumber mills when the ice goes out in the spring. It is a good job and pays well."

"We will pay you to help us here," Ingeborg said with what might have been more force than necessary.

Both of the men turned and looked at her as though she'd spoken out of turn.

"We'll see." Haakan nodded.

"Can't get out on the fields yet. The frost hasn't gone out of the ground, so I been working on the machinery, repairing harnesses and suchlike. We need to make a trip to St. Andrew, and I'd really like to go on down to Grand Forks to the machinery dealers there. Joseph and I been talking about buying a binder together, haven't we, Ingeborg?" Lars glanced at her for confirmation.

Ingeborg nodded. "I've been thinking if you had a steam engine and a threshing machine, you could take it out on the road like you did before. Earn some cash money that way to help get through the winter." She hadn't planned to share this part of her dream with anyone yet, knowing that they hadn't the money to pay for one, and she hated like anything to put more on credit. The debts they owed hung over her like a pall of smoke.

Nothing, nothing could force her off the land, but if they couldn't make the payments on what they owed, their land was the collateral. Before buying more machinery, she wanted to pay off the bank loans Roald had taken out to add another section to the homestead. Two more years and the homesteads would be proved up.

"Yes, if I wanted to leave my family and go out on the road again." Lars shook his head and smiled at his wife. "That's for single men, not for those of us so fortunate to have a wife like mine at home."

"Seems to me after seeing Thorliff's sheep, the shearing needs to be done about now," Haakan added while Lars and Kaaren were exchanging quiet looks of love.

"I was getting to that." Ingeborg leaned forward. "I thought Thorliff and I would wait with the shearing in case there comes another blizzard. You'll find out how winter here always tries to make one last stand." She looked to Lars and Kaaren for support. Didn't they understand how important it was for her to make the decisions concerning her land—Roald's land, the land they slaved over for their children?

"I could get going on that tomorrow. You'd help me, wouldn't you, Thorliff?"

Hadn't he heard her? Ingeborg clasped her hands on the table in front of her. "I think it is not yet time to shear the sheep. I do not want to lose any to a blizzard."

Haakan directed his blue gaze upon her, making her think of nothing but Roald when he was so certain he was always right and would brook no argument from anyone.

She felt her back stiffen.

"But, Mor, I would like to . . ." Thorliff's voice died off at the look his mother shot him.

"It is time for me to go begin chores." Ingeborg rose and bent her head in Haakan's direction. "You can stay here to visit more. In fact, there is a spare bed in *this* soddy." She let the clipped words lay on the table. "Come, Thorliff, I will carry Andrew." She picked up the baby and settled him on her hip. "Mange takk, Kaaren, Lars. I will see you tomorrow."

"I will carry him." Haakan rose also.

"Nei." Ingeborg left the house and strode out across the prairie. The sun slipped behind a layer of clouds stippled above the horizon. Tonight would be a glorious sunset, she was sure. A breeze that had felt welcome before now nipped at her face and tugged at her skirt. Thorliff trudged beside her, Paws trotting beside him at the boy's knee.

The thoughts kept time with her feet as she marched through the snow rather than stomped as she desired. Kaaren would tell her to not be so prickly. Her mor would say that God put men in charge because they were the stronger. Help she didn't mind; in fact, she met help with joy, but not him taking over just because he was a man.

If he still decided to help, she *would* pay him. Of that there would be no further discussion.

She could hear his firm steps coming up behind her. Thorliff turned around and trotted backward to watch Haakan's face.

"I would carry Andrew for you."

"I know." If only she wasn't wearing these confounded skirts, she could walk faster and not get tangled up. All she needed to do right now was to sprawl on her face in the mud.

The thought tugged a grin at the corners of her mouth. Now that would be a sight to see.

"Will you show me how you do the chores? I know every farmer has ways of his, or her, own."

"Ja, if you are sure you want to help." She didn't add, *and not take over,* but it wasn't for want of desire.

"Mr. Bjorklund, I will show you where the hens lay their eggs, and you can help me take the horses and oxen down to drink at the river. That's always more fun than pulling buckets at the well." Thorliff ran forward and skidded on a patch of snow. Paws leaped beside him, barking and nipping at the slush that flew up from the boy's feet. "Good, huh, Mor?"

"Ja, good. But if you fall—"

"I'll get wet and muddy, I know." He repeated his action, laughing at the joy of it, his arms wind-milling to keep his balance when his skid carried him past the snow patch.

"You have a fine son," Haakan said softly for her ears alone.

"I try to tell him that often. Since his father died, Thorliff has felt it his job to care for me and Andrew. He was not happy with Lars at first, because he saw Tante Kaaren being taken away. But Lars brought him Paws, and from then on, the worship began."

"A boy needs a good man in his life."

"Thorliff had one—his father." Ingeborg entered the soddy and blinked in the dimness. She hadn't finished the lamps, and now they would need the light as soon as the chores were done. Of course she could bring in the lantern from the barn.

"Thorliff can show me how to feed the animals after we take the large stock down to drink. Or we can bring up enough water from the well. If we do the barn chores, then you will have more time to do the things you need. It isn't like I haven't milked a cow before." Haakan stood in the door and waited for her answer.

Ingeborg sighed. "That would be welcome. I will have supper ready when you are finished." She leaned down to pick up Andrew, who had been pulling at her skirt.

"What do you usually do with him while you are milking and doing the other chores?"

"He comes along to the barn and plays in the grain bin."

"I see." He patted the little fellow on the back and started to go out the door.

"The milk bucket, Mr. Bjorklund." Ingeborg snagged the bucket from where it sat on the far side of the work table and followed him out the door. He took the handle with a smile and headed across the muddy yard to the barn. Ingeborg lifted her face to track the honking geese in another dark V against the dimming sky. They would be setting down soon for the evening feed. Perhaps tomorrow night she could take the gun and go bag some. Roast goose sounded mighty tempting.

The evening star glowed in the western sky above a narrow band of gold on the horizon when Haakan and Thorliff returned to the house. The lamps were lit, throwing shadows on the dark walls that seemed to suck in the light and hoard it forever. Slices of ham simmered in their own gravy on the back of the stove next to a steaming pot of potatoes, and the smell of baking biscuits permeated the air.

Haakan sniffed appreciatively when he came in. "It smells wonderful in here. Thorliff guessed we were having ham clear out to the barn." He set the pail down on the work counter. "Do you have a strainer?"

"I'll take care of it. You two wash up. There's hot water in the reservoir." Ingeborg drew the baking pan out of the oven and slammed the door. "Thorliff, would you please go out to the root cellar and bring in a jar of jam? I think there is some plum left."

"Do plums grow around here?" Haakan stopped before dipping water out of the reservoir at the cooler end of the stove.

"Ja, plums, chokecherries, June berries, and strawberries. You just need to learn where to find them."

"How did you learn where they were?" He finished dipping hot water into the enameled wash basin and closed the lid on the reservoir. "I'll fill this again after we eat."

"Thank you, but that is not necessary. Thorliff will do it." Ingeborg turned with a biscuit in her hand. She softened her tone. After all, he was only trying to help. "Metiz showed me."

"Metiz?"

"She's a spry old woman who's been a real friend to us. If you stay, you will meet her when she returns from wintering with her family."

"Ingeborg, I said I came to help, and I will stay until the fall."

She could feel his gaze drilling into her back as she fixed the biscuit for Andrew, who'd grown fussy with waiting, even to shedding tears. "Ja, that is what you said."

"I do not go back on my word."

She could hear the water splashing as he washed. Thorliff returned with a jar of jam and set it on the table. She flipped the bail off the top of the jar and scooped some of the sweet jam onto the warm biscuit. Andrew quieted fast as a candle blown out after jabbing a finger in the jam and sticking it in his mouth.

The man's words echoed in her mind and heart as she brought the remaining supper to the table. She understood about keeping one's word. She'd gotten herself lost in New York City on a mission to keep hers. Just as quickly, a thought of the wealthy young man who'd become her guardian angel there flitted through her mind. How was Mr. Gould and his new wife now? She still had the condolence letter he'd sent after Roald died. She'd been amazed at how news traveled. To think he'd somehow heard, even in New York City. She brought her mind back to the present with a snap when Thorliff took his place on the bench next to her chair.

Haakan sat down in the other chair and leaned over to riffle Thorliff's hair. "You have a good hand with the animals, boy. I can see you don't get angry easily. That is good."

Thorliff's face lit up as if candles glowed behind his eyes. "Thank you." He answered in English, which earned him another smile of accolade.

Ingeborg felt a swift stab of resentment, followed by a flash of pride. She had thought to have them talk more English, but slipping back into their native Norwegian was so much easier. If it hadn't been for Agnes and her family having lived in Ohio where more English was spoken, she would have forgotten the little she learned in the months they worked in Fargo. Most of the immigrants were content to stay with their own language and chose to live closer to others who spoke the same.

She knew learning more English would be good for them, of course it would. She told herself that again and bowed her head. "Mr. Bjorklund, will you say grace?" At his silence, she lifted her eyes. "Unless of course, you don't want to."

"No, I will. I mean I can." He began the familiar words, and they joined in.

At the "amen," she looked up at him. "Do you know a grace in English?"

"Ah, no." He shook his head. "We don't go much for saying grace in the logging camps."

"Oh." She passed the plate she had filled for him. "I hope you like our ham."

"Mor and I smoked it ourselves last fall." Thorliff took his plate and inhaled the fragrance. "Nothin' smells good as ham, lessen it be bacon."

"I think you are right." Haakan winked at Thorliff after taking a bite of the ham. "Best I've ever tasted."

"We raised the pigs too. Before that, we had mostly elk and deer. Mor shoots them up the river."

Haakan stopped with a bite of ham halfway to his mouth. "Your mor knows how to shoot a rifle?"

"Sure, she's a better shot than Lars. Far weren't too happy, but Onkel Carl taught her how. I go with her sometimes. Onkel Carl taught me to snare rabbits. In the summer, I fish and get rabbits, then Mor don't have to hunt so much."

"Thorliff, don't talk with your mouth full." Ingeborg wanted to tell him not to talk at all, least ways not about such things, but she thought the better of it. Might as well air all their dirty laundry now. See if the man really would live up to his word. She sliced another bite of ham and chewed with careful concentration.

"See those elk robes on our beds? Mor shot both them, then tanned the hides. Far said they was the warmest quilts we had." Thorliff started to get up, probably to bring one of the robes to the table. At his mother's stern headshake, he sat back down. "You can look at them later. You could sleep in my bed, and Andrew can sleep with Mor. I'll roll up in a robe on the floor."

Ingeborg could feel the heat start low on her neck and work its way up her face. "Mr. Bjorklund will want to sleep over at Tante Kaaren's, I'm sure."

"I thought I could bunk in your barn, if that is all right with you. Save time in the morning."

"I don't mind if you—"

"Thorliff, that's enough." Ingeborg spoke softly, but her message reached her son.

He slumped back in his chair, looking at her from behind the curtain of blond hair that fell over his eyes.

"Would you like more ham?"

He shook his head.

Ingeborg knew she had hurt her son's feelings, but how could she tell him that an unmarried man did not sleep in the same room as a widow and her children. His sleeping in the barn would be bad enough. Good thing they didn't have close neighbors, for even far-flung as they were, news got around amazingly fast.

"I would rather sleep in the barn, Thorliff. That's proper and right." Haakan looked toward Ingeborg. "Your mor knows best."

Ingeborg felt a rush of gratitude. She hadn't always known or acted on what was best, but this time she knew she was. There'd been enough tisking over the actions of Mrs. Roald Bjorklund, and when she donned her britches to hunt or to plow soon as it was warm enough, there'd be more.

⁂

Haakan didn't say any more about shearing the sheep but kept busy with cleaning out the barn and repairing what harness hadn't been taken over to Lars. The two men talked back and forth every day, leaving Ingeborg out of their planning for the spring work.

At first she ignored it, but when Haakan announced one morn-ing a couple of days later that he and Lars were going down to the river to cut wood for the paddle-wheelers that would soon be plying their trade up and down the river, Ingeborg could feel her own steam begin to rise.

Did she want wood cut? Ja, to be sure. Was she grateful the men worked well together and wanted to bring in some cash money? Ja, of course. But why did they go on and on without even asking her what she thought. They just told her what they were going to do.

The first day she let it simmer.

The second day she caught up on the wash, hanging clothes on the line to dance in the warm wind that was drying the prairie as fast as it did her clothes. Another week of this and perhaps they could begin plowing the land they had backset in the fall. Or per-haps they should start with the fallow fields. They would need to make a trip to town for seed. While she'd kept out some of their wheat for seed, the extra animals she bought in the fall had eaten much of their seed store.

The third day she organized her garden seeds, saved so carefully the fall before, and hung all the quilts and robes on the line to have Thorliff beat them with the broom. If she kept busy enough, she could ignore the resentment that tugged at the sides of her mind. But each ring of the ax and crash of a toppling tree reminded her anew.

"Can I take the sheep out to graze yet?" Thorliff asked each morning.

And each time Ingeborg replied, "Not yet."

Late one afternoon she took the boys and headed across the field to Kaaren's. When she got to the door, she paused. Everything was too quiet. A shiver of dread raced down her spine and up again.

"Kaaren?" She motioned Thorliff to stay outside and stepped inside the house. Blinking her eyes to adjust to the dimness, she looked around the room. A mound lay under the covers on the bed. Ingeborg tiptoed across the hard-packed earth floor and stopped at the edge of the bed. Kaaren lay sound asleep.

Ingeborg leaned over and laid the back of her hand gently against Kaaren's cheek. No fever. She breathed a sigh of relief.

Kaaren's eyes fluttered open. "Inge." A smile brightened the paleness of her face. "Oh, my goodness. Have I slept the afternoon away?" She threw back the covers and swung her feet to the floor in the same smooth and unconscious motion as she unpinned her messed hair. Sweeping it up, she wrapped it around her fingers and into its usual bun high on the back of her head. She reached back to the pillow for her precious hairpins and stuck them in place.

"No, of course not. But I was concerned, afraid you might be sick again. You haven't looked well for some time."

Kaaren paused in the act of pulling on her boot. "Oh, Inge, I was going to wait to tell you when I was certain, but here you are, seeing so much. Most women don't call my little problem a sickness, even though—"

"You are going to have a baby." Ingeborg clasped her hands together in delight.

"Ja, we are."

"Does Lars know?"

Kaaren nodded. "He plans for a son, of course."

"These men. They forget that men need wives, and there are surely more men then women on the prairies. We need daughters to raise to be good wives."

"You make it sound like your plan for more cattle." Kaaren got to her feet. "I just get so tired, and Lars insists I must take a nap every afternoon. If my mor saw me sleeping in the middle of the day, she would be thunderstruck."

"I won't tell her." Ingeborg couldn't keep the grin from breaking out. She threw her arms around her sister and friend and hugged her close. "I am so happy for you." Looking into Kaaren's eyes, Ingeborg knew they were thinking about the same thing—the two small bodies that had been laid to rest in the cemetery next to their father. Both of the women wiped a tear away, and after a sigh, they hugged again.

"I was hoping you would take care of Andrew tomorrow afternoon. I need to go hunting, and now that I know we need even more goose down, I'll shoot more geese. A goose down quilt will keep that little one warm after she or he comes to live here."

"Of course I'll watch Andrew. Where is he?"

"Out with Thorliff, throwing sticks for Paws. While scarce, some of the grass is high enough, so tomorrow I will let him take the sheep out."

"Will you be back by dark?" When Ingeborg shrugged, Kaaren continued. "Then you tell Mr. Bjorklund to bring himself and Thorliff over here for supper. And you come when you can. Fresh meat will be such a treat again, and if you get enough, perhaps we can smoke some. I'm almost out of meat, and the root cellar has many bare spots. Soon there should be dandelion for greens, just like at home."

When will we cease to think of Nordland as home? Ingeborg wondered after she left one soddy and headed for the other. She let Andrew walk beside her, keeping hold of the dish towel she'd tied around his waist. More and more each day, he resented being carried and let her know with squirms and wiggles and the plaintive cry that was becoming the watchword. "Down, Mor, down."

Each day he learned new words and could run farther before overtaking his feet and falling flat out. Undaunted, he got up and charged after Paws or Thorliff, repeating his actions till he looked as if he'd been rolling in the mud on purpose. Ingeborg knew she would have to watch him more closely as the prairie grass reached for the sun.

When she put him to bed that night after washing him clean once again, Ingeborg kissed his rosy cheek and tucked the lighter quilt under his chin. "Den lille guten," she whispered. "God bless." She said prayers with Thorliff and kissed him too. Such good sons she had, and how grateful she felt for their good health. Only at evening or when she cuddled Andrew did she think of the one that died stillborn not long after they settled on their homestead. As

Kaaren so often reminded her, those children of theirs who'd gone before were now cradled safe in their heavenly Father's arms.

"God in heaven," she whispered that night after Haakan had gone out to the barn and the house was quiet. "Please watch over that new life growing in Kaaren. She misses her little girls so. Thank you for spring and our health and for sending Haakan to help us. Father, help me to be content to let the men do the fieldwork, although I'm not so sure that is one of your edicts, but rather ours instead. What does it matter who does which work as long as all that is needed gets done?" She lay in her warm bed and waited, wishing she would hear the still small voice of God that the Bible spoke of. She thought of her family in Nordland and prayed for them. "You heard Haakan say he thinks we should begin shearing the sheep. You're the great Shepherd. Tell me, is the time right?" She waited again. Sighing, she turned on her side. "Thank you for listening. Amen."

After a hurried breakfast, Haakan said on the way out, "Lars and I will make a trip to St. Andrew tomorrow. If we leave before daylight, we should be able to make it back before dark."

"Are you asking me or telling me?" Ingeborg could have bit her tongue at the sharp retort.

Haakan gave her a questioning look as he lifted his basket of food for dinner. "Thank you for fixing this." Ax over his shoulder, he strode out toward the river.

She waved Thorliff and his flock of sheep off after giving him a ham sandwich and a water jug. "Now, don't go too far, you hear. Over the winter the sheep might have forgotten how to mind you."

"Mo-or." Thorliff's pained expression gave deeper meaning to his word.

"Just be careful." She watched as the boy headed out, the sheep following him as though they did this every day. The lambs gamboled around their mothers, and the ram brought up the rear. Paws trotted on the outside of the flock to round up any strays. In the places where the snow had melted first, the grass was already a short carpet of green.

Ingeborg hurried around, setting the house to rights and banking the stove. She gave a good stir to the pot of ham and beans she'd set to cooking and added a dollop of molasses. She took the rifle down and inspected it. When she was young, her brother had stressed upon her the importance of keeping the gun cleaned and oiled. Following his instructions, along with those of Carl, had stood her in good stead.

Andrew tagged at her feet, lost without his brother to entertain him. "Mor, go," he whimpered. "Go, Tor."

"No, you can't go with Thorliff. You are going to Tante Kaaren's." Ingeborg started to change into the britches she'd laid out on the bed but changed her mind. Seeing her in men's pants always made Kaaren tighten her lips. Why add any unhappiness to her today?

She left the house carrying Andrew but soon put him down. Quietly riding on her hip, he was heavy enough, but squirming and pushing, he was impossible. Trying to hurry a baby was like trying to scoop up an egg splattered on the floor.

Andrew looked at every blade of grass, every golden dandelion flower, any bug, and if he saw an earthworm, he squealed with delight. This was a three-earthworm trip.

"Get plenty of geese," Kaaren said after scooping Andrew up and planting a big kiss on his cheek. "Does Tante Kaaren's big boy want a cookie?" She'd said the magic words.

Ingeborg felt like running. Free, she was free to go hunting all by herself. Such freedom!

Once back at her own soddy, she swiftly changed from her skirt to the men's pants and heavy wool shirt. With her boots retied, she clapped her hat on her head, grabbed a biscuit from the bowl and, rifle in hand, shut the door behind her.

Lars and Haakan were sitting on a log in the sunshine on the edge of the woods when she strode past them. She waved her rifle in the air and shouted, "Going hunting. Supper is at Kaaren's if I'm not back in time."

She heard only one explosive word as she marched gaily on. "Britches."

She was sure there were more. Haakan Howard Bjorklund wasn't a one-word man.

6

S tolen! Everything was gone! Teeth chattering from the cold of his wet clothes, Hjelmer tried to still the panic. Here he stood in a strange land, unable to speak the language, and he had nothing. All his earthly belongings had been stolen.

A barrel-chested man in a blue wool uniform with gleaming gold buttons stopped in front of him. But the rapid-fire words meant nothing to Hjelmer. He shrugged, the weight of his wool coat dragging at his shoulders. Why hadn't he learned to talk the language?

The official took Hjelmer's arm and pointed to a huge domed building behind tall, sharply tipped posts that formed an impenetrable fence. Hjelmer could feel the panic grab his throat. Was the officer in the blue uniform taking him off to jail?

The woman who had wrapped a blanket around his shoulders now came to stand beside him. "How can I help you?" she asked, her Swedish clear to Hjelmer.

When the officer raised his voice as if they were deaf, she raised a hand. "This young man saved that child's life, and now he needs some help." Her tone stopped the officer in spite of his lack of understanding.

The man shrugged in reply and muttered something that any one with a sense of astuteness would recognize as a slur on their parentage.

One of the immigrants stepped over to the officer and asked in halting English, "You help him?"

"I wuz just takin' 'im to the Castle Garden. They could help there." The officer's brusque tone matched that of officials world over.

The man said again. "Help?"

"Come." The officer stepped back and beckoned with one hand. The three followed him, Hjelmer feeling like a small boy following his mother through the marketplace. The shaking made even walking difficult. The wind off the water sliced through his wet clothes in spite of the blanket.

Who could have taken his things? All he'd had was a beat-up carpetbag and a canvas sack, nothing much of value to anyone else. But to him? The bags contained his carving tools, the gifts he'd made, his clothes, and worst of all, his tickets and the few kroner remaining from the meager store he'd begun with. Would they be surprised to find the coins in the pouch with the seagull! How would he get to Dakota Territory now?

Hjelmer felt a person beside him and looked to see the father of the child he'd saved, flanked by the mother and other children, their confusion as evident as his own. Hearing murmuring behind them, Hjelmer turned to see other families from the ship clustered around, standing silently but with the same determined looks on their faces as on the family beside him.

"Be off, now. This is no concern of yours." The officer raised his voice and waved them away.

No one moved back; they only drew closer.

The officer raised his hands and then let them drop at his side. He spun on his heel, muttering, and headed through the gate.

Danish, Swedish, Norwegian, German, the languages mixed and mingled as the group discussed what would happen next.

Someone laid another blanket over Hjelmer's shoulders. In the lee of the spike wall the wind failed to tear at his skin. But he knew he had to get out of his wet clothes. The child's mother dug in a bag at her feet. She pulled out a pair of wool socks and stuffed them in Hjelmer's hand.

"Mange takk," Hjelmer said around chattering teeth. What would he wear? How could he dry the clothes he had on? The thoughts ricocheted through his mind like bullets glancing off granite.

He had to keep a clear head. *Think*, he commanded himself. *Think!*

The people around him pressed closer, sensing his need for warmth, and beyond that his need of support.

To the surprise of the group, when the officer returned, a round ball of a woman bounced beside him, the white apron that covered her from neck to ankle fluttering in the breeze of her movements.

"Now, then, what do we have here?" Her Norwegian sounded like the song of an angel in Hjelmer's ears.

Everyone in the group started to tell their version of what had happened.

The officer raised his hand for silence, ordering it also in a tone that killed the cacophony. He pointed a finger at Hjelmer. "You!"

"He's saying for you to tell us what happened. I will translate for him. Shame these police don't learn enough of the emigrant languages so they can at least keep from frightening folks right out of a year's growth."

Hjelmer smiled down at her. She sounded wise, just like Tante Anna at home. The feeling of doom that had been driving him into the cobblestones beneath his feet flew off.

He took a deep breath and tried to stall a shudder. He told her about the rescue, downplaying his part in it and the subsequent loss of his belongings. "It wasn't much," he shrugged, raising the mound of quilt and blanket on his shoulders, "but it was all I have in this world."

"Ah, me." She shook her head. "Those hoodlums on the docks would steal the shoes off your feet if you so much as took a nap. First thing we need to do is get you into some dry clothes before you catch your death."

A wool shirt appeared on his right, trousers were handed him from his left. Hjelmer turned in time to be handed a porkpie hat, also of wool. The group around him smiled as one. Those that had an extra piece of clothing had dug into their satchels and shared.

Hjelmer couldn't speak for a moment, and it wasn't due to the shivering. "But you need these things."

"You saved my son's life." The man on his right looked Hjelmer in the eye. "I have not much, but what I have is yours."

A collective sigh agreed with him.

"Now, ain't that just the way of good folks." The aproned woman beamed on all of them. "Young man, what is your name?"

"Hjelmer Bjorklund."

"Well, Mr. Bjorklund, you go on through that gate to the necessary—the one for men is on the far wall—and change out of those wet things. We'll all wait right here for you."

Once he found the place, Hjelmer stripped to the skin and rubbed himself with the wool blanket until he could feel the heat returning. While he'd have to wear wet boots, the pants and shirt, though shorter than his own, were warm and blissfully dry. He toweled his head, and after smoothing his hair back with his fingers, he set the hat at a jaunty angle.

He rolled his own wet things together, folded the blanket and quilt, and returned to the waiting group.

A cheer went up and Hjelmer could feel a blush start at his chest and work its way up to his ears. He held up the quilt and blanket to see who had loaned it to him. No one stepped forward.

"But you will need these when you get to your new homes."

"Ja," said the child's father. "So will you." He dug in his pocket and extended several coins to Hjelmer. "I wish this could be more, but we all have so little." His gesture included the group around them.

Hjelmer shook his head. "You will need . . . you already gave me . . ." He stopped at the look on the man's face. He looked at all the others. "Mange takk."

"Well, now, ain't that a picture of human kindness. I'll show you where to get that changed so you don't go losing anything more. All of you, follow me, and we'll get you through Castle Garden and on your way." She turned and, like the Pied Piper of Hamlin, lead her flock into the fortress.

After he'd said good-bye to his newfound friends, Hjelmer changed his few coins to American money and returned to the woman who'd become another of his benefactors. She checked the amount of money he now had and shook her head slowly.

"That won't barely get you to Chicago, and then where would you be?" She looked up at him. "If you take my advice, I'd say wait till I'm done working here today, and you can come home with me. My late husband—God rest his soul—brought us where a lot of other Norwegian families have gathered. Most of us have been here for a generation or two, and perhaps you could find some work with one of us." She cocked her head, robinlike, and studied him out of merry brown eyes. "What is it you might be good at?"

"I can carve, but I do that more for pleasure—birds and kitchen utensils and such. But my far made all his sons learn farming. . . ."

She shook her head. "Not much of that where we live."

"And blacksmithing. I can shoe horses, rim a wheel, make tools, household things, whatever can be done with a forge, I can do it or learn how." Hjelmer felt like he was bragging, something his mor said was a sin, but he needed work, and soon. How else would he ever make it to Dakota Territory?

She nodded her head. "I see. You look a mite young to be so

skilled." Just then someone called her name and beckoned to her from behind one of the pillars that reached clear to the arch of the domed ceiling. "You wait over there, out of the way of the traffic, and I will be back with you soon." She darted away before he had a chance to answer.

Hjelmer did as she told him, his rolled wet clothes under one arm and his new quilt and blanket under the other. A bench ran along one wall, and as soon as an old woman vacated her seat, he took it and leaned against the wall. The rise and fall of voices seemed to circle the cavernous building and bounce down to pound upon his ears.

The family next to him were stuffing themselves with sausages and bread, making his stomach rumble in response. The child drank from a mug, the white mustache betraying his drink.

Hjelmer thought of the cows at home, remembering the rich taste of milk still warm from the cow. The cheeses his mother made, fresh bread, lefse, sild, and even the hard biscuits his sister had packed marched like a vision through his head. He didn't dare add up the hours since he'd had any food, let alone known a full stomach.

He took his bundles and went in search of a drink of water. Surely they didn't charge for water, although according to what he saw, they charged for everything else. After a long drink that did nothing to stop the rumbles in his belly, he returned to the bench to wait.

"Now then, Mr. Bjorklund, are you ready to go?" The woman stopped in front of him, a shawl covering her dark dress and the apron folded over her arm.

"Yes, ma'am." Hjelmer stood and adjusted his bundles.

"My name is Mrs. Holtenslander, and we have about a mile to walk to the ferry to Brooklyn where I live."

A mile on flat land like this New York City seemed like nothing to the young man used to the hills and mountains of Nordland. He found himself gawking at the brick buildings, some three, even five stories tall. He was dumbfounded by the crush of people speaking in a myriad of strident tongues and the manner of drayage on the streets: horse cabs, phaetons, heavy wagons carrying wood, stone, or beer, lighter wagons with a wooden cover that had pictures of milk cans painted on the sides, fancy carriages pulled by matched teams, and carts hitched to lame nags. Never had he seen and heard such chaos. A steam train thundered by on tracks over his head, making his ears ring and his legs shake.

After it passed, he looked down at his companion to see her smiling. "That's the El or elevated train. Built some years ago, it's one of the wonders of New York. It provides more room on the streets for other kinds of transportation."

"Oh." Hjelmer spun around to see what caused the clanging that had other folks crossing the streets and heading for the sidewalks.

"Fire engine," Mrs. Holtenslander yelled at him over the clamor.

Around the corner raced six white horses, two abreast with ears flat against their heads. The driver slapped the reins as they straightened out, the wagon behind them a tanker painted red with yellow-and-brass trim. Uniformed men hung on the sides of the wagon.

The thunder of the horse hooves and screaming wheels made him long to follow. The way they drove that wagon, they surely needed a blacksmith every day.

As the ferry chugged across the East River to Long Island, he couldn't take his eyes off the city lit up behind them. Up river, huge sand-block towers rose against the night sky, a promise of the Brooklyn Bridge to come. Once on land again, they walked a few more blocks, past small businesses and stores now closed for the night.

Lamplighters, making their way from post to post, lighted their way through the dusk. When Mrs. Holtenslander stopped in front of a narrow two-story house made of brown cut stone, Hjelmer looked from the carved front door at the top of the short flight of stairs to his hostess.

"You live here?"

"Ja."

Hjelmer stared up and down the tree-lined street that ran between similar houses, their walls butted against each other so as not to waste an inch. The noise of the streets they had walked seemed like in another land. A woman pushed a baby buggy and nodded as she passed. A man in a bowler hat, his black overcoat over his arm, did the same.

Windows glowed, welcoming the homeward bound.

Mrs. Holtenslander climbed the four steps to her door, inserted her key, pushed it open, and stood there waiting for Hjelmer. "Please, come in."

Never in his life had he been so conscious of his dirty and still wet boots, the pant legs that didn't quite reach his boot tops, and the smell that had seeped into his skin while on the ship and from his swim in the litter-strewn harbor. His mor would be horrified if she saw him. His ears burned like he'd been standing too close to the forge.

"I . . . I cannot." He shook his head. "Surely you have a barn or a shed where I could sleep. I do not need a bed. I-I'm . . ." He stuttered to a stop.

"Mr. Bjorklund, I would be most pleased to offer you a room in my home until you find some employment and another place to stay. Surely you would do the same for a young person of your own nationality who was in a difficult situation through no fault of his own. If you hadn't been more concerned for that child's life than your belongings or even your own life, you would be on the train for your new home. And that little boy would be dead, his parents grieving their loss, would they not?"

Hjelmer nodded. "But I never thought—I . . . I mean, your house is so grand, and I am so dirty."

"We have a bathtub, young man, and tomorrow, Fulla, the maid, will wash your clothes good as new. In the meantime, I know my cook has supper ready, and if you are not hungry, which I am sure you are, I am." She waved to the inviting hallway. "Please, come in."

Hat in his hands, Hjelmer mounted the stairs and stepped into a whole new world.

ᴥ᙮᙭

On her travois, two poles with willow branches woven between them to carry the results of her hunt, Ingeborg had piled six geese and the gutted carcass of one deer with the horns still in place because she needed new spoons. Deer antlers could be formed into spoons, combs, and all manner of things needed around the house. The brains, mixed with lye from the ashes, would be used in tanning the hide. So Metiz, the old half-breed woman who'd lived and begun to farm the land before the Bjorklunds filed on it, had taught her. Like the Indians, Ingeborg wasted nothing.

Paws yipped and danced around her, meeting her out on the trail and announcing to all that she had come home. Thorliff came running from the barn, a grin lighting his face.

"Mor, I never even heard the shots." He counted the geese and jogged up to add his weight to pulling by taking one of the travois poles.

"I missed one deer and wasted a shell," Ingeborg grumbled good-naturedly. "How did the sheep do?"

"They stayed right with me. Paws is the best sheep dog. You should have seen him when the ram thought he'd stay out to graze. Paws nipped his hocks and ol' Charlie came charging after us. Sheep is still the leader. She stays right with me."

Ingeborg stopped dragging her pole to tousle his hair and knocked his cap askew in the process. "You didn't let them graze too long in one place?"

He looked up at her with wounded eyes. "M-o-r."

"Sorry. I know you know better than to let them dig up the roots, but I have to check sometimes. That's what mothers are for."

"I thought they were for cooking. I'm really hungry."

"Me, too. That's why Tante Kaaren said to come eat supper at her house tonight."

"Good!" He slanted a grin up at her. "You think she had time to bake cookies with Andrew there?"

They stopped the travois by the barn. She could hear Haakan's voice inside, calming the cow as he stripped milk from her udder.

"Mr. Bjorklund is almost finished with the milking. Wait till you see all the wood they cut. Onkel Lars says Mr. Bjorklund is a terror with that ax of his."

Ingeborg stopped and smiled at her son. He hadn't talked this much all last winter. Was he making up for lost time after the long winter that was so hard on all of them that no one talked much? She knew she hadn't. Guilt stabbed her anew. What trials she had put her family through in those months she raged against God for taking Roald and Carl and the two small girls. But now she lived anew in the light of His forgiveness. She sighed and looked up to see the evening star shining above the horizon as a reminder that God's love and forgiveness comes fresh each day and never changes.

Thank you, Father, thank you. Her prayers flowed freely once more as did the joy she passed on to Thorliff with a hug that made him wrap his arms around her waist.

"Let's get this deer and the geese hung. I'll skin and pluck them later." Together they dragged the deer inside the open barn door and attached the pulley to the stick she'd thrust through the tendons on the deer's back legs. With a couple of quick pulls on the rope, the deer hung head down from the rafter. Thorliff knotted the end of the rope around a peg in the post, went back outside, and returned dragging two gray geese.

Haakan stood from the stool beside the cow's flank, and picking up the milk bucket, he set it out of the way on top of the grain bin.

He hung the stool on its peg on the wall and turned as Ingeborg brought in the last of the geese and strung them up beside the others from the line of pegs on another rafter.

"Six geese and a deer?"

"Ja, I missed the other. I didn't see any elk." Ingeborg turned to face him.

"Where did you learn to shoot like that?"

"My brother taught me when I was young, and I practiced since we came here." She wiped her hands on a twist of hay and dusted them together. "While we haven't had a variety of food sometimes, we have always had meat." She pulled some strips of bark from her pockets. "And medicinals. This willow bark, when steeped, is good for headache. I have dandelion greens on the travois. I know Kaaren will be glad for those. They are good for renewing the body in spring, just like their cheery yellow blossoms bring delight to the eye."

She looked up from the bark in her hands to meet his eyes. "The land is good to those who know how to find its treasures."

"Mrs. Bjorklund, you are an amazing woman." He leaned back against the edge of the grain bin and crossed his arms over his chest.

For one insane moment, Ingeborg wished she were wearing a skirt and shirtwaist with a clean apron and had her hair combed, instead of wearing blood-stained britches, a shirt torn at the shoulder where a tree limb had snagged her, and her much-abused straw hat that failed at keeping twigs from sticking in her hair or the sun from dusting freckles across her nose. The faint stinging on her cheekbones made her aware the sun had done its work there, too.

What must he think?

She raised her gaze again, along with her chin. "M—thank you. We will have supper with Kaaren and Lars tonight." She reached for one of the geese. "I'll take three of these over there. I nearly forgot."

"Let me do that." He swung three of them down and knotted a piece of twine around their feet. "How did you bring all this bounty back with you?"

"Mor made a travois, like Metiz taught her. You can carry a lot that way, more than one person could do alone." Thorliff walked backward out the door. "Come see."

As Thorliff described the value of the simple travois, Ingeborg went on to the house to wash the residue of the hunt from her hands. She'd just as soon have stayed and skinned out the deer, but Kaaren would have supper waiting, and she needed to retrieve Andrew. After the boys were in bed, she would go back out to the barn. While the light wasn't good, she knew she could skin a deer or pluck a goose in her sleep by now.

After a quick wash, she changed back into her woman's garb, as she sometimes called the black ankle-length wool skirt and white waister, then she lifted her shawl down from its peg by the door and headed back outside.

"I strained the milk and set it to cool in the pans in the cellar." Haakan said as he swung the string of geese over his shoulder.

"Thank you."

"All the animals are fed and watered. I put six eggs in the basket in the cellar." Thorliff joined her on her other side. "Four of the hens are broody. You think we should let that black one set? She didn't do so well last year."

"If she hadn't laid all winter, she'd have been in the stewpot long ago." Ingeborg clasped the corners of her shawl around her bosom. With the setting of the sun, a real bite had come on the night air.

"She pecked me again." Thorliff rubbed his hand.

"That makes five broody hens then. I think that is enough for now. You let her have eight eggs, and this is her last chance. Some nice young frying chickens will taste mighty good."

When they entered the other soddy, Andrew banged his spoon on the table and crowed with delight. Ingeborg took him up in her arms and snuggled him close, kissing him on the neck to make him giggle.

"Thank you for caring for him," she said to Kaaren and pointed to the geese Haakan laid by the door. "I brought you something. There are three more at our barn, so the down should go a long way to replenish our store."

"Thank you. Roast goose, tomorrow, with stuffing and the last of the rutabagas."

Ingeborg swung her bag of greens on the table. "And these. I thought you might want them also."

"Good, good. Now please be seated. Andrew was ready to eat a long time ago, and I only gave him a bread crust to stave him off. I thought all of us eating together would be a treat."

As soon as Lars finished grace, they passed the bowls of potatoes and gravy, roast chicken and biscuits around the table, each of them filling their plates and eating like they'd not had a meal for days.

When Kaaren got up to pour the second cups of coffee, Haakan said, "Please tell me more about this Metiz. I hear so much good that she has done—"

"Metiz saved Mor's life," Thorliff said around a mouthful of biscuit.

"Yes, she did. She's become a good friend. She taught us much about learning how to find the bounty of the prairie. Things are much different here than in Nordland." Ingeborg laid her fork down and leaned her elbows on the table. "Metiz is the name for the people who are descendants of both French Canadian fur trappers and the Indians, usually Chippewa or one of the Lakota tribes. They were here long before the current settlers, living off the land like their ancestors did and migrating with the buffalo and the seasons. Metiz herself broke that piece of the prairie nearest the river and raised some grain and garden things like tubers and corn. She still leaves to be with her family in the winter and returns in the spring. She should be coming back anytime now."

"Metiz' wolf saved our sheep last year from a pack of wolves," Thorliff added, his eyes shining in the lamplight.

"Yes, you most likely will see Wolf. Metiz saved his life when he was young, and now he guards her; and because we are her friends, he guards us and ours, too."

"A wolf!" Disbelief colored Haakan's tone.

"Ja, you will see his tracks before you see him. His right front foot was caught in a trap, so his paw print is distinctive."

Ingeborg watched as Haakan exchanged a look of wonder with Lars.

"Stranger things have been known to happen." Lars sipped his coffee. "I have heard many tales in my travels with the threshing crew." He turned to Ingeborg. "Haakan and I think it is dry enough now to make a trip to St. Andrew with the wagon, and since we got so much wood cut for the riverboats, tomorrow would be a good time to go. What do you think?"

Ingeborg hid the pleasure she felt at being asked instead of told. She caught her bottom lip between her teeth. "There could still be another blizzard."

"Inge, the grass is nearly ankle-high in places. We might get another dusting of snow, true, but a blizzard? I doubt it."

"You could wait another week."

"By then we could be out in the fields. I'd hate to waste a day that could be spent plowing."

"Kaaren and I could go later. We have eggs and cheese to take to the Bonanza farm."

Lars laid his hand on his wife's. "I don't think Kaaren feels up to a trip in that wagon. And besides, I'm not sure the ferry is running yet."

Ingeborg looked from Kaaren's pale face to Lars. She nodded. It seemed the decision was out of her hands. But a tiny voice deep inside worried at her. Another few days wouldn't matter so much, would it?

With Haakan carrying Andrew, they made their way back to the southern soddy, and after she put the boys to bed, the two adults returned to the barn. Working together, they had the deer skinned and the geese plucked in what seemed like no time. They covered the deer carcass with a cloth and, after salting it heavily, rolled the hide, hair side in.

Ingeborg poured warm water from the reservoir into a pan so they could wash. Haakan's shoulder brushed hers, sending a tingle down her arm. She had felt the same out in the quiet of the barn.

"Thank you for your help." She handed him a cloth to dry his hands.

"You are more than welcome. I've heard it said willing hands make work lighter."

"Ja, that is true." She started to hang the towel on the peg, when he reached out and took something from her hair. She froze, her gaze snagging on the deep blue of his Bjorklund eyes.

He held up a twig. "You had an extra passenger in your hair."

"Oh, ah, mange takk." She took the twig from his fingers, careful not to touch the rough tips, then crossing the small space, she lifted the lid on the stove and dropped the bit of wood in. All the while, she hoped the actions would calm her tripping heart. What was happening with her?

"We will leave before daylight. Lars will use his team."

"You might be wise to hitch up four in case there are places so soft yet to get stuck." Did her words make any sense at all? Ingeborg took in a solid breath and wiped her hands on her skirt.

"Thank you, but no. That is not necessary."

"I will milk the cow, then."

"Good."

Why did he stand with the lamplight glinting off his hair and stare at her that way?

Her heart tripped again.

He turned to leave. "Good night, then."

"Good night, Mr. Bjorklund."

"I remember you said you would call me Haakan." He waited.

"Good night, H-Haakan."

He touched a finger to the brim of his hat and crossed the few steps to the door. He stopped and looked over his shoulder. "I must say I think I liked you in britches better."

Ingeborg felt the flaming reach clear to her hairline. "Uff da."

She crawled into bed still trying to keep her lips from smiling. Such effrontery. She grinned in the darkness. After saying her prayers, she rolled on her side. This "uff da" was definitely the end of a chuckle.

The men were gone when she awoke to the rooster's crowing.

The blizzard struck in the early afternoon, bearing down from the north like a runaway freight train.

He couldn't remember her face. Haakan tried to bring back the memory of the cook in the lumber camp, but he couldn't. In his mind, she stood in front of the huge cookshack stove, birdlike in her swift movements, but when she turned, he couldn't see her face.

"So, this must have seemed a mighty long walk," Lars said as he slapped the reins over the backs of the team trotting between the traces.

"Huh?" Haakan jerked himself back to the present. "What did you say?"

"Long walk. You know, the day you came to the homestead." Lars turned his head and gave Haakan a questioning look.

"Ja, it was, especially since I nearly froze to death in the snowfall the night before. If it hadn't been for that run-down soddy, they would have found my bones out on the prairie."

"The weather here is mighty changeable." Lars shook his head. "I don't like leaving Kaaren when she is feeling so low."

"Is she sick?"

"Feels like it. Women get that way sometimes when they're in the family way. Of course, it's all new to me. Can't say I ever remember my mor having trouble, but then she was good at hiding how she felt. Kaaren is, too, but I can tell."

"How long have you been married?"

"Not even a year yet. We married after harvest was over last fall. She'd been widowed the winter before. Now, that was a hard year for many around here. Blizzards, and then the flu hit, taking entire families. Kaaren lost her husband and two little girls. Way she tells it, if it hadn't been for Ingeborg, she'd have lost her mind, too. A mighty close call it was there for a time."

"Is that when Ingeborg's husband died, too?"

"Ja, he went out to assist the others as soon as the blizzard let up. We don't know if the weather got him or the flu or some combination thereof, but he never came back. Polinski—you'll regret the day you meet him, now there is one lazy farmer—found the headstall of Roald's mule, and Ingeborg found Roald's pocketknife in the duff by a big cottonwood. Wolves must have got the rest."

Haakan barely kept himself from shuddering. What an awful way to die, unless the man just took refuge under the tree and slept his life away. He left such a fine family. "Some man will be fortunate to marry Mrs. Bjorklund."

Lars sent him a slanting look. "What about you?"

Haakan shook his head. "No, I'm not one for farming on this prairie. Too flat for me. If I leave the timber country, think I'll head farther west. I heard tell there are mountains with trees so big you could hold a dance on the cut stump, and hills and valleys with land so rich you can stick a post in a hole and it'll sprout."

"Funny, that's what they say about the Red River Valley. No one's dug down below the topsoil yet. Might be it goes on forever. Indians say there used to be a great sea here." He motioned to the land around him with his chin. "Well, let's hope we don't have no trouble fording the Little Salt, and we can get loaded and head home 'for the sun heads down. These two horses know the way home. They'll take us there after dark if the moon's hiding out."

Haakan stared ahead over the rumps of the team pulling the wagon toward St. Andrew. This was such an easy ride compared to that day he had walked these miles.

The wagon barely had to float to ford the Little Salt, a far different scene than the one he had forded. The horses threw themselves into their collars, and with mud flying from hooves and wheels, they breasted the bank. Lars wrapped the reins around the brake handle and leaped to the ground to make sure the traces remained secure. He checked all the harness and around the wagon before climbing back aboard. With a chirp and a quick flap of the reins, they were on their way again.

"That's the soddy where I spent one night," Haakan said, pointing to the building with one corner of the roof broken in and the doorway gaping open.

"Better'n out in the weather."

"Ja, I'd slept under enough trees to appreciate the shelter. One night I slept in a barn, another in a haystack. Farms on the Minnesota side can be few and far between."

"Out here, too. But settlers are coming in fast as they can hitch their horses to a wagon and drive it. Mark my words, that railroad comes over on our side of the river and you won't be able to more'n throw a rock between the farms. Almost no land left now, leastwise not for homesteading."

"I heard there's still plenty to the west."

"Right. But nothing with the richness of this river valley. I haven't had to dig a rock yet, or a stump. Just get that sod busted and seeds grow. The Indians didn't even bother to plow. They dug a hole with a stick, dropped in the seed and waited for it to come up. Corn, squash, beans they grew. Takes busted sod for wheat and oats, though. You done any of that?"

Haakan shook his head. "I've plowed plenty. Driven freight with six up, loaded ships on the docks of Duluth, anything I needed to put my hand to in order to survive, I did." He looked over at Lars. "There's work for whoever's willing in this country, but I still like working the timber best."

Lars nodded. "Your skill with the ax proves that. Surprised me how much we got cut and stacked. The paddle-wheelers will be happy to load up."

"Don't you need a dock to load from?"

"We'll build something. What they had got washed away in the spring runoff last year. And the two women didn't have wood cut for the ships last year."

"But they got more sod busted?"

Lars nodded. "Mostly that was Ingeborg. She don't let nothing stop her, but Kaaren thought she was working herself into an early grave. They say hard work is good for healing the soul, but I don't figure the good Lord meant for women to bust sod. It's backbreaking work for a strong man."

"Ja, so I've heard." Haakan pulled his coat shut and buttoned it up. "It's getting colder."

"That north wind cuts right through ya." Lars slapped the reins, sending the team into a trot.

By the time they'd made their purchases at The Mercantile and loaded the wagon, wisps of drapery clothed the sun. Once out of town and on the open prairie, they could see the lowering clouds bearing down on them from the north.

"Them clouds are bellied up with snow, sure as sin." Lars slapped the reins and chirped the horses to a faster pace.

Driven before the rising wind, the first snowflakes bit like pin-point daggers. The horses shook their heads and picked up the pace, already blowing heavily from the weight of the loaded wagon.

"Bring up that elk robe," Lars said. "We can huddle under that. Otherwise we'll be frozen clear through before we reach the river."

Haakan did as told, but the robe provided only scant protection. He'd thought to put in a quilt, but they had planned to be home by bedtime, so he didn't take it. The thought of Ingeborg's reluctance to agree to the trip blasted through his mind. And he'd thought her too concerned about spring blizzards or Dakota blizzards in general. Her fear after what she'd been through was not surprising. And more important than her fear, she had been right. They should have waited. Now they were in trouble.

"How will you see the ford?"

"Count on the horses to know the way, I guess. Right now I can't see five feet in front of them."

The jingle of the harness and the grunts of the trotting team could barely be heard above the wind. Wind was such a paltry word for the driving force that seemed intent on blowing them off the prairie.

Haakan pulled a bandanna from his pocket and fastened it over his face, jerking his hat lower on his forehead so it would stay with him. He could feel the shivers start in his arms and legs and move inward.

"What about that soddy?"

"What?"

"That soddy, the one I stopped in." He leaned closer to Lars and shouted in his ear.

"Good idea. Just how we going to see it? Could go right by in this weather."

Their shouts mingled with the driving snow and whirled away.

Haakan turned to face the north, shading his face from the pelting snow, yet watching for the outline of the decaying building. The snow collected on the brim of his hat and on his shoulders covered by the robe.

Lars pulled the horses down to a walk to give them a breather.

How far had they come? Haakan tried to estimate their speed and the distance. He couldn't tell if they were still on the road or had struck off across the prairie. Stories he'd heard of men lost in the blizzard and walking in circles till they lay down and slept their way to a frozen death played in his head.

With the reins clamped between his knees, Lars stamped his feet and slapped his arms against his chest. "And we thought spring was here!"

"What?" Haakan leaned closer.

"Spring. Thought it was here."

"No, I ain't seen it yet." Haakan thought he mentioned the soddy but wasn't sure. The wind took the words away before they could make it to his ear. He pulled his coat collar up higher. If he wasn't careful, he could lose part of his ears to frostbite. He copied Lars' stomping and slapping actions. Sitting up on the wagon seat like they were was just asking for frostbite, let alone freezing to death.

He peered out to the north, trying to see the soddy. His eyes blurred in the effort.

He thought of the women waiting for their return. They'd already been through so much, they surely didn't need any more suffering. He could hear Ingeborg asking them to wait another week. They should have listened to her. He stared out through the driving snow. His chin felt like it had been stabbed by flying bits of glass.

Since arriving in America, Haakan had pretty much left the faith of his fathers, the faith he learned at his mother's knee and from the stern admonitions of Reverend Sjorguard during confirmation. But now he sent a plea heavenward. *God in heaven, please, I beg you, see us through this storm. If you help us now, I promise to return to you.*

Cold. He'd never in his life been so cold. He clutched the elk robe closer around his shoulder. The wind slashed through all the layers of protection and pierced to the very marrow of his bones. Would he ever be warm again?

While shudders racked his body, he fought against closing his eyes. Frost rimmed his eyelashes, making them even heavier. He rubbed the frost away with the back of his mittened hand. He looked over at Lars. His chin rested on his chest.

꙳ ꙳

Surely the men had seen the blizzard coming and remained in St. Andrew.

Ingeborg stared out the window at the swirling snow. Coming thick and fast, it had covered the ground within minutes, creating a world with no dimensions. No sky, no horizon, nothing but swirling, driving white pellets. She knew because she could barely see her hand at the end of her arm when she tightened the rope from the house to the barn.

She clasped her elbows in her hands and turned to face the questions on Thorliff's face. "Not to worry, son. They are in God's hands, and He can part the snow for them. They are most likely standing in the doorway of The Mercantile, deciding where they will spend the night. Lars understands Dakota blizzards. And respects them." *Roald had, too, and yet one had taken him.* Ingeborg crushed the thought beneath her will and crossed the three paces to the stove. "We will make an egg cake so they will have a fine treat when they do return. How about that?"

Thorliff ducked his head. Paws whined and stuck his nose in the little boy's hand. Andrew stirred, rustling the corn husks in the mattress on the bed. When he whimpered, Ingeborg went over and picked him up, snuggling him against her cheek. That side of the room away from the stove was frigid. How could a day go from bright sunshine and Chinook breezes to sub-zero in only a few hours?

She sat Andrew on his block of wood on one of the chairs and tied him in place with a dishtowel, all the while teasing him with nonsense words and funny sounds. While his usually contagious chortle rang out in the dim soddy, Thorliff refused to look up from the book he read in the glow of the kerosene lamp. At one point, he got up and put on a sweater.

After giving Andrew a chunk of pork rind to chew on to relieve his teething, Ingeborg sat down beside Thorliff and stroked the hair back from his forehead. "Listen to me, son." When he didn't raise his head, she tipped his chin up with her finger so he had to look her in the eye. "We believe that God takes care of us, don't we?" He nodded. "And that He knows what is happening here and answers our prayers?"

Thorliff refused to look at her, covering the blue of his eyes so she might not look in.

"We will pray for the men, all right?"

He said nothing, the squaring of his chin mute testimony to his thoughts. When he breathed, the breath going in caught on something, and what might have been a sob in a weaker person only became a sigh.

"Thorliff, are you afraid?"

He started to shake his head, a movement so small that it failed to set the lock of hair on his forehead into motion. Instead, he nodded, and a tear slid from the corner of his eye. "Far didn't come back, and I prayed and prayed." Another tear trickled after the first. "Why, Mor, why?"

"Ah, my son, my son. So young to have to endure such sorrows!" She pulled on his arm, and he flew to the safe haven of her lap. "I do not know the answer to your question. I asked God the same thing for months and weeks, and I never heard an answer. But I do know, now, with all that I am and believe, that God knows best, and He keeps us in His hand."

"Did Far know he was in God's hand?"

Ingeborg nodded. "Oh yes, my son, he knew. And now your far is standing next to the throne of God with all the angels, and knowing your far, I am sure he is reminding God to take care of his family still down here on earth."

Andrew, drool glistening on his chin, waved his rind in the air and jabbered a long string of sounds, ending with "Mor, see me."

"Yes, I see you, den lille guten. Thorliff, you are such a good reader, why don't you get our Bible and find Psalm ninety-one. God tells us not to be afraid, for He is here with us."

Thorliff went to the chest, covered by the flowers, leaves, and vines painted in the rosemaling of his homeland. He lifted the lid, picked up the heavy Bible, and brought it to the table. Carefully, he turned the thin pages, looking for Psalms. When he found the place, he read aloud, his voice barely audible above the shrieking wind.

"So, what does that tell us?" Ingeborg asked her son.

"That God is in charge of the wind and all that is." Thorliff kept his finger on the place. "And that He knows about us and will protect us."

"Good." She leaned forward. "Then right now we will thank Him for just that. Ja?"

"Ja." Thorliff closed his eyes, and together, he and his mother raised their voices in prayer, certain that God could hear above the howling of the wind. At the "amen," Ingeborg sighed and wiped the corner of her eye with the edge of her apron.

"Now, when we feel afraid, we will remember that verse just as if God were standing right here beside us in all His glory." She stood. "Let's bake that cake. It is good you brought in so much wood this afternoon. As soon as the cake is baked, we will do our chores, and then after supper, we will write a letter to our family in Nordland. I wonder where your Onkel Hjelmer is this day."

Haakan shook the man beside him. "Wake up!" He shook him again. "Lars!"

Lars jerked upright. He turned to look at Haakan, struggling to open his eyes. When he brushed the frost off of them, he stared over Haakan's shoulder. Lars' face cracked in a smile. "Look!"

Haakan turned. Sure enough, the wind had slacked just enough that the dark walls of the crumbling soddy could be seen.

Lars turned the team to the building and drew the wagon as close to the wall as possible. The men stood and nearly fell, since legs without feeling are impossible to stand on. With the halting motions of gnarled old men, they climbed out of the wagon, leaning against the wheels until they could move. They bent to unhitch the horses. In the lee of the building, the wind could only howl at them, not tear them limb from frozen limb.

Even so, their clublike hands refused to bend around the snow- and ice-coated traces.

"Go inside. Start a fire," Lars yelled above the screeching wind.

"With what? There wasn't any wood in there." Haakan crammed his hands under his armpits to warm them enough to unhitch the horses.

How easy it would be to lie down and sleep his life away. Instead, he stumbled to the wagon bed and dug under the supplies to retrieve his ax. He found a flint box under the wagon seat and stuffed that in his pocket. Going to the end of the wagon, he hefted his ax and, with a mighty swing, attacked the sideboards. Chunk by chunk he split the wood, and when he had an armful, he hauled it into the soddy.

While dusk had not yet fallen, between the dark walls and the darker storm, he could see only blackness. He stood still until his eyes adjusted to the darkness and he could make out the end of the small room and the fireplace. He dumped the wood in front of it, and using his ax handle as a brace, he knelt on the packed earth floor. He shaved thin curls of wood off the wagon boards and arranged them in a small pile.

Opening the tinderbox was beyond him. His frozen fingers wouldn't form the minute motions needed. Again he clamped his hands under his armpits, this time inside his coat.

A curse exploded from his throat. They had to have fire, or they would die!

"How are you coming?" Lars stumbled into the dark room.

"Slow." Haakan blew on his fingers, and this time the metal box opened. With shaking fingers, he knelt again by the shavings pile and tried to strike a spark into the mound. Between his shaking and lack of control, what sparks he did strike disappeared into the blackness.

Like the sparks, Lars disappeared into the swirling blackness outside the door.

"Come on, come on." Plea or prayer, Haakan muttered and tried breaking the curls into the tiniest slivers. If only he could see. If only he could make his hands work right. If only the fire would start!

꘎꘎ ꘎꘎

Ingeborg did as she'd counseled her son. Every time the fears returned like a pack of wolves circling and seeking to drive in for the kill, she thought of Jesus standing right behind her and added an angel or two for safe measure. She just wished Kaaren were in the soddy with them instead of across the field in the other house all by herself.

Later, in the barn with the comforting noises of the animals around her and her head pressed into the warm flank of the cow, Ingeborg added extra prayers for Kaaren. Even though the wind howled like a gigantic wolf, screaming and tearing at the corners, she sat on the stool, content with the squeeze and pull motion that brought the milk streaming into the bucket. A sheep called her lamb, the cow switched her tail, and one of the horses pulled more hay out of the manger. Simple noises that tuned out the storm and tuned in her feelings of gratitude. The evening turned into one long prayer, and peace filled her heart.

But in the darkness of the night, with the storm howling so loud she kept waking, she could feel the old terrors ripping at the edges of her mind. How would Kaaren survive the loss of yet another man to the storms of the Dakotas? And Thorliff? Would he ever learn to trust in his heavenly Father? Would she? The blackness of soul that had shrouded her for those many months sought entrance again, slithering under the door she kept forcing closed.

꘎꘎ ꘎꘎

Haakan hadn't felt this close to tears since he left his mother waving to him from the station platform. How senseless! He took in a deep breath and let it all out, seeking to control the shaking of his body. He struck the flint again and again, each time feeling more desperate and knowing that calm and concentration accomplished more than desperation, anytime. His father had struggled to teach his sons that the cool head prevailed in a hot situation.

What he wouldn't give for some real heat right now.

He leaned closer and struck the flint again. A bright red eye landed in the shavings and glowed. Afraid he might blow it out, Haakan puffed ever so gently. The eye expanded, slivers of wood curled black and a flame rose, eating the slivers around it and glowing brighter. Haakan chose three slightly larger slivers and set them, teepee fashion, over the flame. He rocked back on his heels and breathed a sigh of relief. Now they might make it through the night. He added more bits and pieces to the now ravenous fire, already feeling the warmth of it on his hands and face. Fire, so simple a thing, and yet without it, men perished. And the blizzards won.

He added the larger pieces, still careful to keep from crushing the precious flame.

"Thank God, you got it started." Lars joined him at the fire.

"Did you get the horses unhitched?"

"Partly."

"You stay here and I'll finish. I can feel the burning in my fingers now, so I should be able to unhitch them." Haakan got to his feet and stepped back into the fury of the storm. He'd been concentrating so hard on his own war with the flint, he'd nearly forgotten the cataclysmic battle raging outside the dirt walls.

He banged the icy traces and chains against the broad side of his axhead and unhooked them. One by one, he led the horses away from the doubletree and into the soddy. Their body heat would help keep all of them warm.

"We're about out of wood." Lars turned his back to the fire.

"I know. Should we unload the wagon and bring the supplies in here? It's going to be a long night."

"I'll help you in a minute." It was hard to understand his words above the chattering of his teeth.

Haakan returned in a moment with the elk robe and wrapped it around the shoulders of the man hunched near the flame. By the time he'd chopped another load of wood from the sides of the wagon, he'd worked off much of the effects of the cold.

One of the horses nickered when he stepped back through the doorway. Compared to the outside, the room already felt warmer. He stacked the wood near to the fire so it could dry some before being added to the flames. Cold as it was, the snow hadn't melted enough to seriously wet the wood.

What could they use to melt snow for the horses to drink, let alone for themselves?

On the next load, he dumped a sack of seed wheat on the floor next to Lars. "Here, sit on this. It'll get you off the cold ground."

Lars didn't move.

"Come on, man." Haakan took hold of his friend's shoulders.

Lars growled and flung out an arm, catching Haakan on the side of the head.

Haakan stumbled backward. His ear rang only slightly. Lars was too weak to do serious damage. In the north woods, he'd seen men go crazy from the cold. All they wanted was to be left alone so they could sleep. He brought in more of the supplies, stacking them a couple of feet from the fireplace. He opened one sack and poured grain in front of each of the horses after first removing their bridles.

"There, that ought to make you feel better." The horses dropped their heads, and the rhythm of their chewing sounded comforting as he removed their harnesses. Snow had drifted in the corner where the roof had caved in, but even so, Haakan could feel the steam rising from the horses. If he could take the elk robe for a bit, he would use it to wipe them down. The snow that had frozen to their hair now melted to make them colder.

Haakan added more wood to the fire. Lars now leaned against the sack of grain, firelight playing over his slack features. Periodically a shudder clattered his teeth together, but his hands had relaxed their grip on the robe. Could he get the man walking again to keep his circulation going? He'd heard of men killing a horse, gutting it, and crawling inside the cavity for warmth and protection. Is that what he needed to do for Lars? But since they were protected at least to a degree, and if he could keep the fire going, they would be safe. Surely this blizzard wouldn't last for days like some he'd heard of.

Back and forth, the ideas waged a war in his mind, much like the blizzard trying to snatch the roof off their heads.

"Try this first," he muttered, hauling Lars to his feet.

Lars mumbled something, and Haakan figured it was better he could not hear it.

"Lars! Listen to me! You are going to walk with me back and forth in front of the fire. Do you hear me?"

Lars mumbled something again, and his head lolled forward.

Haakan held him up with one arm and slapped his cheeks with the other. "It won't help if I carry you. You have to walk." He pulled one of the man's arms up over his own shoulder and clamped his own around Lars' waist. "Now walk!"

He carried dead weight. The thought made him cringe. He might feel like dead weight, but the man was still alive, and he was going to remain that way.

"Lars, Kaaren needs you!" He raised his voice to outshout the wind. "Kaaren needs you. You can't let her down."

Lars lifted his head. His eyes fluttered open. "Walk."

If Haakan hadn't had such a close grip on the man, he never would have heard the word. But walk they did. Back and forth. Forth and back. Haakan stopped only long enough to add more wood to the fire. When he had to go out and pull more wood from the wagon, he lowered Lars to the grain sacks and covered him again with the elk robe.

Neither of them shivered any longer. *Is that good or bad?* Haakan took turns living in his thoughts of home, of the cook at the lumber camp, of a cup of steaming coffee. When he needed to keep awake, he talked to Lars. He sang some of the drinking songs he'd learned in the camps. The German loggers knew the best ones, and he sang them at the top of his lungs. Then he sang the hymns he'd learned as a child.

Back and forth. Lars stumbled and grumbled, but they kept on. One foot in front of the other, turn, and go back.

How long was this night to last? Never had one seemed so long or so dark.

8

Dawn broke the back of the storm and sent it skulking to its lair. While snow again covered much of the land, there were places where the wind had blown the land bare and others where drifts rose in white waves on the flat prairie. Ingeborg stood in her doorway and shaded her eyes with her hand, looking toward the north for sight of the men.

If they came.

She fled from the thought and stepped into the barn, again capturing the peace of the night before, a peace she'd felt in spite of the howling wind. No wonder Roald and Carl had spent so many of their waking winter hours in the barn. *You felt that peace in the house too, remember?* She nodded, grateful for the reminder.

She milked the cows, fed the chickens and pigs, threw hay in for the sheep and horses, and picking up the full milk bucket, she headed for the house. By now the boys would be ready for breakfast. She looked across the drift strewn field between the two soddies. A plume of smoke rose from the other chimney, and a cow bellered from the sod barn, answered by the one she'd just milked.

Since all the troughs needed water, she'd set Thorliff to drawing from the well. They would take the horses and oxen down to the river to drink as soon as they'd eaten so he wouldn't have to lug as many full buckets. *Take the mule and go look for the men.* The thought had come earlier, too, when she was feeding the horses. The one mule remained from the team, the other had died with Roald. She'd hoped to find another mule to fill in, but so far hadn't found one. Like the other draft animals, mules were a premium on the prairie. If only she could find and afford a jack, she could breed him to her mares and sell the mules as fast as they were grown and broke to harness. Roald had bought the team of oxen before they were even old enough to plow for an entire day. She'd learned the lesson well. You bought what you could when you found it.

She purposely kept her thoughts on the future. If she allowed just a moment into the past, she could feel the darkness surge over its boundaries, and like a wave upon the shore, eddy closer to usurp her sanity and pull her back into the depths of despair.

"No!" She shook her head and kicked her boots against the wooden block by the door to remove the snow before stepping into the soddy. She would not allow herself to slip back. She knew she couldn't take the chance, for the darkness might not let her go this time. "I will trust in the Lord with all my heart . . . I will sing praises to my God . . . and in Him is no darkness at all." She ran the verses together, having learned the power of the Word when she had reached back to grab her Lord's hand and live. "He is my strength, my fortress . . . I am not afraid."

"Mor, are you all right?" Thorliff turned from adding wood to the cookstove. "I was just coming to help you."

"I am fine." Ingeborg sat the bucket of milk on the workbench, removed her scarf, then hung it and her coat on the wall pegs. Taking the round flat pans from the shelf, she tied a dish towel over the bucket and poured the milk through it as a strainer and into the flat pans. When the cream had risen to the top, she would skim that off to churn for butter. Butter and cheese they could always exchange for sugar and other needed things at The Mercantile.

"Mr. Bjorklund isn't back yet?"

She shook her head. If only there were some way to keep the fear from leaping into her son's eyes. Was he picking up on the fear she kept trying to drive out of herself?

"Is Tante Kaaren okay?"

"We will go visit her as soon as we eat and water the animals." She drew the kettle of rolled wheat and oats to the front of the stove and lifted the lid. The rich fragrance of cooked grain rose to greet her. She'd set the pot to cook the night before, the grains taking long slow hours of simmering to soften for cereal.

Ingeborg took three bowls down from the warming shelf that ran across the top of the stove. As she dished up the steaming cereal, Thorliff went out to the root cellar for the pitcher of cold milk.

Andrew brought the hard crust of bread Thorliff had given him to chew and rubbed it and his runny nose against her pant leg. "Mor, hungry." He emphasized his point with a line of syllables that made no sense to Ingeborg.

"He wants bread and milk." Thorliff set the pitcher in the center of the table.

Ingeborg set the bowls at their places. "He'll have to make do with cereal."

"Bacon, Mor, bacon." Andrew clutched around her leg as if afraid she might take off before they ate.

"No bacon today." Ingeborg lifted him up on the box Roald had made for the little ones. He'd talked of making a special highchair for them, but like so many other things, that dream had been killed by the storm as well.

"He means meat. He calls everything bacon." Thorliff took his place.

Ingeborg poured milk on Andrew's cereal and added a dollop of jelly. She did the same for Thorliff and then herself, leaving off the jelly. They were too close to out for her to spend any on herself. She sat in her chair and waited for the boys to fold their hands. When they'd finished grace, she looked at Thorliff. "How do you know what he says and means?"·

Thorliff shrugged. "I don't know. Paws and me could run across the field to see about Tante Kaaren."

"We'll water the animals first."

"Wouldn't take me but a minute. Paws and me can run fast."

"There was smoke coming from her chimney, Thorliff. She is all right." *But the men, are they all right?* The thoughts bombarded her like arrows tipped in worry—lethal projectiles.

"Mor, milk." Andrew held out his cup.

Ingeborg poured him some more and refilled her coffee cup. *Could they be lying broken somewhere without fire? Frozen during the night but not dead yet, and no one came to save them? Surely they had stayed overnight in St. Andrew and were well on their way home now.* She shook her head. Two camps warred in her mind, and caught between them she ranged the no-man's-land of indecision.

She slapped her hands on the table. "That's it. Come along, Thorliff. Let's dress Andrew for the cold. We'll water the livestock, and then I'll take the mule to find Lars and Mr. Bjorklund."

"We'll stay at Tante Kaaren's?"

"Ja." Ingeborg scooped the dishes up and set them in the dishpan. "Hurry, Thorliff." Now that her mind was made up, she couldn't get going fast enough.

Though the sheep begged to be let out of the corral, she ignored them and led the team and the mule while Thorliff drove the oxen and cows to the river. Paws made certain none of the charges got out of line, patrolling their heels like a trained cow dog. On the way back, the sun broke through the cloud cover like a warming benediction and then hid itself again. The wind, blowing straight from the north, picked up in intensity and kicked some of the snow pellets up to sting their cheeks.

Andrew squirmed in the backpack she'd fashioned for him to ride in since he'd grown too big for the shawl sling. "Easy, son, it won't be much longer now." The straps bit into her shoulders. It wouldn't be long before he'd outgrown this also, and then how would she be able to work and still keep track of him?

The animals seemed to drink forever. The river level had fallen, but she knew when the snow melted again, it would rise. Earlier in the spring it had nearly reached the top of its banks. So many things there were to be concerned about. If they weren't frozen out, they could be flooded out. Ingeborg reminded herself that she had promised to give thanks in everything. She sighed. Sometimes, like now, when memories pelted her and the present looked bleak, giving thanks didn't make a lot of sense.

The cows didn't want to go back in the corral. As one headed each way, Ingeborg felt like throwing up her hands. "Paws, go get them." She dumped Andrew in his pack in the oat bin, tied the lid up so he would have light, and tied the horses in their stalls. They could go out in the corral later.

Then stabbing a pitchfork full of hay, she carried it into the corral. The oxen followed her docilely. Thorliff yelled and waved his arms, Paws barked and nipped, and the errant cows joined the oxen at the hay. Ingeborg forked in a couple more loads while Thorliff shot home the bars. Retrieving Andrew, who now had oats in his hair and stuck in his mittens, she led the mule toward the house.

After tying the animal at the post by the door, she hurried inside to bank the fire and put a few coals in a tin bucket. She packed ashes around the coals, bundled some small sticks together to use for kindling, and placed that along with several larger pieces of wood in a gunnysack. She had all the necessities for a quick fire. It would be enough at least to warm them; along with the coffee she put in another small pail. Some leftover biscuits joined the coffee tin, and she tightened the lid down. With the entire load tied in two sacks to hang across the mules' withers and a quilt to sit on, she boosted

Thorliff up and Andrew in front of him.

"I'm going after them," she told Kaaren after the greetings.

"But surely they stayed in St. Andrew." Kaaren, her blue eyes looking huge in her pale face, bit her lip.

Who was she trying to convince, Ingeborg wondered. By the looks of her, Kaaren hadn't slept a wink.

"Do you need help with the chores?"

Kaaren shook her head. "No, I got all the stock fed, and since our cow is still dry, there was less to do." She took in a deep breath and wrapped her fingers together. "Oh, Ingeborg, I'm not sure I can bear another loss."

"You pray, I'll ride. If I'm not back by dark, or if the blizzard returns, at least I'll know the boys are safe here with you."

"I can go milk." Thorliff stood straight, as if trying to convince her he was older and stronger than he was.

"Ja, I know you can, but the animals will be all right for one night, even though Boss will beller fit to raise the dead." She flinched when she said that. How often did the saying ring oh, so true.

"Just hurry." Kaaren picked up Andrew and, resting him on her hip, hugged him close. "We will be okay here."

Ingeborg kicked the mule into a bone-jarring trot and finally into a canter that kept her bags from banging him in the shoulders. Long ears flicking forward, then back, the mule settled into a ground-covering lope. The north wind cut clear through her coat and sweater and set her teeth to chattering. "Please, God, please, God," kept pace with the rocking of the mule.

When she could feel her feet no longer, Ingeborg knew she needed to get off and walk to get the circulation going again, but she kept on instead. The sun remained in its cloud cave, letting the wind terrorize the land.

Surely she should have reached the river by now. Had she gotten turned around? If only the sun would peek out again and be looking over her shoulder

꠸ꠓ ꠖꠓ

The stillness hurt their ears after the howling of the wind. The horses shuffled their feet. The ripe odor of horse manure filled the soddy.

Haakan studied the man now sleeping the sleep of healing, cradled in the curve between two seed sacks and covered with the robe. Firelight danced on his face, a face that no longer wore the pallor of death, and other than the white spot of frost bite on the tip of his nose, it bloomed with the ruddy color of windburn and health.

Stepping outside, Haakan felt a laugh burble in the back of his throat. The wagon in its present state would haul nothing. He'd chopped and burned most of the wagon box, and if the storm had lasted much longer, he'd have cut into the frame and axles. The wagon tongue lay buried in the snow. He looked to the east where a thin band of pale gold marked the horizon. Lowering clouds, chilling reminders of the storm, lightened as he watched.

"Haakan?"

He spun at the call and reentered the soddy, blinking in the dimness. "Thank God, you are awake."

"The storm, it is over?"

"Ja."

"And we are still alive." Lars looked around, an expression of wonder on his face. "I feel as though I've walked forty miles."

"Maybe not quite that far, but I think we must have worn grooves in the floor. I had to keep you moving to get you warmed up." The horses snorted and stamped, their breath a cloud that hung in the air.

"Were did you find the wood?"

"Ah, let's just say the wagon looks some different than when we left town yesterday."

"Can it make it home?" Lars pulled himself to a sitting position.

"Ja, but not with any of our supplies. I thought about riding one horse home and bringing back the other team and wagon."

"It's still on the sledges."

"Ja, good thing. There's a foot or more of snow out there, but if the sun comes out, it will be slush by noon."

Lars threw the robe aside and levered himself to his feet. "Ohh," he said with a grimace. "Have you looked at my feet?"

Haakan shook his head. "I thought it best to keep you moving. I hope you don't lose any toes. Your fingers seem to be okay, and there's a white spot on your nose, but I think it'll go away."

Lars raised a hand and felt the end of his nose. "I have feeling."

"That is good. You think we can leave our supplies here?"

"If need be." Lars shuffled to the door, and leaning on the crumbling sod blocks that framed the doorway, he stared at the wagon.

Or what was left of it. "Good thing the blizzard stopped when it did."

"Rebuilding that box won't take long." Haakan hefted his ax. "If you want to stay here, I can cut up that central beam and the footboard. You use it sparingly, it should last till I return."

"No." Lars shook his head. "Let's harness the horses and ride 'em home, pulling this derelict behind."

Within minutes they were on their way, stomachs rumbling but spirits rising like the sun that gleamed as a silver disk in the sky when the clouds occasionally thinned.

Doubts plagued Ingeborg like mosquitoes in the summer. The men would think her foolish if they had remained for the night in St. Andrew and were now well on their way home. But what if they were dying and she didn't get there in time? Please, God, they weren't already dead! Had she swung too far west and missed the ford? It would be easy since snow covered the track north.

One thing she knew for certain. The children were safe with Kaaren.

She slapped her mittened hands against her shoulders and chest. This abominable cold. Just the other day the sheep had been grazing in hock-deep grass, grass that now lay frozen again under the snow. And the violet growing on the south side of the barn? Would it live?

"Don't be silly," she scolded herself, just to hear a human voice. The mule's ears swept back to catch her words, then forward, nearly pricked together at the tips.

"What is it?" Ingeborg sat up high as she could. Was that someone coming on the horizon? She nudged the animal with her heels back into the bone-jarring trot. Leaning back to absorb the jolts, she kept her eyes on the specks. As they drew closer she saw a team of horses, two people riding astride.

The mule brayed, his tone static with the jolting.

A whinny floated back on the wind.

She kicked the mule into a lope. Pounding across the frozen prairie, snow spraying behind her, Ingeborg felt her heart rising right along with the heat from the exertion. Why were they riding? Had something happened to the wagon? She waved a hand above her head.

The riders returned the gesture.

With so many hours behind the plow, she'd recognize her team anywhere. Belle and Bob whinnied again, and the mule answered.

Ingeborg tried to swallow the lump in her throat, but it wouldn't go either down or up. Surely the misting in her eyes was caused by the bitter wind. "You're alive!" she breathed as they came up to her.

"Ja, thanks to Haakan here." Lars nodded at his partner. "He knew of an abandoned soddy, or we wouldn't have made it through the night."

Ingeborg felt her heart race as she stared into eyes so blue and so familiar. "Mange takk." She couldn't force any other words past the lump.

"Your wagon didn't fare so well." Haakan gestured over his shoulder at the skeleton with wheels.

"Wagons can be rebuilt." She couldn't drag her gaze from his, seeming locked in the blue depths.

"Did you by any chance bring us something to eat?" Lars pointed toward the sacks she had slung in front of her.

"Oh, ja, my goodness." Ingeborg glanced once more at the decrepit wagon, then swung off the mule and promptly collapsed on the ground.

Haakan was off his horse and to her almost before she hit the ground. "Ach, woman, how long since you've walked? Your feet are probably frozen clear through." Clutching her elbows, he raised her to stand in front of him, holding her against his chest for support.

Ingeborg prided herself on standing on her own two feet. For the past year, she'd proven to herself and the world that she could. But now the comfort of this man's arms drew her like a candle burning in a window to welcome home a long lost traveler. She tried stamping her feet but felt nothing from the knees down. She moved them again, leaning into the strength of Haakan's arms to hold her upright. Wriggling her toes in her boots did her in. Each movement brought the stabbing of miniature knives.

"Oh." She clamped her teeth against the pain.

"Feeling is returning?" She nodded, unable to talk for fear she would cry.

"Good."

Good that the feeling was returning but not good the pain. God in heaven, please help me. She clutched Haakan's coat and buried her face in his lapels.

"Here." Lars took one of the quilts from the mule's back and wrapped it around her. "We can be thankful your feet have feeling.

Last night Haakan kept me walking to get the blood returning. I know how painful it is."

"Ja." Ingeborg blinked her eyes. She would endure it, such a minor price to pay and such rejoicing she felt. The men were alive! "I brought you coffee. It is cold by now, but there are coals and some wood if you want to start a fire. There are biscuits in the sack, too."

"Inge, you are a woman above women." Lars kissed her windburned cheek and retrieved the tied sacks. "What made you come out to look for us?"

"I couldn't let you die if I could do anything about it." A mighty shiver racked her from head to toe.

"Well, let's put this wood to good use. We'll all get through the trip home better with something hot in our bellies and a little warmth on the outside, too." Lars kicked a patch of ground free of snow, removed the bucket with the coals, then set it to the side while he used Haakan's ax to shave some curls off the wood. Within minutes he had a fire blazing merrily.

Ingeborg hated to leave the warm strong arms of the man who held her. She looked up to see Haakan Bjorklund's eyes gazing down at her. A smile lifted the corners of his mouth and crinkled the edges of his eyes.

"Better?" he asked softly.

"Ja." She took a step back, and he released her but kept one hand on her arm to steady her. The wind buffeted her, making her realize anew the shelter he'd provided.

"You ... you ... ah ..." Where had her tongue gone? She couldn't even string six words together. Was her brain frozen as bad as her feet?

"The coffee will be hot in a moment." Lars squatted by the blaze, the coffee pail nestled against the blazing wood. He'd set the biscuits on the last piece of wood so they could warm, too.

"Sorry I didn't bring any cups." Ingeborg kept wriggling her toes in her boots as she held her hands out to the blaze. How wonderful the heat felt. She moved around the fire to stay out of the smoke. The horses stamped and snorted, then dropped their heads to push the snow away and find the grass beneath. The mule did the same, and the sound of grazing along with the snap of the fire and the jingle of the harness as the horses moved made Ingeborg take in a deep breath of relief. *Thank you, God in heaven. We have so much to be thankful for.*

"Be careful you don't burn your mouth on that tin rim." Lars handed the coffee pail to Haakan. "I tried to keep this side cool enough to drink from, and I know the coffee could be hotter, but why wait?"

Ingeborg felt the heat of the drink puddle clear down to her middle and send tendrils out to the rest of her body. Between the fire outside and the fire within, she felt ready to take on the driving cold of the north wind. Looking up, the thinning clouds allowed the sun to brighten the prairie.

"It may clear." She nodded to the heavens.

"We better be on our way. I'd like to come back for our supplies before the vermin help themselves."

"Or someone steals them," Haakan added.

"That, too, but folks are pretty honest around here. If you get caught on the prairie and find a house with no one home, you are welcome to help yourself to what is there. That's the law of survival out here. With everyone living so far apart, visitors are always treated like long lost relatives, or better," Lars said with a grin. He looked inside the coffee pail. "There's a last swallow here; you take it." He handed the pail to Haakan. "Amazing how good coffee and a biscuit tastes after a night in a blizzard."

"I know one thing, I'll make sure there is a bucket or some such along whenever I travel this prairie again. If I could have gotten some hot liquid into you last night, you'd have fared better. And the horses too." Haakan scooped snow into the pail and set it in the middle of the fire. "Even a swallow or two now will help them along."

Before long, they were on their way. Ingeborg looked back to see the black circle left in the white prairie. They would have made it home without her, but she didn't regret coming to look for them. If she was lucky, she wouldn't lose any toes either. Frostbite happened so quickly. Lars might lose the end of his nose and his toes as well. Then they would have to keep the gangrene from setting in. She thought ahead to her store of medicinals. What herbs and barks and roots might restore circulation to frostbitten flesh? If only Metiz were back, she would know. Onion or bread poultice for drawing? Soaking in salt water?

About an hour later, Lars made them all dismount and walk around. This time the knives returned as soon as her feet hit the ground. That was good news no matter how painful.

As they neared home, Paws came bounding across the prairie to greet them, his joyful barking bringing Kaaren and Thorliff out the door in a rush.

Kaaren flew across the melting snow and into Lars' arms, knocking him backward into Belle's bay shoulder. "Easy, woman, easy." He held her close, murmuring into her ear as she clung to his waist.

"What happened to the wagon?" Thorliff looked up at Haakan, his eyes round with wonder.

"We cut it up for firewood." Haakan dismounted from Bob's back and stood for a moment to get his feet working. He handed the reins to Thorliff. "I'll get these two unhitched, and you can take them over to the well for a long drink. If there's enough water in the reservoir, we'll pour it over their grain and maybe even add some molasses, if there is any. These two deserve a treat."

"Where are all the supplies?" Thorliff held the reins but followed Haakan around the traces.

"In an abandoned soddy." Haakan snapped the traces back up on the harness ring and crossed the tongue to do the other horse. "There now, off you go. I'll be right with you."

"Dinner's ready when you are." Kaaren wiped her eyes on the corner of her apron and sniffed once again. "Oh, poor Andrew! I left him tied to the chair, eating a crust of bread." She darted back to the soddy door and disappeared inside.

Ingeborg led the mule after the team, her feet feeling like lead weights now.

"Here, let me take him." Lars took the reins from her.

Ingeborg nodded. She lifted the quilts and the sacks from the animal's back. *Silly*, she chided herself. *Now that all is well, I wish I could cry for a week. Silly is right.* But that old fear was gnawing at her mind. If she started crying, would she ever be able to stop?

9

H jelmer hated the foundry from the first moment he saw it.

"It is just a job," he promised himself. "For only a short time. You can endure anything for a little while." He sniffed and coughed on the smoke-saturated air. "As soon as you have the rest of the money for a train ticket, you can leave for Dakota."

The man that walked past him and into the foundry gave him a look that questioned his sanity for talking to himself.

Hjelmer felt like returning the rude look with one of his own. So he was talking to himself. Better than running for the river and throwing himself in as he'd seen someone do from the bridge the day before. This time he didn't try to save the man. If the fellow wanted a quick entrance into the next world, so be it. Life or death, that was his own choice.

And if he hadn't played the hero in saving the child, he wouldn't be trapped in New York without enough money for his train ticket. He'd be on his way to the Bjorklund homesteads in Dakota Territory, where the grass grew green and the sky wore a gown of blue, not smudged gray. Here the only way to tell the sun was shining was to locate the silver disk hanging somewhere in the sky. It gave light but little warmth. He pulled his coat more tightly around him.

Nothing to do but go find the man. Mrs. Holtensland had a friend that owned the foundry and had begged a job for her immigrant hero. He was to ask for Einer Torlakson. She'd said at least the man spoke Norwegian. Hjelmer pushed open the door to the cavernous building, the incessant clanging of hammer on metal from rows of forges creating a cacophony of sound fit to split one's head or drive one deaf in short order. Smoke hung in the air, bellows pumped the acrid smell of burning charcoal, and bright eyes of blazing fire waited for the metal it tried to devour but only heated white-hot. Monstrous steam engines provided power for the drill presses, shears, and sizes, all run by the drive shaft that ran the length of the building. Belts slapping, clutches squealing of metal on metal; the noise shrilled of progress in its most basic form.

Once his eyes adjusted to the dimness of the room in spite of the two-story tall windows that formed the walls on either side, he saw a man walking from forge to forge and talking with the smiths. Hjelmer strode down the aisle between stacks of iron pigs and flat steel bars. The pigs would be melted for cast iron and the steel formed into implements and parts for machinery.

How would he be able to work in a place like this? At home the forge had been on one wall of a three-sided shed, open to a view of the pastures and trees, where a breeze off the hills blew the smoke away and wafted in scents of pine and growing grass.

He waited until the man finished giving instructions to the smith on the nearby forge and then cleared his throat to get the foreman's attention. The man walked on. The man on the forge turned to draw out a white-hot steel bar.

"Sir, Mr. Torlakson." Hjelmer started after him.

"Ja?" The man turned around, a frown creasing his forehead. "I am Torlakson. Who are you?" His voice rose in a shout to be heard.

"Mrs. Holtensland sent me. She said you would talk with me, and perhaps I could be hired on here."

"Oh." He nodded. "To be sure." He turned back the way they had come. "Follow me."

Hjelmer did as ordered, keeping his eyes open so he didn't get hit in the head by a bar being swung into place by the overhead hoist.

He followed the foreman up a narrow set of stairs to an office on the second floor with windows that overlooked the work below. As soon as the door closed behind them, the roar subsided to a rumble. Hjelmer took in a deep breath and let it out with a sigh.

"Now then, young fellow, I told Mrs. Holtensland I was hiring if I could find a good man. You look to be but a boy, big though you are. What makes you think you could hold your own with the men you saw below. They have years of experience."

"My father trained me well, said I seem to have a natural bent for working with metal."

"Your father, you say. Have you not worked for anyone else, apprenticed perhaps?"

Hjelmer shook his head. "I did some work for my uncle once,

fashioned him an anchor for his fishing boat. I've sharpened plows, pounded out new plowshares, brackets for the wagon bed, refitted rims on wooden wheels, all things needed on our farm and for some of the neighbors." Hjelmer could feel his heart sinking as the man shook his head. "Please, I need this job."

"So do all the men who come to me." Torlakson studied the young man before him.

"Please, let me work today, and if I cannot do what you need, you owe me nothing."

"A day's free labor? I'd be a fool to turn that down. Get yourself an apron from those on the pegs and gloves if you didn't bring your own. I'll meet you back on the floor." He turned to answer a question asked by a man sitting on a high stool in front of a slab of wood that made a writing surface.

Hjelmer did as told. He had the knee-length cowhide apron tied in place and the gloves tucked into the strings and folded over like he'd seen the others wear before Torlakson made his way back down to the work area. When the man beckoned, Hjelmer followed. They stopped in front of a forge that was lit but not hot enough for re-forming steel. A young boy, black with the dirt of the place, leaped to his feet and began cranking the bellow, adding its ascending scream to the torrent of sounds.

At the end of the day, Hjelmer laid his hammer down and felt like following it to the floor. Never had his arms ached so, or his head rung, or his mouth been so full of grit. He spit but nothing came. He needed water to spit with, and the only water he'd seen all day was what he'd stuck his forged pieces in to cool.

The other workers made their way to the tall doors open now to the street in front of the foundry. Hjelmer followed them until he came to the stairs leading to the offices. They looked steeper than the rock faces of the Nordland mountains where he'd climbed as a boy. It felt like several life times ago.

Was he to find the man or wait here? His stomach rumbled and his knees shook. Tomorrow, if there was to be a tomorrow, he would bring something to eat and drink.

"We start at six." Torlakson appeared beside him. Had he been dozing on his feet that he didn't hear the man approach?

"You mean—"

"Ya, you be here. Payday is on Saturday. You'll get five dollars a week. If you don't show up one day, don't bother to come back the next. I need men who will do a day's work, every day."

"Mange takk, I will. You'll see." Hjelmer felt life flow into his limbs and hope into his heart. Five dollars in a week was more than he'd ever dreamed possible. Four weeks he would have to work, and then he could buy his train ticket west.

By the time he walked the mile and a half to Mrs. Holtensland's house, he could barely place one foot in front of the other. Everything hurt, and what didn't hurt, he couldn't feel. His hands looked like they'd been fed through a meat grinder, and his shoulders—his shoulders burned like he'd been beaten with his own hammer.

"Uff da," said Fulla, the maid, when she opened the door for him. Her nose twitched at the foundry stench that rose from his clothes. "Mrs. Holtensland is in the library. I suggest you don't go in there like that."

Hjelmer nodded. He hadn't planned to. "Is there hot water that I can wash?"

"For certain." Her look asked him what kind of house he thought she ran. She pointed to a room off the back porch. "In there."

"Mange takk."

"Supper will be served in one hour."

The sting of soap on his bloodied hands held little importance to Hjelmer. He scrubbed with both soap and brush to remove the filth of the foundry. Twice he threw out the water and started again with clean. After donning his only other set of clothes, he reentered the kitchen.

"Do you have some strips of cloth I could use to bandage my hands?" he asked the cook who seemed more disposed to be cordial to a newcomer.

"Land sakes, boy." She dropped her stirring spoon and took his hands in hers. "Didn't you wear gloves?"

"Ja, but traveling softens the hands." He wished he could put them in his pockets and forget the favor, but he knew his hands were to be his salvation. If he couldn't hold a hammer, he wouldn't last at the foundry.

Tearing an old sheet into strips, Cook wrapped his hands, tisking all the while.

After a supper where he'd endured the sniffs of the maid, he joined Mrs. Holtensland in the library at her request.

"How was it for you there? Can you understand the language well enough to make a go of it?"

"Mr. Torlakson, he speaks Norwegian to me and many of the others." A pang caught him midsection. Roald and Carl had written, telling him to learn the English language before he came, but he'd been working hard to earn passage money, and no one near home knew the language either. The thought of his sister who'd been exchanging washing laundry for English lessons nipped at his mind.

"You are fortunate now to be in an area where many people speak Norwegian. That is why many of the immigrants settle here. It is easier than crossing the country without the English language. We have classes at the Settlement House in the evenings. You could attend there."

Hjelmer nodded while at the same time wanting to pull his collar away from his neck. Was it so hot in the room? Was she scolding him? He studied the edges of his fingernails where black crescents outlined the skin.

"I will think on it." Right now all he could think about was falling on the bed and never getting up. He stared into the fire where flames curled around chunks of coal in oranges and yellows, not the white hot of the coke fires at the foundry. There was something he'd been meaning to ask Mrs. Holtensland. What was it? He hardly remembered stumbling up the stairs and collapsing.

The next evening when he dragged back to the house in the same filthy condition, the maid sent him around to the back door. "People such as you don't use the front door," she hissed. "People like you shouldn't even be here. Mrs. Holtensland is too kind for her own good, bringing home filthy immigrants like stray kittens. And with just as many diseases."

Hjelmer blinked in astonishment. What had he done to make this woman resent him so? But the rebuke stung, getting under his skin like a bee stinger never removed. He recalled what had been bothering him the night before. He'd planned to ask Mrs. Holtensland for a recommendation on a place for him to rent. He hadn't been planning to stay here indefinitely. He might be an immigrant, but he wasn't dirty and ignorant. His mor would be wounded to her soul to hear one of her sons referred to as a filthy immigrant.

That night he scrubbed doubly long, but still he could see traces of grime under his fingernails. When he returned fully clothed to the kitchen, Cook bustled over and picked up his hands. "Uff da." She shook her head. "There." She pointed at a chair and Hjelmer sat. Cook didn't say much, but when she did, everyone around her jumped to. She smoothed salve over the seeping flesh and applied another bandage, wrapping the strips of cloth around and around to cushion the palm and tying tight knots on the back of the hand. "Two, three more days and the calluses will form. Then you be good again."

"Mange takk." Hjelmer turned his hands both front and back. "You sure know how to bandage good. Never would have gotten through the day without them." He thought to the filthy, bloody strips he had pulled off when he washed. "You want I should wash the used ones?"

"Nei." She shook her head. "I do that. Leave them by the basin."

Hjelmer turned in time to see the glare the maid daggered between his shoulder blades. He turned back to catch the look of disgust on the cook's face.

"Pay no mind to her." Cook levered herself to her feet with beefy arms pushing against her knees. The look she shot the maid could have fried eggs.

He left the room wondering at the attitudes of both the cook and the maid. Why was one so good to him, and the other would dump him in the mud without the slightest hesitation? He shook his head. Women!

"Mrs. Holtensland, please, I have something to ask you." The two of them were again seated in the library after a supper that filled his belly and astounded his mind at the variety of it all. He had to speak before the warmth of the fire put him to sleep.

"What is it?" Mrs. Holtensland looked up from the needlepoint she worked each evening.

"I . . . I—please don't misunderstand me. I appreciate all that you have done for me, far beyond any thing I can say. But I must—I mean, I can't stay here."

"Why not?" She looked at him over the rim of her glasses.

"It . . . it is not seemly. I mean, you took me in, and I don't want to overstay my welcome."

"Why don't you let me be the judge of that?"

"Please, I have nothing to pay you with. Surely there is some place I can go that won't put you at a disadvantage."

"Are you not comfortable here?"

He looked at her like she'd struck him. "Of course I am comfortable. I have never lived anywhere so fine."

"I see." She continued to peer at him over her spectacles.

"I . . . I cannot pay."

She nodded. "I see," she said again.

Hjelmer was glad she did, for he certainly didn't. He should have just picked up his things and gone—but to where?

"I have a proposition for you, young man." She waited for him to nod. "Out in the carriage house is a phaeton that was my husband's pride and joy. After he died, I sold the horses because I can go anywhere I want on the El or the streetcars. As you'll see, the carriage has fallen into disrepair. Above the carriage house are the quarters where the groom lived. Now, if you will refurbish that carriage, you can live in those rooms. If you run out of work on the carriage, now that spring is coming, there is plenty of work in the yard. Cook likes her kitchen garden turned over, and the gardener I employ cannot find time for it all. Oh, and you will continue to take your meals with me. I enjoy your company. Is that too much to ask?"

Hjelmer closed his mouth with a snap. His sister would have been teasing him for letting the flies in. "No, not at all. I . . . I— mange takk. What more can I say?"

"Nothing more is needed. Good night, young man."

By the time Saturday night rolled around, Hjelmer had made an acquaintance with another young man, Tor Heglund, who also had no family of his own. After they picked up their pay envelopes, they followed the stream of weary workers out the doors.

"You want to join us down the street?" Tor asked.

"Where?"

"Down at the tavern. We have a drink or two, play cards, have a good time. Come on, you will like it. You'll find only Norwegian spoken there."

Hjelmer thought of the four dollars in his pay envelope. He'd won many pots on the ship when he played cards with both immigrant and sailor alike. It seemed like months since he'd had a beer. But he needed to start work early in the morning on the carriage.

Surely one drink wouldn't take too much of his money. And after all, he would make more next week. "Ja, I will come. For one drink only."

His pay check was one dollar lighter when he left.

That night he called himself all kinds of fool after ignoring the sniffs of the maid, blushing at the raising of Cook's right eyebrow, and having to apologize to Mrs. Holtensland for being late for supper. Worst of all, he'd wasted a dollar. He'd have to get that back. The card tables and players at the back of the room marched through his dreams.

Guilt gave him speed in the morning, in spite of feeling like a tree being attacked by a flock of woodpeckers. Or was he banging his head on the log without knowing it? He went over the carriage, checking to see what parts needed to be replaced and what could do with only a cleaning or minor repair. The leather was split in places, the wood spokes and wheel pulling away from the steel rim.

Everything needed painting. He looked around the carriage house and found a small forge, along with cupboards and shelves containing tools still in the same place the former owner had left them. He reached out and lifted down a plane, now rusty and dirty with disuse.

He traced the wooden frame. All it needed was some sandpaper, a bit of oil, and sharpening of the blade. Files of all shapes and sizes, hammers, screw drivers, all lined up waiting for him to come along and bring them back to life. What his far wouldn't give for such a wealth of tools. He was deep into cleaning and refurbishing the work area when Fulla appeared in the doorway.

"Mrs. Holtensland wants to know if you are attending church with us this morning?"

"Ah." Hjelmer thought fast. He had nothing to wear but the clothes on his back, since his others were soaking prior to a hard scrubbing. "Tell her no thank you. Perhaps another time."

The woman sniffed and spun on her heel. Hjelmer thought he heard, "Well, I'm not surprised. Filthy heathen," but he wasn't sure. He stared after the steel-spined retreating body. Whatever was the matter with her?

By dinnertime, which was served later on Sunday, the workroom looked more like it must have in its former glory days. But Hjelmer looked as though he'd been rolling in the dirt he'd swept up. A cobweb stretched across his hat.

"I can't be fetching you," Fulla said when she came to announce dinner. "You aren't in the kitchen when it is time to eat, you can go without." She shook her head at his dishevelment. "And if you think we are going to wash your clothes, you can think again."

The bee stinger returned. Hjelmer itched to tell her what he thought of her bitter tirades and he could feel his cheeks flaming at the effort to keep his mouth closed. It wasn't his place to tell her what to do, after all.

Besides that, his clothes were already hanging on the line to dry.

"Mange takk." He'd be polite if it killed him. *The old bag. Some trolls were more friendly than she.*

The week passed swiftly with the twelve-hour workdays at the foundry and his trying to manage some time on restoring the carriage. Hjelmer fell into bed each night with no energy left to think of either home or his destination. Friday night he told Cook he wouldn't be there for supper on Saturday. He not only needed to win back what he'd lost the week before, he planned to add to his small store of cash.

Torlakson stopped by Hjelmer's forge late in the afternoon and asked him how he liked working there.

"Ja, this is a good place to work." Hjelmer delivered a ringing blow to the piece forming beneath his hammer and stuck it back in the forge to heat again. He nodded to the boy on the bellows. The extra whoosh of air made the forge glow hotter instantly.

"Keep on like you are, and you will prove your father right."

Hjelmer stared at the man, barely able to keep his jaw from smacking his chest. "Mange takk, sir. He would be pleased to hear that."

"See you stay out of trouble, then."

"Ja, I am." The thought of the coming card games rolled through his mind. Hjelmer watched the man as he continued down the row of forges, stopping to speak for a moment with each man. He'd overheard men saying what a fair man was Mr. Torlakson, and now he'd heard it for his own ears. Of course, he'd also heard two men cussing and grumbling what a slave driver the man was. But then one of them reeked of booze and the other came late. Said he'd been caught in a traffic jam.

Torlakson said, "Next time don't come back."

Hjelmer left the card game only one dollar down at ten o'clock. He'd planned to leave by eight, but at that time he only had two bits left in his pocket. He'd looked around the table to see delight glinting from the players' eyes at the immigrant sucker.

It was time to turn the tables.

He won the next three hands. Tor clapped him on the shoulder. "Your luck turned, man. Congratulations."

Hjelmer only nodded. Luck had nothing to do with it. He'd finally learned to read the other players, and like back on the ship, he'd set them up to believe the dumb kid didn't know much about playing cards.

Sunday he again declined the invitation to church. Who had time for that? He had one wheel that needed new spokes and the metal rim shrunk to fit the felloe again. When the others left, he laid the wheel flat on the ground and stacked dry wood mixed with coal around and over the rim. He set the finished spokes into the hub and pegged the wooden rim into place again. When the gardener returned from church, he joined Hjelmer in setting fire to the circle of stacked wood. When lit, the fire burned hot, setting the entire metal rim aglow. When it was hot enough, the two men lifted the rim out with tongs, set it over the wooden wheel, and sprinkled water on it to cool. Then, again with the tongs, they lifted the newly rimmed wheel and put it upright in a tub of water, turning it to cool the entire rim. The now shrunken metal fit like a new skin.

"You sure do know what you are doing," the gardener said, admiration coloring both his words and face.

Hjelmer nodded, running the circular traveler around the rim to make sure it was now the proper size. "My far set many a wheel. He always said his sons would never want for bread if they could set a wheel, shoe a horse, or carve a kitchen tool."

"Your far is a wise man."

Hjelmer nodded. More and more he was beginning to appreciate that.

The thought of his far brought a stinger of guilt. What would he say about his son's gambling? Plenty, no doubt, and none of it would be good.

Hjelmer set the wheel back on the axle and stood back to admire his handiwork. The frame was ready for paint. *Someday*, he promised himself, *someday I will have a carriage like this and a pair of fine bay trotters to drive. No more dumb and filthy immigrant me. I'll have my free Dakota land and maybe a wife to boot.* He'd always thought Kaaren a comely woman, and now she needed a husband. She wasn't that much older than he. This way they could keep the homestead within the family.

Saturday night he doubled his money.

"You lucky dog," Tor said, clapping him on the shoulder again.

"A fair man would let us try for our money back," one player grumbled.

"Next week." A man, huge by even Norwegian standards, tented sausage fingers and stared at Hjelmer out of ice blue eyes. "He can't win 'em all."

Hjelmer stared back. "It's just a game, Swen. See you next Saturday?"

"Ja, next Saturday. Unless you vant to come before then."

"Not me. I'll wait till payday." The two young men finished their beer and headed out to the rain-slicked street.

"I wouldn't want that giant looking at me like that." Tor shuddered. "He's a mean one, he is."

When Hjelmer declined the church invitation again, Mrs. Holtensland looked at him over her spectacles. "I am certain your mor made sure you were sitting in the pew every Sunday. You have been confirmed, have you not?"

"Ja, I have, and ja, Mor would be very unhappy with me. But you asked me to refurbish the carriage, and this is the only day I have any length of time." His smile could have melted a heart of cast iron. "As soon as I'm finished, I'll go to church with you."

The maid sniffed and glowered at him from behind Mrs. Holtensland's back. He tipped his hat to her as they walked out the hall.

Cook chuckled behind him. "That Fulla, she sure got it in for you."

"Why? I never did her no harm."

"I ain't be one to carry tales, but let's just say that apple-cheeked young men with angel eyes and a devil's smile remind her of something she'd rather be forgetting." Cook lumbered back to her kitchen and the dough she had rising for dinner rolls.

Hjelmer shook his head. A few more weeks of doubling his money, and he would be heading west anyway. In fact, one big pot could set him on easy street. He spent the morning painting the carriage. The main body gleamed in new black paint, and the red wheels gave a look of class with just a bit of daring. He'd already patched the upholstery and worked enough saddle soap into the leather to make it smooth and supple again. If only there were a team to hitch, he'd drive the ladies to church next Sunday.

"I hear you are close to finished with the carriage," Mrs. Holtensland said one evening at the supper table.

"Ja, you will be pleased, I am sure." Hjelmer laid his fork down. "Shame you don't have horses for it."

"If I bought horses, would you stay?"

Hjelmer blinked and felt his face go slack. "Bought horses? I thought you planned to sell the carriage."

"I did . . . I do . . . Don't fret, it was just a thought. Sometimes I remember my husband's pride in the carriage and pair, and . . ." She fluttered her hand at him. "No, just forget what I said. I must be rambling tonight, getting to be an old woman."

"You're not old."

"Let's just say, my better years are behind me." She straightened her back. "Now, let's talk about something else. It is so rare you don't run right out to work on the carriage. I have missed our evening visits. Tell me, how is it going with your English classes?"

"I haven't begun them yet. Maybe after I finish the carriage." Hjelmer wanted to add, *And besides, I am getting along just fine without taking language classes*, but he didn't.

Mrs. Holtensland looked at him over the rim of her spectacles. "All the rest of the country isn't as benevolent to Norwegian immigrants as here in Brooklyn. You must keep that in mind."

"Ja, I will, and I thank you for your concern." He waited for her to lay her napkin down and begin to push her chair back. That was the signal that he could rise. When she did so, he pulled her chair back, and they walked from the room. "I have a few things left to do on the carriage. I'll see you tomorrow night."

That night, just before he fell asleep, he thought again to what his benefactress had said. If he wanted, he could probably stay in Brooklyn. He had a good job that paid more money than he had ever dreamed possible, a fine place to live, and a way to make extra money to spend as he wished. With a little encouragement, Mrs. Holtensland would buy a team, and he could drive around the city. Perhaps even out into the country for a Sunday outing. Could life get much better than this?

He deliberately lost the first hand on Saturday night. And the second.

"Things not going so good tonight, eh, kid?" one of the men asked.

Swen only quirked one black eyebrow. He wore the dark look of the Norwegians of the far north known as the Sami.

Hjelmer only shrugged. "Deal."

He won the hand, raking in the pot with a nonchalant motion. "Mange takk. That helps make up for the earlier."

He won the next. The stash of coins grew in front of him.

Swen dealt the next hand calling for Five Card Stud. He dealt one card face down to each of the players. Hjelmer checked his card, a three. The next round dealt face up only gave him an eight. He glanced across the table at Swen's hand. Ace up.

"I'm out," he said, pushing his cards toward the center of the table.

Swen nodded, dealt three more times around and raked in the pot. He stared at Hjelmer, his dark eyes never blinking, then passed the deck across.

"Five Card Stud again." Hjelmer split the deck and spliced the cards at the corners, the whir of the shuffle sounding loud in the silence. He dealt one card face down to each player. By the second round he had two Jacks, one up and one down. Swen showed a King and bet four bits. One player folded, leaving four.

Hjelmer dealt a face up round again, giving himself only a queen and the others no better.

Swen raised the bet to six bits.

"Too rich for my blood," said one of the others.

"Mine too," Tor agreed.

On the next flop, Swen paired his King and Hjelmer his Jack. Knowing he needn't, Hjelmer checked his hole card. He knew that third Jack, the Jack of Clubs hadn't gone anywhere. But he could feel the tension tighten.

"Dollar."

"I call it." Slowly, deliberately, Hjelmer peeled the remaining cards off the deck. A five of Spades slipped in front of Swen and the last Jack showed in front of Hjelmer. *Four Jacks!*

One side of Swen's narrow lipped mouth lifted in what might have passed for a smile. "I see three Jacks with a Queen kicker, an impressive hand. Your bet!"

Hjelmer kept his gaze frozen on Swen's. He slid out two dollars.

Swen's smile twitched. "I got those three Jacks beat, which means I got to have that third King in the hole, don't it? Well, I'm a gonna see your two lousy bucks and raise ya another two."

Hjelmer sat without moving a muscle for a good thirty seconds. He didn't even breathe. This was it. His four Jacks gave him the lock on the hand.

Swen's mouth twitched again and nearly broadened into a real smile.

Throwing four silver dollars in the pot, Hjelmer softly but firmly whispered. "I'll see your two dollar raise and bump you back two."

Swen's eyes narrowed, his brows meeting in a straight gash across his forehead. His voice deepened, like a bear about to roar. "You better not have another Queen in the hole for a full house. If you do, I know you been cheating, dealing seconds like I been suspecting." He propped his elbows on the table. "I call your two dollar raise. Whatcha holding?" He flipped over his hole card. "There's my third King."

"I don't have a Queen in the hole." Hjelmer could hear an intake of breath by the spectators.

Swen let a touch of unholy glee light his black eyes for only an instant.

As he rolled over his hole card, Hjelmer murmured. "What I got is four Jacks."

The sparkle turned to lightning. "You been cheatin'!" Swen exploded. He slammed both hands on the table, and a roar of obscenities blistered the ears of those at the table and anyone within a city block. "I'm going to cut your heart out and feed it to the fish. I'll kill you, you . . ." Swen reached across the table with both hands, fingers wide to clamp around Hjelmer's neck. The young man ducked sideways, scooped the remainder of his winnings and leaped to his feet.

The monster came at him, tables, chairs, and bodies flying in all directions. One pile-driver fist caught him a glancing blow on the shoulder, and Hjelmer staggered back, saved from crashing to the floor only by the arms of his friend.

"Run!" Tor yelled in his ear.

The two pelted out the room.

"I'll find you, you thieving whelp. . . ." The thunder behind them leant power to their legs. "You can't run far enough," the giant bellowed behind them. "I'll find you." The string of Norwegian curses promised all manner of damage to his person, his family, and anyone in any way connected to him.

After a mile of turns and pounding feet, Tor leaned against a wall, struggling to catch his breath. "He means it."

"Naa, it will blow over by Monday. I won that hand fair and square."

"I know that, and you know that. But I saw Swen hit a man one time, and the man never got up again."

"The police—"

"You think those Irish loudmouths care what happens here to us Norwegians?" He stood upright again. "You better get your stuff and head west to that homestead you told me about."

The two walked on, feeling safe now that they could no longer hear the raging Swen.

"But my job—"

"Hjelmer, listen to me. That man will kill you. He said he would and he meant it. You took every dime he had. And worse, you made him look the fool."

Hjelmer spun around. Was that footsteps he heard behind them? He saw no one, but the hairs on his arms and neck stood at attention.

L ars' foot will most likely have to come off," Haakan said to Ingeborg one evening at the supper table.

Ingeborg looked up from cutting the venison steak into small
pieces for Andrew. "There must be some other way to save it. How
will Lars get around with one foot missing?"

"I could carve him a new one. Wouldn't be good as the real thing,
but better than nothing. I heard tell of men after The War between
the States who hobbled around on less than that."

"Ja, they hobbled." Ingeborg shook her head. "Kaaren has lost so
much in her life already. How can she endure this one more thing?"

"Lars is the one losing the foot, not Kaaren."

"I know." Ingeborg got up for the coffeepot.

"Is there a doctor in St. Andrew?"

"No. The closest one's in Grand Forks."

"How do you cut off a foot?" Thorliff looked up from mashing
his potatoes.

"Eat your supper."

"I am. How do you cut through the bones?"

"The same way we cut through wood."

"With an ax?"

"No, more likely with a saw."

"What would you do with the foot?" Thorliff propped his elbows
on the table and leaned forward, the light of curiosity gleaming in
his eyes.

"Thorliff Bjorklund, this is not a subject we need at the table.
Finish your supper."

"But, I—" Her look quelled any further questions.

Haakan quailed under the look she shot him, too. Andrew

banged his spoon on the table and laughed as if someone had just told a marvelous joke or tickled his tummy.

Ingeborg rolled her eyes heavenward. "Hu tu me tu!"

After the children were tucked in bed and sleeping, she brought up the subject again. "We have been massaging Lars' foot and using both hot and cold water soaks, but the blood circulation doesn't return, and the pain is getting worse." She thought about her dwindling supply of herbs. Something in there should be good for frostbite and the blisters that were now forming, but if the gangrene took hold, she had no idea what to do. Either cutting off the entire foot or amputation back into the healthy flesh seemed the only options.

"I will take the foot off if we need to." Haakan sat by the fire carving on a piece of wood. The shavings mounded at his feet and released the sweet smell of cedar into the warm air.

"Have you done such before?"

He shook his head. "Have you or Kaaren?"

"Nei. In Nordland we had a doctor who attended such things. My mor was the local midwife, so I learned much from her, and then after we arrived here, Metiz taught me about the local roots and herbs. I need to grind up some more willow bark to help ease the pain. I wish we had some laudanum. That works so much better."

"You want I should go to St. Andrew to get some?"

"If you rode, you could make the trip fairly quickly." Ingeborg picked up her knitting that always lay ready for her in the basket by her chair. As the needles began their clicking song, she heaved a sigh. "Somehow we have to save that foot."

Later, after Haakan had made his way to the barn and his bed in the far stall, Ingeborg took out her Bible and turned to the stories of Jesus healing the lepers. Wasn't this chilblain much like leprosy, only instead of the diseased part falling off, it had to be cut off? Either way, the sufferer lost a part of himself. And for a man without a foot, the prairie could exact a terrible price.

She closed her eyes and leaned her head against the carved back of the chair. "Father in heaven, I know not what to do. The pain is making Lars talk gibberish at times, and Kaaren is weak from the little one she is carrying. Please, help us. As you healed the lepers with your touch, I ask you do so again." She rocked and prayed, prayed and rocked. Wood settled in the stove with a gentle whoosh. Paws barked outside the door, then settled back down again just as she was about to go see what was bothering him.

"Thank you for Haakan who has come to help for the summer."

He'd looked chastened like a small boy when she scolded him and Thorliff at the supper table. She could feel the smile that rose from her midsection and bloomed on her face. He made her laugh at times, and he made Thorliff laugh, which was even more important. No eight-year-old boy should bear the responsibilities that he did. A sigh followed the smile. What would they do when the man left to return to the Minnesota north woods as he planned?

She could hear her own mor's voice as if she stood right behind the rocker. "Let the day's own troubles be sufficient for the day." She couldn't worry about fall. She had to get through the spring first.

And the red blisters forming on the dead, white flesh of Lars' foot.

She took the willow bark over to Kaaren's in the morning. "Here, make a tea of this for him to drink. It will help ease the pain."

"I know." Kaaren accepted the packet of powder. "Willow bark." She rubbed her forehead with one hand. "I think I'll drink some, too."

"Haakan said he'd go to St. Andrew for laudanum."

"But Haakan needs to be out in the fields. Besides the pain, being unable to help with the work is what's driving Lars insane. We had such big plans for this season." She poured water from the steaming teapot into a small kettle and added some of the willow bark. "How much should I use?"

"About that much again. I've been wracking my brain for something else to try." A line of shouted gibberish erupted from the bed. Andrew tangled his fists in her skirt and stared, big eyed, at the bed. Ingeborg picked him up and jiggled him on her hip. "There now, it is only Onkel Lars." At another shout, Andrew buried his face in her shoulder and whimpered.

Kaaren poured some of the steeped liquid into a cup and crossed the room. "Lars, here, drink this." She sat down on the board that edged the rope-strung bed and leaned forward to help her husband sit up to drink. Instead, he waved an arm, catching her on the side of her head and knocking her backward. The cup flew up in the air, liquid flying every which way.

"Hu tu mi tu!" Ingeborg ran across the room and helped Kaaren sit upright. "Has that happened before?"

Kaaren shook her head. "He's not been violent. I know that the pain is driving him wild, but this—" She rubbed at a reddening spot on her cheek. Tears filled her eyes and she dashed them away. "We have to do something, Ingeborg. Haakan is needed in the field, and knowing you, you'd like to be out there, too. I will ride into St. Andrew."

"And who will watch over Lars?" *And the boys?* Ingeborg thought but didn't add.

Kaaren shook her head. "I don't know what to do!" She wrapped her arms around her middle and swayed back and forth, trying to rock the pain away.

Ingeborg tied Andrew in the rocker with a couple of spoons to play with, returned to the stove, and once again filled the cup with warm liquid. "First, we must get this into him so he can endure the pain." She carried the cup back to the bed. "Lars! Lars! Listen to me." His eyes fluttered open, vague and without sense. "Lars!" The command in her voice cut through the vapors clouding his head.

"I hear you, Ingeborg. Need you holler so?"

"Thanks be to God," Kaaren whispered.

"Drink this. It will help with the pain." Ingeborg propped him up with an arm beneath his shoulders and held the cup to his lips.

He made a face but drank the brown liquid. Pain had sculpted canyons in his face from nose to chin and furrows across his brow. He lay back when finished and took in a deep breath. "It's bad, isn't it?"

Ingeborg and Kaaren swapped looks of consternation.

"You don't have to treat me like I'm an invalid, you know. I've seen people with frostbite and chilblains before. I know how the treatment must go." He looked to his wife, now sitting on the edge of the bed again. "If we must take off the foot to save the man, so be it. Just don't wait too long to make the decision. I want to be around to see that babe of ours born and help him grow up."

"Him, him. Don't these men ever think about having daughters to care for them in their old age?" Ingeborg set the cup on the table. The twinkle in her eye belied the brusqueness of her tone.

"After a boy, we will have girls, then more boys and then more girls."

"Ja, you will keep me breeding all the time. Who will teach that school all of these children of ours are going to need?" Kaaren laid a hand protectively on her belly. "And besides, I think this one is a girl. She will help me with all those boys you want."

Andrew, tired of playing with his spoons, began to whimper in his chair.

"I better get about my chores." Ingeborg stood and crossed to the rocker where Andrew beamed her a smile fit to break any woman's heart. She untied the dish towel and lifted him into the air, kissing his ruddy cheeks and blowing on his neck. The child's chortles made even Lars smile around his pain. "I will see you later."

Kaaren followed Ingeborg out the door. "If you want to ride to St. Andrew, I will care for the boys and make the supper. If you go now, you would be back in time."

"Ja, I thought of that, too. Let me tell Haakan what we plan. I just wish Metiz would come back. She might know of something to help. Laudanum will only dull the pain, not cure the foot."

Ingeborg strode across the field to her own soddy, carrying Andrew because she had no time for him to examine every worm and leaf along the way. If curiosity were wealth, Andrew would be the richest child in the world. Thorliff was out with his sheep, and Haakan was plowing to the west. She could see him moving slowly down the furrows, the rich earth turning over behind him. They should have two teams out there so the planting could be finished. If it wouldn't scandalize Haakan too much, she would join him in the morning. Why was it men reacted so strongly to a woman's being capable of handling teams and machinery? If one of them felt like washing dishes or baking bread, she surely wouldn't be offended.

She quickly slipped her men's pants on under her skirt, bundled some bread and cheese into her pockets, and snatched up Andrew as she went out to the corral to bridle the mule. One of these days, they should think seriously about getting a saddle. She led the mule and carried Andrew out to the field to tell Haakan the plan.

"I'm riding to St. Andrew for the laudanum. Kaaren will care for Andrew and make the meals for the day. Would you please tell Thorliff what is happening?" The words came out in a rush, for with the first ones, she could tell he wasn't pleased.

"I told you I could go." He pushed his hat back on his head.

"I know that. But there is so much to be done in the fields, and with only one man—well, I just thought I am the most dispensable one."

"But you don't have a sidesaddle or a saddle of any kind." One of the horses stamped its feet and started to move forward. "Whoa, there." He tugged on the reins. "It's . . . it's—"

"Unseemly, I know." Ingeborg heaved a sigh of frustration. "But out here on the prairie some things are more important than what's *seemly* or not." Her inflection on the word said clearly what she thought of it. "Besides, I have my britches on." She lifted the edge of her skirt to show the hem of the men's pants she wore. "I will be all right, and with both on, I'll be warmer, too." A brisk breeze had sprung up. While not as warm as it had been, still the prairie would dry quickly because of it.

Andrew began to wriggle on her hip. "Down, Mor, down."

"In a minute. You want to ride on the mule with me?"

A grin turned his cheeks to rosy apples. "Me ride." He reached for the mule's bridle, so close beside him. The mule jerked back.

"I better be going."

"You'll be careful?" The look of concern that creased Haakan's forehead made a warm glow begin in Ingeborg's middle.

"Ja. This old mule can lope all day. We'll be back before dark."

"We'll have lamps in the windows, just in case."

The glow spread. "Here, if you could hand him up to me?"

Haakan took Andrew. Ingeborg turned to belly herself up on the mule.

"Let me help you."

She paused and turned to face him. He offered a hand on one bent knee, Andrew clutched in the other arm. While the baby tipped the man's hat off his head and chortled in glee, the man held her gaze with his.

Frissons of delight raced each other up and down Ingeborg's back. With a swallow and a nod, she placed her foot in his hand and swung aboard the mule, settling her skirts down as far as possible on her legs. When she looked down at him from her fussing, he stared up at her, his eyes blue like bits of the sky above had come down to visit earth.

Her breath caught in her throat. "M-mange takk." The words cracked. The wind lifted his hair, giving her the insane urge to smooth it back. He held the baby up to her, and in the passing, his fingers touched hers, warm, safe, and comforting.

"Hurry home."

She thought of his words as she turned the mule to go. Looking back once, she saw him retrieve his hat and slap the dirt off it on his knee before settling it back in place with both strong hands. "Gidup, Jack." She clapped her legs against the animal's washboard sides. Was that a promise she'd seen in his eyes? Surely he had felt the same when their hands touched?

She shook her head. What was the use? He was leaving in the fall, so she'd best not be mooning over a man about to leave. "Come on, mule." She hugged Andrew to her, and the mule broke into the same ground-covering lope that would take her to St. Andrew and back.

After depositing Andrew in Kaaren's waiting arms, Ingeborg again set off north across the prairie. She let her straw hat fall behind her shoulders on its ribbons and lifted her face to the sun. She had freedom for the day. What a heady thought. There were no meals to cook, no bread to bake, no cows to milk, and although she would probably be back in time for evening chores, no child clung to her skirts. She was free!

The temptation to take her braids down and let the wind blow through her hair shocked her back to sensibility. She shook her head and laughed at herself. One would think she were twelve instead of twenty-eight. Ducks quacked overhead on their northward flight. A meadowlark sang his spring courting song. The rich smell of burgeoning spring on the prairie made her sniff more than once. She gazed ahead at the hurt-your-eyes green of the growing grasses rippling before the wind. "Mange takk, Lord above. What a wondrous thing you have created here." And since there was no one around to remind her that whistling was not proper for women, she pursed her lips and, in the cadence of the cantering mule, whistled "O God, Our Help in Ages Past" while the words ran through her mind at the same time.

By the time the sun reached its zenith, Ingeborg was wishing she'd brought a flask of water along. She chewed the dry biscuits with a slab of cheese in each and reminded herself to be grateful for the food and to quit wanting more. The brown water that flowed in the Little Salt didn't appeal, so she knew she wasn't too thirsty.

The first thing she asked of Mrs. Mackenzie, the wife of the proprietor of The Mercantile, was a drink of water.

"Of course, of course." She trundled off to the living area behind the store and returned with a cup of cold, fresh water.

"Mange takk," Ingeborg said before draining the cup. "That surely was good."

"I have the coffeepot on. Would you like to take a few minutes and join me in a cup?" The woman with hair the color of a robin's breast, and the same habit of cocking her head to see better as a robin on a worm hunt, smiled and motioned to the door leading to the parlor.

While Ingeborg had enjoyed the ride, the thought of a chair rather than the ridged back of the mule sounded mighty tempting. "Only for a minute. I need to get home before dark." She followed her hostess around the counter and through a curtain into their living quarters. She sank into the indicated chair and leaned back with a sigh. Oh, how good the cushioned seat with a back felt.

"Here we go." The woman returned with a tray that held two steaming coffee cups and a plate of cookies.

Ingeborg raised one of the cups and sniffed, her eyes closing in bliss. "Ah, coffee. The smell alone makes the heart brighten." Taking one of the cookies, she dunked it in the coffee and bit off a hunk. "Now this is perfect." She gazed around the room, comparing it to the dark soddy in spite of herself. Real glass windows on two walls let the sun in, and white wallpaper with blushing peonies trailing in stripes made the heart glad. A braided rug lay in front of each rocker, and another with an orange cat curled on it fronted the round heating stove.

"Such a cheerful home you have made here." She listened in delight to the bonging of a grandfather clock that stood tall by the door to the kitchen. "So long since I've heard a clock. Funny, the things we used to take for granted have so much more value now."

"That is so. Mr. Mackenzie gave me that clock for our anniversary. Fifteen years we been married, ten of them here in St. Andrew."

"You came when the town was nothing but a dream, then?" Ingeborg sipped her coffee. She shouldn't be here enjoying herself when Lars needed the laudanum so desperately. *One more minute*, she promised herself. *That is all I'll take.*

"Yes. My husband believed the settlers would come, and when people come, they need a store. He didn't want to homestead, too backbreaking he said." She looked around the room and then back at Ingeborg. "'Sides, he'd been raised in a store, and his daddy gave him a start for this one. I thank the good Lord for bringing people like yourselves to settle here. We will have a fine town here, lessen the railroad passes us by."

"The railroad is coming this far north on the west side of the river?" All thoughts of staying for only one more minute flew out of Ingeborg's head. "I knew they went to Canada on the east side of the river, but will they be coming over here, too?"

"That Mr. Hill, he plans to cover Dakota Territory with railroads. The farmers can ship their crops easy that way. You mark my words, there's big changes coming."

Ingeborg set down her cup. "Well, I thank you for the coffee and the information, but I better be on my way. Lars Knutson, my brother-in-law, is suffering from frostbite and the chilblains mighty bad. He and Mr. Bjorklund got caught in that last blizzard on their way home from here."

"Oh, my. We wondered about them when the storm hit. Land sakes, bad frostbite is nothing to joke about." She rose to her feet. "Come, Mrs. Bjorklund, let's get you on your way. What is it you'll be needing today?"

Ingeborg followed the bustling woman back into the store. "I need medicinals for treating his foot. A bottle of laudanum, and . . ."

Ingeborg stared at the bottle of whiskey Mrs. Mackenzie set on the counter. Should she take that along with the laudanum? Her far always swore by the disinfecting power of liquor in addition to its medicinal properties to help pain. But then, he liked a drop or two on occasion, besides.

Mrs. Mackenzie set the small bottle of laudanum beside it. "Is there anything else I can get for you?"

Ingeborg looked at the jar with peppermint sticks. "I'll take two of those, both the bottles, and please wrap them well so they won't break in the sack on the way home."

"That I will do. When will you be bringing cheese again?" the woman asked as she wrapped the bottles in several layers of paper. "I swear there must be a line from house to house here. When folks hear there are Bjorklund cheeses in the store, they line up on the porch." She finished her bundling, wrote the list in her book, and smiled across the counter. "You come back soon. It's time we women had a quilting bee, or some such, so we could all get to know each other. Oh—" She slapped her hands on the counter. "I have something for you." She disappeared through the curtain and returned a minute later. "This here's a slip of the geranium I have growing in my kitchen window. I thought you might enjoy a bit of color, too."

At Ingeborg's "mange—" Mrs. Mackenzie raised a hand. "No, don't say thank-you. That'll put a blight on it. Just pretend you snipped this off yourself." She passed the sack over the counter. "We'll be praying for Mr. Knutson, too. You be careful going home, now."

"Mange takk for the coffee and cookies." Ingeborg smiled and nodded in response to Mrs. Mackenzie's raised hand. "I know. And one day soon I will have a start to give someone else." Ingeborg left the store with the sting of tears behind her eyes. She sniffed as she unlooped the mule's reins from the hitching post. Did she dare mount here?

She looked up and down the street. There was no one in sight, so she led the mule to stand sideways beside the steps. Then she swung aboard and trotted west, out past the church and the few remaining houses. At the end of town, she kicked Jack into a canter and headed home, her treasured sack clutched in front of her so it wouldn't get banged around and break anything.

Cold, stiff, and sure she had sores where she'd sat, Ingeborg swung off the mule as the first stars poked holes in the heavens and winked at the earth below. A warm spot glowed around her heart at the lamp beckoning in the window. Paws yipped beside her, bringing Thorliff through the door to fling his arms around her waist.

"What is this, my son? Is something wrong?"

"No, I'm just glad you are home." He hugged her tighter.

"Did you think I would not come?" She stroked his hair back and tipped his face up to look at her. "I am here and all is well. You take the mule out to the barn and give him a good feeding, all right? No water yet, though."

Thorliff hugged her again. "I will." He grasped the mule's reins and swung up on his back. "Tante Kaaren has supper ready. We already ate." With that he drummed his heels on the mule's ribs and trotted across the field.

Andrew met her at the door and clung to her skirts. Kaaren stood at the stove, already dishing up a plate of food.

"You had a good trip?" She set the plate on the table and reached for Andrew. "You let your mor have some supper, now, den lille guten."

Ingeborg handed her the sack. "I bought some whiskey, too, and there is a treat in there for the boys when Thorliff comes back. How is Lars?"

"Sleeping for now. I gave him enough willow bark tea to drown a cow. Thorliff read to him for a while after the men decided what needs to be done next in the fields."

Ingeborg squashed the instant flair of resentment that again they had decided farm matters without her. "He should sleep real well with some of this." She raised the small brown bottle of laudanum. "You just put a couple of drops in a cup of water. I thought perhaps we could use the whiskey in between times. My mother used it for cleansing wounds. It might help on the open blisters."

"Mange takk, Inge, for going to town like this. I know that is a long ride by wagon, let alone on horseback."

"Horseback might not have been so bad, but that mule has a ridge for a backbone big enough to—" She looked up to see a smile curving Haakan's mouth. The heat rushing up from her neck flamed across her face. "Excuse me, I . . . I better wash." Turning to bury her hands in the bowl on the cabinet counter made her wish she could bury her face as well. Anything to cool it off.

She sat down to eat, composed at least on the outside. Haakan took the chair across from her and Kaaren the one on the end. Between them, they peppered her with questions until she raised her hands in surrender. "How am I supposed to eat and answer all you've asked?"

Kaaren rested her cheek on Andrew's soft hair. "Sorry, Inge, I didn't think. Tomorrow we will plant that slip of geranium. It will bloom so pretty in your window."

Lars moaned from his bed. "Kaaren." His voice sounded weaker than when she left in the morning.

"Coming." Kaaren dipped a cup of warm water from the reservoir, added three drops of the vile brown liquid, and crossed the room. If this didn't work, what would they do?

Y ou better cut if off," Lars muttered a day or so later.

"No, not yet. There must be something more we can do." As Kaaren and Ingeborg stood by the side of the bed, Kaaren reached for the whiskey bottle.

"If you're going to pour that over my foot again, give me a swig or two of it first. What a waste of good whiskey." Lars reached for the bottle, at the same time lifting his foot. "Looks awful bad, don't it?" He tipped the bottle to his lips and chugged. "Whew." With a grimace, he handed the bottle to his wife and wiped his mouth with the back of his hand. "Now, if I was a drinkin' man, I might appreciate that, but as I ain't, that burns something fierce both inside and out."

Ingeborg studied his swollen foot. "What if we made a dressing and soaked it in the whiskey. That would keep the alcohol in place and might do some leaching of the poison."

"Well, put me under first. I can hardly stand to have you touch the thing, let alone wrap it."

Kaaren went for the laudanum, while Ingeborg, with one finger on her bottom lip, continued studying the foot. *Father God, I just don't understand. I've been praying for you to heal this foot and also for wisdom to know what to do. Do you want Lars to lose his foot? That doesn't seem fitting with what I read in the Scriptures.* She looked from the foot up to Lars' face. How could she ask him such a personal question?

She sucked in a deep breath. This could be no more difficult than birthing the twin lambs with a fractious, frightened ewe. "Lars, you remember the stories of Christ healing the lepers in the Scriptures?"

He shrugged. "Well, kind of . . . I mean, I heard them a long time ago when I went to church with my family and all. Ain't been no church out here, you know."

"I know, but Kaaren reads out of the Bible every day."

"Sure, but we ain't been reading about the lepers."

Ingeborg nodded. Knowing Kaaren, she was reading from her favorites, the Psalms or Proverbs. Whenever there was trouble, those were the first places she headed. "For some reason my Bible fell open to one of the leper passages, so I read it and then the others. In all cases, the lepers had to ask for Christ to heal them, and then do something He commanded."

"So?" He closed his eyes and leaned back against the pillows Kaaren had stacked behind him. "You think I haven't been praying for this foot of mine? What kind of idjit do you think I am? Of course I've been praying." He sat forward, wincing at the action. "I pray and pray, and my foot looks worse and worse. You got an answer for that? Do you?" He shook his finger in her face.

Ingeborg stepped back. Was this what she'd been like when she had questioned God? No wonder people stayed away from her. "I don't have an answer." She softened her voice. "All I know is that God loves us and promised to be beside us through all the trials on this earth."

"Yeah, well, right now I think God is looking the other way, too busy with some other part of the world." He laid the back of his hand over his eyes. "Thanks for trying, Inge, but I need to resign myself to losing this foot, and if we don't take care of that soon, I'll lose my life, too."

"If onlys" flashed through Ingeborg's mind. If only they hadn't gone to town; if only they had listened to her; if only . . . if only . . . She closed her eyes and mind against the memories. Blizzards, indeed, had taken their toll on the Bjorklunds.

"We have to deal with what's now." She said the words as much to herself as to the man in the bed.

"Mor!" Thorliff threw himself through the door and stopped in front of her, puffing heavily.

"What is it?" Ingeborg looked from her grinning son to follow where he pointed. "Metiz!"

The old woman, a descendent of marriages between the French Canadian trappers and the Lakota and Chippewa Indians, stood grinning in the doorway. She'd lost a front tooth to the winter, but her silvered hair was still pulled back in a single braid, her black eyes still snapped with delight, and the lines in her face resembled a dried apple more than ever. "We come back."

"We?" Ingeborg crossed the room and, extending her hand, drew her old friend into the room. "Oh, Metiz, I am so glad you came.

We need your wisdom so desperately."

Metiz gestured behind her. A sturdy boy with the same bright eyes and dusky skin as hers stepped forward. He wore a combination of skin vest, bright red shirt, and leather leggings, while a thong held back his thick, black hair. "My grandson. Baptiste. He friend for Thorliff."

Thorliff wore a grin that would have split a more tender face. He looked up at Ingeborg.

She nodded. "Perhaps you'd like to show Baptiste your sheep."

"Come on." Thorliff straightened his back, shot a grin over his shoulder at his mother, and walked over to the newcomer. "You want to see my new lambs? I have," he wrinkled his forehead in thought, "twenty-three. Two black ones."

Baptiste nodded. He glanced up at his grandmother for permission and, at her nod, followed Thorliff out the door.

Thorliff whistled. "Paws, come here. That's my dog." His words floated back into the silent soddy.

"They be good together." Metiz nodded. Her mixture of French, English, and her native tongue, along with a smattering of Norwegian made it possible for them to communicate. Sometimes they needed no words, using signs and actions to convey what they meant.

"I am so happy you came. I don't know what else to use to make Lars' foot better."

"What happen?" She moved to stand beside the bed and looked the sick man in the eyes.

"Frostbite. We got caught out by that last blizzard."

"Bad one, that." She sniffed, leaning over the bed to peer at the swollen reddened foot, now seeping from the open sores. "Foot bad."

"Ja, that it is." Lars shrugged his shoulders, but the furrow between his brows belied the lighter words. "I think we need to cut it off before it poisons the rest of me."

"What done?" She turned to Ingeborg.

"Rubbing it, hot and cold soaking, willow bark tea for pain, now laudanum, and I poured whiskey over it to clean it again."

"I drink the stuff, too. Maybe it does more good on the inside than out." Lar's attempt at humor fell as flat as the lefse Kaaren had made the day before.

Kaaren entered the house. She'd been outside hanging clothes on the line and stirring the wash in a kettle over the fire outside. "So good to see you, Metiz. Welcome home." Kaaren's knowledge of French made it easier for her to talk with the old woman.

In French, Metiz asked, "Has he run a fever?" Kaaren nodded. "Out of his head at times?"

"Only with the pain. He sleeps a lot now that we have the laudanum for him."

Metiz nodded. She cupped her hands over the foot, pressing gently, exploring the festering member.

Lars blanched, sweat popped out in his forehead, and he clamped his teeth together. Kaaren took his hand, wincing at the force with which he grasped it.

Metiz sniffed again, and closing her eyes, she pressed up the leg. She turned to see the man's reaction. "Better?"

"Up there, yes. I ain't never had anything hurt like this." He took in a deep breath and let it out, the air whooshing from his lungs.

Metiz pondered the man in front of her, one finger tip massaging her chin. "I think not cut off whole foot. Two small toes, save rest. Put foot up high. I bring medicine." She turned and headed for the door. "Boy stay with your boy?"

"Of course." Ingeborg followed the old woman out the door. "What can I do?"

"Make him drink." She mimicked tipping up a bottle.

"We have the laudanum."

"Later. Make knife sharp. Very sharp. Heat poker." She set out for her encampment at the ground-eating trot that Ingeborg had learned Metiz could endure for hours.

Ingeborg watched her go and then headed across the field to her own soddy. She could hear the boys talking from the barn when she reached the door. Off in the distance, Haakan continued to widen the rich brown strip of field as the plow laid over furrow after furrow. "Thorliff," she called, "I need you for a minute."

"Coming." The two boys appeared in the barn door, Paws at Thorliff's knee. The boy trotted up to his mother. "What do you want?"

"Would you please go get Mr. Bjorklund for me? Tell him it isn't an emergency, but I need help soon."

Thorliff nodded and with a "Come on, Baptiste," the two boys raced each other across the rippling prairie grass.

Ingeborg watched them go. How good it would be for her son to have a friend, someone that lived close enough to be with often and to do boy things with. She worried sometimes about this lad growing up with no one his age, always the oldest and responsible beyond his years. When she was eight, she had brothers and sisters both older and younger and went to school. They needed to get the school going, that was one sure thing. And now Kaaren's husband might not live. "No, I will not even think such!" Her words rang loud and firm in the prairie silence.

By the time Metiz returned with a bundle on her back, Ingeborg and Kaaren had all the supplies ready. Haakan had come in from the field to help hold Lars down if need be. Ingeborg had put Andrew down for a nap with strict instructions to Thorliff that he must stay by the house to hear the baby when he woke.

"I'm not drunk, yet," Lars sang, a silly grin belying his words. He hefted the bottle and took another swig.

"I think I could use a swig of that, too," Haakan muttered for Ingeborg's ears alone.

She shot him a nod of agreement. Her stomach was doing small flip-flops at the thought of the work ahead. Would it be enough to just remove the toes? Or would they have to repeat it with the re-mainder of the foot? *God, help us, guide us, and bring healing to this son of yours. And please, I'm so frightened. Give me strength.* She caught Kaaren's eye and knew she'd been thinking and doing the same.

"Drink more." Metiz sat on a chair by the bed. "We use table?"

"I know," Kaaren answered. "I have a sheet ready to put on it. We can get more light over there. I have all the lamps ready to light."

Ingeborg looked around and saw that it was so. The room felt stifling with the fire going to heat plenty of water. The poker she'd brought back with her lay on top of the stove, ready to insert in the firebox. She closed her eyes at the sight of the knives, their edges gleaming in the lamplight, newly ground on the whetstone to a fine edge. *Dear God, please get us through this.*

"Are we ready then?" Haakan asked. At their nods, he leaned over the bed and slipped his arm under Lars' shoulders. "All right, my friend, let's get this over with. You use your strength, and I'll use mine, and we'll get you on that table before you pass out."

Lars mumbled some kind of answer but did as ordered. Once they had him standing on his good foot with his arms over the shoulders of Haakan and Ingeborg, they half carried, half walked him to the table, and he crumbled onto it. He slipped into uncon-sciousness from the alcohol and the pain of the jarring.

"You hold him." Metiz nodded to Ingeborg and Haakan.

"How about if we run a rope around him and the table from chest to foot?" Haakan asked.

"Good. You do."

Haakan wrapped a rope around the snoring man and the table.

Then he and Ingeborg took their positions, Haakan beside the diminutive woman. With a quick slash, Metiz began the operation.

Behind them, Kaaren gagged and rushed out of the house.

Ingeborg was torn between caring for her sister in distress or for the man beneath her hands, but she held to her post. She turned her face away from the sight of the welling blood. By the time the toes and part of the side of the foot were cut off and another area cut open to bleed and drain the poison, she felt dizzy from the heat and the smell of blood and putrefaction. *Don't you dare faint*, she ordered herself. *This is no different than butchering a deer*. If only she could believe that. But the deer were always dead, and this was a living, breathing human being cut.

Metiz motioned for Haakan to retrieve the poker from the stove where it now glowed white at the end. "Place there." She pointed to the cut side of the foot.

Haakan did as told but looked across the man on the table and into Ingeborg's eyes, as if asking permission. She nodded slightly and shut her eyes against the sight. The stench of burning flesh made her gag, but with all the strength she possessed, she held her place. She gripped Lars' leg till her muscles screamed in protest as, in spite of the rope binding him, he bucked beneath their hands.

Sweat poured down her face and into her eyes. The tears streaming down her cheeks added to the flow. She peered across the table to see Metiz spreading a paste on the ravaged foot and gently wrapping clean cloths around it.

"Now, him we put in bed."

"Let's carry the table over there. It will be easier on him." Haakan, too, wore rivers of sweat, the hair draped over his brow glistening dark with it. Together they lifted the table, and once it stood by the bed, they untied the unconscious man and laid him on the bed.

"Make high place for foot. Evil drain away." Metiz piled the quilts and propped up the leg.

"I'll bring in the feedbox. That should work better." Haakan dashed the back of his wrist across his forehead. He laid a comforting hand on Ingeborg's shoulder as he passed and headed out to the barn.

"I . . . I'm sorry." Kaaren crossed the room and stood shivering by the table. "I couldn't keep it down. I'm so sorry."

Ingeborg snatched one of the quilts and wrapped it around the quivering woman. "Here, sit in the rocker and drink something hot. You needn't feel bad. Things affect you more when you're increasing." She poured a cup of coffee and laced it with honey. "Drink this." Placing the cup in Kaaren's hands, she watched Metiz move silently about the injured man, settling the covers, laying a hand on the green-tinged brow. The old woman seemed to be listening as she moved, as if sensing the inner workings of the man she cared for. She'd stop, close her eyes, then lay her hand on the foot, the knee, the shoulder.

The sound of Kaaren sipping the sweetened coffee kept time with the stentorious snoring of the man on the bed. Lars sounded more drunk than wounded, and for that, Ingeborg was glad. She had the laudanum ready if he should begin to stir. Surely the pain from his mutilated foot would intrude on his drunken stupor soon.

"Here." Haakan returned with a feedbox from the barn. He wrapped it in a blanket and slipped it under the foot when Metiz raised it. Lars snored on.

Metiz looked up from her study of the injured man. "We done all." She nodded and looked at each of the others in the room, waiting until they met her gaze. "Now we pray. You to your God, me to Great Spirit. Me"—she touched her chest with her thumb—"me, I tink one and same." She raised her hands above her head and, face looking upward, began a chant in a language all her own.

Ingeborg took Kaaren's hand in hers and reached out for Haakan. "You take hold of Lars' hand," she said softly. When he had done that, she bowed her head, waiting silently for the man beside her to begin praying. When he didn't, she looked up to see a look of total consternation, fear, resentment—she had no idea which was plastered on his face. When he caught her gaze, he shook his head.

Oh, my. Ingeborg bit her lip. *So the man doesn't pray? Doesn't he believe either?* She was sure he did. Hadn't he joined in on grace at the supper table? Yes, he had.

The soft words of Metiz bathed them like a song.

Ingeborg bowed her head again. "God in heaven, our Father. You have commanded that we pray for what we need, and healing Lars' foot is surely that. Please, we ask that you restore life to the frozen flesh and heal the part that was cut." She could feel herself begin to shake. Never had she led prayer like this, with a group of both men and women, and for healing.

"Father, forgive my weakness and give my husband the strength to mend and the grace to ask you for help." Kaaren's gentle voice whispered the pleas of her heart.

Ingeborg could feel Haakan's hand begin to relax in hers.

Lars shifted on the bed and slipped into the easy breath of one asleep.

Ingeborg knew that if she looked up, she would see their prayers winding heavenward like tendrils of smoke or the incense she read about in the Bible. Never in her life had she felt such peace, such an absolute certainty that God heard their prayers, that He cared beyond human understanding. She kept her eyes closed, suddenly afraid that if she looked at the foot of the bed and Jesus wasn't standing there like she saw in her mind, she'd break down with sobs too deep to stop.

"Amen." Haakan's strong voice broke the spell. Only at that instant did she realize there had been a male voice adding words of prayer.

Like a cloud on a mountain, silence rested upon the room.

When Ingeborg opened her eyes, Metiz was gone.

Haakan wiped away the tears that had overflowed and streamed down his tanned cheeks.

Kaaren blew her nose and leaned her head against the back of the rocker.

Ingeborg could hear her pastor from Nordland as if he stood beside them. "The Lord bless thee and keep thee, the Lord lift his countenance upon thee and give thee his peace. Amen."

"Amen," she whispered in return. "Amen."

"Mor," Thorliff called from outside. "Can we come in now? Andrew wants you."

"Ja. We will have some dinner now. I know everyone is hungry." Kaaren levered herself up from the rocker. "I have soup hot on the back of the stove. Inge, you cut the bread, and, Thorliff, you go out to the cellar and bring a jug of milk out of the water tank." She swept Andrew up in her arms and, squeezing him tight, plunked him on his raised chair.

Ingeborg looked over at Haakan, who still hadn't said a word. He raised one eyebrow in a question mark. She shook her head and shrugged. She really didn't know what had happened to them all either. But time would tell. Indeed, time would tell.

Mid-May 1884

Hjelmer kept looking over his shoulder even as he mounted the train steps at the station in New Jersey. Every time he saw a big man with dark hair, his heart started to race. No matter how many names he called himself and how many times he promised he wouldn't react like that again, the feeling persisted.

Swen wanted him dead.

He was well into Pennsylvania before he finally felt his mind and muscles begin to relax. Swen wouldn't spend the cost of a train ticket to follow him. No man in his right mind would do that. He began to take an interest in the sights out his window, and soon the discomfort of the hard seats and the noise of the squabbling children and chattering parents faded from his awareness. The beauty of the land captured him.

When the conductor said that Pittsburgh, Pennsylvania, was coming in two stops, Hjelmer struggled with a hard decision. As much as he loved working with metal, this city, the home of the steel mills, would be a good place to find a job. Dark had fallen by the time they entered the city, and all he could think of was the fires of hell. Mills lined the tracks, smoke and flames their heart. Flat train cars lined the tracks, piled high with lengths of steel waiting to be shipped to far-flung places.

Hjelmer got off the train at the next station. The smell of carbon and smoke and metal filled his nostrils. Did he want to stay here? He had ten minutes to make up his mind.

"All abo-a-r-d!" The conductor placed the step into its traveling position and swung his lantern.

Hjelmer grabbed his valise and leaped back aboard as the train began to move. He'd wasted enough time on his quest for land of his own. Dakota Territory, his family, his life. Another big city was not for him.

Five days later he still couldn't sleep, not wanting to miss a single sight. He stared out the train window. They hadn't been exaggerating. The letters home hadn't begun to describe the flat expanse of the prairie or the immensity of it.

Surely there was room for half the inhabitants of the world to farm here and still have space for towns and cities. He shook his head. His brothers had been men of vision, but had they really learned to love this flat land after living in the mountain grandeur of home?

He checked the gifts he'd purchased at the stop in Chicago. Mrs. Holtensland had given him a valise with some of her husband's clothes, along with her blessing when he had to flee New York for his life. On top of the pants he'd packed lay a book for Thorliff, a carved pony for Andrew, a crystal vase for Ingeborg who loved her flowers, and a book of poetry for Kaaren. He knew she loved to read. For himself, he'd purchased several carving tools to replace the ones stolen. He'd wanted to buy a forge and some tools, but he wasn't sure what they had at the homestead. The dream of riding up on a horse had faded, too, when he checked the price. One could buy a hundred acres of prime farmland for far less than a horse.

The money remaining in the leather pouch Mrs. Holtensland had also given him had dwindled faster than the snow under spring sun. While he'd seen four men at a card game in the lounge car, he'd kept from joining in. *You learned your lesson*, he told himself. *Gambling is not for you and never will be again.* He shuddered at the thought of what his far would say if he knew his son, his only remaining son, had been chased out of New York on a death threat for supposedly cheating at cards. He shuddered again. If Swen ever did catch him, that would be the end of him for sure. One thing he knew with absolute certainty. He hadn't cheated. He'd won fair and square. But one other thing he'd learned, size and rage counted for more than honest play.

He leaned back in the seat, letting his thoughts keep time with the clacking wheels. If he understood right, the land he now rode so quickly across his brothers had traversed with horse and wagon and much adversity. He glanced out the window facing east and leaped from his seat to cross the aisle and press his nose against the glass. A line of ten, no, more like fifteen teams were pulling the new-fangled plows he'd read about. Plows one sat on instead of walked behind. The stair-stepped line of teams were turning over a wide swath of rich black soil. Roald had written of the wonders of the Bonanza farms, and this must be one in action. Hjelmer shook his head in total wonder. How many acres could be turned under in one day with such luxury? Did Ingeborg have such a plow? Could he make such a plow if she didn't?

He threw himself back in his seat, visions of new machinery plowing through his mind. How much would one cost? He jingled the change in his pocket. More than he had, that was certain. He straightened in the seat. One thing he knew, if he couldn't make one, he could sure repair them. They had to be metal, and he knew the repairing of iron and steel.

Roald, too, had written that there was not a rock to be found on the homestead. What would it be like to plow without hauling off a sledge loaded with rocks? Norwegian soil grew rocks better than anything.

"Grand Forks, next stop." The conductor stopped in the doorway and repeated his announcement. As he made his way down the aisle, he stopped at Hjelmer's seat. "If you be wanting to take the St. Paul, Minneapolis, and Manitoba Railway to Grafton, you'll cross the river here and walk to the other train station. Tain't far for a young sprout like you."

Hjelmer had been grateful ever since boarding in St. Paul that the conductor spoke Norwegian. There'd been a couple of times when he nearly got off at the wrong station because he didn't understand the language. Once he did get off, but the conductor called him back. It seemed he'd never make it to his destination, so many were the miles he crossed. Seven days now he'd been cooped up.

"Mange takk." He corrected himself, "Thank you." With a grin he added, "Much obliged," his latest phrase.

"You'll do, son, you'll do." The conductor shook Hjelmer's offered hand and went on down the aisle, his voice carrying the announcement of the coming stop to all ears.

Hjelmer swung down to the wooden platform after the train coughed and snorted to a stop. He swung the rope around his quilt over his shoulder, picked up the valise in one hand, and set out for the river, the bridge looming down at the end of the street. He stopped before crossing the steel-girded structure. It looked large from here, but compared to the long, massive bridges he'd crossed on his westward trek, this one rated low. He'd seen the long curved Rockville Bridge in Harrisburg, Pennsylvania, which, according to the conductor, was the longest bridge in America. He'd been so impressed, he'd asked someone to translate what the conductor had said. Now that bridge was a work of man that challenged the elements. And the Brooklyn bridge, he'd been watching it grow the month he lived in New York. Nearly finished now, it was touted as one of the wonders of the world. He had seen some country, indeed, he had. He stopped in the middle of the bridge and looked over the side at the teeming brown water. Looked like nothing more than liquefied mud. Why in the world did they call it the Red River? Hawking a glob of spit, he sent it to join the murky water passing below. Give him the sparkling blue rivers of home any day.

Would he ever be able to go back? *Mor wants to come over here,* he reminded himself. *One day I'll have enough money I can return to Norway and bring her back here with me. Far will never come, but Mor will.* Why he knew that with such certainty didn't bother his mind, but knew it he did.

At the western station they were unloading new farm machinery. He stood amazed. Green, red, and white, the bright colors gleamed on equipment he could only hope he figured out right. The one with the sharp teeth would be for mowing. It was easy to tell the plows because the shares were much the same as the hand models, and the wheels that carried what looked like skinny curved teeth could only be a rake, but what a job that would do. He stroked a loving hand down the cold metal. He would have one of these, yes, someday he would.

The sun had died a glorious death on the western horizon by the time he stepped off the train in Grafton. Miles of track were being laid at an astonishing speed, but for now, this was the end of the line. He knew the Red River lay to the east, and the Bjorklund homestead was somewhere to the north, so he began his walk back to the river. For certain he couldn't get lost if he followed the river.

Walking felt good after all the hours of sitting on the train. Hjelmer strode out, quickly leaving behind the hamlet of Grafton. Birds sang good-bye to the day, and he marveled at the purpling of the land as the sky deepened to azure and the stars poked their way through the heavenly canopy. The wind at his back cooled the sweat that had beaded under his shirt and coat, and laid the grass on its side to rest for the night. Only the whine of the mosquitoes sounded discordant in the peace. Far off, a cow bellered, a dog barked, and another answered. Ahead he could still see the outline of the trees in the dimness. Strange that no matter how fast he walked, they didn't seem to draw any closer.

He slapped at a mosquito on his neck. You'd think with the wind they'd be in hiding, but no such luck. He stopped for the night far short of the trees. Their being close was definitely an illusion of the flat land. One could see almost too far for comfort. He thought of angling south to the light he could see in the distance. Must be a farm, but knowing how far away he could see the trees, the light might be just as far off.

After eating the roll and cheese he'd purchased in Grand Forks, he rolled in his quilt and pillowed his head on the valise. Before long, he pulled his coat over his head so he'd still have some blood left in the morning. Frogs croaked and peeped, an owl hooted on its ghostly passing, and another bird cried a song he knew not. But when he pushed his coat back so he could see the stars shimmering above, he quickly retreated. Close darkness was definitely preferable to the blood-letting. Already he itched.

He woke with the dawn only a promise on the eastern horizon. Sometime during the night he must have discarded his coat as a head protection, for any skin that had been exposed to the marauding mosquitoes now itched unbearably. Unable to ignore his discomfort, he got to his feet, folded his quilt and rolled it, and with his bundles tied to his back, he set out again.

The glory of the morning restored him. The rising sun gilded each blade of grass and bespangled every spider's web until the earth lay encrusted in gold and jewels. He took in a deep breath of spring perfume—the blend of grass and earth and growing things mixed with a sweet overlay of blooming flowers. Soft air caressed his cheeks, and the breeze lifted his hair when he removed his hat.

If he'd been younger, he'd have spun around and around, dancing the music of spring. His feet shuffled a couple of steps, then walked on. He couldn't stop grinning, and he could feel the stretch of it in his cheeks. His arms insisted on rising above his head, and his hands clapped, much against his better judgment. The song burst forth from his throat, playing baritone to the lark's soprano. The river, when he reached it, sang bass while the cottonwood trees rustled sibilant secrets of symphonic strings. All sang of spring, a prairie overture.

While he wanted a drink, the mud-brown water made him hesitate. Was it drinkable? Animal and bird tracks showed him the wildlife of the area frequented the riverbank. He dipped his hand

and raised the water to his mouth. Nothing like the sparkling waterfalls of home, that was for certain. But it was wet and revived him just the same.

He inquired at one soddy if they knew of the Bjorklunds, but they shook their heads and pointed north. Surely their language had been some form of German. Again, Hjelmer regretted never having learned other languages, especially English.

The sun was nearing straight up when he saw smoke rising from two chimneys fairly close together. He broke into a trot, his bags bumping against his shoulders. A flock of sheep raised their heads, poised to flee at a moment's notice. A dog barked and soon came racing to accost him.

Hjelmer stopped and let the dog, hackles raised and stalking on tiptoe, sniff his shoes and pant legs. "Easy, boy. I mean you no harm."

"Paws, come." The boy's command rang across the meadow.

The dog lifted his head, looked back at his master, and whined deep in his throat.

"Come, I said." Staff in his hand and porkpie hat pushed back on his head, the boy strode toward the visitor. "God dag." He stopped and slapped his knee. The sheep had gone back to grazing.

"You're Thorliff, aren't you?" Hjelmer nodded as he spoke. No one with eyes could fail to recognize this young version of his older brother, the likeness was so exact.

"How'd you know?"

"Because I'm your onkel Hjelmer, and I'd recognize a Bjorklund like you anywhere. Do you remember me at all?"

Thorliff cocked his head. "Sort of. Come on, Mor will be pleased to see you. We were beginning to wonder what had happened to you." He turned to lead the way, then spun back and extended his hand. "Velkommen." He stopped and started again. "Welcome to Dakota Territory."

"Mange takk." Hjelmer shook the boy's hand. "You have grown up so fast. How my mor, your bestemor, would love to see you." He matched his longer strides to the boy's as they headed for the house, burning with questions as to who it was with the team out in the far field and how they all were.

"Mor! Mor!" Thorliff called when they neared the sod house. "Come quick."

A woman came charging out the only door, drying her hands on her apron as she came.

"We have company!" Thorliff dashed forward. "Onkel Hjelmer is finally here."

Ingeborg wiped her hands again and extended them to the new-comer, her smile of greeting bringing warmth to his heart immediately. "Hjelmer Bjorklund, you grew up while we were away." She clasped his hands in hers and squeezed. "How are you? Why did you come that way? How long since you've eaten?" The questions tumbled out while at the same time she pulled him toward the door where a small child, wearing the long dress of a baby yet, clutched the doorframe.

Ingeborg scooped up the child. "Hjelmer, this is Andrew. He's nearly two now." The little boy buried his face in her shoulder, first finger in his mouth. "Come in, come in. Dinner will be ready soon. Would you like a cup of coffee in the meantime?"

Hjelmer looked around the soddy, his first reaction one of dismay. This was the way his brothers lived, like rabbits in a burrow? But as his eyes adjusted to the gloom, he recognized the trunk his mother had painted for the emigrants and saw his brother's hand in the chairs around the table and the rocking chair by the stove. All the Bjorklund sons had been well taught on the intricacies of fashioning wood into useful and functional items. Gustaf started them young with their first carving knife and slowly graduated them to lathes and saws and planes.

He raised a hand to scratch his face and the back of his neck. "Ah, ja, that would be wonderful."

"What did you get into?" Ingeborg stepped closer to peer at his face.

"Not what did I get into, but what got at me. No one warned me that the mosquitoes would try to eat me alive."

"Uff da. They can be bad." She glanced down at the boy waiting by the door. "Go get some buttermilk from the cooler. It is in the crock on the right." While Thorliff scampered off, Ingeborg set Andrew in the rocking chair, from where he immediately scrambled down and twined himself in her skirts. In spite of the difficulty, she poured coffee into a cup and motioned Hjelmer to the table where she set the saucer down.

"Mange takk." Hjelmer sucked in a deep breath, the air redolent of simmering stew or soup, fresh baked bread, and now the coffee before him. Under it all lay the musky scent of dirt walls and floor. *How can they stand it so dark? And yet, I'm sure more windows are too costly.* "You have made a comfortable home here." He wanted so badly to ask about the man out plowing the field, but he restrained himself.

Thorliff returned and set down the jug of buttermilk, then sat in the chair and leaned his elbows on the table. "We thought you was coming a long time ago."

"Thorliff!" Ingeborg turned from slicing the bread. She picked up a cloth and took it to the table. Pouring some buttermilk into a dish, she dipped the cloth and started to smooth the thick liquid on the young man's neck. She drew back.

Hjelmer looked up and saw her cheeks flame red. He grinned at her and reached for the cloth.

"I . . . I forget you are not one of the children any longer." Ingeborg raised a hand to her face. "Cover well wherever there are bites. That should take the itch out and the swelling."

"Mange takk." He did as told and felt immediate relief. He sighed. "Between this and the coffee, I'm not sure which is more welcome." He spread the soothing buttermilk on the back of his neck, pulling his shirt away to let the skin dry. "Where did you learn this remedy?"

"A friend of mine, Metiz, she knows everything about medicinals." Ingeborg held the bowl out so he could dip the rag again.

"Metiz, that is a strange sounding name." He dabbed the cloth at the swollen bites on the back of his hands, grateful he'd kept his cuffs buttoned instead of rolled back. The bites ended at the cloth line.

"Metiz brought Baptiste with her when she came back this spring. He's my friend." Thorliff picked up Andrew, who had plunked himself on the floor and begun to whimper. "He helps me graze the sheep." He bobbled the child on his knee and made funny faces to make the little one laugh.

Paws let out a yip in welcome that brought Thorliff to his feet and to the doorway with a delighted cry. "We have company. You get to meet another one of your relations."

Hjelmer turned in his chair. The man filled the doorway, backlit against the sun outside. He had to duck to enter the same as Hjelmer had. Hjelmer laid the cloth on the table, at once aware that with buttermilk all over his face and hands, he must look a sight. This was not the best impression for whoever this man was.

Ingeborg performed the introductions. "Haakan Bjorklund, meet Hjelmer Bjorklund, your cousin twice removed. Hjelmer is the youngest of Gustaf Bjorklund's sons."

The two men shook hands and sized each other up through matching blue eyes. They looked enough alike to be brothers.

"Welcome," Haakan said in English.

"Ja, mange takk," Hjelmer answered while his thoughts raced. *What cousin? Who is he? What right does he have here? He acts like he owns the place.*

"Haakan's mor wrote to him in the north woods of Minnesota and asked him to come here and help out Kaaren and me." Ingeborg turned back to the stove and handed Thorliff the plates she had warming on the shelf of the stove. "Here, you set the table."

"Good that you could do that." Hjelmer felt a bit more at ease. "I understood they needed a man to work the fields. That is why I came as soon as I could." He caught the look exchanged between Ingeborg and Haakan. What else was there he didn't know?

"Lars has been working Kaaren's fields since last fall," Ingeborg said. "They were married after harvest."

Hjelmer sat down, feeling like he'd just been gut-punched. *Why hadn't Mor told him this bit of news?*

13

W*hat is the matter with the boy?* Ingeborg could not yet think of Hjelmer as a man, no matter that he stood nearly as tall as Roald had. Breadth of shoulder ranked somewhere between Carl and Roald, but the boy promised to resemble Roald more. He still had some growing to do. She tried to study him without his knowledge. The two men conversed politely while she settled the children and remembered to bring the jam for their bread.

If she hadn't known Roald so well, the tightening of lips and deepening furrow between the younger man's eyes would have gone unnoticed. Something was definitely bothering him. She seated herself and clasped her hands for grace. After a moment of silence, she nodded to Thorliff, who began, "E Yesu naven . . ." Hjelmer joined in, as did she. And when she glanced up from under her eyelashes, she could see Haakan with his head bowed. Although he wasn't saying anything, she could feel a difference about him, too. Something wonderful, beyond mortal man's understanding, had happened at that bedside three nights before.

As soon as the meal was dished up, they fell to with a vengeance. Hjelmer asked for seconds and accepted the third helping that Ingeborg encouraged him to take.

"I . . . I'm sorry," he finally said, pushing his plate away. "I didn't know I was so hungry. I don't always eat that much."

"Mor likes us to eat a lot." Thorliff gazed up at his newfound uncle. "Sometimes she makes cookies, too, but Tante Kaaren makes the best."

"Do you think Tante Kaaren would let me taste her cookies sometime?" Hjelmer asked.

Thorliff nodded. "We can go over to her house after dinner and ask."

"I thought we would go over as soon as we are finished. She will be so pleased to see you again." Ingeborg took away the spoon that Andrew banged on the table.

"Onkel Lars got frostbite, so we cut off part of his foot."

"Thorliff!"

"Well, he did." He looked back at Hjelmer. "But he is lots better now. Metiz is making him get better."

"Along with God's help." Ingeborg stood to clear away the dishes. "You help me with this, young man." She glanced over at Haakan to catch a glint of amusement dancing in his eyes. She could feel the answering smile curve her own lips. What was he seeing that made him laugh inside like that? A wink sent her way made the familiar warmth pool around her middle.

Haakan stretched his hands above his head. "Much as I'd like to accompany you, I think I'll head back to the field instead. From the looks of those clouds, we'll get rain before dark, so I need to put in every minute I can. Perhaps tomorrow you can work with the other team, Hjelmer. With the bad weather and all, we're late getting out on the fields. We're plowing now, working the soil that's already been busted so we can get it seeded."

"Ja, that will be good."

"I could drive the oxen to disc what you've plowed," Ingeborg said to the stove.

Silence, thicker than sheep's wool and heavier than rain-soaked soil fell on the room.

A man cleared his throat. It had to be Haakan. She turned around. Hjelmer stared at her like she'd just sprouted horns. Haakan shook his head, but the smile hadn't left his face.

Andrew took that moment to let out a shriek, disgruntled at the lack of attention.

"But . . . but your children." Hjelmer blinked once and then again.

Who do you think did the work here the last months? Ingeborg felt like yelling in his shocked face. *Didn't you read the letters I've written to your mother?* She thought a moment, remembering how much of the last year she had carefully neglected to mention.

"Come, let's go now before Andrew falls asleep or gets any crankier." Without waiting for a reply, she set the child on her hip and strode out the door, closely followed by Thorliff.

"Down, Mor, down," Andrew pleaded.

"Mor, are you angry?" Thorliff asked softly from by her side. Paws whined and danced in front of her.

"Nei!" The sharpness of her voice made the dog's ears go down.

Andrew whimpered in her arms, his weight pulling her off center. Any other time she would have let him walk, but now she was in a hurry. She hitched him higher and continued the pace. She could hear Hjelmer coming up behind her.

"I could carry him for you."

"He don't take too good to strangers," Thorliff answered for her.

"Mange takk, but we have done this many times before." *And will continue to do so long after you are gone.* She kept the thought to herself. *Who does he think he is, coming here and making judgments about what I can and cannot do?*

"Thorliff!" Baptiste's voice came from the sod barn.

"Coming." Thorliff looked up to his mother for permission, and at her nod he scampered across the grassy expanse.

Baptiste stepped into the sunshine from the barn door.

"Why . . . why, he's Indian!" The shock in Hjelmer's voice needled Ingeborg again.

"Partly. He's from the Lakota tribe, part of the Chippewa Nation, and he's also French Canadian."

"He's a half-breed?"

"No, he's Metiz." Ingeborg spoke from between clenched teeth. Why was she letting this young man get to her like this?

"Metiz? Isn't that the name of the woman who is helping Lars?"

"Ja, it is." Ingeborg knocked on the doorframe and stepped into the soddy. "I have brought you company, Lars, Kaaren. Hjelmer has finally made it to Dakota Territory."

"Oh, Hjelmer, little brother, how wonderful to see you." Kaaren made him blush by throwing her arms around him. She stepped back after the hug and looked into his eyes. "I've spent many hours praying for your safe arrival, and now you are finally here, safe and sound. The Lord be praised."

Ingeborg set Andrew down and rubbed the crick in her back with her fists. "You look like a new man, Lars."

"Thanks, I am a new man." For the first time since the amputation, Lars was sitting in the rocking chair, his foot propped up on pillows on a stool. He reached out a hand to greet the newcomer. "Welcome, I've heard so much about you."

Kaaren took Hjelmer by the arm. "I want you to meet my husband, Lars Knutson. We were beginning to think you had fallen into the drink and never come out."

"Well, I didn't fall, I dove. But you are not far off." Hjelmer shook hands with Lars. "It is a long story, but I am glad to finally be here."

"Sit down, sit down. I could use a good story. Kaaren, is the coffee hot?" He leaned over to pick up Andrew. "And this young one here would like a cookie. I know he would." He settled the little boy on his lap. Andrew wriggled himself into a comfortable position and beamed up at Kaaren when she handed him a cookie.

"Takk."

"You're welcome, little one." Kaaren smiled over at Ingeborg, who had taken a chair at the table. "He's getting more words every day."

Ingeborg nodded her head. "Thanks to Thorliff."

"Takk." Andrew said it again and waved his cookie in the air, scattering crumbs all over Lars.

"And he even used it in the right place." Lars gently pinched Andrew's foot, drawing a giggle. Another pinch and the baby's deep belly laugh filled the room. At that same moment, Thorliff and Baptiste came through the door, laughing along with the little one.

"I know, I know. You smelled the cookies." Kaaren passed them the crock she had set in the middle of the table.

"Baptiste is finished cleaning out the stalls. Can we go fishing?"

"Where do you fish?" Hjelmer asked, then nodded his thanks when Kaaren placed a cup of coffee in front of him.

Thorliff looked at him, a question mark all over his face. "Didn't you see the river?"

"Ja, the one that's more mud than water?"

"We catch fish from it."

"We used to drink from it before we dug the wells," Ingeborg added, and saw the surprise register on Hjelmer's face. This was certainly a day of shocks for him, she mused, noticing how careful he was to ignore Baptiste after that first stunned appraisal. *Doesn't he realize how precious water is here on the prairie? It isn't like Norway, that's for certain.*

"Ja, you have earned some time off, and a mess of fish would taste mighty good for supper. Have you kept any worms?" Ingeborg sipped her coffee and watched Hjelmer try to corral his thoughts.

"No, I'll get them from the edge of the manure pile." He grabbed two more cookies from the jar. "Come on, Baptiste, before they change their minds."

"Thank you for cleaning the barn," Lars called after them.

"You are welcome" floated back on the breeze they left behind. Hjelmer sat like he had a steel rod up his back.

Ingeborg left Hjelmer visiting with Lars and Kaaren, saying she needed to put Andrew down for a nap. When Kaaren nodded toward the bed, Ingeborg shook her head. Kaaren followed her out the door.

"What is it, Inge? Something is bothering you."

"He has a lot of set ideas for so young a man." Ingeborg cuddled Andrew close and swayed back and forth as he snuggled into her shoulder. She kept her voice low so the men wouldn't hear her.

"Sounds like Roald all over again, if you ask me." Kaaren shaded her eyes with her hand to watch the two boys laughing their way to the river.

"He doesn't like Indians."

"Why should he not? He's never met one before." Kaaren shook her head.

"Probably heard too many stories." Andrew snuffled, so Ingeborg swayed some more. "Who does he think he is, anyway?"

"Probably thinks he came to save the Bjorklund women from the perils of the prairie." Kaaren took in a deep breath of the pure air. "Since tomorrow is Sunday, why don't we send the boys over to the Baards and invite them for dinner? They can meet Hjelmer, and he'll get a better idea of what life is like out here. Lars wants to talk to Joseph about borrowing his nephew to help out until he can get back on his feet."

Ingeborg continued to sway so Andrew wouldn't wake. "Work is what Hjelmer came for, so let him do it. We don't want our young savior to feel less than wanted."

"Inge." Kaaren cautioned with a smile.

"I know, I know. I just get tired of these men thinking they know it all and we have heads stuffed with cotton wool." She shook her head, setting her straw hat to bobbing.

"You want to work in the fields."

"Ja."

"I see. And you just happened to mention it at dinner?" Kaaren rolled her lips together to keep from laughing out loud.

"Ja. Sometimes things just slip out." Ingeborg laid her cheek against the downy hair of her child. She chuckled along with Kaaren when their gazes met.

"Oh, Inge, what will we do with you? If working in the field is so important, you bring the boys over, and I will do the cooking again. I know we are getting behind, and Lars feels just terrible about it. He'll huff about you donning britches again, but a little huffing never hurt anyone."

Ingeborg reached out a hand and clasped Kaaren's. "Mange takk, sister mine. Now you get that young man to tell you all his traveling stories. I have a feeling there is more there than we have any idea. Monday morning I'll head for the fields, also. Right now I better go set some beans to soaking so we can have baked beans tomorrow. You know Agnes will bring plenty of food, too."

"I'll make my dried plum pie. Joseph would crawl over here on his hands and knees for plum pie."

"I'll go call the boys and have them take the mule over. Looks like we won't have fish tonight after all." She thought a moment. "No, I'll drive the wagon over to Baards and Andrew can sleep on the way."

"You could leave him here."

"Are you sure?"

The look Kaaren gave her made Ingeborg smile. "Mange takk. Please tell Thorliff where I went when he comes home; although I might be back before he is. Oh, and just in case, I have a ham I'll put in the oven for supper."

"I know, for if the fish aren't biting." Kaaren took the sleeping Andrew from his mother and turned back toward the house. "Enjoy your ride."

"I promised myself I'd get a saddle for that ridge-backed mule before I rode him again, but quilts will have to do." She set off across the prairie to her own soddy, whistling beneath her breath. Freedom, she was being allowed a moment, an hour or two of freedom.

She filled the firebox with wood and turned the damper down so it would burn long and slow, then plopped the ham she had soaking on the counter into the roaster and slipped it into the oven. They only had one more ham in the cellar, and the smoked venison was running low, too. The deer she'd shot hadn't lasted long. She needed time to hunt again. Now wouldn't that sizzle Hjelmer's beard, if he had one?

Within minutes she had the mule bridled and pulled over to the corral fence, where she stood on the bottom rail to make slinging her britches-covered leg over his back easier. Once aboard, she nudged him into a canter instead of the innards-jolting trot and headed west across the prairie.

On reaching the newly turned furrows, she pulled up to tell

Haakan where she was going and then set off again. The wind caught the brim of her straw hat, and only thanks to the ribbons around her chin did it keep from cartwheeling across the prairie. After a time Jack started to puff, so she drew him down to an easy jog. When a bevy of grouse flew up from a clump of bushes off the track, she berated herself for not bringing the gun. Raising her face to the sun guaranteed a new rash of freckles on her nose, but she didn't care. The sun and wind kissed her cheeks to cherry red and tugged strands of golden hair from her coronet of braids.

It seemed only minutes had passed when she waved at Joseph, plowing the eastern half of his section. One of the boys had the other team and was plowing the next furrow slightly behind. The Baards were fortunate. They had two sons and a nephew old enough to help Joseph with the farm work.

"Land sakes, look who's here." Agnes followed the sound of the dog barking and met Ingeborg before she could dismount. "What a wonderful surprise for the day. And how are you, my dear?" She tisked a bit at Ingeborg's choice of attire, but the grin on her round face and the raised eyebrow meant she was only teasing. Two small children, a boy and a girl, had gone from tumbling and playing at her feet to hiding behind her skirts, staring out at the newcomer with wide eyes. Agnes held the youngest of her brood of five, six-month-old Rebecca, on her solid hip.

"Good, good." Ingeborg swung to the ground. "We have company. Roald's youngest brother, Hjelmer, has arrived, and we thought you might like to come meet him tomorrow. Since it is Sunday, we could all use a break."

"Ja, we will do that. My Joseph will say yes for certain when we get an invitation like that. What do you want me to bring?" She took Ingeborg by the arm and drew her into the soddy. "Come, you have time for coffee. Penny, will you cut some of that cake, please?" While she talked she brought the coffeepot closer to the front to heat it. "Did he bring a letter from Norway?"

"No, come to think of it, he never mentioned a letter. Something happened to delay him somewhere. He should have been here over a month ago by the last letter we received." Ingeborg undid the ribbons of her hat and laid it on the table. "How's the baby?"

"Growing like a weed. How is Lars' foot?"

Ingeborg almost told her friend about the bedside experience, but something held her back. "He's still in a lot of pain but on the mend, finally, thanks to Metiz and the good Lord's answer to a lot of prayer."

By the time they caught up on the news and finished their coffee, Ingeborg sat back with a sigh. "I better be heading back. I have a ham in the oven for supper in case the boys don't catch any fish. Fresh meat of any kind sounds so good. We had dandelion greens the other day, cooked with bacon."

"Land, we ran out of bacon months ago. Feeding this horde is like hosting locusts." Agnes pushed herself to her feet. "We will see you late in the morning, then. Sure do wish we had that church built and could call a preacher. Ain't been one through here in months. You think they forgot we exist?"

The two women walked out to where one of the boys had watered Ingeborg's mule and tossed him a forkful of hay.

"You surely can be thankful for Metiz and all her medicinals," Agnes said. "She's a mighty good friend to have."

"Which reminds me, I want to invite her to come tomorrow, too. Maybe if she felt more a member of the community, she would build a better house and stay through the winter, especially if we have a real school here next year. Baptiste needs schooling bad as our own young'uns do."

"Prob'ly more. You think she's taught him his letters and his numbers?"

Ingeborg shrugged. "Mange takk for the respite. See you in the morning." She used the corral fence to swing aboard like she had at home. Agnes shook her head.

"If you wasn't such a good woman, I'd think you should have been borned a man the way you like to wear men's britches."

"You should try them sometime. Beats skirts any day." Ingeborg waved and kicked the mule into a lope again, this time with the sun sinking toward the horizon behind her.

She was careful to change back to a skirt before going to Kaaren's for supper.

"That's all right," Hjelmer said after supper at Kaaren's. "I'll sleep in the barn, same as Haakan. I have my quilt one of the people gave me in New York." He'd told them the story of his saving the drowning child and the subsequent loss of his belongings. He hadn't mentioned being forced to flee New York before Swen could kill him.

"If you are sure, then." Kaaren paused to give him time to change his mind. "We have the extra bed here."

How can I sleep in the same room with you and your new husband?

I'd thought to share that bed with you. He kept his face averted in case his thoughts showed through his eyes. The dreams of marrying Kaaren and having his own land immediately were not fading like they should. Would he have to marry Ingeborg? That thought brought him no pleasure at all. He could tell he'd managed to get on the wrong side of her several times already.

"I'll work with Haakan first thing in the morning till I get the hang of it, and then I can work your fields." He nodded to Lars. "You just get better. You don't want to lose more of that foot."

"Him no lose more." Metiz spoke quietly from her chair by the bed.

"Ja, well, let's not take any chances."

"You sound just like Roald." Ingeborg shook her head. "It's uncanny."

"So I've been told. Mor says I look enough like him to be his twin." He lifted one shoulder in a shrug. "Sometimes I have a hard time remembering him. It seems much longer than four years since he left Nordland." He glanced up to see moisture gathering in Ingeborg's eyes. "Sorry to bring that up."

"No, no, I've learned that the more I—we talk about him, the easier it gets." Ingeborg sat in the rocker with Andrew sound asleep in her lap. Baptiste and Thorliff sat at the table, a book before them, with Thorliff reading softly to his friend. With all of them crowded into the soddy, Hjelmer felt the walls closing in on them.

"How did you all manage to live in one soddy, especially during the winter?" The question blurted passed his reserve.

Kaaren smiled and nodded. "It wasn't easy. What with the babies underfoot and keeping them out of the fireplace."

"Roald and Carl spent much of their time out in the barn, working on furniture and farming implements."

That's where I'd be. I'd have that forge fired up and go at it. "I saw the forge. You need new plowshares or some such?"

"We always need those. I brought back two from St. Andrew, but I'm better with wood than iron." Haakan rocked his chair back on two legs. "If we can run three teams, that'll leave two shares free each night to be pounded out again. We always have to sharpen the blade at dinnertime."

Metiz removed the poultice she had covering Lars' foot, and after spreading a paste over the healing tissue, she rebandaged it. "Come, Baptiste, we go now." She picked up her pouch of medicinals. "You drink tea."

Lars nodded. "You made a believer out of me. No matter how terrible your tea tastes, it works. Thank you, Metiz."

"Pray too." Her black eyes twinkled in the lamplight. "Great Spirit hear."

"Ja, God is good." Lars reached out a hand to clasp hers. "You come tomorrow to share a meal with all of us, you hear?"

Metiz nodded. "We bring more fish."

Baptiste looked up from the story. "I set line tonight."

Hjelmer watched and listened. *Was this what all Indians were like? What about the warriors slaughtering the settlers?* More than once he'd heard the phrase, "Only good Indian is a dead Indian." *Were there more around here or only Metiz?*

As the good-nights were said, Haakan took Andrew from Ingeborg. "I'll carry him."

The canopy of stars arched above them, lighted by a sickle moon hanging low in the sky. The wind blew from the west, bringing the rich fragrance of freshly turned soil, overlaid with the spicy aroma of night-blooming flowers. Paws sniffed the ground and followed the trail of some nocturnal animal off into the prairie grass.

If it hadn't been for the mosquitoes, Hjelmer would have stopped to admire the heavens. Instead he kept pace with the others, and his thoughts and questions he kept to himself. Things surely were different than he had planned.

The next day brought further surprises. The morning chores went quickly with the extra pair of hands, so as soon as they finished breakfast, Haakan headed back out to the barn where the sheep remained corralled. "We're so far behind that the fleece are beginning to lose quality. Maybe we can finish the shearing before the Baards get here, then we'll be free to start the field on Monday. You know how to sheer sheep?"

"Ja, we had a flock at home."

"Good. Thorliff has been learning, and he's getting pretty good at it." He ruffled the boy's hair, knocking his tweedy hat to the ground.

Thorliff picked it up and dusted it off before squaring it on his head again. "I can almost keep up to you now."

"Should have been done with this a month ago, but the time just got away from us. On a homestead, there are always too many things that need doing *now*."

"They might have frozen in that last snowstorm then." Thorliff swung open the gate, and the three entered the corral. "You want I should let the sheared ones out to graze?"

"Sure, Paws can keep them close by." The two men stood by the gate and snagged each unshorn sheep before it could escape. With the flock divided, Haakan handed Hjelmer a pair of shears. "You take these, I'll sharpen the others. Thorliff, get me a file, will you."

Sweat soon ran in rivers down his back as Hjelmer bent over each bleating sheep, clipping away with the shears, being careful not to nick the squirming animal. The flies would torment any cuts, and besides, a blood-free sheep was just as much a matter of pride as was removing the fleece in one pelt.

"You want a drink?" Thorliff appeared at his side with a bucket of water and a dipper.

"Ja, when I finish this one." Hjelmer clipped the last row and set the sheep free. He tossed the fleece on the pile by the barn wall and wiped his forehead with the back of his hand. Taking a long drink of water, he wiped his mouth this time and arched his back to get the kinks out. "Mange takk."

"You do a good job. Better'n me." Thorliff helped capture another sheep. With only three remaining in the corral, catching them was getting more difficult.

"You want to do this one?"

"Ja, I could."

Just then Paws barked and ran down the lane. Thorliff ran over to the fence and clambered up on the rails, leaning out to see what the dog was barking at.

"The Baards. They're here." He leaped down on the outside of the corral and ran after the dog, waving his arm and shouting hello.

"I think we get to finish this ourselves." Haakan let his disgruntled sheep go. "He doesn't get to play much, and with the Baard boys here, there'll be roughhousing a plenty."

Hjelmer kept his opinion to himself. The boy could have stayed to help them catch the remaining sheep. His far would never have let his sons run off like that. He looked up to see a quizzical look pass over Haakan's face. Had his thoughts been that obvious?

He could hear the high humor of greetings going on over by the soddy, but he and Haakan doggedly kept after the last two sheep in the pen.

"We'll help you catch them." Two boys joined Thorliff on the corral fence and leaped into the pen. The sheep exploded to the other side. Hjelmer felt himself grabbing thin air, and only quick footwork and a hand in the dirt had he kept from falling flat. He'd had one in his grasp. He glared at the three young ones.

Wiping the sweat from his brow again, he settled his hat and turned back to the fray.

Out of the corner of his eye, he caught sight of a skirt. He turned to look. A young woman with curls of gold cascading down her back set one neatly shod foot on the bottom rail and leaned slender arms on the top. Her smile surely had captured part of the sun, and the sky leant bits of blue to her eyes.

He reached for his hat, shifting his weight to the forward foot. The sheep the boys chased darted through the opening. Hjelmer fell flat forward on the packed dirt.

"Oomph." His breath left him.

erves him right. Haakan had to look away to keep from laughing.

"Are you all right?" The feminine voice sounded foreign amidst the raucous laughter of the boys.

Hjelmer spit dirt mixed with dried sheep dung from his mouth and raised to his hands and knees. He spit again and wiped the dirt from his sweaty face. It smeared wherever he touched, creating mud and a doleful expression.

Haakan could feel the embarrassment radiating from the young man now getting to his feet. "Good day, Penny. How have you been?"

"Good, Mr. Bjorklund." She dropped to the ground from her place on the fence and dusted off her hands. "I see you're nearly finished shearing. You need some help bundling the fleece?"

Haakan shook his head. "Thanks, though." Never in both times he'd seen Penny had she been so friendly. It couldn't have anything to do with the young man retrieving his hat and slapping it against a dirty pant leg, could it? He let Hjelmer finish dusting himself off. "You met the other Mr. Bjorklund, Hjelmer, here yet?" When she shook her head, setting the curls to bouncing, he finished the introduction. "Hjelmer, Miss Penny Baard, meet your new neighbor, and so forth." He never had paid much attention to the niceties of introducing folks. Howdy seemed good enough for him, but then he was beyond courting age.

A vision of Ingeborg with flour on her nose and a smile on her mouth flashed through his mind. He tried to bring up a picture of another cook he had known, but Mrs. Landsverk had faded into a distant memory.

Hjelmer ducked his head. "God dag."

Penny flashed Haakan a look of dismay. "Doesn't he speak English?"

"No, he just came over from Norway. Give him a chance."

She shifted her attention back to Hjelmer. "God dag."

Hjelmer nodded and without another word strode out through the corral gate toward the wash bench on the side of the soddy.

Haakan wondered if the red on the back of his neck was from sunburn or wounded pride. Picking oneself up from the leavings in the corral didn't do much for one's pride, especially since the younger boys had laughed in delight at the tumble. What fun it would be to tell Ingeborg about this little set-to.

Thorliff and one of the boys dragged the sheep they'd finally cornered by the barn wall over to Haakan. "What's the matter with him?" Thorliff nodded toward the retreating figure of Hjelmer. "Did he get hurt?"

"Not so's you can see." Haakan flipped the ewe over on her back and clamped her between his knees. "Soon as we're done here, why don't you take the flock out to graze on that field between the soddies? Then you can keep an eye on them and still have dinner with the rest of us."

"Ja, they're pretty hungry," Thorliff put his hands on his hips. "They sure look funny without their wool."

"Like us, they look better in their clothes."

The boys thought that a real knee slapper. Their hoots of laughter rang out as they ran to the fence, clambered up and over, dropping to the ground at a dead run.

Haakan shook his head. Oh, to have such energy again. He finished clipping and let the last sheep scramble to her feet, then held open the gate while she ran back and forth, bleating at her flock mates. "Come on, you stupid creature, the gate's open." The sheep continued running and bleating, now trying to get out between the corral poles. "If you had half the brains God gave a goose, you'd see that gate and hightail it outa here. I've half a mind to let you stay by yourself." When he'd finally herded the animal out the gate, he looked up to see Joseph coming across the lot.

"Ornery, ain't they?"

"No, just stupid. Kinda like some of the people I met in my travels." Haakan settled his hat on his head and dropped the rope loop over the gate pole to fasten it. "How you been?"

"Tolerable. You need some help with the plowing with Lars still down?" The two men ambled back toward the soddy where Ingeborg and Agnes were loading food and the table into the back of the wagon.

"Thanks, but now that Hjelmer is here, we'll manage. I know you got your own work to do."

"We're about to seed. When that's done, we'll come your way. We can hold off busting more sod for a few days."

"How come you're so far ahead of us?"

"My fields dry out a mite faster, and there's been two of us working all spring. Knute's been a big help, too, with switching teams and the like. He's about big enough to handle a team. Sure wish I bought one of them newfangled plows last fall. Wait till you see how slick our mower works. Me'n Ingeborg bought it together last year. Put up hay on all three places faster'n we coulda done one before." He tipped his hat back. "Shore do like that new machinery."

Haakan listened and nodded. "Saw a whole shed full of those plows over on the Bonanza farm east of St. Andrew. Hard to believe any one farm could use so many. Never seen such a thing before." He went in the house and brought out two chairs. "Need anything else?"

Ingeborg shook her head. "That's it, then."

Agnes looked down from her place on the wagon seat. "Now you young'uns set down 'fore you fall down." The three little ones in the space behind her did as told. She clucked to the team and sent a ripple of command through the reins. While the wagon creaked off, the three older boys ran and hoisted themselves to sit on the open tailgate.

"Where's Petar?" asked Ingeborg.

"Oh, that nephew of mine, he's sparkin' a gal west of us. When we said we was takin' today off, he said he'd rather go visit with her. Cain't understand it myself." Joseph spit a glob of tobacco juice off to the right. He chuckled at his own joke. "Must be spring, all right. All the world's got matin' on their minds."

"Joseph Remson Baard, how you talk," Agnes scolded. She glanced further behind and then nodded for the others to do the same. Penny and a cleaned-up Hjelmer were walking together, albeit four feet apart.

Ingeborg slanted a sideways glance at the man striding beside her. Was that what these buzzy feelings were all about whenever he was in the same room as she? Just spring? It was a good thing, because with him going back to the north woods, she'd probably never see him again.

Was it just spring? Haakan caught the glance Ingeborg sent him. The urge to take her hand in his made him falter in his stride. And he didn't want to stop with her hand. How would she feel in his arms?

Joseph began whistling a carefree sound that brought the same from the three boys on the wagon rear.

"You better check your sheep," Ingeborg called to her son. When she motioned to the flock grazing between the soddies, all could see their heads were raised, and they were watching something coming from the river.

"Metiz and Baptiste are coming." Thorliff leaped from the wagon. "Come on, let's go meet them."

The sheep grew more restless, shifting toward the wagon.

"Look! There's a wolf!" Hjelmer spun around and headed toward the soddy.

"Where are you going?" Ingeborg's voice carried, frightening the sheep even more.

"To get the rifle," Hjelmer yelled over his shoulder.

"No!"

Hjelmer stopped. He turned around.

"That's Wolf, Metiz' wolf. He won't hurt our sheep."

"He's a pet?" Hjelmer stared at her, then looked toward the wolf that had melted back into the trees.

"No . . . yes . . . not really." Ingeborg shook her head. "It's hard to explain, but I will tell you the stories later." She dropped her voice as Hjelmer caught up with the rest of the party. "Just don't be afraid of him. Once he knows you belong here, he will never bother you."

"That's mighty hard to believe," Hjelmer muttered under his breath, but Ingeborg heard him.

"You'll find there are many things that are hard to believe out here on the prairie, but that doesn't make them untrue."

"Are you all right? I heard shouting." Kaaren came out in the yard to meet them.

"As right as one can be when a huge gray wolf was about to attack the sheep." Hjelmer again muttered under his breath.

The look Ingeborg sent him said she'd heard and didn't appreciate his comments.

Agnes threw him a similar look as she picked one of the little ones out of the wagon and set her on the ground with a pat on the bottom. "Go play."

Haakan helped set the table in the shade of the soddy and put the chairs around it. In spite of the black flies, it would be cooler outside, especially in the shade with the wind blowing just enough to cool sweaty faces. From the look of him, Hjelmer could use a northerner.

When they were all gathered, the men picked up the chair Lars sat in and carried him outside. The women set out the food on the indoor table, and everyone dished up their plates and took them outside. The group divided as usual, with the men discussing crops and new farming methods while the women watched the little children and talked about things of the house and garden. Hjelmer and Penny sat off by themselves, and the four boys ate as fast as possible and took off to play by the sheep.

When the little ones wound down, they were put to sleep on the beds inside, and the conversation shifted to the neighbors and all the happenings around the area.

"What's this I hear about the railroad running a line through this area?" Haakan asked.

"Roald and me, we talked about if that ever were to happen," Joseph said. "I can see an elevator right near here where we can ship our grain from. You know they put up a water stop about every twenty miles."

"Roald dreamed of more than a water stop and grain elevator. He saw a town growing up right at that corner where we're going to build the school, where the cemetery is. He said one day we'd have a doctor out here, stores, a hotel. He had big dreams, he did." For a change it felt good to Ingeborg to be talking about Roald. He and Carl spent many an evening discussing their plans for the future. She looked up to see Haakan send a small nod her way.

"Ja, dat Roald, he some fine man," one of the other men added. "He and dat brother."

"I heard Polinski is pulling up stakes," Joseph said after stuffing a chaw of tobacco in his cheek.

"None too soon, far as I can tell." Ingeborg kept her voice low. "I'd sure like to buy up his homestead."

"Now, Joseph, you promised." Agnes raised both her voice and an eyebrow.

"I know, I know, but there's no harm in wishing."

"Ja, well, in your case, wishes too often come true between you and that bank manager."

"It would make a good home for Petar, should he up and decide to get hitched to the Johnson girl." He clasped his hands behind his head. "You gotta admit that."

"Then let him buy it."

Ingeborg listened to their arguing, but her mind played with another thought. *Wouldn't that make a fine addition to the Bjorklund lands?*

"How much land does he have?" Haakan leaned forward and rested his elbows on his knees.

"A full section. Worked the bare minimum, though. Ol' Abel, he weren't too much for breaking sod."

"Or anything else. He's the laziest—"

"Inge." Kaaren's gentle voice broke into Ingeborg's harsh words. *Forgiving is easier than forgetting, and I sometimes wonder if I've even begun to forgive that lowlife.* "Ja, I heard you." She looked over at her sister-in-law, whose pale face showed all the love and concern her gentle spirit shared. But as far as Ingeborg was concerned, it had been the Polinskis who caused Roald's death. She still struggled at times with the bitterness that had nearly driven her into the ground.

Agnes reached over and patted Ingeborg's hand, her touch reminding Inge of her mother's healing hands.

Ingeborg shook her head and sighed. "I will let it go again. I know Roald is in God's hand, and there is no better place to be."

"As is Carl and Gunny and baby Lizzie. Sometimes I miss them so, I feel like I am being ripped apart." Kaaren took Ingeborg's hand. "So much we have lost to this land." She blinked a couple of times and smiled. "But it has given us much, also." She smiled at Lars and back at Ingeborg. "We have much to be thankful for."

"Ja, I know." Ingeborg tuned back into the discussion between the men. Haakan was asking questions and Hjelmer and Penny had moved closer so they could join in.

"Do you know when he is leaving?" Haakan asked.

Joseph shook his head. "No telling with that feller. I know he's not working his fields, though, so he must plan on being gone before fall, else they won't have nothing to eat."

"They'll be begging at our doorstep again, that's what." Agnes had no more use for the man than Ingeborg did. "Anyone that treats his wife no better'n his mule don't deserve—"

"Now, Agnes." Joseph's eyebrows became a straight line.

"Sounds like a real fine piece of humanity." Haakan turned to Kaaren. "Say, is there any more of that plum pie? If I could get it before Joseph does, I'd call this a good day."

"Now, that ain't fair." Baard got to his feet. "If'n I get there first . . ."

"Gentlemen, gentlemen." Kaaren stood and waved them back.

"Me help." Metiz, who had been watching and as usual saying little, spoke up. She and Kaaren headed into the house and the discussion turned to other things.

Ingeborg shot Haakan a grateful look. She knew what he had done, broken the discussion before it got any hotter and in the most pleasant way.

They'd all settled back with more coffee and either pie or cookies when they heard Paws barking in the distance.

"That's his 'someone is coming bark,' " Ingeborg said after tilting her head to listen better.

"Mor, we have company," Thorliff yelled a moment later.

The wagon had followed the riverbank up from the south and now turned on the trail they had made from Ingeborg's soddy to the river. White canvas covered the hoops and horses pulled the wagon. A man on a horse rode alongside it. A cow bellered, to be answered by one of their own.

"Tell them to come over here," Ingeborg called to Thorliff. "They can water their stock and make camp by the barn." She turned to Kaaren and Lars. "If that's all right with you?"

"Of course." Kaaren headed for the kitchen. "I'll heat up the leftovers and the coffee. They are probably hungry by now and sick and tired of living in that wagon."

"Our first settlers this season." Ingeborg followed Kaaren into the soddy. "Do you think they will find land near here? What if they bought Polinskis?"

"I wouldn't mention that if I were you." Kaaren lifted the lids on the stove and stirred the coals before adding more wood.

"Why not?"

"If anyone is going to buy Abel out, I would like our men to have first chance at it."

"Our men?"

"You saw the light in Haakan's eyes. I say, just keep quiet about it and warn the others."

Ingeborg nodded. "I will."

"Paws, come here! Paws!" Thorliff came running to the men outside. "There's gonna be a dogfight if something isn't done. Paws, he don't like that dog with them new people."

"Paws!" Haakan could be heard trotting past the house.

Ingeborg went to the doorway and shaded her eyes. Paws and a big black dog were tiptoeing around each other, hackles raised and tails no longer wagging.

The man on the horse drove between them, shouting and waving a rope. Paws rolled head over heels and got to his feet, teeth still bared and ready to go at it again.

"Paws, come here, Paws." Ingeborg whistled and slapped her knees. "Come on, boy."

Since the black dog had slunk under the wagon, Paws turned and limped back to the soddy.

"He's hurt." Thorliff knelt beside his dog and examined him for cuts. He looked up at his mother. "That dog could have killed him. Paws was just protecting his home." Paws licked Thorliff's hand and thumped his tail.

Paws whimpered and lay on his side. Haakan knelt beside the boy and ran gentle hands over the caramel-colored fur, checking for broken bones. "I think it's just a bruise, son. He'll be okay in a few days." He rubbed the dog's ears and shoulder. Paws flinched but licked his hand. "Good dog."

Haakan stood and spoke close to Ingeborg's ear. "It wasn't the dog that hurt Paws but that horse. Man should be more careful with his animals."

Ingeborg nodded. She'd seen the same thing. She felt a tightening in her chest, the same way she'd felt when Roald set out and when Lars and Haakan had left for St. Andrew. She glanced up to see a shadow cross Metiz' face. Something wasn't right here.

The visitors stopped their wagon by the well. The man dismounted and began helping his wife down over the wagon wheel.

"Howdy," he said as Haakan and Ingeborg walked over to them.

"God dag." For some reason Ingeborg spoke in Norwegian.

"Oh, heaven above, you speak Norwegian, too." The woman switched to a broken Norwegian with ease. "Both of us come from good Norwegian stock, although we be second generation." The woman looked like a giant coming toward them. Nearly as tall as Haakan and with a girth that made two of Ingeborg, she strode across the dusty yard as if she owned it. "Now ain't that fine?" Her husband, not a small man by any means, looked to be only half her size until they joined together, both with their hands extended. "I'm Elmira Strand and this be my husband Oscar." She waved a hand and a horde of children flowed out of the wagon. How they had any room for supplies was beyond Ingeborg.

Mrs. Strand introduced them all, but the only name that stayed with a face in Ingeborg's mind was the eldest daughter. While she carried a young child when descending from the back of the wagon, she quickly handed the baby to her mother and smiled sweetly at a spot over Ingeborg's right shoulder. Mary Ruth looked more like a Jezebel, her knowing eyes roving the young man with a look that said, *You're mine.*

Ingeborg half turned to see flames rush up Hjelmer's neck and over his face.

Over his shoulder, she could also see Penny, who had enjoyed the attentions of Hjelmer all day. The look on her face promised rain showers ahead.

Ingeborg felt like ordering the newcomers out and on their way immediately, but her mother's good training in hospitality took over. "I am Ingeborg Bjorklund, and this is a cousin of my husband's family, Haakan Bjorklund. Why don't you let the boys"—she gestured to Thorliff and Knute—"water your stock. My sister Kaaren has food laid out for you. Come and join us. We are having a party of sorts."

"Well, now, ain't that nice." Mrs. Strand settled the child in her arms against her massive bosom. The child whimpered and drew back. "You have to forgive little Ansom, here. He ain't been feeling too good. Might have a heat rash or something. We come from the other side of Minneapolis looking for a new start. Ain't that right, Oscar?"

He nodded. Obviously, she was the talker in the family.

Ingeborg introduced them to the others, except for Metiz, who had disappeared. Once the newcomers were all seated and had filled their plates, Kaaren stopped at Mrs. Strand's shoulder. "Why don't I take the baby, and then you can enjoy your meal?"

"Why, that would be right neighborly"—Mrs. Strand handed the fussy child to Kaaren—"wouldn't it, Oscar?" Without waiting for his answering nod, she continued. "Perhaps a wet cloth on his face would feel good. Broke out in those spots just this morning, but he ain't too sick. Just feeling a mite puny."

When Ingeborg returned from taking Andrew to stay with Kaaren the next morning, she found the team of horses along with the mule all harnessed and tied to the corral. Haakan had yoked the oxen for the first part of the day and already left for the field. They alternated so one team could be resting while the others worked. Thorliff was out with the sheep. She checked on the soup simmering on the back of the stove, and after donning her britches, she clapped her straw hat on her head and tied the strings under her chin as she strode out to the barn.

Freedom. Freedom from the dimness of the soddy and freedom from washing and cooking. She glanced over at her garden spot. Perhaps they could take time out to plow that one day soon. She was torn between the fieldwork and planting the garden. It was a typical spring; everything needed doing at once.

She untied the horses, slapped the reins on their backs, and drove them toward the field where the disc waited. Meadowlarks sang and the jingle of the harness made its own melody. Bob and Bell nodded, snorting once in a while, as if to be part of the bur- geoning spring symphony. She could feel the pull of the team in her shoulders and the stretching of her legs to keep the pace.

"Ingeborg, what are you—" Hjelmer stared at her, trying not to look at her pant-encased legs. "You . . . that's not . . ." He stammered to a close, his cheeks bright red from the sun or the shock, she knew not which.

Oh, not again, I'm so tired of this. "Hjelmer, let's get one thing straight right now." Ingeborg hooked the reins to the metal ring high on Belle's rump. "Things are different here on the prairie. I know my wearing britches isn't considered proper, but you ought to try plowing in a skirt." He started to say something, but she raised a hand to shush him. "This is my land, and if I hadn't worked the soil, planted and harvested, we would have starved and perhaps lost our homestead. Now, which is more important, a woman in britches or the land?"

She waited for his answer. He looked everywhere but into her face.

"Well?"

"The land, but—"

"No buts. If you want to help us here and perhaps find land of your own, you'll have to put up with my britches and probably a good deal else."

He stole a peek out of the corner of his eye at Haakan who was just bringing the oxen even with them.

"Ja, Haakan too. We do what we have to do, Hjelmer. You'll understand that better some day down the road. It ain't always comfortable, but God willing, we'll keep the land and build good homes here for the children."

"There a problem here?" Haakan stopped the oxen and settled the plow blade by pushing down on the handles.

"No. I think not." Ingeborg shook her head. "Is there?" She looked to Hjelmer, who also shook his head. But instead of looking at her, he studied the toe of his boot as if it were the prettiest face west of the Mississippi.

"You ready to take the plow?" Haakan asked.

"Ja." The curt reply spoke volumes. Hjelmer traded places with Haakan and clucked the oxen forward. Immediately the handles bucked, and the plowshare rose out of the soil as if it had a life of its own.

"No. Keep it solid and point the blade down." Haakan paced beside him.

Hjelmer gripped the handles and wrestled the plow back into submission.

"Now, the oxen respond to voice commands. You heard me giving them. Gee is for—"

"I know."

"Now, don't fight it. Guide it."

"I am."

Haakan stopped, looked back at Ingeborg, and shook his head. "I'll leave you to it, then." He paused a moment as if waiting for an answer, and when none came, he returned to help Ingeborg hitch the three to the disc. "If he'd only listen."

"Ja, he'll learn. Near as I can tell, Bjorklund men have a stubborn streak sky wide and a hard time asking for help." She stood from hooking the last trace to the doubletree.

"Only the men?"

She glanced his way and grinned back when she could see he was teasing her. "It happens to the rest of us when we marry them." Her gaze snagged on his and wouldn't let go. Blue eyes looked directly into gray, both shaded by broad-brimmed hats that failed to dim the intensity.

Ingeborg's breath left her body. Taking another made her feel light-headed. Was it the air or the fact that her heart had accelerated to running speed? Her fingers tingled.

A horse stomping its hoof shattered the moment.

Ingeborg took in another deep breath and blinked. "Ja, well, I . . . we . . . ah . . ." She snatched the reins like they were lifelines and strode to the rear of the four-foot-wide row of sharpened steel discs. "Git-up there, Bob, Belle. Come on, Jack."

"I'll get Lars' team out."

"Fine."

She could feel his eyes drilling into her back and fought the urge to turn around. She looked up toward the trees bordering the Red River and made herself think of fishing, of hunting, of hauling water, of anything to keep her mind off the man behind her. In spite of the heavy rocks lashed to the edges of the disc to give it weight, it bounced on a thick clod of dirt, bringing her mind back to the task at hand.

What can we do to make it safe to ride the disc? What would add enough extra weight and make the job easier for the driver? With her mind engaged thusly, she forgot the man and thought only of discing and planting and the thrill of seeing a sheen of green cover the newly turned land when the grain sprouted and poked its way through the soil.

She passed Hjelmer and the oxen as she continued round and round the field. Soon her legs ached, her shoulders burned as if they'd been stung by a hive of bees, and her mouth felt as though she'd been chewing the dirt, not just discing it. When she glanced up at the sun to tell the time, it looked to have been stuck in place. She gritted her teeth and kept on going. After all the trouble over her working the fields, she wasn't about to back down now just because of a few aches and pains. It would take more than one day to get her strength back.

At noon she unhooked the traces, then hooked them to the rump ring and guided the horses toward the barn. She would love to ride one, but right now Belle's back looked high as a two-story building.

Neither said, "I told you so," but the look the two men exchanged said it for them. Ingeborg was too tired to care. They unharnessed and unyoked the teams, and after allowing a short drink, they hobbled the oxen and horses on the shorter grass between the houses. From there they walked on over to Kaaren's for dinner.

Ingeborg had forgotten she was wearing britches and had forgotten the Strands were still camped by Kaaren's barn, until she heard Mr. Strand call a greeting and Mrs. Strand suck in her breath loud enough to choke.

"Well, I never!" Her words exploded.

Ingeborg bit off the comment she was about to make to Haakan. She looked over to see the mountainous Mrs. Strand with her hands on her hips and a look of absolute horror on her pie-round face. She struggled for words, obviously an unusual occurrence for her. The woman settled with an "uff da" and clamped fists.

Haakan tipped the brim of his hat. "God dag to you, too, Mrs. Strand. Fine day, is it not?"

Ingeborg could swear he was laughing.

Hjelmer muttered a good day and walked faster, as if hoping he could leave the embarrassment of his sister-in-law behind.

Ingeborg slanted a look at Haakan, expecting maybe to see his brows lowering and his eyes flashing—with what? Anger, resentment, astonishment? *Well, too bad for him, I—* She looked again. She'd been right before. He *was* laughing and fighting hard to keep it from showing. *Bless the man.* She could feel the warmth curl in her stomach like a kitten contented from being stroked.

"I have a favor to ask, Haakan," Lars said after they'd all chuckled quietly so the Strand's wouldn't hear about the britches incident. Only Hjelmer had failed to see the humor in it.

"What's that?" Haakan laid down his fork and looked at Lars.

"I need a crutch."

Haakan looked from Lars to Kaaren. When she nodded, he said, "So?"

"Could you bring me a sapling or a tree branch from the river that I can carve and smooth into a crutch? Needs to be tall enough to fit under my arm. I figure that by the time I have it smoothed down, my foot will be well enough to hobble around. I could at least do some of the barn chores."

"With all the pain you're still suffering from, you sure you're ready for this?"

"Ja, or I will be when the crutch is. If I have to look at the finished stick for a few days, that will make me want to heal even faster. I just thank God over and over for how good I'm doing." His voice caught on the last words.

"And Metiz agrees?"

"Metiz hasn't been back since she disappeared yesterday when the Strands drove in. Don't know what got into her."

I do, thought Ingeborg. *She smelled bigotry and ran before it bit her. Don't blame her at all.* She twisted her back, trying to work the kinks out. If she didn't get moving pretty soon, she'd have a hard time moving at all.

"You know, I been thinking," Haakan nodded as he spoke. He pointed to the bandages on Lars' foot, still swollen somewhat. "I think we should build you a special shoe that would protect your foot when you start moving around. You'll be a long time getting it into a regular boot."

"You thinking wood or iron?" Lars studied his foot.

"Hjelmer, what do you think?" Haakan nudged the young man next to him.

"I . . . ah . . . um . . ." Hjelmer blinked and swallowed what he'd been chewing. "I guess I was off woolgathering somewhere." At their knowing looks, the red crept up his neck.

"About us making a shoe for Lars to keep that foot from getting bumped."

Leaving the men to their discussion and to keep herself from falling asleep at the table, Ingeborg leaned forward, lifted Andrew down from his chair, and cuddled him on her lap.

"Mor's den lille gutten?" She kissed his fair hair.

"Mor, down." Andrew tried to slide out from under her arms.

She let him go and looked across the table at Kaaren. "I can tell he misses me."

"He's gotten to be a busy one, he has. On the go from the moment you brought him." She watched the little fellow go to the door.

"Tor!" Andrew called. "TOR!"

"Thorliff is out with the sheep." Ingeborg turned in her chair to keep an eye on him.

"Me go." Andrew stepped over the door sill, clutching the frame with one hand.

"No. You stay here." Ingeborg rose from her chair, squelching a groan in the process, and snatched up her son. Tickling his tummy brought out the belly laugh that made them all smile. The child twisted in her arms.

"See Tor."

"See Andrew." She nibbled on the finger he thrust toward her mouth. He giggled again.

"He is such a good baby." Kaaren finished pouring another round of coffee. "But he sure misses Thorliff. If I've heard 'see Tor' once today, I've heard it a hundred times."

"Stubborn little fellow, aren't you?" Haakan gently poked Andrew in the side, causing more giggles. Turning back to Lars, he said, "How about if I cut you a branch tonight after the plowing. I'll quit early enough to go look for a prime one."

"Thanks. When I can hobble better, maybe I'll even be able to go do some fishing. Or I could watch the sheep while Thorliff and Baptiste fish." He ran his fingers through his hair, standing it upright. "I feel so terribly useless."

"I'll bring you some harness to mend. That ought to keep you busy." Haakan pushed back from the table. "Takk for matten."

"Velbekomme." Kaaren answered with a smile.

When their meal finished, the men and Ingeborg trooped out the door to ringing cries of "me go, Mor, me go." She didn't even glance over her shoulder, knowing that doing so would only make Andrew yell more.

"Let's yoke Lars' oxen to the disc since they're fresh. Hjelmer, why don't you take the team I had—they didn't put in a full stint— and I'll take your oxen, Ingeborg. That leaves Bob and Belle to rest. We can use them this evening to plow the garden."

Ingeborg flashed him an astonished look. She'd not mentioned the garden. How had he known her desire to work there? Or was he just trying to keep her out of the fields? The latter thought drove out the joy of the former. Why was she so suspicious?

When she collapsed in bed that night, her entire body ached. Her hands, in spite of her leather gloves, felt as raw as if she'd laid them flat on a hot stove. She thought back to the days, weeks, and months of fighting the plow handles. And breaking sod was much harder than plowing an already harvested field. How on earth had she done it all? *Better enjoy the help while you can, woman*, she.

thought. *When Haakan leaves, it'll all be back on your shoulders. Lars will have enough to do of his own. Unless of course, Hjelmer stays.* Right now, that was scant comfort. He'd looked to be in nearly as bad a shape as she was. Neither one of them had done such hard labor for too long a time.

She thought, too, about the plowshares that had been pounded out and resharpened after the fieldwork was done. Haakan and Hjelmer had worked together at the forge, but Hjelmer was clearly the better blacksmith. From the look on his face, one could tell the young man really enjoyed working the iron and the fire.

"Thank you, Father, for all we got done today and for the perfect weather you are sending our way. Thank you that Lars is doing so well. You worked a mighty miracle there." She forced herself to get back out of bed so she could finish her prayers. Falling asleep was a bit more difficult when on one's knees. She also forced herself to pray for the Strand family. But when she bowed her head to listen to God, she caught herself just before she fell over. Sleep could come in any position if one was tired enough.

The same routine continued over the next few days. When Ingeborg caught up with the discing, she switched to seeding. She didn't need a team for that since she hand-broadcast the seed, so the animals got a bit of rest. Every afternoon, Mary Ruth Strand, with a wide-brimmed straw hat covering her fall of auburn hair and shading her pert nose, brought a water jug out to the field workers, ostensibly to be a good neighbor. But it was amazing how most of her time was spent with Hjelmer.

"You know, watching her sashay across those furrows makes me wonder . . ." Ingeborg clamped a lid on her words and thoughts. "Nobody's lips are that red naturally."

Kaaren looked up from the iron pot full of clothes she was stirring over the coals outside the soddy. Ingeborg had taken a day off from fieldwork and the two women were doing the laundry together. To keep the peace, Ingeborg had reverted to her skirts.

"Shh." Kaaren nodded toward the wagon still sitting beside the sod barn.

Ingeborg looked over her shoulder and groaned. Here came Mrs. Strand in full sail. "Whatever did I do to deserve this?" Her mutter was for Kaaren's ears alone.

"God dag." The woman's voice carried like a cow calling her calf. "I just came to thank you for allowing us to camp here."

"You are welcome," Kaaren answered in careful English.

This must mean they are leaving. Ingeborg hid her glee in the shirts she was wringing out to hang on the clothesline.

"Thank you, too, for that delicious cheese you sent over. I haven't had cheese like that in a month of Sundays. Our cow is so close to dry it's barely worth milking her." She paused. "I'd be willing to pay for some more of that cheese, if you have some."

"Oh no, we couldn't charge you." Kaaren wiped her hands on her apron. "I'll get you some right now so you can have it for dinner."

Ingeborg nearly choked. Far as she knew, Kaaren would be cutting into the last wheel. The next ones weren't all the way cured yet. Why didn't she just turn over the entire homestead?

"Your brother-in-law, that Hjelmer, seems to be a right fine young man." Mrs. Strand came close enough to Ingeborg to talk, but not too close, as if wearing britches and other manly pursuits that Ingeborg engaged in might be catching.

At least that was Ingeborg's thought.

"Ja, he is." Swish and dip, dip and swish and wring. Another shirt plopped into the basket for hanging.

"My Mary Ruth speaks quite highly of him."

"I'm sure she does."

"He mention anything about her? Like—"

"Here you are." Kaaren handed the woman a fat hunk of cheese. "And I brought you some potatoes, too. Thought they might be tasty."

"Why, glory be. Thank you so much. You sure I can't pay you, now?"

"Ja, that will—" Ingeborg began to speak, but Kaaren silenced her with a look.

"No, we don't charge our guests."

Ingeborg knew that statement was as much for her as for Mrs. Strand, but then Kaaren hadn't been on the receiving end of the lady's pointed remarks and withering looks.

Mary Ruth continued to bring a water jug across the fields every afternoon. Sometimes she made a midmorning trek also, acting such the good neighbor. Her green eyes sparkled up at Haakan, too, but most of her sparkle she reserved for Hjelmer. Ingeborg barely got a drink.

Sunday, Hjelmer asked if he could use Jack the mule.

"Of course," Ingeborg answered.

"I thought I'd go call on the Baards. Since Roald thought so much of them, I think I'd like to get to know them better."

Ingeborg blinked. Since when had Roald ever mentioned the Baards? Had he ever written a letter home? She thought hard. Maybe once, but she and Kaaren were the letter writers, as if that went along with being the wife.

"I'm glad to hear that. Agnes and Joseph are fine people and so is their niece Penny." Ingeborg couldn't resist the jibe.

Hjelmer's ears turned red, bright enough to see in the dim light of the soddy. "If there's nothing else you need me to do?"

"You could go fishing with me." Thorliff looked up from his mush.

"Maybe another day." Hjelmer pushed back from the table. "Takk for matten." He paused in his rush out the door. "I'll be back in time to do the chores for Lars."

Haakan looked after him. "I thought Miss Mary Ruth had—" He caught Ingeborg's cautioning glance at Thorliff. "Ah, yes. Well, how about if I go fishing with you, Thorliff? Would that be all right?"

"All right? You mean you'd go?" Thorliff gripped the edge of the table.

"If you want."

"Mor, too?" He swung his excited gaze to his mother.

"Ah, well, I—" She thought of the garden waiting for her. All morning she'd been thinking of the garden and planting her seeds, but the look on her son's face decided it. "Ja, I will go, too, and bring Andrew."

"But he's too little." The words burst out and immediately she could see he would like to snatch them back. He took in a deep breath and let it out. "Sorry, but he will have to learn to be quiet."

Ingeborg tousled Thorliff's hair. "If he isn't quiet, he and I will take a walk till the fish jump on your line."

"I'll get the worms." Thorliff leaped off his chair and out the door without touching the floor.

Ingeborg looked up to see Haakan staring at her, nodding slightly.

"What?"

"You are a good mother, Ingeborg Bjorklund."

"Mange takk." Their gaze remained locked.

"Mor, down!" Andrew broke the tension, his heels drumming on the chair.

Ingeborg leaned forward and untied the towel she had wrapped around the child's waist. She lifted him down, all without losing eye contact with the man sitting at the end of the table.

"I . . . I—" She slapped her hands on the table and rose. "I will pack a box for a picnic." She leaned out the door and said, "Thorliff, watch out for Andrew, he's coming after you."

"Ja, I will." The reply came from behind the barn where Ingeborg knew he was digging at the cool edge of the manure pile where the earthworms diligently mixed earth and manure to create a fine soil for raising little worms.

She stepped outside the door to watch Andrew head after his brother. Off to the side of the house, she could hear Hjelmer sloshing water at the wash bench, preparing for his visit to Agnes and Joseph. She smiled to herself. Did he really think they believed he would visit the parents instead of the young woman he'd shown such interest in?

The breeze fanned her warm face. Why was it every time she got in an eye duel with Haakan she had this inordinate need for fresh air? Was it because she forgot to breathe? Or because she wanted to go closer and knew such a move to be dangerous?

Her practical side took over. Dangerous for what? He was just a kinsman who had come to help out for the summer. When fall came, he would return to the north woods, and she most likely would never see him again. She would write his mother and tell her mange takk for encouraging her son to come help, and someday his mother would write and say her son had married, and—

She cut off the thought and laid a hand over her heart to still the tiny pain.

While Haakan finished up some chores of his own, she debated what to wear. The britches would be so much easier if she needed to cross logs or marshy places, depending upon where they fished. She reached for the grubby pants, hanging on the row of nails by the bed where she kept her few extra garments. She thought again of his gaze at the breakfast table, so blue, so deep, so . . . She left the britches where they hung, and untying the apron from around her waist, she picked up the basket with the food and started for the door.

The tiny bit of mirror she owned caught her eye. She stopped to take a peek. She checked her hair, tucked a few strands back in their proper place, made sure she had no smudges on her face, and sighed. What was the matter with her? It certainly wasn't necessary to pinch her cheeks to make them pink, the sun had done plenty of that already.

She sighed again. If creamy white skin, perfect hair, and soft hands were what drew a man's fancy, she failed on all accounts. And on top of that, she spoke her own mind. She could see her mor shaking her head and muttering prayers for the sake of her daughter. She'd seen it many times, too many to count. And at that point, she'd never in her life donned britches. If she only knew, poor Mor.

Ingeborg plunked her straw hat on her head and marched out the door. "Andrew, where are you?"

Her two boys had come around the corner of the barn by the time she reached the middle of the yard and was about to call again.

"See, Mor, worm." Andrew clutched a fat, wriggling one in three pudgy fingers. The worm squirmed and looped itself over his fingers, making the little boy squeal in delight.

"Don't let Andrew eat that." Ingeborg leaped forward and grabbed the worm just as it reached her son's mouth. "Thorliff, you know he puts everything in his mouth."

"I know."

"You know what?" Ingeborg stared at her elder son's face.

"I know he puts everything in his mouth." He made a gagging sound.

"He didn't." Ingeborg scooped up the grinning baby. "Andrew, did you eat a worm?"

"Worm." Andrew giggled. "Worm."

She pried his jaw open. Traces of dirt lingered at the corners of his smiling lips and a bit on his tongue. Ingeborg closed her eyes. He did. He ate the worm. She forced herself not to gag.

"I'm sorry, Mor. He ate it before I could grab him."

"Worm good." Andrew opened his mouth again.

"If this child lives to be five, it will be a miracle." She took him back in the house to wash his face, but when she tried to wash out his mouth, he only swallowed the water anyway, so she stopped. What good would washing his mouth do when he'd already swallowed a worm with all the dirt that went along with it?

"Oh, Lord, please remember your words about it's not what goes into the mouth that defiles a man but what comes out. Please protect this innocent child from what he has eaten." She put on a stern expression. "Andrew, worms are not to be eaten. Do not eat worms. You hear me?"

"Mor." His cheery face fell at the tone of her voice. His chin quivered, and he hung his head. "Worm."

"No worms."

A fat tear slithered down his cheek.

"Oh, Andrew, what am I to do with you?" Wiping the tear away, she hugged him close and, after closing the door behind her, made her way back to the picnic basket. Paws jumped back at her approach. He'd been sniffing the contents.

Thorliff and Haakan were nowhere to be seen. Hjelmer led the mule out of the corral and swung aboard. "Bye." He waved with one hand and tightened his hat down on his forehead with the other, then kicked the trotting mule into a lope westward across the prairie.

"Thorliff? Haakan?"

"Ja, in the barn." The two of them came out moments later, Thorliff carrying the worm can and Haakan with a bundle over his shoulder.

"How about I take the youngster, there?" Haakan reached out his arms and Andrew went right into them. With a smooth motion, Haakan swung the little boy up to sit on his shoulders. "Hang on, now." Andrew grabbed for a hold on the man's hair and knocked his hat to the dust. "Ouch." Haakan hung on to the child with one hand and retrieved his hat with the other. "Now listen, we got to work this out."

Andrew bounced up and down, shrieking his glee.

"Andrew, sit still." Ingeborg tried to keep her mouth straight but failed. When Andrew chortled his belly laugh, they all joined in. She took Haakan's hat and set it on the baby's head, covering him almost to his shoulders.

"Guess that won't work, either."

Andrew bounced again. "Go."

Thorliff backpedaled in front of them, waving his arms to make Andrew laugh again and bounce some more.

"Here." Ingeborg took the hat, set it atop her own, and strode out, picnic basket on her arm. Within two strides Haakan caught up to her.

"I'm glad you wore your abominable skirts."

Her cheeks instantly adopted the sunburned look and feel. He'd heard her call them that?

They returned in time for chores with two long strings of fish, a few mosquito bites, a baby asleep on Haakan's head, and a glow around Ingeborg's heart. Wasn't this what families were supposed to be like? She knew that this would be a memory to lighten the long dark days when the cold winds howled across the plains in winter.

Two days later, she walked into Kaaren's for dinner to find Thorliff sitting at the table already. His cut lip oozed a few drops of blood, one eye was swollen to the size of a double-yoked egg, and the other was barely open.

"Thorliff, what happened to you?" She dropped to her knees beside him and clutched him to her shoulder. "Who . . . what. . . ?" She looked up at Kaaren, frantic for an answer.

"Thorliff, tell me. What happened to you?" Ingeborg smoothed the hair back from his dirt-streaked forehead. Traces of blood smeared under his nose told her he'd had a nosebleed also.

He sniffed and tried to keep his head ducked so he couldn't see her.

"Kaaren?"

"I don't know. He wouldn't tell me." Kaaren brought a warm cloth and began washing the dirt and blood from his face.

A sharp rap on the door drew all their attention.

"Mrs. Bjorklund, I need to talk with you." The order in Mrs. Strand's voice brooked no argument.

"Come in, please." Kaaren opened the screen door and beckoned the woman inside.

"Your dog bit my son right on the back of his leg, and it is bleeding. Mind you, not just a nip but an out-and-out vicious attack." She clamped her arms over her humphing bosom, much like an army officer disciplining his troops. "What are you going to do about it?"

Ingeborg rose to her feet with one hand on Thorliff's shoulder. "Why, I don't know at the moment. Does your son need stitches to stop the bleeding?" She knew she was stalling for time, but something told her this was not all that it seemed to be. "Paws has never bitten anyone before."

She bent down and looked Thorliff in the face. "What do you know about this, son?"

Thorliff sniffed and flinched away when Kaaren touched his eye.

"What happened to your boy, there?"

"I don't know, but you can be sure I will find out." Falling over a tree or some such hadn't inflicted these battle scars on her son, but she had a good idea what did. Fists, that's what. She looked at the woman who stood there waiting as if it were her due.

"Mrs. Strand, we will tie our dog up for the moment."

"No. It wasn't Paws' fault. He was just protecting me." Thorliff finally found his voice.

"From what, son? Were there coyotes out there?"

Thorliff shook his head.

"Was Baptiste there?"

"He went home."

"Why? He usually spends the day with you."

Thorliff shook his head.

Ingeborg stood to her full height and squared her shoulders.

Mrs. Strand made a harrumphing sound at the sight of Ingeborg's britches.

"Excuse me, but I need to get to the bottom of this with my son. If you would be so kind." Ingeborg ushered the woman out before she realized what happened.

"I will be back."

"Oh, I'm sure you will," Ingeborg muttered under her breath. She looked from Kaaren to Lars, who both shrugged, and then back to Thorliff.

"All right, Thorliff, now I want the full story." Her tone said it all.

Thorliff looked up, and a tear welling under one swollen eyelid rolled down his bruised cheek. "I started it. The fight."

"A fight! Did you and Baptiste have a fight?"

"Oh no! Baptiste is my friend. It was those others." He swiped the back of his hand under his nose and came up with a bloody smear.

"Those others?" Ingeborg felt like she was one step off in a marching parade.

"Arnie and Bert Strand."

"Thorliff Bjorklund, I want the entire story right now. And don't leave anything out!"

Thorliff sniffed and began with a bit of a quaver. "I took the sheep down to the river to drink, like I always do, and Baptiste came over, like always. After they drank, we took them to the next patch of good grass. They don't like the real deep grass, so we let them graze, and Baptiste and I kind of knocked the tall stuff down."

Ingeborg nodded for him to continue.

"And then they came, just like the other day. Baptiste kinda faded into the woods like Metiz has taught him, 'cause the other day they were teasing him and being mean. They called Baptiste a . . ." He paused and sniffed again.

"Go on."

"A dirty Indian. Mor, he's not a dirty Indian! He's cleaner than they are. They wear dirty clothes and talk bad. So I . . . I jumped on Arnie and punched him hard."

"Good for you." Lars leaned forward in his chair. "You should have told us."

"And then what happened?" Ingeborg spoke softly, knowing if she raised her voice her fury would overflow and scare Thorliff more than he already was.

Thorliff shot Lars a look of gratitude, then looked back at his mother. "Bert jumped on my back, and we were rolling all around, and I kept trying to push them off of me, and then Paws bit him. He punched me one more time and went running back to their wagon. Paws didn't mean to hurt him, Mor. He was just protecting me."

"Oh yes, he did." Lars slammed his fist on the arm of the chair. "If I could get out there, I'd give them a lick or two myself."

"And, here, we've been helping them out!" Kaaren in full fury was a sight to behold. She headed for the door, rage turning her pale face to bright red.

"No! Kaaren, wait." Ingeborg leaped to her feet and went after Kaaren. "We need to hear the whole story first, and then we will decide."

"Now, Thorliff." Ingeborg took the chair facing her son again. "Why didn't you tell me this had been going on?"

"I . . . I wanted to take care of it myself. You are working so hard, and you said I'm a big boy, and you trusted me with the sheep, and . . ." His voice ran down, his shoulders slumped, and he hung his head.

"Hitting someone is always wrong. You know that." Ingeborg reminded him softly.

"Not when someone beats up your friend," Lars said with a snort. Kaaren laid a hand on his shoulder and tightened her grip.

"After all we have done for them." Kaaren shook her head again. "You know, children don't come up with things like this without first hearing it from a grown-up. If that's the way the mister and missus feel, I don't want them squatting on our land."

Surprise making the edges of her mouth twitch, Ingeborg looked up at the usually peaceable Kaaren. "Squatting? You invited them, remember?"

"Not if I'd known they could act like this."

Ingeborg remembered how Metiz disappeared the day the Strands drove up. "Has Metiz been back since they came?"

Kaaren and Lars shook their heads.

"I wish I hit them harder." Thorliff's lower lip stuck out to match the swollen upper one.

"What's going on?" Haakan and Hjelmer arrived at the same time.

By the time Ingeborg told them the story, a black thundercloud had settled on Haakan's brow. "I will go talk with Oscar. He's on his way in from the field now." He turned to answer the question before Lars could ask. "He came to me and asked if there was anything he could do to repay us for our generosity, so I sent him out to your far west field to plow. His team has had a good rest and about grazed off the entire center field here, so why not?"

"I was going to tell them to move on." Ingeborg sighed. She stroked the hair back again from Thorliff's forehead.

"They need to have a wheel tightened, as the rim is about to fall off. Oscar asked if I could help him do that." Hjelmer stood, turning his hat in his hands. "I told him I would, but maybe I shouldn't."

"I think it would be a good thing for you to do tomorrow. We have enough wood cut?" Haakan asked.

"I think so, but it will leave us tight."

"You could let him cut his own wood." On one hand Ingeborg appreciated the men discussing the arrangements, and on the other, she resented when they didn't include her in the conversation. *Don't be silly*, she chided herself. *Just be grateful you and Kaaren are no longer here alone*. The thought of Haakan being gone by the winter sent frost quivering up her back.

"But that would delay them one more day or even more." Haakan squatted down in front of Thorliff. "I had hoped they would be good friends for you, but I can see that I was wrong. You did good, boy, sticking up for your friend that way. But next time, think it through first so you can do them some real damage without getting beat up yourself."

"Haakan!" Ingeborg tried to look indignant.

"Just teaching him the lay of the land." Haakan turned to go outside. "Let's get washed up so we can eat. Those fields are waiting."

He stopped at the door. "Where are your sheep, boy?"

"In the corral at home."

"Good job, son, you did real well."

When the men returned from washing and sat down at the table, Kaaren served the meal without a word. Thorliff still sniffed once in a while, and Andrew kept reaching out, trying to touch his brother's swollen eye. "Tor, bad owie." Each time he said it, the little one shook his head, a doleful look on his face.

About the third repeat, Thorliff's fat-lipped mouth began to twitch. He looked at his mother, who was shaking her head and trying not to laugh.

"Poor Tor, bad owie." This time Andrew patted Thorliff's head.

Ingeborg looked at Haakan, who winked back at her. Lars let out a snort. Only Hjelmer continued to eat, seeming to be off in a land of his own.

"Poor . . ."

Ingeborg bit her lip, but it didn't do any good. She started to laugh. Thorliff looked at her and joined in. Kaaren hid her giggle behind her hands, but Lars and Haakan broke loose. Andrew looked at each laughing person as if trying to understand what the joke was. They laughed harder, so he joined in, his belly laugh making the others laugh still more. When Thorliff laughed, it hurt his lip, so he yipped an "ow."

Andrew sobered instantly. "Poor Tor—" He began again but cut it off when the others burst into another round of laughter. Banging his spoon on the table, he waved his other hand in the air.

"What's so funny?" asked Hjelmer, coming out of his daze.

Haakan shrugged. "Nothing I guess, if you didn't see or hear it." He lifted his cup. "Could I please have some more coffee."

Ingeborg jumped up to get it. If anyone had walked in on them, they would certainly have thought the Bjorklunds on the verge of lunacy. That laugh of Andrew's could make a stump smile.

"So what are we going to do about the bite on the boy's leg?" Kaaren asked, sipping her coffee.

"It won't be a problem after I talk with Oscar, I'm sure." Haakan pushed his chair back. "Lars, I have that hunk of wood you requested. You can start working on your crutch after dinner." He grabbed his hat off the peg on his way out. "Hjelmer, I'll meet you at the corral. Ingeborg, why don't you and Thorliff go work in the garden this afternoon. Better keep Paws with you. I don't like the look of that black beast of theirs."

The look he shot her kept Ingeborg in her seat. He was going to deal with the Strands. It really should be her place to speak to them, but instead she poured herself another cup of coffee. How come it felt so good and right to let him shoulder this responsibility? If she weren't careful, all her hard earned decision-making power might fall by the wayside.

Thorliff drank the last of his milk and started to go after Haakan.

"Wait right there, young man. We have some talking to do." Ingeborg pointed at his chair. The boy slid back in place. "Now, we've never had to talk about this because it's never come up before, but there are better ways of dealing with problems than trying to beat someone up."

"Yes, ma'am."

"When you get in an argument with one of the Baard boys, what do you do?"

"I don't never get in an argument with them. They are my friends."

"Well, why can't Arnie and Bert be your friends?"

" 'Cause they don't like me, and they called Baptiste a bad name. The Bible says to stick up for your friends."

Ingeborg shook her head. "Where?"

"In the David and Jonathan story. Saul was going to kill David, but David's friend Jonathan stopped him. And Saul was the king, besides being Jonathan's father."

"Ah, yes." Ingeborg paused, trying to think fast enough to get around this one. "But Jonathan didn't start to hit Saul, did he?"

"No, ma'am."

"Sometimes a well-delivered punch turns away wrath," Lars offered. Thorliff shot him a hopeful look.

"And sometimes it gets the stuffing beat out of you." Ingeborg glared at him. "Thorliff, you're good enough with words that you should be able to talk your way out of problems. I want you to try that in the future. Remember the Bible also says, 'A soft answer turneth away wrath.' "

It says, "Love thine enemies," too, a little voice inside accused her. Ingeborg tousled Thorliff's hair and stroked her hand down his cheek, feeling the swelling around his eye. Right now, love wasn't what she felt for those Strand terrors or for their mother, either.

Later, while she and her boys were marking rows and dropping in the precious seeds, she looked up to see Mary Ruth waltzing across the field with the water jug to give Hjelmer his afternoon sustenance. To her mind, they spent a mighty long time over the water jug. Then, when Hjelmer finally did hup the oxen into motion again, Mary Ruth strolled along right beside him.

And he's spending Sunday afternoons calling on Penny Sjornson. What's with that boy, playing two girls along like that? He's asking for trouble sure as shooting.

It took several more days before the Strands hitched up their wagon and were ready to head on west. The morning dawned with a cloud cover that looked like rain, but no one offered to let them stay longer.

Ingeborg was on her way out to the barn to check on the cow that was about to drop her calf when she heard two voices. She turned the sod corner in time to see Mary Ruth and Hjelmer in an embrace that brought the heat blazing up her throat. She ducked back before they saw her, but then, it would have taken a herd of buffalo to catch their attention, so engrossed were they in each other.

She had a string of names for the two of them that lasted about a mile long. *Don't matter to me what girl he marries or doesn't as the case may be.* She put her palms to her still sizzling cheeks. Why, no one had ever kissed her like that before the marriage bed, that was for certain. Her mor would have flayed the skin from her daughter's bones had she ever caught her in such a compromising situation. Only girls of low morals acted like that.

And, here, that was Roald's brother going right along with it. What was the matter with him? She felt the cow's distended bag and patted her with soothing words, words hard come by when she really wanted to lay into those two young people. Far as she knew, they were still there. She left the cow and stormed back to the soddy. Did trouble naturally follow that young man, or did he invite it?

She wrapped a loaf of bread in a cloth and added a large hunk of cheese. If they weren't so low on meat, she'd have included a venison haunch. All the while she wondered at what she was doing. Much as she disliked the woman, her daughter, and the two middle boys, it seemed to Ingeborg that Oscar Strand and the little ones shouldn't suffer want because of the others. Unless they headed into St. Andrew for supplies, it was a long way west before they'd run into another town. Had Haakan told them about Grafton to the southwest?

When Ingeborg and Andrew arrived at the wagon, Mary Ruth was just climbing in the tailgate, and Hjelmer was no where in sight.

"Here, I brought this for your dinner. Hope you find some land you are happy with." She handed the packet to Oscar, who smiled down at her.

"Mange takk for this and all you've done for us. You're good folks."

Mrs. Strand sniffed and turned to say something to her children. A smack, a cry, and with the reins slapping the horses' backs, they left.

"Good riddance," Kaaren said for Ingeborg's ears alone.

"I have a feeling we're going to see more of them, yet." Ingeborg stood clutching her elbows. Andrew pulled up a dandelion and held it up to her.

"Mor, pretty fowler."

"Yes, my son, it is, and so are you." She picked him up and hugged him to her. Was he hot? She felt his forehead. Sure enough, and was that a mosquito bite on his face? By midafternoon he was covered with spots and fussing, wanting only to be held in his mother's arms. Ingeborg remembered the spotty baby that had arrived when the Strands drove in. Mrs. Strand had said it was heat rash but Ingeborg now knew better. Was it measles or scarlet fever?

athing Andrew in cool water brought down his fever. Haakan
stood beside her, his presence a comfort in her fear. All the while
she bathed the little boy's hot spotted body, she prayed for God to
make him better and protect all the rest of them in case this was
something dangerous.

"You know, Ingeborg, when Strand's baby had it, the spots were
gone in a couple of days."

"You think I am overly concerned?" She wrung out the cloth and
laid it on Andrew's tummy.

"No, I am just trying to make you feel better." He nudged her
aside. "You go make supper, and I will do this."

Ingeborg raised her gaze to his. "You would do that?"

"Of course. Once he falls asleep, I will go do the chores. Thorliff
has already started them." Haakan dipped the cloth in the basin.
When he tickled Andrew's tummy, the baby smiled, but his eyes
drifted closed, only to open and whimper for his mother.

After Haakan and Hjelmer had gone to the barn for the night,
Ingeborg sat in the rocking chair holding the sleeping Andrew. Too
easily the memories returned of that terrible winter when cool
cloths were not enough to save Kaaren's two little girls nor Carl. A
tear meandered down Ingeborg's cheek, soon joined by another.
Gunny would be four years old now and Lizzie two, like Andrew.
What good friends these cousins would have been. *What do parents
do when they don't believe in our Heavenly Father and a place where
we will all be together again*, she wondered. *And the baby I lost, I will
see him or her, too. God must have a special place for those unborn
souls.*

She tucked Andrew into her bed and leaned over to kiss Thorliff's cheek.

"'Night, Mor," Thorliff whispered, not even opening his eyes.

"'Night, my son." She stroked his hair back. The swelling had diminished somewhat in the bad eye and gone away in the other. His bruises showed black-and-purple, edged in green splotches. Would that all his bruises in life healed so easily.

Andrew twitched restlessly beside her, whimpering in his sleep. She laid a hand on his belly to feel him burning with fever. With all her strength, Ingeborg fought against the demons of the year before. She picked the child up and rocked him against her shoulder while she poured more water in a basin. Sitting in the rocking chair, she stripped off his nightclothes and dipped and wrung the cloth to spread on him till it, too, was hot.

Trying to keep Gunny, Kaaren, and Carl alive had taken the same motions, the only difference being that no blizzard howled about the house this time.

"Dear Lord, please." She could barely mouth the words. They kept pace in the frantic corridors of her mind. *Gunny, Lizzie, Kaaren, and Carl so sick. Dear Lord, deliver us.*

With both hands she grabbed back her sanity from the marauding wolf of depression and whispered her verses over and over. "God is my strength and my fortress. I will rejoice in God my Savior." And finally, as the little body on her lap cooled, and the child slept comfortably, she whispered the name above all names. "Jesus, thank you. Jesus. Jesus. Amen."

Haakan found her and Andrew asleep in the chair. He took the baby from her arms.

"No!" Ingeborg clasped Andrew to her breast. But when she opened her eyes and saw it was Haakan, she blinked and stared around the room.

"I was just going to put him in the bed. Why didn't you call me? I would have helped you."

"I . . . I didn't think of it." She rubbed her gritty eyes with her fingertips. "Put him in my bed," she whispered. "I don't want Thorliff to catch whatever it is."

The next day while Andrew alternately slept, whimpered, and scratched, Ingeborg resolutely kept her mind from the still little bodies she had laid to rest that dreadful winter and kept up her litany of prayer and praise. The time spent rocking Andrew gave her needed rest and time to pray for all the others of the family. "Thank you, Jesus" said over and over brought a song to her heart and music to her lips. "Thank you, Jesus" could be set to all kinds of melodies.

Within two days Andrew was back to full speed and calling her to come see. Everything was exciting for him, and he wanted to share his finds with both Mor and Tante Kaaren. Keeping track of Andrew was becoming more and more of a chore.

"It must have been a kind of measles," Kaaren said. "Scarlet fever would have lasted longer."

"I know. I am just so grateful that was all of it."

On Sunday, Hjelmer again left to visit the Baards.

"Tell Agnes and Joseph hello for me," Ingeborg called as the young man trotted Jack out of the yard.

"Ja, I will."

"And Penny, too." Ingeborg couldn't resist the barb. To that she received no answer.

"I have an idea," she said to Lars and Haakan later as they leaned back in their chairs, full from a meal of fried fish, thanks to the efforts of Thorliff and Baptiste the day before.

"What's that?" Lars asked.

"What if we made a three-sided fence, kind of a cage or platform, and attached it to the frame of the disc. That way the person could ride, and the added weight would drive the disc deeper."

Haakan looked at her through squinted eyes that showed he was giving her idea consideration. He leaned back in his chair. "It could be dangerous."

"Not really. Falling backward in case of an accident or something wouldn't be so bad, depending on how hard the ground was. With a waist-high or even higher railing, you could make it double-barred for more safety. Seems to me the chances of one getting flipped over the front would be pretty slim. If the team bolted for some reason, you'd fall out the back, wouldn't you?"

"I can see you've given this some thought."

"Ja, I thought about a seat like the one on our mower, but one could get dumped easily that way."

"Speaking of which, we better get those teeth sharpened and the thing well oiled. The hay looks about ready to cut."

"Ja, and if ours is about ready, Joseph's must be ready now. His fields dry out faster." Lars polished a bowl he'd been carving for Kaaren.

Ingeborg started to interrupt but thought the better of it. She'd given them her idea, and now she would wait to see if something came of it. If she had her way, she'd be outside with the disc right now figuring how to make it work. But today was supposed to be a day of rest.

Later in the garden when she stooped to pull a handful of weeds, she could hear her mor's voice. "All the weeds you pull on Sunday will be double there on Monday." Ingeborg had never checked it out, but to be sure there were always more weeds every day. Her fingers itched to get the hoe and go at them.

Would hunting be considered work? No more than fishing, she decided. If Thorliff kept an eye on Andrew when he woke up from his nap, she could be at the game trail at dusk when the deer were going down for a drink.

She told Thorliff what she planned, and with Haakan still at Kaaren's talking to Lars, she slipped into her britches and left at a trot. One of these days, she would have to teach Thorliff to shoot the gun. While he kept them in rabbits with his snares and fish from the river, he had pleaded more than once to learn to shoot. So far, they hadn't dried any fish, just eaten all he caught.

Entering the woods that bordered the river was like stepping into another world. The leafy green bower shaded her from the hot sun now sinking toward its rest. Birds stopped their tweeping and twittering at her arrival but resumed as she walked on. Much of the underbrush had been cleared in their quest for firewood, so now slipping through the woods was much easier. The river sang its own song, more restful since the spring runoff was past. She watched the paddlewheel boat slosh its way downstream without hallooing it. The short stacks of wood Lars and Haakan cut had been purchased on one of the first runs. In other years the wood had gone a long way to paying for their supplies. Perhaps this winter Lars and Hjelmer would be able to cut enough again to make a difference.

Lars and Hjelmer. As she leaned against a rough-barked tree, she thought of the man who wielded an ax with such dexterity. If he were here to help through the winter, there'd be no end to the amount of wood to sell. She sighed. But he wouldn't be here, and there was no use wasting time dreaming about it. She pushed herself away from the comforting tree and made her way to the game trail, where she hunkered down in the brush behind a fallen tree they'd left there for this very purpose. Resting the rifle at the perfect angle, she settled down to wait.

Soon the birds began their music again, and the rustlings resumed in the underbrush. Ingeborg sat so still that a rabbit stopped not three feet away, and raising on its haunches, nose twitching, it inspected her carefully before hopping on about its business.

With the setting sun, the woods deepened to purple, and the whine of the mosquitoes about drowned out the evening calls of the other flying creatures. A bat darted about, scooping up the flying bugs. Out of the corner of her eye, she saw the buck stop and test the breeze. Two does followed him with their fawns—still wearing the spots of babyhood—at their sides.

Ingeborg gripped the butt of the rifle, snugging it into her shoulder and lining the sights on the head of the buck. She used to go for heart or neck shots because they were more sure, but no longer. None of the meat or hide was destroyed with a head shot. Lars would be pleased with the antlers, too.

He took another step and paused. One more step and she had him lined up perfectly. She squeezed the trigger. The woods exploded with crows screeching, the roar of the gun, and the does bounding away. The buck lay where he'd stood. She quickly leaped over the log, and with knife in one hand and rifle in the other, she crept up on the prostrate animal. When she nudged him with the toe of her boot, he didn't move, but she wasn't surprised. He'd been dead before he hit the ground. She cut the jugular so he could bleed out and looked around for some saplings to cut for poles to drag him on a travois. Metiz had shown her how to create such a handy cart without wheels.

"That was some shot." Haakan stepped from behind a giant oak.

"Oh!" Ingeborg put her hand over her heart. "You near frightened me to death. Why didn't you tell me you were here?"

"I'd have scared the deer away." He crouched beside her and shook his head in amazement. "You are an incredible shot. No wonder they let you do the hunting."

"Mange takk." Ingeborg slit the belly and carefully cut out the musk glands before gutting the animal. She tossed the intestines into the woods. "To feed the other creatures," she explained, keeping the heart and liver for their own meals.

"You want me to cut a pole? We can carry it together."

"If you'd like. I was about to make a travois." She wiped her knife blade off on some leaves and stuck it back in its sheath. She'd noticed he had his ax. He wore it like another arm and just as naturally.

Within minutes he'd cut a sapling and tied the feet of the deer to it with the vine of a creeper. They boosted the ends of the pole to their shoulders and started the half-mile trek for home. Ingeborg could feel the grin tip up the corners of her mouth. She couldn't stop it, but then she didn't try very hard. He'd come for her, come to help her bring home the deer.

He stopped, and she nearly stumbled at the jolt on her shoulder. He pointed off to the right and ahead of them. The gray wolf sat next to a tree, nearly invisible in the dusk.

"Don't worry, that's only Wolf." Ingeborg sucked in a deep breath. The pole had grown heavy and the stop brought relief. To think of all the times she'd dragged the game back by herself.

"How do you know?"

"What other wolf would sit there like that? They'd be gone long before we saw them, or there would be a pack and they'd attack. But with all the game available now, they'd never attack." She raised her voice. "I left the innards for you back there. If you hurry you can get them before anything else does." The wolf faded out of sight, silent as a shadow.

"Well, I'll be. He didn't understand you." Haakan looked at her over his shoulder. "Did he?"

"Who knows? But he usually shows up when I've shot a deer or elk. He hunts, but more important, he keeps the predators away from my sheep and my family. Metiz says it's because he has accepted us as part of his pack." She could feel his doubts as if they were fingers touching her arm. *So be it, he'll learn.*

The next morning Ingeborg had moved the table outside so she could cut the meat in thin slices for smoking. She already had the haunches soaking in salt water to be cured and smoked. Thorliff had a good bed of coals going and was stringing the meat on the drying racks as fast as his mother could slice it.

"Mor, come see." Andrew called from the front of the house. When she didn't respond, he called again, more urgently. "Mor, come."

"Andrew, I will in a minute. Right now I'm busy."

"Please."

Shaking her head at his wheedling, she left the knife on the table and followed his voice. He stood next to the wild rose bush Roald had planted two years earlier. Taking her hand, he pointed to a pink rose, petals opened flat and the golden center reflecting the sun. "See, pretty." He looked up at her. "Mor's fowler." He had some trouble getting all his sounds in the right order.

"Ja, den lille guten, that is Mor's flower." She picked him up so he could see it more closely. "Smell." She leaned forward to sniff the sweet fragrance. Andrew stuck his nose in the bloom and blew, knocking one of the petals off to float to the ground.

"Broken." The little boy struggled to get down. "Broken, Mor."

"No, it's not broken." She picked up the petal and held it to his nose. "See? It smells good. Sniff." He blew again and giggled at her chuckle.

"He don't sniff good, does he?" Thorliff joined them. "See, Andy, sniff like this." Kneeling in front of the child, Thorliff made an exaggerated sniffing motion.

Andrew blew a spray of drops all over his brother's face.

Thorliff wiped his face and shook his head. "He don't get it, Mor."

"Well, that's okay. He sure has the idea of pretty fowlers down pat."

"Pretty fowlers, pretty fowlers." Andrew stuck his finger in Thorliff's nose. "You pretty fowler."

"Now, you stay right here and don't go near the fire," Ingeborg reminded her youngest child. "Go get your digger and you can dig by the house in the shade." Andrew trundled off in search of the small shovel Lars had carved for him.

Paws leaped from his place in the shade and charged off across the field yipping and barking. Thorliff followed. "Onkel Lars! Mor, Onkel Lars is walking with his crutch."

Ingeborg followed her children around the corner of the house. "Land sakes, look at you. Are you"—she caught Kaaren's shushing motion—"ready for a cup of coffee?" She changed questions in midword.

"I'm ready to sit down, that's for certain sure." Lars collapsed on the bench that held the wash basin. "I never thought one-foot-hopping with a crutch was such a killer." He wiped his sweat streaked brow. "Takes some getting used to."

"He said if he didn't see some different scenery, he was going to go raving loco, but when I offered to hitch up the wagon . . ." Kaaren shook her head. "Men can be so stubborn."

"I made it, didn't I?"

"Ja, that you did."

Ingeborg left the two of them to their discussion and the loving attention of Thorliff and Andrew and danced inside to add kindling to the stove so it would heat the coffee more quickly. Lars was navigating on his own again, thank the good Lord above for His tender mercies.

That night Haakan and Hjelmer brought the shoe they'd fashioned over to Lars. They'd attached leather straps to a wooden sole and cushioned the upper part of the sole with sheepskin.

"Try that and see how it works." Haakan and Hjelmer exchanged looks of foreboding.

"If it don't work, we can do better." Hjelmer knelt down to help Lars with the leather thongs that laced the straps together.

When Lars put his crutch under his arm and stood, he looked down at the shod foot. "Well, you two came up with a good thing, that is for sure." He took a step forward and put his injured foot to the ground. He flinched, but a grin spread across his face. "It works."

"I'm thinking that if I curve some thin metal and nail it around the front, it would protect your foot even more." Hjelmer continued to study the movement of the foot in the new shoe. "Keep you from bumping it."

Haakan nodded. "You got a good idea there. Lars, give us back the shoe."

"Not on your life, you might mess it up." He pretended to face them off with his crutch.

"Lars." Kaaren scolded him, the smile on her thin face belying any words of censure.

The next evening he handed the shoe back with a sheepish grin. "When I dropped that chunk of wood on it today, I thought I was going to die. Go ahead and add the roof on it with my blessing."

When the field hands came in at noon, Metiz was inspecting the finished shoe. "That be good." She nodded and smiled up at Lars. "You take easy some."

"Thanks to you," Lars said.

"Took more than me . . . us." She gestured to the others and glanced upward. "Him . . . He heal."

"Amen to that." Kaaren laid a hand on Lars' shoulder. "Metiz, won't you please join us for dinner? I've set an extra plate."

Ingeborg looked up to see Hjelmer wince, but he covered it instantly. He was learning.

❧ ❧

With the grain sprouting a veil of green over the land, the families turned to haying. They started mowing at the Baards, and with the sulky mower, they kept going from dawn till dark, switching teams and drivers. As soon as the moon rose, they set out again.

Then, while Joseph's grass dried, they cut the Bjorklund fields.

"Well, I never." Agnes shook her head in amazement. "To think all that hay is down and ready to rake, and I ain't had to lift a finger."

"You think cooking for all these hungry mouths ain't lifting a finger?" Ingeborg bent down to pick up Andrew.

"Sure beats cooking, raking, and stacking too, don't it?"

Ingeborg watched as Penny took a jug of water out to the men. She and Hjelmer managed to be together more often than not. It seemed a rerun of what she'd seen before, but she kept that to herself. Of the two, Penny Sjornson or Mary Ruth Strand, the one crossing the field now was far and above her favorite.

"I think we should invest in a sulky plow or two, along with another mower and rake," Joseph said, as if he were continuing a discussion started earlier. They'd gathered around the tables for dinner, and if she hadn't been pouring coffee just then, Ingeborg might have missed his comment.

"I thought you wanted a threshing machine next?" She set the pot down between Haakan and Joseph.

"That, too." Joseph grinned up at her, the line between white skin and tanned visible on his forehead with his hat tipped back.

"Just how are we supposed to pay for all this machinery? My egg money can't carry it all."

"The bank will extend our loans, or the machinery companies will carry a loan. They want to sell that newfangled stuff pretty bad."

"Joseph, you know how I feel about borrowing more money."

"Lars thinks it's a good idea."

"So do I." Haakan lifted his cup for her to fill.

But it's not your money, she wanted to say. *You'll be gone, and I'll be left holding the loan papers.*

"I think we should do it, too." Hjelmer looked back from grinning up at Penny, who had just given him another helping of pie. "Look at how much we've gotten done in such little time. Why, another two weeks and we'll be finished. I've never seen hay put up so fast."

"Ja, well, we don't have to decide today."

"Ingeborg," Joseph said as they were about to head back to the field. "How about you drive the mower for a while? I know you been dying to."

"Don't worry, you old fox, I've driven it before, and I like it as well as you do."

"Sure has been easy on the arms compared to that old scythe."

"I know, I know. Please, let me think about it some more. If I could, I'd buy ten plows and do like the Bonanza farmers and string 'em out wheel-to-wheel like beads on a necklace. That sod would all be busted by the end of this season that way."

Feeling almost unneeded with the haying going so smoothly, Ingeborg started butchering chickens one morning at sunrise, and by midmorning, she had the wagon loaded with cheeses, eggs packed between layers of straw, butter formed in squares and in molds with a leaf design on top, crocks of buttermilk, and chickens ready for the frying pan. She'd spread water-soaked quilts over the entire load and covered that with hides and straw to keep it all cool. Whatever they didn't want at the Bonanza farm, she knew Mrs. Mac-kenzie at The Mercantile would gladly take. But she'd never brought things back from the Bonanza farm yet.

"You want anything from St. Andrew?" she asked Kaaren when she dropped Andrew off for the day.

"Just bring back a letter from home," Kaaren answered. She drew a paper from her pocket. "And whatever you can get from this list."

Ingeborg took the paper with a smile and a shake of the head. "And here I was beginning to think you was pure noble." She slapped the reins over the horses' backs and set out for town. How nice it would have been to have Kaaren go along. They could have enjoyed the day off together. But she hated to leave Lars alone yet, and this way, supper would be ready for the men when they came home. She waved at Thorliff and Baptiste and their family of sheep. She would have breeding stock to sell this summer and fall as the settlers moving west continued to pass them by.

The flood of pioneers had slowed down some with the railroad gone north of them to the west. Those who could afford to take the train did so. The government was still giving out homesteads to those who would settle farther west, beyond the Red River Valley. She'd heard tell the land wasn't near as good out there. More rocks, for one thing, and less water.

The drive gave her plenty of time to think. She thought about buying more machinery, about going further into debt, about Polin-ski moving on and the possibility of buying up his homestead. She thought about the Strands and tried to wish them well, but com-mitting them to God's care was about as far as she could go. If the truth were to be told, and she had to 'fess up, most of her thoughts were about the man who'd walked into her life a little more than two months before and about how fast the time was flying until he would walk right on out again.

"The Bible says to let the day's own troubles be sufficient for the day." The horses flicked their ears back and forth to listen and check out the things ahead. "So, that's what I got to do. Rejoice, it says, and again rejoice." She tried to put the life of the day into her words, but the thought of Haakan leaving made it more than a mite difficult.

After crossing the river on the flat barge that served as a ferry, she clucked the horses up the small grade and broke out on the eastern plain of the Red River Valley. Bonanza farms lined both sides of the road, and about half a mile up, she turned to the right to the Franklin Farm. Every time she came, she had to fight the insidious worm of envy that wriggled into her heart. There were barns and sheds of sawed lumber, a two-story house painted white, an entire corral of horses, besides the ones already at work in the fields. Machine sheds accommodated machinery she'd never even heard of, and silos held extra grain until it could be shipped.

Farming Bonanza style seemed to not even dwell in the same world as homesteading.

Mrs. Carlson, the mother of the manager, came out the back door as soon as Ingeborg halted the horses. "Oh, Mrs. Bjorklund, I have been wondering about you and hoping you would return." With her white hair pulled back in a bun and her stiff black bombazine dress, she looked the lady of the manor to Ingeborg, and yet she always welcomed the guest like a long lost relative.

"I finally had both enough produce to bring you and the time to do so." Ingeborg wrapped the lines around the brake handle and climbed down from the wagon. "How have you been?"

The two women exchanged small talk as Ingeborg displayed her wares. Mrs. Carlson declared she hadn't had cheese like these since last fall from the Bjorklunds' final trip of the season.

Her son George strolled up to the wagon and tipped his hat to Ingeborg.

"Oh, George, can you get one of the men to load these things into the springhouse? Tell Cook we will be having fried chicken for supper. How many did you say you have here?" When Ingeborg told her fifteen, the woman nodded. "Good, that should feed everyone tonight."

George nodded to his mother. "I will." Then he turned to smile at their guest. "How are you? I hope this year has been better for you than last." Slender and not much taller than Ingeborg, George had an easy smile and brown eyes that about matched his hair. Both had golden highlights, more visible when he tipped his tan fedora back on his head. She'd heard rumors that he'd never been married, but not for want of available applicants, even sparse as women were in the valley.

"Ja, it has." Ingeborg looked around her. "You have made more improvements, I see."

"We painted this spring and built a new shed. Those new reapers can't take the weather like some of the other machinery."

"Surely you can come in for a cup of coffee and some cake." Mrs. Carlson waved toward the house.

"Please, don't say no. My mother doesn't have many women to visit with. She gets lonely out here." This last was meant for Ingeborg's ears alone.

"Ja, but I cannot stay long. It is a long trip home again." Ingeborg let him lead her toward the house, opening the door for her and ushering her in. Never before had he joined the women for coffee. He was always about the job of overseeing the many workers, the teams, and all the myriad details of running such a huge operation.

Mrs. Carlson returned from her library with a purse full of cash. "Now, how much do I owe you?" When Ingeborg named a sum, the woman counted it into her hand. "Are you sure that is enough? You bring us such good cheese and fresh eggs. I keep telling George we should have hens and milk cows of our own, but he insists he has no time for such. If it weren't for people like you, I swear we should starve."

"Now, Mother." George folded his lank form into the chair by the long oak table. He set his hat on the chair next to him and motioned the two women to sit.

"I will in a moment. Let me go tell Hannah—that's our maid—to serve." She bustled down the hall to the kitchen in the rear of the house.

Ingeborg forced her gaze to the man across from her, but she really wanted to admire the lovely furniture, the rugs, the pictures on the walls. Such wealth. Managing a Bonanza farm must be very lucrative.

"Mrs. Bjorklund, before my mother returns there is something I would like to ask you."

"Ja?"

He rubbed one finger over a knuckle on the other hand. "I . . .

ah . . . I know it has been some time now since your husband died, and I was wondering if . . . that is . . . could you . . . would you be willing to let me call on you?"

"Call on me?"

"Yes. Maybe we could go for a buggy ride, or—"

"Mr. Carlson, my farm is a far piece to go for a buggy ride."

"Ah, here we are." His mother took her seat at the table and pointed to the place in front of her for the maid to set the tray. "Thank you, Hannah. Now, Mrs. Bjorklund, I hope you enjoy this cake. I know your sister-in-law makes an egg cake that knows no parallel, but many visitors have told Cook how tasty this one is." She passed the rich spicy cake on a china plate to Ingeborg and followed it with a cup of coffee. Tiny purple violets trimmed both the plate and cup. "You take it black, if I remember?"

"Ja, mange takk. Ah, thank you." Ingeborg couldn't bring herself to look George in the face again. Did he mean he wanted to court her? Or was he planning to purchase more supplies from them at the farm? Why ever would he want to take her on a buggy ride?

The time passed swiftly, and knowing the distance home, Ingeborg refused a third cup of coffee and pushed back from the table. "Thank you for the cake and coffee. I must be going now. I will return in a few weeks when the next cheeses are ripe."

George and Mrs. Carlson rose, too. "Oh, I wish you could stay longer, my dear. I'm sure those boys of yours are about full grown by now. When you come next, please consider bringing them to visit. This house needs the sound of children's laughter." She took Ingeborg's hand in hers. "Now you take care of yourself and tell the other Mrs. Bjorklund hello for me. I hope she is happy in her new marriage."

"Oh, she is, and by late fall there will be another little Bjorklund living on our farm."

"That is such good news. She has been through so much, and you, too." By this time they'd reached the door, and while George escorted Ingeborg out, his mother stayed inside, waving from the door.

"Good-bye." Ingeborg turned again to wave. "Your mother is such a fine woman."

"My mother would like nothing more than for me to fill this house with small children. You heard her subtle hints."

"Subtle?" Ingeborg raised an eyebrow.

"About as subtle as a charging buffalo. But she means well." He helped her up into the wagon. "I can come calling, then?" He looked up at her, his brown eyes serious under the brim of his tan felt hat.

"I . . . I don't know. Let me think about that, please?"

He nodded and stepped back. "Until I see you again." He touched the brim of his hat and stood still while she drove the team out of the yard. When she looked back, he waved.

Now what have you gotten yourself into? Did she want him to come calling? He was a fine figure of a man, to be sure. But what did he see in her? The thought made her chuckle. Talk about a radish blooming in a rose garden. That's what she would be. She slapped the reins on the horses' backs. "Giddyup there, Belle, Bob. We've got a long way to go before dark."

She stopped at The Mercantile and got Kaaren's order and the things her own house needed as quickly as possible. Then tucking a precious letter in her pocket, Ingeborg headed for home. It would be dark or close to it by the time she got back.

The boys were already in bed when she entered the soddy after leaving off the supplies and the letter from home at Kaaren's. She'd read it herself on the way. Bridget had asked about Hjelmer, if he arrived yet or if they'd heard from him. Ingeborg hoped he felt guilty as sin for not writing in all this time.

"I'll go take care of the horses." Haakan met her at the door.

"Mange takk." She sighed when the musty smell of the dirt walls closed in around her. That lovely home across the river, with shiny tables and tall windows that let in all the light, made the soddy seem even smaller. She placed her hat on the peg reserved for it and her shawl next.

"Mor?"

"Ja, Thorliff, I am home."

"Did you see the surprise?"

"No." She crossed the room and bent over the bed. "What is it?"

"It's a surprise." He turned over and went back to sleep.

18

She discovered them in the morning. Nodding bluebells sur-rounded the base of the wild rose bush.

"Haakan dug them for you." Thorliff looked up to watch her face.

Ingeborg rolled her lips together and blinked back the moisture that gathered behind her eyes and at the back of her throat. She knelt down and touched one of the delicate blue blossoms with a trembling finger.

"He thought you might like them. He said I had to keep the rose bush, the bluebells, and the cottonwood tree you planted by the cor-ner of the house watered. Is it okay, Mor? Do you like them?"

"Oh, Thorliff, my son, I don't just like them, I love them and you too. I know you had something to do with this." She wrapped her arms around him and hugged him close.

"If you love them, why are you crying?"

"Because I'm so happy."

Thorliff put his hands flat on her cheeks and looked deep into her eyes. "Mor, sometimes you make no sense."

"Ah, Thorliff, sometimes beauty just makes me cry. Good things make me cry. It's all right." She pressed her hands over his. "It's okay."

Thorliff studied her intently. "You sure?"

"I'm sure." Ingeborg got to her feet. "Now, I hear Andrew waking up. Let's get him and have some breakfast."

"I need to take the sheep out." Thorliff danced in front of her.

"Ja, as soon as you're done eating." Ingeborg took one more look at her bluebells, then up to the blossoms on the rose bush. Such beauty at her doorstep, and both were gifts from two fine men. How rich her life. She sent the Father another thank-you when she picked Andrew up from where he knelt in the middle of the bed.

About the man who planted your bluebells, a voice inside seemed to ask. *Do you love him?*

Well of course, she could hear herself answer. *He is a relative, of course I love him.*

But is your love for him more than that for a relative? Aren't you in fact in love with him? That was a question she was not ready to answer or even admit to the possibility. After all, he was leaving in the fall. A gentle voice whispered, *He could always return in the spring.*

She finished pulling Andrew's dress over his head and tied him onto the chair for breakfast. If not tied, he slipped away, always determined to find Thorliff.

Thorliff took the other chair. He extended his hand, flat on the table and palm up for Andrew to play slap-and-get-grabbed. Every time the little one got his hand away in time, he let out his belly laugh that set the bluebells to ringing.

Ingeborg set thick slices of bread covered with heavy cream and dotted with choke cherry jelly in front of them. She tied a dish towel around Andrew's neck, cut the bread in small pieces, and handed him a spoon. Lately he'd been adamant that he should feed himself.

She turned away so she couldn't be appalled by the mess he made. She should have waited to dress him until he was done eating and she had stood him in the dishpan and washed him down. The sheep bleated from the corral by the barn, pleading to be let loose for their morning feed. Paws sat right by Andrew's chair so he could catch any spills before they decorated the hard-packed dirt floor.

Ingeborg listened to the boys' prattle with one ear while she quickly finished the morning chores, all the while listing in her mind the things that needed to be done that day. She needed to finish drying the venison, scrape the putrefying meat and tissue from the hide, and salt it down to remove the hair since this was spring and the coat was still blotchy with unshed spots. Once tanned, she would turn the hide into gloves, or—she paused and kept her smile carefully concealed. She would make a leather shirt for Thorliff, much like the one that Metiz had made for Baptiste. Wouldn't he be thrilled?

She turned to look, to truly look at the boy at the table. Suntanned skin and peeling shoulder tops told of the hours he spent outside without a shirt on. The freckles on his face ran together to form a darker bridge across his nose and cheeks, and now with his second teeth grown in, his smile looked different, too, like he still had some growing to do to catch up with his mouth. He'd outgrown his boots that thankfully lasted until he could go barefoot, and there wasn't a shirt in the house with long enough sleeves.

The next time she went to The Mercantile, she'd need to get him pants, but the boots would have to wait for Lars to make, or she would buy him a pair in the fall. She studied the baby beside him, also growing like the proverbial dandelion or the sunflowers that nodded by the trail to the Baard's house. He, too, would need boots in the fall and pants and shirts cut down from some of Thorliff's garments.

Too much to do. Always too much to do. What she really wanted was to continue plowing and breaking the sod that needed to decay over the summer. Instead, as soon as she and Andrew were ready, she would take him to Kaaren's and take the extra team over to the Baard's to help bring the hay in to stack by the barn. One or two more days, and they would start to stack here on their own fields. From the looks of the thick windrows, they would have plenty of hay, even if she bought more stock. And, if the rains fell right, they might get a second cutting.

"Bye, Mor." Thorliff had his hat on his head and his dinner of bread, cheese, and dried venison in a sack over his shoulder.

"Me go, Mor, me go." Andrew struggled against his bonds.

"You have enough for Baptiste, too?"

"Ja, and he brings some."

"I know. If you come home before we do, go on over to Kaaren's."

"I could start the chores." He shifted from foot to restless foot.

"Ja. Mange takk, Thorliff."

"Or I could go fishing." His eyes lit up.

"Fishing, me fishing." Andrew slammed his spoon down on the table.

"When you get big." Thorliff darted out the door, ignoring the wails of his little brother.

Hjelmer glared at her when she showed up in her britches.

I'd like to see you out here in skirts, you pompous young pup. Ingeborg restrained herself from commenting, but it wasn't easy. *Who does he think he is, anyway?* She'd seen the lowering looks he'd been directing at Haakan lately, too, especially whenever Haakan asked the younger man to do something. *If one wanted to dignify him with the title "man."* The thoughts made her want to go over and shake him.

Instead, she helped hitch the team to a wagon tongue and pulled the empty flat wagon back out in the field to be loaded again. The men had constructed wide, flat beds for the wagon frames, with a tall rack in front so the driver had something to brace against as the wagon filled. They had three wagons running so the men in the field were kept busy forking hay onto a wagon, while others at the barn forked hay from the wagon to a stack. The younger children did their part by tramping the hay down. The tighter it was packed, the less chance there was for spoilage.

"Hey, Ingeborg, welcome," Joseph called.

"Ja, thank you." Ingeborg waved at Penny, who though in skirts, drove the other team back to the barn. Ingeborg steered the team to the spot where the men leaned on their pitchforks taking a moment's breather. She wanted to leap off the wagon and throw her arms around Haakan in thanks for the bluebells. She wanted to feel his strong arms close around her and hear his heart beat beneath her cheek. She wanted to . . .

"Uff da," she muttered. Such thoughts. She could feel her cheeks flame, and it wasn't from the sun. Now she was almost embarrassed to look at him. But when he tossed up the first forkful, their eyes met. The warmth unfolded itself and stretched in her midsection, sending little tendrils of excitement clear to her fingertips.

"Thank you for my flowers."

"You are welcome. They reminded me of your eyes."

The warmth curled again and purred. "I . . . ah . . . giddyup, there." She stared straight ahead and flicked the reins for the horses to pick up the pace.

With the flat wagon bed covered with hay, Swen and Knute climbed aboard to begin the packing job.

"How come you didn't bring Thorliff? He would have fun with us." They tramped the hay down as they talked.

"He had to feed the sheep. You can all play tomorrow when you come to our house." Her mouth spoke with the boys, but her gaze followed the broad-shouldered man slightly ahead of the team who was filling his fork with hay. Again, in a smooth motion he swung his load up, twisted the fork, and dumped the hay on the lowest spot. Sweat darkened the back of his shirt, and sleeves rolled to the elbows revealed tanned arms.

She jerked herself back to the team. It was a good thing they knew what they were supposed to do, because her mind had certainly been off elsewhere—not far away, just following the man who noticed bluebells and saw them in her eyes.

When they stopped for dinner, she joined Agnes in the serving before sitting down to eat. Haakan moved over so a space opened beside him. Ingeborg stepped over the bench and sat down. When she looked up, Hjelmer sat directly across from her, his brows in a straight line that told her he was not pleased with her choice of seating, among other things. But when Penny sat next to him, the sun chased his angry furrows away, and the smile he gave the girl said more than a polite hello.

Ingeborg stifled her frustration with him and turned to smile at Haakan, pleased that he, too, had noted the younger man's infatuation with Penny. The twinkle in his eyes said it all. She dug into the food on her plate, grateful for the chance to sit down, for the food, and for the warmth of the shoulder so close to hers.

You're acting like a love-starved maiden, she scolded herself. *Remember, he is leaving in the fall.*

That night, back at Kaaren's for supper since they finished haying at the Baards' in time to come home and do their own chores first, Lars asked the blessing on the food. Afterward, he looked up to Ingeborg and Haakan. "I've been thinking. How about if we have a church service here at our house on Sunday. I know there's no preacher, but we can sing and pray and read the Scriptures without one."

"We could probably find someone to preach, too." Haakan looked at Kaaren. "Since you like to teach, you could do that."

Kaaren dropped her fork so it rang on the plate and tumbled to the floor. When she retrieved it, she stared at him, shaking her head. "But, Haakan, I am a woman. Women aren't pastors."

"Seems to me that out here on the prairie, we make do with what we got. You could find a passage or two of Scripture to read and then talk about them. Tell what they mean, a sort of reminder of how we should act. You could do that."

"Would she wear a white robe?" Thorliff asked. "She'd look like an angel."

"Why, Thorliff Bjorklund, how beautiful." Kaaren laid a hand on his shoulder. "I think you are going to be a writer or a poet someday. You so often say just the right words."

He ducked his head. "I want to write a book."

Ingeborg looked at him, shock causing her mouth to drop open.

"You are a farmer. This will be your farm, Thorliff."

"I know." He raised his deep blue gaze to meet hers. "But I like to write things, Mor."

Ingeborg turned to take the spoon Andrew was banging on her arm. "We'll see, son, we'll see."

That Sunday the Baards and two other families arrived before noon to take part in the service. Since the sun shone and a breeze blew, they met in the shade of the soddy, and soon everyone was seated on the grass Haakan had scythed short for them. Kaaren started the first hymn, her clear soprano winging its way across the prairie. Their voices raised in praise to the Heavenly Father as they went from hymn to hymn with different ones starting their favorite.

When the lull fell, Lars said, "Shall we pray? Father in heaven, we come before Thee without a church or a place of worship but knowing that Thou art here with us. Forgive us our trespasses as we confess them now before Thee."

A silence fell, and even the small children sat without squirming. With heads bowed, each one recounted their sins in the silence of their hearts. Someone sniffed, another blew his nose. A meadowlark soared above them, spilling a song of blessing on the people gathered reverently below.

Kaaren opened her Bible. "This is from the first letter of John, chapter one, verses nine and ten. 'If we confess our sins, he is faithful and just to forgive us our sins and to cleanse us from all unrighteousness. If we say that we have not sinned, we make him a liar and his word is not in us.'" She closed her Bible. "We who have no pastor are called to be pastors one of another. We can worship together, confess our sins, and learn God's Word. Even though we live so far apart and the years have been hard, we have no excuse not to worship together like this. God says for us to gather together, and we are following His orders. So, if any of you have a favorite verse, say so, and we will read it. God, himself, will preach to us through His Word."

Agnes asked for Psalm 139, and one of the neighboring men asked for the twenty-third Psalm. Kaaren read each section and then turned to the Sermon on the Mount. When she finished reading that, someone began humming "Oh, God, Our Help in Ages Past," and the entire group picked up the words. When they finished, Thorliff asked for the story of the boy Samuel.

When Kaaren finished reading, Lars cleared his throat after a moment of silence. "Let's close with prayer and then the benediction. 'Our father, who art in heaven . . .' " The voices joined together as young and old, male and female recited the Norwegian words memorized at their mothers' knees. At the "amen," Lars stood and raised his right hand. "The Lord bless thee and keep thee . . ." The age-old words floated across the gathering and settled as a mantle of peace on those assembled. ". . . And give thee His peace." The "amen" rang sure and true.

The children leaped to their feet and chased each other around the building. Mothers bustled to set up the food they'd brought, and the men grouped together to discuss the haying and the latest news.

Ingeborg stopped for a moment and looked over the joyous gathering. Such a far cry from last year at this time. So many changes, so much to be grateful for. Tears threatened to spill at the burst of thanksgiving that swelled up in her heart. "Thank you, Father," she whispered, snatching the bug that almost disappeared into Andrew's mouth.

"No, den lille guten. Bugs belong on the ground, not in your mouth." She picked up the child and hugged him to her breast. Right now, she felt like hugging the whole world.

"I think our service went real well," Lars said later that evening after everyone had left for home to do their chores. The Bjorklunds, except Hjelmer who had walked Penny home and not yet returned, were gathered at Kaaren's house.

"You did just fine, Kaaren." Haakan held up his coffee cup in salute.

"To think we will do this again next week at the Baards'." Kaaren leaned back in her chair. "We will truly have a church here one day, and I don't think it will be too long coming." She leaned forward to tousle Thorliff's hair. "And by the time you are ready for confirmation, we most likely will even have a pastor. Won't that be wonderful?"

"I guess." He looked up at his aunt. "When are we going to have school again?"

Kaaren looked from him to the two men and to Ingeborg. "We will have a schoolhouse for next winter, Thorliff, and this summer I will help you again. Forgive me for letting your lessons go. Every afternoon, after the sheep have grazed their fill, you and Baptiste can come over here, and we will start your lessons again."

Ingeborg took in a deep breath. How would Kaaren care for Andrew, cook for all of them, and manage studies for the boys as well? Keeping track of Andrew was problem enough when she was busy.

Was it time she hung up her britches and let the men do the field-work? At least for now? Lars would soon be able to join them. She rolled her lips together. It wasn't as if she hadn't enough to do at her own soddy. The garden was getting ahead of her, the weeds coming up like she'd liberated the plot from the sod just for them. There was washing to do, cleaning out the root cellar, cream to churn for butter, and milk to set for cheese. She stopped the listing right there before it overwhelmed her.

But she loved being out in the field, turning the sod, raking the hay. She looked up to see Haakan's gaze on her face. What was it she saw in his eyes, in the quirk of his mouth?

Decisions, decisions. So many decisions to make.

They finished the haying on Saturday. Three haystacks now stood guard beside the sod barns on both Bjorklund homesteads. After the Baards waved good-bye and headed home, the Bjorklunds finished their chores—Lars had now taken over the milking—and settled down with their second cups of coffee.

Ingeborg leaned her elbows on the table, the cup cradled between both hands. "I think we, or one of us, should go look for breeding stock, both for oxen and horses. We have three mares that could be bred, and a couple more cows would—"

"Would give us more milk to dispose of. You can't keep up with the cheese as it is." Kaaren held Andrew on her lap.

"Ja, that is true. We might need a larger cellar for storing ripening cheeses. But the offspring can be trained as oxen, and we can sell them. There are plenty of people heading to the western side of the territory, and they all need horses and oxen."

"Along with milk cows, sheep, pigs . . ." Lars added. He had his foot propped up on a stool topped with a pillow. Even with his specially designed shoe, his foot swelled, growing even more painful when he walked very much. Though he limped, he grew stronger day by day.

"If we fenced off some of the land for pasture, you could let them graze without hobbling. You'll need to do that for a larger herd." Haakan rocked the chair on its back legs.

"For the sheep too." Thorliff looked up from the book he was reading in the lamplight.

"Ja, although they take a lot of grazing room, more than we'd want to fence this first year."

Ingeborg lifted her gaze from studying the rim of the cup to

Haakan's face. Was he planning to stay, then? Had she heard right? He said 'we.'

"We could buy the barbed wire. We haven't enough trees to split for rails." Lars nodded. "I saw some pretty big pastures when I was out with the threshing machine. Everyone isn't as lucky to have a good herder like our Thorliff." He leaned forward and tousled the boy's hair.

Thorliff brushed it back off his forehead and grinned at his uncle. "Me and Baptiste."

"So, where would we go to find more stock?"

"And who would go?" Kaaren looked around the circle. "Who has time?"

All eyes looked at Ingeborg. She shook her head. "Not me. I think Lars should go."

"I'll be able to work in the fields soon."

"You could go to work out there Monday if we had a sulky plow. I think you're strong enough to push the foot pedals, and if not, we could arrange a pad on it or something."

"Buy a sulky plow now?" Ingeborg heard her voice squeak.

"You have enough produce to make a run to the Bonanza farm. You could order the sulky plow at The Mercantile at the same time, stable the team in St. Andrew, and catch the boat for Pembina to look for more cows and mares. Didn't you say that Roald bought the one team of oxen up there?"

"Ja, but I don't know where, and . . ." Ingeborg sputtered to a stop. Hadn't this been her dream, buying more stock and raising animals to sell? Then why was she hesitating? Did she know how to tell if an animal was sound? Of course. Could she drive a hard bargain? If needed. Did she want to go? No!

She looked up to see Hjelmer looking at her from under lowering eyebrows. "You have been very quiet," she said. "What do you think?"

"I think it is not a woman's place to do this. Buying livestock is a man's job."

Ingeborg was sorry she'd asked. Should they send him? She looked to Lars, who sat off to the side of Hjelmer and slightly behind. The slight shake of his head could have been a trick of the light. She watched without seeming to look at him, and he did so again.

Haakan rubbed his fingertip around the rim of the cup.

"Would anyone like more coffee?" Kaaren asked, getting to her feet and handing the nodding Andrew to Lars.

"I don't think we need to make the decision tonight, do we? Let's think about it."

"And pray about it," Kaaren added as she refilled Ingeborg's cup.

"Ja, that too. But even if we don't buy more stock right now, that plow would make a big difference."

Hjelmer strode ahead of them on the walk back to the other soddy. The rigid set of his shoulders shouted his resentment. Haakan carried the sleeping Andrew. A sickle moon hung in the west with a star dangling below the tip. The horizon still bore the lighter blue from the long set sun, and above them, the Milky Way spread its canopy of distant pinpricks of light.

Ingeborg drew in a deep breath and let it out on a sigh.

"Is there something wrong?" Haakan asked in a low voice.

"Just the not knowing exactly what to do." Ingeborg stuffed her hands in her pockets. "I'd like to depend more on Hjelmer, but . . ." She looked ahead to where Thorliff tried to match his uncle's long strides. Hjelmer paid the lad no attention.

"He is self-centered."

"Ja, and opinionated."

"That too." Haakan shifted the baby to his other arm.

"You want I should take him?" Ingeborg slowed her steps as they neared the house. Hjelmer headed straight to the barn and his bed.

"No, he is fine. Do you want to know what I think?"

Ingeborg stopped by the corner of the house. "Of course."

"I think you should go order the sulky plow. If it were my decision, and I had the money or was willing to borrow more, I would order two. Once your own sod was broken, you could let Hjelmer go break sod for others, thus bringing in some more cash."

"Would anyone have money for that?"

"Some do."

"Ja." Ingeborg nodded and rubbed her chin with a callused finger. "I will think about that."

The next morning they hurried to finish the chores and after breakfast harnessed the team for the drive to the Baards' house for church. Ingeborg wrapped the roasting pan that held two baked hens in a blanket to keep it warm and nestled the loaves of bread around it. A pot of beans that had been baking all night completed her contribution to the community meal. Hjelmer rode Jack so he wouldn't have to walk home later that night after spending the afternoon with Penny.

When Thorliff had pleaded to ride with him, Hjelmer had started to say no, but one look at Ingeborg changed his mind. Swinging the boy up behind him, the two rode off.

"Me ride. Me ride." Andrew sent his plea after them, but to no avail.

"Hush now. When you get bigger you can ride." Ingeborg sat him on her lap and got him giggling by playing the "what is this?" game. "What is this?" She poked him in the tummy. "And this?" She gently pinched his chin, then his cheek and pointed to his nose.

"Eye, Andrew, say eye." She touched the side of his right eye.

"Eye." He pointed to his nose. "Nose." He stretched up his hand and pointed to hers. "Nose." He turned to Haakan and reached as far as his arm would. "Nose?"

Haakan leaned sideways until Andrew could reach.

"Nose!" The little one shrieked and kicked his feet. His chuckle made Thorliff turn back to look to see what was happening.

"You are one smart little boy." Haakan grabbed a tiny foot and shook it. Andrew gurgled again.

"Nose. Eye."

"He'll probably tell everyone his new words," Ingeborg said, a loving smile curving her lips. "I can just hear him in the middle of prayer time. Eye, nose!"

"Eye, nose." Andrew laughed and kicked his feet again.

If contentment were a piece of the sunshine, Ingeborg knew how it felt. Just like now. They stopped their horses by the sod barn at the Baards' and tied the team to the wagon wheels. Haakan removed the harnesses and hooked the bridles over the hams before pouring a measure of oats for each of the team. Then he helped Ingeborg get out the food.

"You watch Andrew, now," she called to Thorliff, who made a face but did as bid. "Just until we help Agnes get things set up."

They were all set to begin the service when another wagon drew up.

Ingeborg groaned. "The Strands. Here comes trouble."

19

He's just asking for trouble. Haakan debated whether it was time for a little man-to-man talk with Hjelmer. The looks he constantly arrowed at Ingeborg were not only unnecessary but growing more unkind by the day. *I wonder what his problem is?* He thought some more, the jingle of the harness and clopping of trotting hooves providing the perfect counterpoint for deep thinking.

It had been bothering him for some time.

Ingeborg had been nothing but gracious, treating the boy with the same loving concern she treated everyone. Was the issue of her wearing britches the root of it? He could feel an inward chuckle. You had to admit the woman had spunk. He slanted a glance sideways to where she sat, properly attired since this was Sunday and they were meeting with the neighbors. She was quietly playing with Andrew, who could draw a smile from the soberest face.

Except from Hjelmer.

Haakan had watched the boy-man—Haakan was never sure which he was—fight against enjoying the little one. He usually left the house in the evening as soon as supper was finished. Granted he worked hard like the rest of them. One couldn't fault him for that.

Andrew's chortle and Ingeborg's chuckle drew Haakan's attention again. He leaned over so Andrew could touch his nose. At the action and accompanying laugh, a lump big as a burl on a Minnesota pine tree clogged his throat.

Dear Lord, was this to be his family? When had he begun to fall in love with Ingeborg? With a love that made the feelings he'd had for Mrs. Landsverk seem like a seedling next to an aged giant. He'd seen it that night at Lars' bedside when they all prayed for God to heal the foot. He shuddered at the remembrance of Metiz so calmly removing the putrefying flesh.

He could never remember a time when he had felt Jesus right in the room with them, but it had been unmistakable. If that didn't turn one into a praying, believing man, no doubt nothing would.

If you'd prayed the night of the blizzard, the frostbite might never have happened. That sly voice had been tormenting him lately. But leaving the God of his fathers on the shores of Norway had seemed a natural thing to do. After all, this was a new land with unbelievable opportunities, and he was young and strong and healthy—and dumb.

Haakan reached over and tickled Andrew's tummy. At the deep chortle, Haakan could feel the moisture threaten to overflow behind his eyes. Ach, how he loved these two boys. They'd reached right out with their child's hands and snagged his heart good.

What if Ingeborg wouldn't accept him? What if she didn't love him as he loved her? He thought he'd been reading the signs right, but about the time he'd get up the nerve to kiss her, she'd pull away or someone would interrupt. Would they ever have any time alone? Just the two of them?

He never tired of watching her, the way her smile lit the room, her laugh—oh, her laugh! Would that he could keep her laughing all the while. She needed more to laugh about in her life. It had been so hard.

Oh, Lord, help me bring joy to her heart and laughter to her lips. Let me be a father to these boys. Dear God, let her say yes. He could feel sweat trickling down his temple. *What if she says no?* He shook his head to clear away the abject terror at the thought of the rest of his life, spread before him like the pictures he'd seen of a desert, without Ingeborg.

Perhaps if he presented it like a business proposal, she would accept. The thought comforted him. He clucked the horses into a faster trot. Surely God would speak to him through the reading this morning. His mor always said that when you asked God for something, you should listen real hard to His Word, because that was how He answered.

Haakan knew, though, that wasn't the only way God spoke.

He heard a team coming up behind them and turned to see who it was. Lars sat on the bench seat, his ailing foot propped on the board in front of him where Kaaren had secured a quilt or some such for padding. But he was driving. The welcoming grin he tossed

Haakan brightened the day even further.

"Kaaren," Haakan called. "How about reading the 'this is the day' Psalm?"

"I planned on it," she called back. "I think we should open with that one every Sunday."

Haakan could feel the question in the steady gaze Ingeborg leveled at him. Soon, probably sooner than he was ready for, he would explain all.

Soon he would see her. Hjelmer felt like kicking the mule into a dead run. Penny would be waiting. Granted he couldn't do more than sit by her during the service, and then she would help serve the meal. But after the cleanup, they would elude the smaller children and walk across the prairie. Last Sunday they'd sat in the loose hay at the bottom of one of the stacks so carefully built by the haying crew and talked. And talked. Never had he been able to talk to anyone like he could with Penny. She made him feel like, like—

"Onkel Hjelmer, I'm about trotted out. Jack's got a backbone like a pole," Thorliff said, his voice jolting with the bounce of the mule.

"Sorry." Hjelmer pulled the mule back to a walk. Why had he let Thorliff ride with him, anyway? That was stupid.

Hjelmer retreated once again to his daydream. He'd told Penny of his dream of owning his own blacksmith shop and she'd shared hers about working in a store full of general merchandise like The Mercantile she'd seen only once. He wondered sometimes how he could break land for his own farm and run a blacksmith, too. Perhaps he'd have a livery with it. That way he could have a shiny black surrey with red wheels and a team of matched bays that would never see a lick of fieldwork. He'd even braid their manes like a pair he'd seen trotting on the streets of New York. When he rented that rig out, people would come for more.

He squeezed his knees, and Jack broke into a lope when they neared the Baard homestead. Other wagons were already there. One he didn't recognize, and he saw a couple others coming across the prairie.

Thorliff swung to the ground. "Mange takk." He stopped. "Thank you for letting me ride." All of them were trying to remember to use American words rather than Norwegian. It wasn't easy, so sometimes their sentences were a jumble of both kinds.

"You're welcome." Hjelmer didn't look at the boy. He was too busy searching the gathering for a glimpse of Penny. He'd even thought one night when sleep wouldn't come that maybe he should go to Grand Forks and find a poker game. That was a quick way to raise some money. Unless he had some prospects, Joseph wouldn't look kindly on a marriage proposal for his niece.

Ah, there she was. Their eyes met across the intervening space. Hjelmer could feel his heart leap. Yes, Penny, she was the one. He could see the blush pinking her cheeks clear from where he stood. The look she sent him as she turned to answer a question made his blood pound.

✦ ✦

Haakan stopped the wagon next to the young man and followed his gaze to see the silent interchange. Just as he'd thought, Hjelmer was suffering the same pangs as he. Ah, spring fancies that turn to summer love. He stopped himself. He, Haakan Bjorklund, thinking poetry? He swung down from the wagon and, after lifting Andrew down to the ground, helped Ingeborg over the wagon wheel.

"Come help me unharness these beasts." He clapped Hjelmer on the shoulder. "She'll wait a few minutes more for you."

Hjelmer shot him a startled look.

"Come on, son," Haakan lowered his voice, "you think we haven't noticed? Don't get your back up, she's a wonderful girl, and you are a fine strapping Norwegian man. What more could a future uncle-in-law ask?"

"He could ask that the man have money or at least a livelihood to support his niece."

"Ah, that. You have a skill, several in fact." He swung the heavy harness off Belle's broad back. "You can go west and homestead."

"Ja, I've thought of that." Hjelmer leaned his hands on the wagon side. "But I would like to stay around here and open a blacksmith shop."

Haakan paused in tying Bob to the wagon wheel. "Would you now?" He nodded. "If you begin at a crossroads where the settlers can stop, you might have a good idea there."

"I thought by the schoolhouse. That is, when a schoolhouse is built."

"Have you mentioned this to Ingeborg?"

Hjelmer got that squared-jawed look that told anyone watching he'd either bit a sour lemon or someone said something he didn't like. "What would be the use?" He slapped his hands on the wagon sideboard and turned and strode off across the packed dirt toward the sod house.

Haakan stared after him. Whatever had rubbed a hot spot under his collar? He finished giving each of the horses and Jack the mule a measure of oats, and then with hands in his pockets, he strolled across to the gathering. Greeting the others, he kept an eye on Hjelmer. While his jaw had relaxed, he still kept as far from the remainder of the family as possible, being a bit more civil to Kaaren and Lars, but not much. It looked to be about time they took a certain young man to task. Perhaps that was a job for him and Lars. Maybe they could handle it without causing either of the women any further grief or concern.

He looked out to see another wagon nearing the farmstead and groaned when he recognized the woman sitting so upright beside the driver. The Strands. He'd heard they'd camped on another neighbor's land, seeming to be in no hurry to travel farther west or north to where homesteads were still available.

Another wagon, this one with a wheel that looked about to fall off, arrived from the north. Haakan glanced over to Ingeborg to see if she recognized the family. Sure as shooting, it had to be the Polinskis. While Ingeborg hadn't told him all the story of the Winter of Death as he'd heard it called, she'd mentioned the Polinskis. Her jaw had tightened at the name.

He caught the look of concern that Agnes shot Ingeborg and the way the woman edged closer to her friend. Kaaren, too, found her way to her sister-in-law's side. A hush fell over the group as Abel Polinski looped the reins around the broken brake handle and climbed to the ground. Instead of helping his wife down and removing the harness from his team, he left them and ambled toward the gathering. Mrs. Polinski climbed over the wheel. Her brood tumbled out the back of the wagon, and though she tried to straighten the hair of one girl and smooth the youngest's dress, it didn't do much for the look of them. They were a sorry lot indeed.

Joseph and Agnes welcomed the newcomers as they had all the others, only this time their greeting was more than a mite forced. "You know all the others here?" Joseph asked.

"Other'n those two over there, and by the look of them eyes, they must be Bjorklunds." Abel pointed to Haakan and then Hjelmer.

Joseph finished the introductions and called the meeting to order. Everyone began singing "Holy, Holy, Holy" as if their lives depended upon it.

Haakan felt a deep ripple go through his chest. He looked down at the woman beside him, her contralto voice carrying the alto line as if she had a hymnbook in front of her. She held Andrew on one hip and her other hand rested on Thorliff's shoulder. *Dear Lord, make this my family, please. Why else did you bring me out here. It certainly wasn't in my plans.* He laid his hand on Thorliff's other shoulder and joined in the next stanza.

By the time the service was over and dinner had been set out, it was obvious to everyone that Hjelmer had a problem. Mary Ruth Strand picked up real quick that Hjelmer and Penny Sjornson had eyes for each other, and she didn't like it one bit. Though she smiled sweetly and her trilling laugh could be heard frequently, all was not well.

Haakan caught the surreptitious glances between the adults and the gentle snickerings behind hands and handkerchiefs.

Polinski soon revealed the reason he'd driven this far to join the worship, and it wasn't because he longed to hear the Word and sing the hymns. "I just want to know if any of you here are interested in buying me out. I'm asking two dollars an acre, and I got half a section there with about twenty acres broke."

"Twenty?" Joseph asked. "Looks to me more like maybe ten and part of that ain't backset."

"Wa-ll there's a sod house on it, and that ought to be worth something, too. Dowser said there was water, but I ain't had time to dig me a well." Abel pushed a felt hat back on his head that looked like the dog had used it for a pillow. "It's good land, nary a rock on it, and we ain't too far from a crick."

"Is the crick on your land?" Haakan asked.

"Don't rightly think so, but since that section belongs to the gov'-ment fer schools, nobody never said I couldn't draw water from it. It went purty close to dry last summer, anyhows."

Haakan leaned close to Joseph's shoulder so only he could hear. "Seems a bit much for unbroken land."

Joseph gave a barely perceptible nod. "And the soddy ain't worth nothing but pulling down. The man never did put a weatherproof roof on it. Miracle they didn't all freeze to death last winter." He turned his head slightly toward Haakan. "I thought he had a full section so he had timber rights like the rest of us."

Haakan nodded. "I see."

"You thinkin' on it?"

Haakan nodded again. He looked up to see Ingeborg watching him with one eyebrow raised, curiosity rampant in her gaze.

"Better not wait too long. If'n he gets to the bank, they'll snap those homestead rights up in a minute and jack the price out of sight. I'd buy it if I didn't think I'd do better investing in more machinery right now. I bid on more land and Agnes is gonna make me sleep in the barn."

"Let me tell you, it's fine for a time, but come winter, I'd rather be back in a real bed."

"That so?" Joseph glanced over at Ingeborg and back at Haakan. He tipped his hat back. " 'Pears to me that spring has bit more'n just the young sprouts here."

"Just keep your 'pears' to yourself." Haakan slapped the man on the shoulder.

"Ja, well, let me give you some advice. You take good care of her or you got others to answer to. If'n I were you, I wouldn't want to get on the bad side of these women here. They might tear you limb from limb if you hurt our Ingeborg. She's seen hurt enough." He glanced over at the other men grouped together where a laugh had just erupted. "Let alone the men."

"You'll know soon enough if she accepts me." Haakan joined the others around the table, and they sang the grace together. After filling their plates, everyone found a place to sit and enjoyed the visit as well as the food.

After they were all done eating and Polinski was herding his brood back to the wagon, Haakan stopped him just before he slapped the lines over the sorry pair they called a team of horses. "How about if I come over tomorrow and look your place over?"

"Wa-ll now, that would be right fine, you know." Polinski shot a gob of tobacco over the wheel. "I'm right glad to know there is someone here who is interested. We'll be seein' ya, then."

"Are you serious?"

Haakan had been staring after the rickety rig and didn't hear Ingeborg come up.

"Yes, I am. Guess I've grown to like the flat prairie after all, much to my surprise. Of course, the people here might have something to do with that." He gave her a look fit to set the fires burning inside.

"You'd give up logging?"

"Yes and no. Yes, I wouldn't go back to the north woods unless I could do that in the winter to make some extra money. But I think

I would do better setting up a mill of my own. There's plenty of hardwood along the riverbanks, and if we cut and sawed that into lumber instead of just firewood, might be a pretty good cash crop."

"Sounds like you've given this some thought?"

"Guess you could say that, yes."

Ingeborg reached down and picked up Andrew, who was tugging at her skirts. "I wish you all the best." She turned at a call from Agnes. "Let me know when you are ready to leave for home."

Haakan strolled over to a group of men gathered by the corral.

"So, you heard any more about when the railroad is coming through?" asked one of the men.

Haakan shook his head. "Nor where. If you look at a map, a good line would be right through this area on the way to Drayton, if they go this way rather than straight north from Grafton and due east. Of course, they might skip Drayton, too."

"Who knows?" The fellow shook his head. He made more a statement than a question.

Haakan looked across the group to Oscar Strand, who had their attention and was asking about available land.

"There's that piece of Po—" Joseph gave the man a sharp jab to the ribs.

The man coughed, "Excuse me for a minute." He turned and spit, at the same time looking toward Joseph, who gave a brief shake of his head.

"What was that?" Strand asked.

"Oh, nothing."

Joseph turned the tide of the conversation to haying, which for most of the farmers was still in full swing. "You want my nephew, Petar, to come cut for you with our new mower? As you can see, all our hay and that of our partners, the Bjorklunds, is stacked and ready for winter."

Within minutes Petar had more work than he could manage.

Haakan looked over to where Hjelmer stood talking with Penny Sjornson and Mary Ruth Strand. If he'd had his head out of the clouds, he could have gotten some extra work, too. Sometimes joining in with the men was important.

So he will be going away. Ingeborg kept her thoughts veiled behind her eyes, attempting to appear perfectly normal. *And sooner than I dreamed—or feared. At least it isn't as far as the north woods, but I'll lose my help once again. Good thing Hjelmer will be here.* But the thought of having to depend on Roald's youngest brother didn't bring a leap of joy to her heart. Only Haakan did that. *Of course he wouldn't be so far away he couldn't come help in an emergency.* Her thoughts seemed to be having a discussion of their own. So much for having thought they might . . . they might . . . She took in a deep breath and swallowed the tears burning at the back of her throat.

There was no chance he could work both places. Cleaning up the Polinski mess would take more time than starting from scratch. She hiked Andrew farther up on her hip and leaned her head against the soft down of his hair. That was all right. She and her sons, they would make it. She wouldn't lose the land, and she'd do what was needed—herself.

"Thorliff!" She looked around for the group of boys who'd been running and playing all afternoon. "Thorliff, time to go home."

"I could come with Hjelmer." He came to a stop in front of her, blue eyes pleading for a few more moments of play, something he so rarely got to do.

"No, he might ride home after dark. You say good-bye to your friends and come now."

Thorliff did as asked and joined them in the wagon. Haakan clucked to the team and turned them in a wide circle to head east for home. The jingle of the harness, the clupf, clupf of the horses' hooves in the dust, Thorliff whistling and swinging his legs over the tailgate of the wagon—sounds emanated from everywhere but from the man and woman sitting on the plank seat. Ingeborg had laid Andrew down on the quilts in the back to continue his nap.

"So, what do you think of my taking over the Polinski place?" Haakan finally asked.

"Fine, I guess." She stared at the swaying rumps of the horses in front of her. Even to her own ears, her response sounded about as lukewarm as dishwater sitting all morning and about as appealing.

"Does that mean you like the idea or you don't?"

"I don't know." She tried to be flippant but knew she failed even as the words came from her mouth.

"Ingeborg, what is wrong?" The words dropped into the stillness.

"Nothing."

A bird tweeped and twittered on a thistle by the side of the trail. Another answered. A horse snorted. Thorliff continued to whistle.

"Ingeborg, I won't leave you to work again the way you have in the past. I just thought that if you would marry me, we could join the two pieces. I'm not going to homestead it, so I won't have to remain on the land. I'll buy the land outright—I think I have enough saved—or I will use some of that for machinery and take out a loan at the bank, like all the other respectable farmers around here." He waited for her answer, then glanced over to search her face. She kept her gaze straight ahead, chin lifted and shoulders rigid like she didn't dare move for fear she would crumble or crack. *Oh, Inge, my darling Inge. You don't have to bear it all alone anymore. I am here, and I won't leave you. Only if God calls me home will I leave.*

He continued to wait, the lines to the horses' bits easy in his hands.

A bolt shot through her at the word *marry. Marry! He wants to marry me. Haakan Bjorklund wants to marry me. How can I marry him? I don't love him.*

You don't? The gentle questioner prodded. *Are you sure?*

"But you don't love me," she finally blurted out.

"What makes you think I don't? You think I would stay around and work like I have been for just anyone?"

She stared at him with her mouth open. She hadn't thought along those lines. She was just grateful for all he did.

"The question is, do *you* love me? Or do you think you could learn to?" His voice came softly through the late afternoon stillness.

Ingeborg didn't say anything. She couldn't. The incredible joy that welled out when he said he loved her took her breath away. The thought of being alone again had been almost more than she could bear. But is that all she felt? Fear of being alone again? The thoughts ran through her mind as the silence lengthened. She glanced back to check on the children. Andrew still slept soundly in the back of the wagon, and Thorliff was now curled up sleeping on the quilt, also. Birds chirped and twittered in the weeds by the track, and the horses snorted and picked up the pace as they neared home.

"Well?"

"Yes."

"Yes, what?"

"Yes, I'll marry you."

"And?"

"Yes, I love you. The reason I hesitate to say it is because I feel so different this time than I did with Roald."

"That is good."

"That is good?" Ingeborg looked at him, wondering if she heard her right.

"That is good because I am a different man than Roald, and after all you've been through in the last years, you are a different woman.

Our love will be good and will only get better."

Ingeborg slipped her hand under his arm and laid her head on his shoulder. The air felt incredibly sweet and gentle, the shoulder under her ear strong and secure.

Haakan pulled the horses to a halt, and turning on the seat beside her, he grasped her chin with his fingers. He pulled her to him carefully, slowly, as if fearful of breaking the magic of the moment. When she faced him, he tipped his head and fitted his lips to hers. Her sigh of wonder melded their mouths together.

"I think we should be married soon," he whispered when he finally released her mouth.

"How soon is soon?" She leaned into him, resting her forehead against his chin.

"Next week."

"Next week!" Her eyes flew open, and she bolted upright.

Andrew whimpered from his bed in the quilts.

"Next week! Are you mad?"

20

Three days later, Haakan headed for Grand Forks to settle the deed for his property. The previous day he had spent hassling over the details with Polinski. When he finally convinced the man to accept a lower offer, he also had to volunteer to pay Abel's way to Grand Forks and back on the riverboat since he wanted the deal done quickly.

More than once he'd already regretted that decision. Abel Polinski only knew one tune, "poor me." Haakan wanted to stuff a rag in the man's mouth. Tossing the lazy brute overboard would have been doing his wife and young'uns a favor. Twice Haakan excused himself and made his way to another part of the noisy vessel, but each time Polinski found him and resumed his litany of despair.

By the time they'd been to the land office and finalized their deal, Haakan gave the man a brief handshake and left him in the middle of the street. Afraid to look over his shoulder in case Abel followed him, Haakan ducked into a men's clothing store and stood looking out the window. When the other man finally turned and ambled toward the river again, Haakan breathed a sigh of relief.

"Can I help you, sir?" a quiet voice behind him asked.

"Ah, no, no thank you. I'm . . . ah . . ." Haakan started for the door and then thought the better of it. He'd be getting married in just a few days. Wasn't a man entitled to a new suit for his wedding? "Ah, yes, I guess you can, if we can find something that you can have ready by morning when I catch the paddle boat back upstream. I'd like a new suit."

"And what color would you like?"

"Black."

"We have a navy blue one that would look very good on you."

The man looked over his spectacles. "I think I have one in that color that can be made to fit. Here, let me show it to you."

A few minutes later, Haakan stared at himself in the mirror. A spanking white shirt complemented a navy jacket with sleeves above his wrists and matching trousers with the same problem. "You can make these fit?"

"Surely, sir."

"Then I'll take them." Haakan stood patiently while the man measured his arm and leg lengths. After counting out what was getting close to the last of his money, he promised to return in the morning. Checking to see if Polinski was in sight, he stepped out the door when he saw the coast was clear. Now the bank.

With the deed in hand, getting a loan was easy. Haakan left that building and headed for the ladies' dress shop. If he got a new suit, Ingeborg needed a new dress. By the time he finished shopping, he had also purchased two sulky plows that would be loaded on the paddle-wheeler in the morning, three books for Thorliff, a red wagon for Andrew, a vise for Hjelmer, ten peppermint sticks, and a white enameled teakettle for Kaaren and Lars. Never in his life had he felt so wealthy. He now owned a half section of land, had money for the needed machinery, and if he had anything to say about it, he'd buy lumber for a new house for his intended the next time he came to town. He knew how much the darkness of the soddy oppressed Ingeborg, and he intended to remedy that situation as quickly as possible.

He fell asleep dreaming of her rocking in front of a sun-filled window, knitting the socks she turned out so neatly.

Just before boarding the next day, he found his final gift.

Lars had the raft ready when the riverboat reached the Bjorklund homestead. He poled out to the paddle boat and Haakan lowered a package to him before swinging down the ladder. The raft tipped a bit when he stepped onto it, and Lars shifted to redistribute the weight. They waved the captain on, and with the toot of the whistle, the swish and thump began again, and the boat continued downstream.

"So, how was it?" Lars asked.

"The land is mine." Haakan thumped his chest where the deed burned a hole in his breast pocket.

"What about Polinski?"

"I'm not sure. He wasn't on the boat." Haakan looked at Lars and groaned. "He wouldn't take the money and run out on his family, would he?"

"I have no idea." Lars poled them into the shore, then stepped onto land and tied off the raft. Together the two men climbed the low bank to the field above. "I've always thought the man a weasel but never dreamed he'd do something like this."

"We could be borrowing trouble."

"Let's hope so." Lars snagged the metal open toe of his boot on a clump of grass and winced.

"Still sore?" Haakan hefted his package up onto his shoulder.

"Some."

Haakan clapped him on the shoulder. "Well, I've got good news for you. You can go back to working in the fields as soon as someone makes a trip to St. Andrew."

"You bought the plow?"

"Two of them. We have a lot of sod to break. Everything I bought I shipped through to St. Andrew, so we need to make a trip up there to pick it up right away." As they neared the soddy, Paws charged out from around the barn, barking to warn the family that strangers were on the land. When he saw who it was, he lowered his tail and bellied out to them.

"Good dog. You just got to improve your eyesight, that's all." Haakan leaned over and stroked the caramel-colored muzzle. One white ear stood back up, and Paws leaped to his feet, rejoicing as if he was forgiven his gaffe.

Thorliff came around the corner of the soddy and catapulted himself into Haakan's surprised arms. The package he carried fell to the ground, but he ignored that and hugged the boy close.

"I thought you weren't coming back."

"I'll always come back, understand? Until the good Lord calls me home, I'll always come back. You hear me?"

"Ja, I hear, but my far didn't come back."

"I know. Do you still miss him?"

"Ja." Thorliff nodded. "But I can't see him so good anymore." He dug one grimy toe in the dirt. "Are you going to be my far?"

Haakan nodded. "Yes, I am. That okay with you?"

Blue eyes met blue. Thorliff nodded.

"You've done a fine job taking care of your mother since your far left, and now, if you don't mind, I'll take over some of that. Give you more time to go fishing."

"You come, too?"

"Sometimes."

Thorliff nodded again and a sigh escaped as if the load of responsibility had just sprung a leak and lightened with each passing moment. He glanced up at Haakan from the corner of his eye. "Good."

Haakan hugged the boy again and looked up to see the mother standing by the soddy.

He felt like the sun had just burst forth from behind heavy clouds, sun he hadn't seen for what seemed forever. If only he dared to fly to her like Thorliff had come to him. Or she would run to meet him. Instead, she stood waiting, her forehead wrinkled as if in doubt.

"What are you waiting for, woman?" He spread his arms and braced his feet.

She hesitated, then skirts aflying, she ran and threw herself at his chest. With both arms around his neck, she clasped him to her as if he might let go. When she raised her tear-stained face to his, he kissed her with all the warmth and passion he'd been storing since they met.

When she pulled away, she noticed Lars standing a few steps away, a grin on his face that said he'd probably tease her about this unseemly public display of affection for the rest of her natural life and beyond. She buried her face in Haakan's broad shirt front, the heat of the blush scorching his chest.

"Remind me to go away more often," Haakan whispered in her ear.

"I cannot believe I acted the hussy like that." She muttered the words into his third button.

"It's okay. Lars and Kaaren, they gave us their blessing, remember?"

"Ja, but—"

"But nothing. I am not so proud I cannot kiss my wife-to-be in front of our family. Now, I promise to behave in public, but Lars and that grinning son of yours are not the public." He dropped a kiss on the end of her nose and tucked her next to his side, an arm over her shoulders as if afraid she might step away.

He bent over and picked up the paper-wrapped package that had fallen to the dirt in Thorliff's onslaught. "I have a present here for you." He handed her the bundle. "Careful."

Ingeborg flinched when something stabbed her finger. "Ouch."

"I warned you."

"Ja, but not soon enough." She looked from him to the packet and back again.

"Open it, Mor. Open it!" Thorliff fairly danced beside her.

"Thorliff, run to the barn and get a shovel." Haakan took back the package Ingeborg hadn't begun to unwrap yet, and with his jackknife he cut the string.

"Oh, be careful, we need the string." Ingeborg reached for the thin twine, carefully stuffing it into her apron pocket. Then she assisted Haakan in unrolling the layers of paper around the gift.

"A rose bush." She looked from the wilted stalks to Haakan's grinning face.

"Ja, a white one. We will plant it on the other side of the doorway, and since this is a climbing variety, you will have an arch of roses over your door. The woman who sold it to me said they have the sweetest perfume."

Ingeborg stroked a wilted petal. "We will water it well to bring it back to life." She leaned her head against his shoulder to veil the tears that swelled at the thoughtful offering now cradled gently in her hands.

He turned his head and covered her lips with his. "Pure sweetness, like you," he whispered against her mouth. "But you must watch out for the thorns." He nipped her bottom lip gently.

Ingeborg's laugh rang out across the prairie, lifted by the wind and blessed by the sun.

"If you two are going to keep up such nonsense, I believe I'll take myself home where I am needed." Lars clapped Haakan on the shoulder. "Are we going to St. Andrew today or should we get an early start in the morning?"

Thorliff returned with the shovel. "Here."

Haakan took it. "Now, how about a bucket of water?"

"Okay." The boy headed for the well.

"Let's go tomorrow. I don't want to drive home in total darkness. There's not even a moon tonight. Remember what happened last time we tried to make a fast trip?"

Lars tipped up his open-toed boot. "I'm not likely to forget that. But it can't snow in July." He glanced at Ingeborg. "Can it?"

Ingeborg shrugged. If only they had listened to her last time— she stopped that train of thought. One couldn't change the past, that much she'd learned.

"Well, I'll be heading home. Ingeborg, you have some produce you want to send to The Mercantile in the morning?"

"I should take a load to the Bonanza farm. They've grown accustomed to regular deliveries." She thought of the hours she spent after the field chores, cutting the curd and draining it for cheese, then firming it and letting it ripen. And the pounds of butter churned in her wooden churn. How many dozen eggs did she have ready to send? And what could be pulled from the garden? The young hogs weren't ready yet, and while she had a couple of hens not laying, they would eat those themselves. She did have that haunch of smoked venison.

"Ja, I think there is enough to take to the Bonanza farm. I will have it ready."

"Would you rather go? You could pick up the plows and the other supplies on your way back." Haakan motioned Thorliff toward the corner of the house where the man began digging a hole for the rose bush.

What she really wanted was to go with Haakan, just the two of them, no children, no other family, just them.

Lars winked at her. "Why don't the two of you go. Leave Andrew with Kaaren, and Thorliff will be out with the sheep until his lessons. That sounds the best arrangement to me."

Ingeborg could have thrown her arms around him and kissed him.

Lars winked again and took a step back as if he could read her mind.

Haakan pushed the dirt in over the rose's roots and beckoned Thorliff to pour water in the hole. He looked up at Ingeborg. "Sounds like a good idea to me. If you can be ready to go on time, that is."

Ingeborg nudged him with the toe of her boot. "Try me."

"Oh, I will. You can bet I will." Haakan sent her a look that painted her face with the rosy glow of sunset, only the sun wasn't anywhere near going down. Ingeborg's hands involuntarily covered her cheeks.

"Haakan Bjorklund!"

"With that, I'll be on my way." Lars left whistling, his hands in his pockets.

"Pour more water, son. Let's get this bush in the ground so we can get on with other things."

The promise in Haakan's words sent Ingeborg into the house with enough heat in her face to start the stove. But once inside, she giggled.

Still grinning, she scooped the yawning Andrew out of his bed and blew on his tummy, causing more giggles. He wrapped his arms around her neck and laid his head on her shoulder. With a departure from her normal scurrying, Ingeborg sat down in the rocker, settled the little one into her arms, and set the chair to rocking. Andrew popped his first finger in his mouth and began sucking contentedly as he leaned against his mother's shoulder.

Haakan found them that way a few minutes later. The scene tugged at his heart and brought a lump to his throat. Much as he already loved these two boys of hers, the thought of Ingeborg birthing and rocking a son of his brought a picture of the future and the joy of it to his soul. While he hoped for more sons, he dreamed their daughters would have golden hair and a firm jaw like hers, and at least half her spunk to carry them through life's difficulties.

He knelt beside the chair. "I'm going out to start chores. Is there anything you need before then?"

Ingeborg looked at him as if he'd left his mind on the steamboat. No one ever asked if she needed anything, and he would only be out in the barn.

"Ah . . ." She couldn't gather her thoughts back from where they'd roamed the past and make a sensible answer. "No, but mange takk for asking."

He patted her arm and laid a gentle hand on Andrew's head before he rose to leave.

She listened to the sound of his footsteps until they died out. Why on earth was she doubting that marriage to this man was anything but God's will? Surely God brought him here, and surely He had put the love within their hearts.

But—there was that *but* again. Was it too soon? Was it for the best? Was it a selfish move on her part? No . . . yes . . . no! And contrary to the gossipy murmurings of Mrs. Strand, there had been no improprieties. He slept in the barn, as did Hjelmer. And both of them spent most of their days in the fields. What gossip could come of that?

Andrew sat up with the smile of an angel for her, slid to the floor, and headed out the door. "Bye, Mor," he called. "See Tor."

Ingeborg sat still only a moment more. She took off after the child. Who only knew where Thorliff was? "Thorliff!" She called him as she snatched Andrew off his feet and swung him in the air.

"Here, in the barn."

She set the little one back on his feet. "Andrew is coming to see you. Watch for him."

"All right." Thorliff stuck his head out the open barn door. "Come on, Andrew, run."

Paws trotted by the child, reaching to lick his face any chance he got. More than once she'd seen the dog edge the baby out of harm's way, like the day he tried to toddle under the team of horses. Thanking the Lord for His constant presence, she turned back to the house to begin getting things ready for the trek in the morning.

"Who was that out in the field with you," she asked at the supper table after fixing Andrew's plate. She looked up to see a scowl on Hjelmer's face.

"Mary Ruth." His curt reply invited no more questions.

"Aha, still bringing you afternoon refreshments, is she?" Haakan bit into his slice of buttered bread.

"I didn't ask her to." Hjelmer reached for the bowl of stew.

"No, I don't suppose you did. I have a feeling no one needs to ask that young lady for anything once she sets her mind on you."

"What do you mean by that?" The words snapped across the table.

"Easy, son."

"I'm not your son." Hjelmer pushed back from the table. "And what I—what she—well, it's no one's business but my own." The screen door slammed behind him.

Haakan and Ingeborg exchanged looks of total bewilderment.

"What was that all about?" Ingeborg shook her head.

"Heaven only knows, but methinks that young man is about to be caught in a triangle not of his own making." He glanced at Thorliff, who had quit eating to watch what was going on.

Thorliff licked his fork. "I like Penny better than Mary Ruth."

"Eat your supper." Ingeborg fought to keep the smile from her face. He spoke her thoughts exactly.

"I am." He took another mouthful and chewed. "Is Hjelmer going to marry up with Penny like you and Haakan?"

"Maybe."

"I saw him kissing her."

Haakan and Ingeborg swapped glances of consternation. "Really, when?"

"Out behind the barn. They didn't know I was there." His wrinkled nose said what he thought about kissing. "But if you want to kiss Mor, that's okay."

Ingeborg felt the familiar heat begin on her neck and work its way upward. "Finish your supper." She knew if she looked at Haakan she'd see a grin that would make her cheeks even hotter.

That night Ingeborg wrote a letter to the families in Norway, knowing that Kaaren would be doing the same. She asked them to thank Haakan's mother for sending him west to help out the widows and finished with the news of the coming wedding. She didn't mention much about Hjelmer, other than to say he was hard at work in the fields. While she wanted to ask if he'd always been so surly, she didn't. He certainly wasn't the same lad she remembered from home.

She went to bed praying for him, wondering what she had done to cause the friction and what she could do to make matters better.

When she was loading the wagon in the morning, Haakan came in from milking. "I think we should have Lars make the trip. I can do the fieldwork where he can't."

Ingeborg nodded. "It would do Kaaren good to go along, too; she needs a time away. She can skip the boy's lessons for today."

With that decided on their part, she crossed the field to the other soddy. "Good morning," she called as she approached the soddy.

Kaaren came to the door, letter in hand. "You are early, where's the wagon?"

"Haakan is finishing the loading. We think the two of you should take the trip to St. Andrew and on to the Bonanza farm. It's been months since you've been away from the farm, and—"

"Oh, Inge, that's a wonderful idea." Kaaren's eyes sparkled in delight. She nodded. "I know, I will buy cloth to make you a dress for the wedding."

Ingeborg shook her head. "No, I have the blue silk Roald gave me, remember? I have been thinking of cutting that out, but I just haven't had time." She blinked at the bit of a lie. The truth was she hadn't *wanted* to take the time, as if cutting the cloth given to her by a former husband might cause a jinx on the new marriage.

"That will be a beautiful dress."

"But so impractical. Where would I wear a dress like that?"

"To church. By winter we will have a church and school building."

Lars came to the house, carrying two frothing buckets of milk. "Where do you want these, the house or the cellar?"

"Pour them into the rising pans. How would you like to drive me to town today, dear husband?" Kaaren gave him a mock curtsey.

"I'd be honored. What about the boys?"

"I will oversee their lessons. Surely they can put up with me for one day. You two just go and have a good time. Haakan will be over with the wagon in a few minutes." She handed Kaaren the letters. "The top one is for Roald's family, so it can go in the envelope with yours if you wrote them."

"Maybe I'll be bringing back a letter, too. What a marvelous day." Kaaren clasped the papers to her bosom. "I'm going to town."

Ingeborg nodded and turned to leave. "You know, Lars, perhaps you could take this ecstatic woman to dinner at the hotel in St. Andrew. I think you both earned the treat."

"Inge!" Kaaren stopped stock still, her mouth dropping open. "We can't afford something like that."

"After you sell all the produce to the Bonanza farm, you will have cash." She watched Lars go into the cellar. Lowering her voice, she leaned closer. "Please tell Mrs. Carlson that I am getting married." At the questioning look on Kaaren's face, Ingeborg continued. "Ja, the last time I was there, her son, George, asked if he could come calling on me."

"Inge, a suitor."

"Ja, well, I'm not like Hjelmer, dangling two on the string. One is enough for me."

"And a better man you'd find only in my Lars."

"And he is taken. Mange takk and have a good time." Ingeborg turned and headed for home.

"Thorliff will tell you what the lesson is," Kaaren called after her. "He can come over and pick up the slates and books."

Ingeborg waved to say she heard and continued on. There would be no time to take a team out to plow, that was for certain.

She appreciated Kaaren's teaching skills more than ever when she finally had Thorliff and Baptiste washed up and sitting at the table. Both heads, one dark and the other fair, were damp from the wash basin, and the spots of clean on their tanned chests showed the paths of a water fight. They hadn't worn shirts or shoes since the frost left the ground.

In sheer desperation, she sat Andrew in his chair and tied the dish towel around his middle. Each day she threatened to tie him on a long line to the clothesline so he wouldn't wander off. Today she'd caught him beyond the barn. "See Tor, Mor. Me see Tor," the little one insisted.

Baptiste grinned at Andrew and reached over to tickle the little one's tummy. As usual, no one could resist his giggling and both boys fell in with the distraction.

"Now, that's enough." She moved Andrew out of tickle range and gave him a hard cookie to gnaw on so she could go back to teaching. "Thorliff, please read page 126 aloud, and, Baptiste, you be ready to ask him questions about what he read." When they'd finished that, she made them switch places. Baptiste was much better at asking questions than reading aloud. Thorliff helped him sound out the words. Since they were reading in English, half the time Ingeborg didn't know if they were saying the words right or what they meant.

When they finished the reading assignment, she handed them slates and told them to write a description of something they had seen that day. When they read them aloud, she was amazed. Both boys showed a remarkable ability to see with more than the eye. Baptiste wrote about his grandmother working to soften a rabbit pelt so he would have warm mittens in the winter. Thorliff described the newly hatched chicks out in the barn and explained how the mother hen kept them under her wings to be safe from the hawk.

"You are both poets, I think," Ingeborg said after she read their stories. "Have you chosen what you will memorize next?"

Thorliff grinned up at her. "Psalm 100."

Baptiste, his dark eyes snapping, said, "Because it is short." Both boys giggled.

"All right, but first we work on sums." She looked at the notes Kaaren had left her. "I see you are in addition, Baptiste, and Thorliff is in multiplication."

"We could work better if we had a cookie or something." Thorliff tried to look woeful.

"Cookie! Cookie!" shouted Andrew, who had been putting buttons back into a tin.

When Ingeborg could finally send them out the door, reminding Thorliff to watch Andrew, she breathed a sigh of relief. She'd rather plow ten acres any day. She checked the dinner cooking in the oven and went outside herself to take up hoeing the garden. She'd hardly begun when she heard the clump and harness jingling of the approaching teams.

When Haakan and Hjelmer came in for dinner after washing up, Haakan said, "I've been thinking we should build a house this fall so that there will be room for all of us. We could order the lumber when we're in Grand Forks."

Ingeborg stared at him like he'd lost his mind. "When are we going to be in Grand Forks?"

"I thought maybe we could take a little trip after the wedding. Kaaren suggested it, and I think it's a good idea. Hjelmer, here, can do the chores, right?" He glanced at the young man shoveling in food is if someone were going to take his plate away any moment.

"Ja."

"Kaaren said she would take care of the boys. What do you think?"

What did she think? He wanted to build a house, a real house with windows and rooms and—"We can't build a house that soon. A barn is much more important."

"Spoken like a true farmer," Haakan muttered.

"We could look at machinery and maybe even find someone to sell us breeding stock."

"I suppose you want a roll of barbed wire for a wedding present?"

She ignored the teasing in his tone and cocked her head in thought. "One wouldn't go very far."

At Haakan's shout of laughter, Andrew banged his spoon on the table, and Thorliff giggled into his cup of milk. Only Hjelmer failed to see the humor. He finished his plate and pushed back his chair. "I'll take Lars' oxen out this afternoon."

"Don't you want any cake?" Her comment was wasted in the banging of the door.

"I'll take his piece," Thorliff offered.

"Me cake." Andrew set his spoon down and lifted up his plate.

"You want me to talk with him?"

"No, it is me he's so surly with. I need to get to the bottom of it." Ingeborg passed out pieces of apple cake—she'd used the last of the dried apples—and sat back down with a cup of coffee. What would be the best way to pursue this?

She put Andrew down for a nap, and after shutting the screen door to make sure he couldn't get out should he wake sooner than usual, she started out to where she could see Hjelmer working with the oxen. Only he wasn't alone. A young woman walked beside him, her head bare to show the dark red ringlets of Mary Ruth. Penny always kept her sunbonnet on because her nose burned so easily.

"Uff da!" Ingeborg turned and went back to her garden. "That young man is asking for trouble, that is for certain."

21

Hjelmer, I need to talk with you." Ingeborg stopped beside the young man as he unhitched the plow by the barn. The brindle pair of oxen that belonged to Lars stood patiently, their hides darkened and curled by sweat.

"Ja?"

You won't make it easy, will you?

"Look, if it is about Mary Ruth coming out in the afternoon, she doesn't keep me from working, if that is what's bothering you." He let the tongue of the plow hit the ground with a thud.

"It's not about what is bothering me, but what is bothering you." Ingeborg clutched her elbows with the palms of her hands.

"Why should something be bothering me?"

"That's a good question. One I keep asking myself." *Dear Lord, please give me wisdom.* She waited, though the strain of it made her chew her lower lip. She waited while he winched up a bucket of water from the well and poured it into the trough. The oxen dipped their muzzles and drank till it was gone. They raised dripping faces and looked at him, pleading for more.

"That's all for now." He started to draw them back from the trough but paused. "All right, you want to know what's bothering me, here it is. You keep me so busy in the field I hardly have time to build my own business, and that is what I want to do more than anything."

"Doing what?" Ingeborg nodded. "Blacksmithing? You want to be a blacksmith?"

"Ja, I have no land of my own to farm, no money—"

"Hjelmer, I will pay you wages when the harvest is done."

But it was as if she'd not spoken.

"No way to make a living for myself, let alone a wife. And you, you run around in britches, go hunting, work the fields, let someone else raise Roald's sons . . ."

She couldn't have stopped the torrent if she'd tried. Instead she stood listening to his bitter tirade, wishing she had armor to protect herself from his slinging barbs.

"And now you're getting married to a man you hardly know—"

"He is *your* cousin. And Roald's."

"And he has all kinds of high-sounding ideas for this place." He spun around to face her. "My brothers' land."

The light dawned for Ingeborg. *His brothers' land. He'd thought to come in and take over the land his brothers had fought to wrest from the prairie.* With a supreme effort, she kept her own counsel. When he finally wound down, she looked up from the pigweed she'd been studying near the tip of her toe. She felt like hitting him over the head with the heavy oxen yoke, but instead, she just looked at him.

Within a few moments, he dropped his gaze and his shoulders slumped. "I . . . I'm sorry, that was uncalled-for."

"Sometimes it helps to get things off your chest. Now I have listened to you, will you do me the honor of doing the same?"

He nodded, one hand stroking the ox nearest him.

"You have used the forge and what tools we do have to fix our plows and such." At his nod, she continued. "And you have repaired and sharpened plowshares for others and re-rimmed wheels." She let a silence hold. "Did I ask you to give me the money they paid you?"

"They didn't pay me much."

"I know. Few here have any spare cash. We usually trade for what we need and pray for a good harvest." She sighed. "Hjelmer, this land is for Roald's children and for Carl's, had they lived. In the meantime, it is my land and Kaaren's. If it means so much to you, I would give you a parcel, but—"

"But?"

"You said you wanted to be a blacksmith. Where would you go? Have you thought about that?"

He leaned his elbows on the ox's broad back. "I would build a house and a blacksmith shop down where you plan to build the school and church. That is a crossroads and would be a central place for people to bring their tools. Roald talked long ago of building a town on Bjorklund land. Penny wants to have a store, and we could do this—"

"Penny?" Ingeborg kept a straight face.

Hjelmer nodded. "I can't ask her to marry me until I have something to offer her. Joseph would not allow it, but we have talked. We have dreams."

"What about Mary Ruth?"

The shutters dropped over his eager face. "I don't invite her, she just comes. What am I to do?"

"Are you asking my advice?" Ingeborg prayed again for wisdom.

Hjelmer paused. "I . . . I guess I am."

"Then you need to tell her you are interested in another."

"Ja, I know. I . . . I tried, but she laughed me off. And then she got mad. You don't want to be around when Mary Ruth gets mad."

Ingeborg nodded. That was something he would have to work out. "Let me tell you what I will do. If you want to build a shop by the cemetery, I will deed you five acres for all the work you've done since you came and up through harvest. If you continue to help out here, I will pay you wages."

"You would do that?" He studied a hair sworl on the ox's back, then looked up at Ingeborg. "After the way I have treated you?"

"Hjelmer, you are my family. All you have to do is ask for forgiveness, and it is there for you. Did you learn nothing in confirmation?"

"Ja, but you are not God. He forgives more easily than people do."

"Are you asking?"

He nodded.

She waited.

He took in a deep breath. "Please forgive me for the way I have acted."

While she could barely hear him since he spoke to the cow's backbone, she nodded. "Of course. You are forgiven." She stepped forward and patted his shoulder. "And now, can we please be friends like I remember in Nordland? I have missed that boy with the cheeky smile and the ready whistle." She caught a shadow in the depths of his Bjorklund blue eyes. Was there something else he was still hiding?

"Ja, we are more than friends. You are my sister, and heaven help anyone who ever hurts you." The last was said with typical Bjorklund emphasis.

She breathed a prayer of relief on the way to the soddy. Thorliff and Andrew were playing by the side of the house and ran out to greet Hjelmer when he drove the oxen by.

"Can we have a ride? Please?" Thorliff begged.

"Ja, you can. But you hang on to Andrew good so he don't fall off." As he spoke, Hjelmer swung Thorliff aboard and then settled Andrew in front of him. The oxen plodded on with only a switch of their tails, and Hjelmer began to whistle a cheerful tune.

"Oh, Lord, why did I wait so long?" Ingeborg shook her head as she entered the soddy. Could this have been settled long ago and saved them all the heartache? God only knew. How had she managed to keep a lock on her tongue? Again, God only knew. She kept her thanks going through the remainder of the meal preparation.

After hearing Hjelmer laugh with Thorliff out at the washstand, Haakan looked at her with a questioning eyebrow. She only tipped her head in a gesture of "I'll tell you later" and finished settling Andrew onto his chair. When she thought about Lars and Kaaren not being back yet, she pushed the little drill of fear back into hiding. Tonight she would rejoice with the change in Hjelmer. As God's Word said, "Let the day's own troubles be sufficient for the day." She was sure they were on the way back, and all was well. After all, when she made the trip she usually returned after dark, also. She'd learned long ago that waiting was always harder than doing.

Paws alerted them to the arrival before the jingle of harness reached their ears. His yip said it was family, not a stranger, so they all rushed to the door.

"Looks to me like you did a right bit of buying in Grand Forks," Lars called to Haakan when he whoaed the team.

"The packages stayed wrapped, didn't they?" Haakan raised high the lantern and peered into the wagon bed.

"No way you could wrap these two beauties." Lars climbed down from the wagon and clapped a hand on the frame of one of the plows. "Tomorrow, I will be out before daybreak."

"They sure are something." Hjelmer had climbed into the wagon and was exploring every inch of the newfangled machines. "You think they will hold up in this heavy soil, busting sod and all?"

"Man selling them said they were reinforced special for the prairie. 'Cording to him, you could plow a section a day, but then we all know what they'll promise when they're trying to sell you something."

"Looks to me like he sold you right well." Lars walked around the wagon to help Kaaren down. Turning to Ingeborg, he asked, "You got supper ready? I could eat a mule."

"Onkel Lars," Thorliff protested.

"Not Jack, some other tough old thing."

"Ja, I will just warm it up some. How did it go at the Bonanza farm?"

"They wish we'd come more often is all." Kaaren reached in the wagon bed and lifted out a package. "Mrs. Carlson was right surprised to get your message, but she sent you her blessings. Said you deserved whatever happiness the good Lord had in store for you."

Ingeborg started to reach in to help with the unloading, but Haakan shooed her and Kaaren away. "You go on in and get that supper on the table. We'll take care of this."

"I don't know," Kaaren said in answer to Ingeborg's questioning look. "But, Inge, wait till you see what we bought. Four metal milk buckets, so shiny you can see your face in them, and a separator for the cream. No more skimming the pans for us. The cheese and butter will go much faster now."

"And for you, my little pumpkin"—she grabbed Andrew's hands and danced him in a circle—"we brought—"

"No, don't tell him. Let him open the package," Lars interrupted. She handed a flat parcel to Thorliff. "Use this with our love."

Thorliff carefully untied the string and unwrapped the paper. Both were far too precious to waste. His eyes widened into circles. "Oh, Tante Kaaren, Onkel Lars, mange takk, mange takk." He sank down on a chair, caressing the tablet of lined writing paper. Two pencils were tied to the tablet.

"So you can save your writings, Thorliff. Someday we will all be proud of what you write, and I want to be able to look back and see where I helped you get better." She sat down beside him. "I think if you write on the slate first, and when the writing is the best you can make it, then you can copy your work to the paper."

Andrew reached up a grubby hand to grab the treasure. "Me see."

"No!" At the baby's crestfallen look, Thorliff held his precious tablet down to be seen. "But do not touch. This is not for Andrew."

"But this is." Kaaren handed the child a round wrapped parcel. She helped him untie the string and unwrap the red object. "This is a ball." She showed him how it bounced on the floor. Andrew crowed in delight and tried to grab the bouncing toy. It skittered away from him and away he went after it.

"That should keep him occupied for a while." Lars took a chair at the table. He propped his foot up on his knee and sighed. "Sure is good to be home."

Ingeborg dished up plates of venison stew and slices of bread and set them before the travelers. Just as she finished pouring the coffee, Haakan came through the door. "I can't seem to pry Hjelmer away from the plows, but I guess the rest of us can have a party." He set a package before each of them. "We'll just call these wedding presents."

"For all of us?" Lars stopped the forkful of food halfway to his mouth. "You got it wrong, man. For weddings the groom gets gifts. He doesn't give them."

"Ja, well, I've never been one to follow conventions." He waved his hands. "Open them. Children first."

Andrew was so busy chasing his ball, he ignored the goings on, but Thorliff, eyes sparkling, carefully unwrapped yet a second present. "Books." He looked up at the man leaning against the wall. "Three books. Mor, look, I never had three new books before." He opened one and sniffed the pages. "Wait till Baptiste sees these. And they smell so good." He sniffed again and held the book to his mother.

Andrew came to his mother's knee and dutifully stuck his nose on the page, but Thorliff removed the book quickly. Andrew still hadn't gotten down the idea of sniffing, but he did understand blowing. Haakan took Andrew's hand and led him outside. When they returned, the little boy was riding in a red wagon.

"Merciful heavens, you must have spent a fortune." Ingeborg sank back in her chair.

"A man gets married to a woman like you with two fine strapping sons only once in his life. I want us all to remember it."

"I'm sure we will."

"Open yours." Haakan pulled the wagon around the table, bumping into chair legs, which only made Andrew bounce and crow more.

Ingeborg followed Thorliff's care in unwrapping the package. She laid the paper flat on the table, the folded garment in the middle. "A dress! It . . . it's beautiful."

"I hope it fits. The lady said that since you was such a good seamstress, you could take it in if you had to." Haakan stopped behind her. "You'll look lovely in it, I know."

Ingeborg raised the dress by the shoulders and held the lovely rose-colored garment to her. The lace at the oval neckline and at the hems of the short sleeves felt rich beneath her fingers.

"I was right." Haakan's voice cracked on the words, and Ingeborg felt the familiar warmth curl around her heart once again.

"Man, those plows are the best thing that—" Hjelmer burst through the door. "Oh! Well shoot, if that's going to be your wedding dress, you'll do us all some proud. Sorry for bustin' in like that."

"I brought you a gift, too." Haakan handed the young man a package.

Hjelmer hefted it and cocked his head sideways just a bit. "It's heavy enough I wouldn't want to drop it on my toe."

"Open it!" Thorliff demanded, looking up from his book.

Hjelmer did as instructed, being as careful of the string and paper as everyone else. He held up a vise, the pleasure cracking his face wide. "I've sure needed one of these." He stroked the length of metal. "That'll help when I have to make new parts for them fancy plows out there."

"The man at the machinery store said they'd always carry replacement parts."

"Ja, well, Grand Forks is a mite far to go when the plow breaks down. Unless you plan to keep a full set of extras here, I'll plan on using this to make and repair the old ones." He saluted Ingeborg. "Just the beginning, right?"

She nodded.

"Hey, I did as you asked," Lars said to Haakan when they were ready to leave.

"And?"

"Pastor will be downright happy to marry up the two of you a week from Saturday."

Ingeborg felt her stomach bounce somewhere down about her knees. Nine days till the wedding.

"Lars and I have a gift for you, but you have to agree to it in advance." Kaaren smoothed the papers in front of her.

Lars nodded at the look Haakan gave him. They all focused on Ingeborg.

"We want you and Haakan to take a wedding trip. Now I know it won't be long and far, but we will keep the boys, and between Lars and Hjelmer, the fieldwork will continue." When Ingeborg tried to say something, Kaaren held up her hand. "Now just quit shaking your head, Inge. You are going on a wedding trip, and that's final."

"You make a mighty forceful schoolmarm when you talk like that." Ingeborg took in and released a deep breath. "I take it we all agree on where we will be going?" They all nodded.

"Well, if we don't come back with more machinery and livestock, it won't be for not trying. Grand Forks, here we come!"

But as the days passed, Ingeborg developed what Kaaren called the pre-wedding jitters or a near terminal case of cold feet. She came up with a thousand reasons why they should wait, or not get married at all. Sometimes she couldn't figure out which side she argued on. Instead of smiling and laughing like she had been, she wore a frown that sent even Paws scurrying. She attacked the soddy like a general on a mission. Death to dirt. Unless, of course, it was on the walls or what fell sometimes from the ceiling. Outside, it was death to weeds, and all in the garden fell before the onslaught of her hoe.

When Haakan tried to reassure her, she slumped against his chest, then straightened her spine and shoved upright. "I know, I will be fine when . . ." Her voice trailed off.

"When what?"

When she rested her weary head in her hands, Haakan kissed the nape of her neck and held her close. "Not to worry, my dear. As you've said, the waiting is always worse than the doing."

"Or the not doing."

On Sunday, church was held at one of the neighbor's, and Haakan announced that everyone was invited to the wedding the next Saturday in St. Andrew.

Ingeborg tried to smile, but knew it had been a miserable mistake. Accepting everyone's congratulations and best wishes felt like the first stages of labor. Painful.

On Tuesday she donned her britches and went hunting. When she'd taken up her favorite place by the game trail, she rested her chin on her hands and closed her eyes. "Father, God," she whispered, "why am I so afraid? I would rather meet a wild wolf than feel this way. Is it fear? Is it—what is it? What's wrong with me? I know I love Haakan, and I believe he loves me. I should be rejoicing, yet I'm like a bear whose paw is caught in a trap. What is wrong?" The deer started and bounded back the way they'd come, crashing into the brush.

She jerked upright. She saw their rumps going away. Today she couldn't even hunt right!

On the way home, she shot at a grouse and missed. At this rate they'd have to have beans for their wedding party.

She slumped down against a tree, too tired, too frustrated to go any farther. A shadow off to the right caught her attention. Wolf had slipped into the clearing and sat at the base of another tree.

"We're a pair, you and I. If you were hoping for a handout, I missed."

He whined and lay down.

"You'd fare better on your own. There are plenty of rabbits, but I probably couldn't even hit one of them."

He rested his muzzle on his paws, his yellow eyes unblinking.

"If it isn't fear of being married, what is it?" The tip of his tail wagged.

"I was afraid of you and look what it got me—a crack on the noggin and the loss of a baby. That's what fear does for you."

"Well, I'm not going to be afraid anymore. If something happens to Haakan, I'll just keep on going. God won't leave me." She stopped. That's what was frightening her: those terrible losses and the depth of despair afterward. She let the tears flow. "Can I do that again, God? Would you ask that?"

She raised tear-stained cheeks and looked up at the blue sky peeking between the leaves of the oak above her. A verse trickled through her mind like sweet water in a dry land. "And lo, I am with you always." She repeated the verse and yet again, each time thinking on a different word. *Always* was key here. He would be with her *always*. Always meant that no matter what happened, He would be here.

When she rose to her feet and rested the gun on her shoulder, she looked around. Wolf was gone. The sun slid on its downward trek. Cottonwood leaves whispered in the breeze.

And like the wolf, the fear had faded away, too.

When she got home, Joseph had just driven his team into the yard.

"Got you a letter here from Norway." He held out the envelope.

"Can you stay for a cup of coffee?"

"No, thanks. I need to get on home. See you Saturday."

"Thank you for swinging by." She waved again as he trotted the team and his well-filled wagon out on the lane. With one finger, she slit open the envelope flap, careful not to rip the precious paper. Thorliff would use the inside for some of his lessons.

"My dearest Ingeborg and all our family there. I have sad news to share with you. Gustaf has gone home to be with the Lord. It was his heart. It had been bothering him for some time. . . ." Ingeborg could read no further. She stuffed the letter in her pocket and headed for Kaaren's house. Now there could be no wedding after all.

22

"What do you mean we won't be getting married next Saturday?" Haakan fought to keep his voice calm and level.

"We need to observe a time of mourning for Gustaf." Ingeborg pointed at the letter as if that would back her up.

Haakan rose from his chair by the table and began pacing the floor. Three steps and turn. Three steps and turn. *Lord God, what do I do?* He rammed his fingers through his hair, feeling like tearing it out by the handful. This woman would try the patience of a saint, and that was a title he certainly did not consider fitting for himself. When he could talk without shouting, he knelt in front of her.

"Ingeborg, what is the date on that letter?"

She handed it to him.

"Just as I thought, dear one. He died three weeks ago. It would be different if we lived in Norway still and were there with all the families. But we aren't. We're here in Dakota Territory."

"Haakan, they observe a time of mourning in this country, too."

He shook his head. "I know, but it isn't the same." Oh, to find the words. He took her cold hands in his. "Listen, Inge, please listen with your heart. I love you, and I want to marry you. You love me, and you said you were willing to marry me. I know you've been struggling with all of this—"

"How do you know that?"

"I love you, remember? I watch you and you are not so good as you think at hiding your turmoil. I want to take the burden from you, but you wage your wars alone." He stroked the backs of her hands with his thumbs. "Yes, we grieve for Gustaf. Remember, he is . . . was Hjelmer's far. Like you, tonight the boy grieves alone. But it is easier when we are together. I help you, and you help me, and

God helps us all." His voice cracked, and he rested his forehead on their hands.

"What if this is God's way of saying 'wait'?" She removed her hand from his and began stroking his hair.

"Ja, it could be that." Tonight he had no strength left to fight with. Her hand felt like an angel's wing must feel, soft yet firm and filled with love. He knew she loved him, without a doubt. "Go to sleep, my love, and we will talk again in the morning. Perhaps God will get through to one of us this night."

After kissing her good-night, Haakan strolled out to the barn. Inside, he heard the sound of weeping.

❧ ❧

"You told him what?" Kaaren clamped her hands on her hips.

"That we need to observe a time of mourning for Gustaf, and we should postpone the wedding." Ingeborg's words came in a rush. This morning she didn't feel half as sure of this as she had last night. "It is seemly, that's all."

"That is the most . . . the most . . ." Kaaren threw her hands in the air. "I can't believe this is you saying that. Yes, I can. You used the same argument on me when I was to marry Lars, but Carl had been gone only six months then. Ingeborg, listen to me. You wear britches because you can get more work done, and it is more comfortable. Seemly or not, you do it. You plow and plant and harvest because the work needs to be done. It is thanks to you that when we lost our husbands we did not also lose our land. Was your doing man's work seemly? No, of course not! Is it *seemly* when you go hunting? No, but we surely do appreciate the results of your labors."

"I . . . I . . ." Ingeborg leaned her head against the back of the rocker. "All right! All right! I'll marry Haakan on Saturday, but if anyone comes talking to me about *seemly*, I will send them to you."

"Let's hope Mrs. Strand didn't hear the invitation."

"Who cares!" Ingeborg looked up at Kaaren and tried to still the twitching at the side of her mouth. But the smile insisted on life and brought with it laughter and joy.

"Mrs. Strand will s-s-say you are n-never s-seemly." Kaaren could hardly talk around the laughter bubbling in her throat.

"Wh-who c-cares." Ingeborg wiped her eyes. "That woman will try to tell St. Peter how to run the heavenly gates."

Haakan stopped just inside the doorway, Andrew on his shoulders. Thorliff slipped in beside him and looked up at him. Andrew banged his fists on Haakan's head and laughed along with his mother.

"I take it we *are* getting married?" Haakan hardly dared voice the hope he felt springing in his heart.

"Ja, if you will still have me and promise to protect me from Mrs. Strand." Ingeborg wiped a tear from her eye. "Uff da!"

Saturday dawned with a thunder and lightning storm that lasted just long enough for Ingeborg to think it another "no" sign, and Haakan wanted to throw her over his shoulder and carry her away.

But when the sun came out and the land steamed around them, they loaded all their cooked food, the new good clothes, and their carpetbags in the wagon. The drive to St. Andrew took more time than usual because of the other wagons they met on the way. But the steamy air did nothing to dampen the joy of the day, and the storm accomplished at least one good thing—it cut the dust.

When they arrived at the white clapboard-sided church with the steeple above the front door, they discovered that some women of the church had brought flowers from their gardens to decorate. Roses and pinks, baby's breath and delphinium, the rich colors and richer fragrances welcomed the wedding guests.

Agnes had a crew setting up sawhorses and boards to make tables to hold the food, and off to one side another table already held an array of gifts.

Ingeborg sat in the wagon and stared. All this for her and Haakan? Surely, there must be some mistake.

Penny came over to the wagon and smiled up at Ingeborg. "I took some of the flowers the ladies brought and fashioned you a bouquet. It's in the vestibule. The minister says we will start right at twelve o'clock noon if'n everybody's here or not. If that's all right with you, that is."

Haakan came around and helped Ingeborg down. "Now, you and Kaaren go change your clothes and don't worry about any of this. Agnes has it all under control."

"Thank you, Penny. What a thoughtful thing to do." Ingeborg turned to retrieve her parcels from the bed of the wagon, but Haakan was there before her. Only once before in her entire life had she been treated so . . . so . . . she couldn't think of the word. But a picture came to mind of a man in a gray topcoat handing her into a carriage in New York. She'd always called him her New York angel, even when he found her in Fargo at the Headquarters Hotel.

Funny, she hadn't thought of him in months. David Jonathan Gould, wouldn't he be pleased and happy for her? The thought made her smile. So many friends she had made on her journey. She stopped for a moment and looked around. It appeared as if many of them were either already here or on their way.

Once inside the church, she turned to Kaaren. "I wonder how Mrs. Johnson at the hotel in Fargo is?"

"What brought that on?" Kaaren shook out the rose-colored dress she'd folded so carefully in a quilt to keep it from wrinkling.

"I don't know, just thinking back, I guess. She would be glad for me."

"Ja, that she would. Now change your clothes, and I will button you up. Imagine Haakan being able to pick out a dress that fit so perfectly we didn't have to alter a thing! Some men are surprising."

When Ingeborg was dressed, Kaaren studied her for a moment, fingertips to her bottom lip. "I know just the thing." She left the room and returned a few moments later with several small rosebuds in pink and white. Quickly she picked the thorns off the stems and wove the blossoms into the coronet of golden hair that crowned Ingeborg's head. "Now you are just perfect."

"If it takes all this fussing to make me perfect, I'd just as soon do without," Ingeborg muttered, but when she looked in the full-length mirror on the wall, she caught her breath. Was that really her? But when she grasped the cheek she saw in the mirror between two fingers and pinched, it was she who felt the pain.

"Where are Andrew and Thorliff?"

"Right down front with Penny and Agnes so they won't miss a thing."

The organ began to play, and a hush fell over the gathering. Kaaren prodded Ingeborg until she stood by the door. "Now, Hjelmer is right outside to walk down the aisle with you. Haakan and Lars will be up front like we said. You just come when you are ready."

Ingeborg nodded. Getting married in Norway had been nothing like this. She and Roald just went and stood before the minister. He said the vows, and it was over.

Kaaren turned back and hugged her. "You'll be fine. It's only our friends and family out there. Now, come on." She stepped through the door, nodded at Hjelmer who looked uncomfortable in a too-tight jacket, and walked down the aisle as if she did this every day of the week.

Ingeborg squared her shoulders, put her hand through Hjelmer's arm and swallowed. "Let's go."

The organ played louder, all the people stood up, and Ingeborg walked down the aisle, trying hard to smile around quivering lips.

Tears glittered in Haakan's eyes. The smile he sent her wobbled at the corners.

Ingeborg ignored the tear that spilled out and stepped forward to take Haakan's arm. Together they turned toward the minister. The Norwegian words rolled out over the congregation, and both of them answered in all the right places, Haakan's voice deep and sure.

"I, Haakan Howard Bjorklund, take thee, Ingeborg Bjorklund, to be my lawfully wedded wife."

Ingeborg repeated her vows after the minister, her "I do." ringing sure and true.

The pastor raised his hand one final time. "The Lord bless thee and keep thee. The Lord make his face to shine upon thee and give thee his peace. In the name of the Father, and of the Son, and of the Holy Ghost. Amen." He smiled at the two of them. "You may kiss the bride."

Haakan placed his hands on either side of Ingeborg's face as if she were bone china of the most fragile kind. His lips rested on hers for only a moment, but the joy of it seared clear to her heart. They turned and faced the gathering, and with the organ playing a triumphant march, they walked back up the aisle and out into the sunshine.

Even Mrs. Strand gossiping behind her hand couldn't dim the sun for Ingeborg. After everyone ate their fill, Joseph and another guest took out their fiddles, and the dancing began. They stopped only long enough for the bride and groom to open their gifts: a pig in a crate, a braided rag rug, a carved box for small keepsakes, and the one thing that made Ingeborg cry—a wedding-ring quilt, pieced by Agnes and the other women of the area. The pieces looked like jewels spread on a light background.

"How did you . . . when . . . oh, this is so lovely. I've never had anything so nice." Ingeborg wiped the tears away before they dripped on her dress.

"We been burning the midnight oil, that's for certain," Agnes said, fingering the design. "It did turn out mighty pretty, didn't it?" She leaned close so Ingeborg could hear her whisper. "I'm thinking we better start another one right away." She glanced over to Penny and Hjelmer, who were dancing as if their feet had wings.

Ingeborg turned and noticed someone else looking at the dancing couple. A shudder ran through her at the sight of the girl's face. Mary Ruth Strand was not a happy young woman.

When the steam whistle of the boat blew, Haakan hustled her toward the wagon. Ingeborg kissed Thorliff good-bye and gave Andrew one last squeeze. "We'll be home soon. You be good for Tante Kaaren, now."

Thorliff gave her a disgusted look. "Mor, we're always good." He started back to his friends. "Come home soon."

"We will." After they had waved good-bye to everyone, Lars drove them to the landing.

"You two have a good time now and don't worry about anything."

Taking the valises in one hand, Haakan put the other under Ingeborg's arm. "Come, wife, or the boat will leave without us."

Ingeborg hesitated when she stepped on the dock. She looked over her shoulder once and then strode up the gangplank.

✒ ✒

If the success of the wedding trip were to be measured by the amount of things purchased, theirs was successful beyond measure. If laughter were the key, all locks were opened, and if love were the final yardstick, the trip reached clear to the moon. Or so Haakan said as the steamboat neared St. Andrew again.

"Half the baggage on this boat belongs to us," he pretended to mutter.

"I told you to quit spending money a long time ago. We didn't need all this now."

"We don't have it all. I need to go back and get the horses and cows."

"Don't remind me. The bank owns my soul now."

"Oh no. Your soul is God's, and your heart is mine. Don't ever forget it. The bank only has claims on the harvest." He pulled her into a sheltered corner so he could put his arm around her again.

"You say the nicest things." Ingeborg leaned into his chest.

"You make it easy to say good things." He tipped up her chin so he could look into her eyes. "You are not to worry about the bank loans. I am your husband now, and that is my job. We will pay them all off within two years, so that by the time your homestead is proven, we will be debt free."

"Ja, if the harvest is good, and—"

He laid a finger over her lips. "Hush. The machinery will more than pay for itself, and you aren't married to just a farmer. Remember, I will be a lumberman in the winter, too." He looked deep into her eyes, as if he could see clear to her soul. "I will take care of you and our family, Ingeborg Bjorklund, have no fear."

"You and God?"

"No, God and me. He comes first."

Ingeborg rested her forehead on his chest. "Are you sure Lars will be there to meet us?"

"Yes, he and I, we made the arrangements. You can trust us to do what we say."

"I know."

The boat shuddered to a stop, and the crew threw out the hawsers. As soon as the gangplank clunked into place, men began hauling bundles down to the dock.

Ingeborg looked out, and sure enough, Lars stood in the wagon, waving his hat above his head so they would see him. She breathed a prayer of thankfulness and leaned down to pick up her valise. Inside it were presents for the boys and for the family.

"Mor! Mor!" Thorliff darted around the busy workmen and dashed up the gangplank to throw himself into her arms. "Oh, Mor, I missed you so."

She clutched him to her and rested her cheek on his hair. "I missed you, too." She let him wiggle out of her hug and took his hand. "Come, let's go home."

"Now you're back, we're a family, right?"

"What do you mean?" Ingeborg looked down into his upturned face.

"I mean, now Andrew and me, we have both a far and a mor like we used to. And you won't have to work so hard in the fields anymore." He squeezed her hand and finished with a serious nod. "Unless you want to, right?"

Haakan caught up with them and laid a hand on Thorliff's shoulder.

Thorliff took his hand, looking up to the man beside him. "Do I call you Far now?"

"If . . . if you want to," Haakan answered.

"I do, 'cause we're a family now." Thorliff dropped their hands and ran toward the wagon. "Onkel Lars, wait up."

Ingeborg watched the flying bare feet of her son. As one who'd lost both a mor and a far in his short lifetime, he'd learned to take things as they came.

Haakan cleared his throat. "Yes, I guess that makes us official." While he didn't touch Ingeborg, the look he gave her shouted of love and loving.

When will I learn not to blush when he gives me looks like that?

Telling all of the news took until after midnight by the time they got home, so when the rooster crowed in the morning, Ingeborg had a hard time leaving the shelter of her new husband's arms and beginning the day.

Haakan kissed her once more for good measure before he went out to the barn to milk. Ingeborg didn't pay much attention to Paw's barking until the timbre changed to a deep-throated growl. She hurried to the door to see Mr. Strand standing in his wagon, his gun pointed at Paws.

"Call off your dog," he thundered, "'afore I blow his head off."

"Paws, come here." Ingeborg slapped her thighs. "Paws!"

Growling, the dog came, looking back over his shoulder with teeth bared. He took his place right next to Ingeborg, slightly in front of her knee.

"Whatever is going on out here?" Haakan burst from the barn, followed by Hjelmer.

"I come to make an honest man of that whelp there." Strand pointed an accusing finger at Hjelmer. "He got my daughter in the family way, and he's goin' to marry her, and that's the God's truth."

23

I did no such thing!"

"Are you calling me a liar? My daughter a liar?" Strand leveled the gun at Hjelmer's chest.

"No, sir, not exactly." Hjelmer took a step forward.

"Go back in the barn." Haakan spoke the words softly, for Hjelmer's ears alone.

"But—"

"Go back in the barn, easy like, one backward step at a time." He stepped forward, and now the gun was aimed at him. "Mr. Strand, put the gun away. I'm sure we can sit down and talk about this without a gun."

Ingeborg clasped her hands in front of her.

Haakan knew she was praying. He kept his gaze locked on that of the intruder. "Please, as a friend and neighbor, I ask you to come in and sit at our table. You have the honor of being our first guest since we got married. I'm sure Ingeborg has the coffee ready, or it soon will be." All the while he kept his voice even and soothing, same as when he was calming a fractious animal.

Right on cue, Ingeborg chimed in. "Of course. You're welcome to stay for breakfast, too, if you'd like."

Haakan dared not look behind him to see if Hjelmer had obeyed or not. Walking forward, he took hold of the horse's reins, right below the bit. He could see Strand was beginning to relax. The gun barrel now pointed down, and the man's finger no longer clutched the trigger. "How about if we tie your horses up over by the barn? They might want a drink from the trough there, and I'm sure a feed of oats would be welcome. We'll be mighty happy to have the new crop harvested. How are things looking over where you are staying?"

Strand laid his rifle down and climbed out of the wagon. "You won't be pulling any funny business now, will you?"

Haakan could smell liquor on the man's breath now that he was up closer. Had it taken some artificial courage to get over here? What in the world had happened to cause all this? As far as he knew, Hjelmer was truthful. The look of stark shock and horror on his face told them that, if nothing else. There'd been no ducking with a shamed face.

If the girl hadn't been a tramp before she got here, the dream of Hjelmer must have done it to her. What a pity.

Haakan led the team over to the barn and tied them up. He asked Strand again about his family, anything to get the man talking about something else. "You found a homestead yet?"

"No! That's another thing! I was all set to bid on the Polinski place, and you bought it right out from under me. I went over there the other day, and Mrs. Polinski said she hadn't seen hide nor hair of that worthless husband of hers since the day he went into Grand Forks with you."

Haakan groaned. In all the wedding excitement, he hadn't gotten over there yet. But he'd expected the Polinskis to be gone by now. Abel had said they'd move immediately. Now what would he do?

"That low-down polecat. You don't suppose he took off and left them, do you?"

Strand obviously enjoyed being the bearer of bad tidings. He perked right up, a grin coming to the corner of his mouth. He spat a plug of tobacco juice at the bottom of the rose bushes and wiped his chin with the back of his hand. "Couldn't rightly say, but it sure looked that way to me."

Ingeborg shot a look at Haakan that said she was simmering. When she slammed a plate of pancakes in front of the man, he was lucky he didn't wear them or the coffee that hovered near his back while Ingeborg poured the cup full.

"Now, I didn't plan to come for breakfast." He looked up at Ingeborg. "But this sure looks mighty good."

"Now, Mr. Strand—" Haakan began.

"Call me Oscar." Strand wiped up the sour cream and jelly with the last bite of pancake. "And thank you, Mrs. Bjorklund. Now, weren't that easy? You got married and you didn't even have to change your name." The skin tightened around his eyes. "Not like my girl. She'll be changing her name right soon, if'n I have anything to say about it."

"Don't you think you should ask Hjelmer for his side of the story?"

"Story be . . ." He followed with a string of cuss words and slapped his hands flat on the table, making the dishes jump.

Andrew whimpered from the bed where he'd still been sleeping. Ingeborg went to get him, glad Thorliff was out in the barn.

"Now, Mr. Strand, we don't allow for that kind of talking in our home, so if you can't calm down, we better step outside away from innocent ears."

"Sorry." Strand sent the apology Ingeborg's way. "Didn't mean to wake the little one, there."

Haakan rested his elbows on the table and tented his fingers to tap his chin. "Here is what I propose. Let me talk with Hjelmer, and then we'll come over later and talk with you and Mary Ruth."

"My girl, she been raised right. We don't do with no lying in our house neither."

"I'm sure you don't. But a few days one way or the other won't make a difference in the long run."

"Just so he does right by her. I want grandsons, but not on the wrong side of the blanket. And my Mary Ruth is a good girl."

Who's he trying to convince, me or himself? Haakan nodded but remembered the girl bringing afternoon cold water and cookies clear from where they were staying to Hjelmer out in the fields of the Bjorklund homestead. Did the father know about those little adventures, or was it strictly between mother and daughter? Sniffing out a polecat had never been difficult for Haakan.

The man rubbed the bridge of his nose. "I give that young pup three days to make this right, or I'm coming back with the gun, and this time no fancy talk is going to help a'tall." He got to his feet. "Thankee for the meal, and my missus hopes you'll come calling, soon like." He clapped his hat on his head as he strode out the door.

"Like about when we have a thunderstorm in January!" Ingeborg sank onto a chair. "He means it, doesn't he?"

"Yes, I thought we were getting through to him, but that conniving old sawhorse. He ate our food as if he would be a good neighbor, but he had no intention of changing his mind. Then to invite us to come calling! The nerve of the man!" Haakan leaned back in his chair and swiped both hands over his head, smoothing his hair for a few seconds. A grin started about midmouth and worked its way to the edges, then added strength with a chuckle and broke forth in full laughter like a spring freshet briefly dammed up by rubble.

"Haakan Bjorklund, what is so funny?"

Andrew looked up at his mother, then over at Haakan. When Ingeborg smiled down at him, he grinned and waved his pudgy fist in the air. When Haakan laughed again, Andrew let forth with the belly laugh of all belly laughs.

"What's so funny?" Hjelmer and Thorliff walked in the door.

"M-Mr. Strand." Haakan wiped his eyes.

"He wants to shoot me, and you think that's funny?" Hjelmer stared from one to the other.

"He'd rather you married his d-daughter." Ingeborg waved Andrew's fist at them.

"That's funny?"

"No, not funny at all, but you should have seen him."

"I did. I don't like looking down the end of a loaded shotgun." Haakan planted all four chair legs back on the dirt floor and swiped at his hair again. "Oh, my. Well, son, if you want my opinion, I think the best thing is for you to disappear for a time. Since you swear you aren't the father to that girl's baby, and I've seen how she's after you, I have a hunch there is no baby."

"She'd lie?"

"Appears so. How quick do you think you can be ready to leave?"

"Where would I go?"

"My guess is Fargo. Go work on the railroad like your brothers did. The pay is good, and they are always looking for strong backs. With your blacksmithing skills, you'd be a real asset."

"But . . . but what about Penny?"

"You'd have to leave her here. Her folks wouldn't hold too well with you and her running off. Besides, you don't want to start married life on the run. In a couple of months, you'll get a letter from us saying the baby never showed, and Mary Ruth is still slim and trim as ever."

"And then you can come home." Ingeborg set Andrew in his seat and went to the stove to begin frying pancakes again.

"But . . . but what if. . . ?"

"What if she really is in the family way?"

Hjelmer nodded.

"Do you swear that you are not the father?"

Hjelmer nodded again. "On a stack of Bibles, if I must."

"Then all will turn out all right in the end. You eat yourself a good breakfast. Got any cash?"

"Some. Lessen twenty dollars, I think."

"Good, that's enough to hold you till you get paid." Haakan got to his feet. "And if Strand comes back here, well, we'll deal with that when it comes. But I don't think he will. Let us know in a couple of weeks where you are, so before then we can honestly say we don't know. That should shorten some of that old . . ."

"Haakan."

"I won't say it." He raised his hands. "But it sure is hard not to think it."

Within the hour, Haakan and Ingeborg, with Thorliff and Andrew in front of them, stood watching Hjelmer stride off across the prairie, heading south.

"I wonder when we will see him again?" Ingeborg said with a catch in her throat.

"Only God knows, but He will watch over him." Haakan swung Andrew up to his shoulders. "Come on, let's go fishing."

"Fishing!" Thorliff jumped up and down. "I'll get the worms." He headed for the manure pile on the other side of the barn.

"Worms!" Andrew squirmed to get down. "Me, worms."

"You're a worm all right." Ingeborg set him on the ground. "Thorliff, he's coming with you." She started into the house and turned back. "And don't let him eat the worms."

"I won't."

They returned late that afternoon with enough fish for them, for Kaaren and Lars, and some left for smoking. Lars took over the scaling job until the others finished chores, and then they all joined in. Ingeborg had scales clear to her elbows. Haakan even picked a few from her hair. At supper that night, they all ate fried fish till they complained of stomachs popping.

"Where do you suppose Hjelmer is by now?" Kaaren asked.

"I hope he's far away, either by boat or train. I don't trust that Strand fellow any farther than I can throw him." Lars locked his hands behind his head.

"Or his wife, either," Haakan added.

"Haakan!" Ingeborg shook her head with a glance to the boys.

"Where would you throw him?" Thorliff looked up from drawing on one of the pieces of brown wrapping paper.

"See?" Ingeborg's look said more than that.

"Nowhere." Haakan tousled the boy's hair. "It's just a figure of speech."

"Me and Baptiste, along with Swen and Knute, we threw each other into the haystacks. That was fun. But no one's big enough to throw Mrs. Strand."

"You could build a . . ."

"Haakan Bjorklund."

He winked at her but saved the rest of his comment for later. After the boys were sleeping, he leaned close to the rocking chair where she sat knitting a thumb on a mitten that looked to be about Andrew's size. "Build a catapult and throw her into the next state. The next state after Minnesota."

Ingeborg kept her voice low in case Thorliff really wasn't asleep yet. "Shush. You have to watch what you say around those boys of mine. They repeat everything, and you know Thorliff believes every word you say."

"You are right. But he needs to learn to tease and be teased, too. Otherwise how will he get along in school?"

"He'll be fine." She put her knitting away and picked up her Bible. "What should we read tonight?"

Haakan listened as Ingeborg read of Christ's miracles. As far as he was concerned, being here and married to this woman who seemed to glow in the lamplight was miracle aplenty. And later, when she lay tucked snugly against his side, he thanked God for the miracle of their love, and that he no longer had to sleep in the barn.

<hr/>

Hjelmer strode south, a pack containing clothes and bread and cheese over his shoulder, leaving all his tools but the carving knife behind. With each step, his rage at Mary Ruth deepened and spread. Here he was running again and through no fault of his own. Just like it had been in New York, where he was falsely accused of cheating and had to run for his life. Only this time the pursuer was a furious father. One not afraid to use a shotgun.

Hjelmer called Strand every name he could think of and a few he made up. When he was done with him, he started on Mary Ruth. When he closed his eyes, all he could see was the hurt in Penny's gentle gaze. Who would tell her? Would she believe the gossip that surely would arise? Would she wait for him, or marry another?

What if Mary Ruth really was pregnant? Who was the father? Not him, that was for certain.

Without conscious thought, he veered to the west and made a beeline for the Baard homestead.

"Mrs. Baard, is Penny home? I need to talk with her."

"Hjelmer, what is that pack? Where are you going?" Agnes dusted her hands and wiped them on her apron.

"I'll tell you later, but it is really important that I speak with her." He clutched his hat in his hands. *Please let her be near, I must talk with her.* If someone had told Hjelmer he was praying, he would have laughed them off, but he repeated the phrase while Agnes wrinkled her brow to think.

"I know, she's out with the boys cleaning the springhouse. Go on out." She followed him to the door. "Everything is all right at home, isn't it?"

"I hope so." Hjelmer left her and headed for the room dug into the ground. He could hear someone laughing. As he got near, Swen bolted from a hole in the ground that was covered by a low roof of sod.

"I'll get you!" Penny shot after him, skirts flying in the race to catch her cousin. From the look on her face, he must have been tormenting her again. "You ever throw a mouse at me again, and I'll—" She stopped as if she'd slammed into a wall. "Oh." Her hands went to her hair and then covered her face. "I'm a mess."

Hjelmer reached out with a long arm and snagged the running boy. "Here, now you can do to him whatever you want." He smiled at her distress. "And you are not a mess."

He loved the way her cheeks flared red, the way she tried to smooth her hair and had to bite her lip to keep from laughing at her young cousin flailing in Hjelmer's grip. *I could lose her!* The thought made him drop the boy.

"Please, can I talk with you for a few minutes?"

"Of course." She studied him from serious eyes. "You are going somewhere?"

"Ja, I must." He took her by the arm and together they walked out toward the prairie.

"She did what?" Penny spun around and faced him when he finished telling her the story. "That . . . that witch! Mary Ruth, I could scratch her eyes out. To think she would accuse you of—" She stopped and looked up at him. Her voice dropped to a whisper. "It's not true, is it? I mean, I could understand if—"

Hjelmer clutched her shoulders with both hands. "No, I never even told her I liked her, not ever. She wanted me to, but I never did. Oh, please, Penny, you got to believe me."

She threw her arms around his neck. "Oh, Hjelmer, I believe you. I don't want you to leave."

"Haakan said I should go work on the railroad for a while. I will do that, and when I come back, I will have money to start a blacksmith shop. Ingeborg said she will deed me five acres by the school and . . . and . . ." He wrapped both arms around her slender body and buried his face in her soft neck. "Penny, when I come back, will you marry me?"

"Yes! Yes! A thousand times, yes!"

When he kissed her, she melted into his arms. A few minutes later, they pulled apart and stood breathing hard. "I love you, Penelope Sjornson, and I always will. You remember that, you hear?"

"I will. I love you too much to forget."

"Then I best be going." He touched the tip of her nose with the tip of his finger. "Tell your aunt and uncle what has happened. Tell them good-bye for me."

"For now. The good-bye is only for now."

He nodded and turned to leave before the moisture in his eyes brimmed over. Why was he feeling so desolate? He'd only be gone for a short couple of months after all. Wouldn't he?

～⊛ ⊛～

The next afternoon when Paws announced a visitor, Metiz could be heard talking to the dog. Before Ingeborg could close the lids on the stove and greet her, the old woman appeared in the door.

"Berries me bring." She held out one of her hand-woven baskets full of plump, purple-blue June berries.

"Metiz, how good to see you, and what a wonderful present. Where did you find them ripe already?" Ingeborg popped one of the juicy berries in her mouth and closed her eyes, the better to savor the sweetness.

"Plenty more."

"Good, perhaps I can send the boys out to pick tomorrow, if you will show them where. These will make delicious jam."

"Good pemmican."

"I should dry some, shouldn't I?" Ingeborg nodded. "Perhaps Kaaren and I can go, too."

Visiting with Metiz was growing easier all the time, with them both learning new words of the other's language and understanding the signs better too.

"Strand come?"

"You heard?"

"He loud voice. Mean."

Ingeborg poured them each a cup of coffee and set the leftover cornbread on the table. "Ja, that he is."

"Lars' foot?"

"He'll be able to put his boot on soon, I think. Thanks to you, that man can walk."

"Thank Great Spirit." She finished her piece of cornbread and drained her coffee. "Takk."

"You are welcome." Ingeborg got to her feet. "Come, I have something for you out in the root cellar." A few minutes later, she shaded her eyes as she watched Metiz trot back toward the river, the basket now containing six eggs and a hunk of cheese. She would have given her friend more, but Metiz turned it down. *Thank you, Lord, for Metiz. Guess we could call her our prairie angel, she's helped us so much.* Ingeborg sighed. She'd better get going in the garden before the weeds took over.

⚶ ⚶

Hot July ran into a hotter August, and the uncut prairie grass stood tall as a man's chest. Ingeborg spent much of her days weeding the garden, caring for her livestock, and keeping Andrew out of trouble. "I don't remember Thorliff being such a problem," she said one afternoon to Kaaren.

"You didn't know him at two, but he wasn't as busy as Andrew. Thorliff could sit and play with a couple of sticks and a pile of dirt by the hour. I would hear him telling the sticks what to do, as if they were humans. I think he started telling stories before he could really talk."

"Ja, I'm not surprised." Ingeborg studied the woman before her. "Why don't you lie down and put your feet up for a time. Look how swollen your ankles are."

"It's this little one." Kaaren stroked her burgeoning belly. "You'd think there were two of them fighting it out in there."

"Are there twins in your family?"

"Ja, now that I think of it. Wouldn't that be a miracle?"

"A miracle all right. And I can't keep up to one little one."

"Mor, get Andrew please. He's eating the grasshopper."

Ingeborg leaped to her feet. "Carl Andrew Bjorklund, put that down this instant." She flew out the door. "Be glad yours are still safe inside."

She dusted her son off and stuck her head back in the door. "Take a rest, there's no law against it. I'll cook supper for tonight."

"Inside what?" Thorliff paced beside her.

"What?"

"You told Tante Kaaren to be glad hers were still safe inside. Inside what?"

"Thorliff, sometimes grown-ups talk about things that are not for little boys to hear. Can you understand that?"

"Oh." He thought for a moment, then asked, "Like when you and Haakan laugh in bed?"

Ingeborg rolled her eyes toward heaven. How could she ever keep ahead of this child? These children? And to think Haakan wanted more.

The next time family immigrated from Norway, it was going to be a girl. One who could help with the young children.

A couple of days later, Ingeborg settled Andrew down for a nap, determined she would finish the hides she had salted while she had some peace. Thorliff and Baptiste were out with the sheep, and the men were breaking sod to the west. She carefully set the bars in place across the doorway and headed for the barn. Deep in her task, she failed to keep track of the time.

Paws yipping with joy meant the boys were back with the sheep. She stepped from the barn and waved to the boys on her way to the house. Andrew rarely slept this long. Was he coming down with something?

"Mor, we're hungry," Thorliff called.

"Come get some bread and sugar after you corral the sheep." She stopped for a moment to smell the white roses that twined now to the top of the door. Each blossom beckoned her attention, and she spent a few moments picking off the spent flowers. She left the rose hips on the pink one, planning to use them for her medicinals since they were the wild kind that grew to thumb size.

Silence from in the house. She bent to remove the bars and stepped inside. Blinking to adjust her eyes to the dimness, she crossed to the stove and lifted the lids to check the firebox. Out.

"Thorliff, could you bring in some wood?"

"Ja, we will."

Ingeborg crossed the room and stopped by the bed. No little body mounded the covers. The bed was empty.

24

"A ndrew, Andrew, where are you?" Ingeborg spun around, frantically searching each nook and cranny. "If you are hiding, come on out, I have bread and sugar for you." But Andrew was not in the soddy.

"Thorliff, go call for Andrew, will you? He must have climbed over the bars. You and Baptiste search the barn." Thoughts of what could happen to a little one who climbed into the boar's pen tore through her mind. Or what if he fell in the well, or the mule kicked him? All the possible tragedies raced through her head. *Perhaps he went out to find Haakan. Or over to Kaaren's.* As each place on her own homestead yielded no laughing little boy, she grew more desperate. Her heart thundered in her ears as she ran across the field to Kaaren's house.

"No, he's not here. I haven't seen him." Kaaren left the house and headed for their barn. "I'll look around here. Send Thorliff out for the men."

Oh, God, dear God, watch over my son. I failed to keep close watch on him. Please don't punish such an innocent child for the carelessness of his mother.

"Andrew, Andrew, where are you?" she called, her voice ringing out across the prairie. She called again. But there was no answering giggle. No "Mor, see me."

She ran to Haakan's arms as soon as he drove the team into the yard.

"When did you see him last?"

"When I put him down for his nap. I put up the bars, but he must have crawled over them or through them or something. Haakan, he is gone, and we cannot find him." She looked out across the waving grasses of the prairie, beyond the area immediately around the house and barn. The hayfields stood knee-high again and beyond. A man could, and at times had, gotten lost in the sea of rippling grasses. If a man could get lost, so much more would a little boy be swallowed up.

"The river!" Suddenly remembering the river, Ingeborg wrenched herself from Haakan's arms and raced across the garden, heading for the meandering Red River.

"Ingeborg, wait!" Haakan tore the harness from Belle and leaped aboard. He swerved to miss the garden and galloped after the running woman. When he caught up with her, he pulled the horse to a halt and braced his foot for her to use as a step. "Come, get on." She put her foot on top of his and grasped his proffered hand. With a grunt, he swung her up behind him. "Has anyone sent for Metiz?"

"Baptiste went after her." Ingeborg scanned the ground, the grasses, the trees, but nowhere did she see any sign of the missing child.

They entered the trees at the road cleared for hauling wood and water, but before they reached the water's edge, Metiz waved them back. "He no here. I look." She waved up and down the riverbank.

"How far could he get? He wasn't alone that long. Oh, how could I let him get lost like this?"

Dusk was falling by the time the neighbors arrived. Thorliff had taken Jack and gone to tell the Baards and the others. Within each arriving wagon lay a pile of quilts and hides, lanterns and food. People brought whatever they had on hand, for no one knew how long the search would last.

Haakan sent groups out combing the fields and woods and the prairie grasses. Hours later, they returned empty-handed. No little boy in a calf-length dress accompanied them.

"We can't see anymore tonight, and the mosquitoes are driving everyone crazy," Joseph said in an undertone to Haakan. "We'd best start again at dawn."

The mosquitoes, poor baby, the insects would be eating him alive— if he was still alive. Oh, God, I can't stand this. Where are you? Don't you care about my son?

One by one as the searchers returned, they ate a sandwich, drank some hot coffee or cold water, and fell asleep on whatever was handy, the ground, the haystacks, wagon beds.

"What are you doing?" Haakan laid a hand on Ingeborg's shoulder.

She shrugged him off. "I'm lighting a lantern, what does it look like? I will go look again. Surely if he hears my voice, he will answer."

"Where will you go? Do you think you can see better than all the others?"

"No, but maybe they frightened him, their strange voices and all. Maybe he's hiding, too afraid to come out." She slid the glass chimney in place on the lantern. "Oh, Haakan, he's all alone out there. I want my baby." Her voice broke as he took her in his arms and held her close.

"I know, I know." When she quieted, he tipped her chin up with gentle fingers. "Promise me you won't go out tonight. Your lantern could go out, and we could lose you too. Please, it isn't long until dawn, and then we will begin the search again. One thing to be grateful for—it isn't cold, so he won't freeze to death."

"Ja, but it might rain." She glanced up at the starless sky. "Oh, what if he's caught in the rain?"

"Ingeborg, listen to me. We prayed for Lars' foot and God healed him. Would He do less for our beloved son?"

"Sometimes God doesn't answer prayers like that. I should know." The pit of despair yawned before her, threatening to suck her into its whirling depths as it had before. "If I lose Andrew, I know I shall lose my mind."

"Oh, Inge, no. We are one now, you and me. We are stronger together. You don't have to bear this alone. I am here, and God never left."

Ingeborg raised her lantern and blew it out. The yard fell dark, the wind blew, and the howl of a hunting coyote could be heard in the distance. She shuddered and wrapped her arms around her sides. "You go sleep, if you can. Tomorrow, or rather today, may be the longest day of our lives."

"Inge—"

"No, I need to be alone now." She listened as he made his way back to the house. He wouldn't find a bed there, she knew. Someone else had already usurped that soft surface.

She wandered around the barn listening to the sheep, restless at the coyote's song. Was the animal finding a new kind of prey? *Oh, God, please keep my child safe.* Metiz hadn't returned either. Was she far up the river searching? A little one like Andrew would drown so easily. Why hadn't she taught him to swim? The whys drove her around to the corral. The horses slumbered, the hogs snorted in their sleep. All appeared peaceful, but for a small child lost in the miles of never-ending prairie grass.

She sank down on the washstand at the side of the house. "Oh, God, how can I bear this?" *My grace is sufficient for thee.* The verse stole softly through her mind, followed by another, *Lo, I am with you always*, and bits of another. She leaned her head against the rough slabs of dry sod and swatted a mosquito away. They seemed to come in swarms, their whine louder than the wind singing through the grasses.

Behold, I am thy God . . . The Lord is my Shepherd. "Dear God, tend your little wandering lamb tonight." She breathed in the stillness, redolent with the smells of a summer night. The roses sent their fragrance wafting around the corner, the earth damp with dew, the moisture of a storm in the distance, all part and parcel of their land. But where was Andrew?

Slowly the sky lightened, so faintly at first she thought she might be imagining it. But the band in the east brightened and broadened, giving promise of the returning sun. She could hear someone bustling around inside the soddy, the clank of stove lids, the thud of wood.

The sky lightened further, chasing the clouds so a few stars directly above glittered in their perfect splendor. Far away, beyond time and help—like God. She shook her head. *No, I will not go back to that. God is here and now, as He says He is.* She stumbled to her feet and followed the path to the outhouse. On her return, with Paws padding beside her, she walked around the barn and looked to the south, to the prairie grasses bending before the breeze, illuminated with the dawn.

The prairie. It hadn't broken her before. It wouldn't break her now. *As God holds my hand*, she promised the flat land, *you will not break me.* She shook her fist at the rising sun as it painted the few remaining clouds in shades of purple, lavender, and pink. "You will not!"

She retrieved a hayfork from the barn and began forking hay from the middle stack into the sheep pen. Today, no one would take them out to graze. They would all look for Andrew. But no matter what despair shattered the human heart, the animals still had to be fed and watered.

Paws yipped and streaked out across the pasture just south of the barn. Ingeborg stabbed her fork into the stack and wandered around to see what had excited the dog.

Stumbling across the stubble, a hand buried in the hair of the gray wolf padding slowly beside him, the little lost child arrived home.

"Andrew!" Ingeborg screamed his name and flew across the ground separating them. "Thank you, God, thank you, thank you." She babbled as she ran toward her son, and the tears she'd been too terrified to shed poured down her face. The wolf sat, and Andrew ran to her on his own. She swept him up in her arms, hugging him as though she'd never let him go again. "Oh, Andrew, Andrew, thank God, you are safe!"

"Mor, big dog." He pointed back to the wolf, who sat panting quietly.

"No, Andrew. That is Wolf, Metiz' Wolf. He is our friend."

"Big dog," Andrew insisted.

"Mange takk, Wolf."

The animal blinked and faded back, disappearing into the morning mist just as Haakan ran across the field to stand beside her.

"Was that really a wolf?"

Ingeborg nodded.

"And he brought Andrew back?"

"Ja, he did." Ingeborg kissed her son's filthy cheek and brushed her hand over the welts on his face and arms caused by a myriad of mosquito bites. "Uff da, so terrible you are bitten."

Haakan stared at the space where Wolf had been. "Well, I'll be. God surely used a strange way to protect our son."

Our son, how good that sounded.

"Mor, me hungry." The little one shook his head. "No Tor, Mor."

"You think he went hunting for Thorliff?" Haakan reached over to carry the boy, who went right into his arms.

"No doubt." Together they entered the yard where all the rescuers waited.

"Praise God, He saved our boy." Agnes called from the door, "Food's on, folks. Come eat, and then you can all go home and do your chores."

"The good Lord saved our boy"—Haakan pointed to the east—"just in time to see a new day rising." He put his other arm around Ingeborg's waist.

"Praise God, indeed." She felt the strength of the man beside her, one more thing to be thankful for.

"Mor, I hungry."

"So, let's get some food in you, little one." Haakan carried the child through the crowd of well-wishers, who shook the man's hand and patted the child on his back or on his cheek.

Ingeborg watched them go, the tears still streaming unnoticed down her face. God certainly did provide in an unusual way. But then, didn't He always? During all the heartache of the last four years, all the deaths, the body-breaking labor, God had been there all the time, when she turned to look for Him. And now with all the joys, friends, family, crops, a child found, He was here, too, all the time. And He would not leave them. As Haakan said, this was surely a new day rising.

"Mor, you're crying," Thorliff said at her elbow.

"I know, but these are tears of joy, from a heart overflowing with thanksgiving." She laid a hand on his shoulder.

Thorliff shook his head. "Be easier just to say mange takk."

Acknowledgments

In writing the second book in the RED RIVER OF THE NORTH series, I used many of the same resources as I did for *Untamed Land*, and they are listed there. In appreciation for their willingness to share their time and knowledge of this era, I add:

Bill Grant, who grew up in the area in which the story for this series is set and knows well the history of Walsh County. He also loaned us a book that proved invaluable.

John Jogoda is a veritable walking encyclopedia of firearms history, the tanning of hides, and hunting practices, both current and historical.

Don Peterson added to his resume by becoming a consultant on poker playing to the point of rough-drafting the card game scene for me.

Sharon Tissue read the manuscript and added many valuable comments.

As always, Sharon Madison and Sharon Asmus, from Bethany House Publishers, helped shape the final copy.

To all of these, along with my family and friends, who always encouraged, sometimes prodded, and often listened to me groan, my heartfelt thanks.

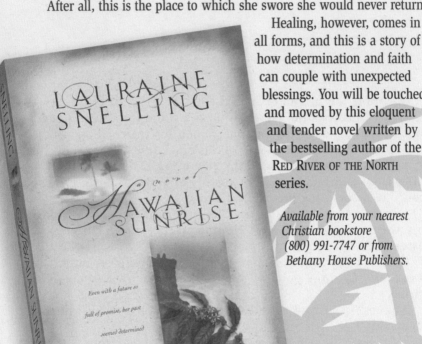